THE DOOMSDAY VIRUS

THE DOOMSDAY VIRUS

Barry Silverstein

To John—
May you always avoid
viruses of all kinds!

iUniverse, Inc.
New York Lincoln Shanghai

The Doomsday Virus

iUniverse, Inc.

For information address:
iUniverse, Inc.
2021 Pine Lake Road, Suite 100
Lincoln, NE 68512
www.iuniverse.com

ISBN: 0-595-26883-8

Printed in the United States of America

To Sharon
For everything you are to me.

PART I

1993

CHAPTER 1

Marty Gladstone had gone to his office in Kendall Square, Cambridge before dawn, as he had done seven days a week for longer than he cared to remember. From the windows of the converted old manufacturing plant, Marty could see the sun rising over Boston, its golden sheen glimmering on the Charles. He had a pang of guilt as he saw the early morning runners' breaths because he had all but abandoned jogging of late.

Marty sipped his hot herb tea from the trade show mug. It read, "The brightest ideas come from Incandescent." He looked at it momentarily, smiling to himself in the hope that the phrase would prove prophetic.

Marty's company, Incandescent, was on the verge of launching a remarkable software program that could fundamentally change the way PCs operated. Maybe it could even change the way all computing was done.

This wasn't vaporware. Marty and his team had finally developed nothing short of a monumental breakthrough in operating systems. It was the company's most stunning achievement since Marty founded Incandescent in 1978, only three years out of MIT. The big question was, could Incandescent get its OS to market before GWare, Incandescent's much larger rival.

Marty had reason to worry. Managing the daily snafus associated with software development was one thing, but keeping the project confidential was another. Sure, his staff was under non-disclosure, as were vendors, freelancers, partners, and anyone who came in contact with Incandescent now, but he knew it could all blow in an instant. If the news leaked out, he'd lose the element of surprise over GWare.

Marty envisioned Incandescent as a giant dike, with himself and Henry Chu running around, plugging their fingers in newly springing holes. Well at least Marty could depend on Henry, he thought, the chief developer of Incandescent's soon-to-be released multimedia operating system. Over the past six months, Marty and Henry had practically lived together, roaming the halls of Incandescent at all hours, days, nights, and weekends, readying the product for its launch.

Henry was a remarkable guy, someone who had that natural ability to succeed at most anything. But the product they were close to finishing was truly Henry's *tour de force*. He had been laboring over it for so long it seemed a part of him. And his pride in it was not unlike that of an expectant father.

As if to enter Marty's thoughts, Henry suddenly appeared in Marty's cube.

"Morning boss," Henry said with his standard bemused expression. His unshaven face and rumpled shirt testified to another all-nighter.

"Is it that time already?" Marty asked with a smirk. "Well, where does the bug count stand as of today?"

"'bout a dozen, but nothing serious. Easy fixes for the code jockeys."

Marty acknowledged the report with a satisfied grunt. Bugs were a natural part of software development, and Henry was a master at both finding and classifying them. Henry worked closely with the "code jockeys," as he called them, known more commonly as programmers, to come up with the most economical way to fix the bugs.

The more code it took to fix a bug, the more likely additional bugs would occur. The chain would continue and, eventually, it could lead a software program down a rat-hole. More than once, a major software operating system or application program had to be recalled because of serious bugs.

Incandescent's chief competitors, GWare and Microsoft, were well known for issuing software programs that weren't fully de-bugged, in an effort to rush a product to market. Consumers became the victims in the high-stakes game. Even worse, bugs could lead to security holes in the software...and that meant computer viruses could easily infect the operating systems. Software products were increasingly vulnerable to virus attacks, either from within the OS itself or using the operating system as a carrier. Marty and Henry had both worried about the potential for a virus attack. In fact, they were feverishly trying to build a viral deterrent into the program code.

The code jockeys didn't really care much about the bugs their work created, or even the "back doors" they might leave open, making the program vulnerable to a virus. Their job was to churn out the code needed to build insanely great functionality into the software program. They figured it was the job of the QA engineers to fix the bugs and patch the security holes.

Sometimes this aspect of the software business drove Marty crazy. Over the years, he had to temper his perfectionism with the realization that *nothing* was ever perfect in the software world. He loved the unbridled creativity, the invigorating feeling of working as part of a well-oiled team to turn out elegant, meaningful products—technology that really mattered. But the pressure associated with making a marketable product was at times unbearable.

Working with people like Henry Chu made the effort worth it. Henry proved his value day in and day out. Henry was just one of those guys who made things happen, no matter what the odds. He had gained the respect of even the hard-core nerds at Incandescent; they referred to him as "Doc" because of his reputation as a code doctor beyond comparison. The nickname stuck, even if Henry never did complete his doctorate at MIT.

"How's the AV coming, Doc?" AV was Marty's short-hand for the OS anti-virus component.

"Slow but sure," Henry replied. "Only one snafu in the last week."

"That's encouraging."

Henry nodded, sighing audibly. He didn't want to tell Marty that the AV schedule was beginning to slip, at least not until he determined if he could do something about it. Henry was considering calling in a contractor, but with the extreme secrecy surrounding this portion of the project, he was loathe to do so.

Henry understood things could and often did go wrong. He was paid to expect the unexpected and to make the unanticipated problems manageable. But this time, Henry felt an unusual sense of fatigue, even a sense of dread. Why, he wondered? Yes, the stakes were higher this time, but he had been here before. So what was bothering him?

He knew what it was. This time Henry secretly doubted Incandescent's ability to succeed at releasing their OS before GWare beat them to it. He felt that it could be the damn anti-virus component that could actually ruin it all. Henry visibly shuddered at the thought.

Henry Chu had never thought much of GWare's technical proficiency at putting out software products, but he had to admit they had the ability to flood the market and bully competitors out of the way. He knew that GWare was exceptional at product marketing and distribution, and that would make the real difference in the fight for market share. The idea that Incandescent could produce a far better product that might get overwhelmed by GWare's sheer marketing might stuck in Henry's craw.

More than that, Henry wondered if battling against such a giant was really worth it anymore. How much more could he take banging his head against the wall, day after day? He still enjoyed working at the company, sure he did, and he had a deep affection for Marty and his friendship with him. But sometimes, sometimes he wondered if it would be different elsewhere…

"Something wrong, Doc?" Marty's question snapped Henry back to the moment.

Henry shrugged it off. "Nah, just a bit too much night-owling, that's all."

Marty nodded dismissively as Henry turned to leave.

It seemed like hours later when Marty took the call from Erin Keliher, but it was only 8:30 AM–5:30 AM San Francisco time.

"Erin, what are you doing up at this ungodly hour?"

"Journalists never sleep…kind of like software developers," Erin answered, her smile coming through the phone.

Marty chuckled. "So what can I do for you?"

Never one to mince words, Erin got right to the point. "Rumors are flying about what you're up to, Marty. Thought I'd get the story straight from the top."

Marty stood up and began to pace around his desk, the phone cradled on his shoulder. "What kind of rumors?"

"Oh, you know, multimedia, interoperability, viral deterrents…that kind of stuff." She paused, lowering her voice. "I figure it's going to break soon…and I'd like to be first with the story."

Marty swore to himself. Just what he had hoped wouldn't happen…the press was ready to break the story about his operating system. It was staring him in the face, seen through the eyes of Erin Keliher. Well it could be worse. After all, who better but Erin, the influential technology columnist for *The Wall Street Journal*, to write about it first. At least it wasn't one of the other two-bit reporters who would have butchered the product and tried to smear Incandescent. If anyone would tell it accurately, instead of doling out a load of misquoted crap, it would be Erin.

Marty did a quick assessment in his head. What if Erin wanted to see the real thing, which she would likely ask for? How would he pull it off? If he and Henry scrambled, he thought, they could have a rough working prototype put together in as little as 48 hours. At least they could have something to show Erin…something he hoped liked hell would impress her.

"Marty, you still there?"

Marty cleared his throat audibly. "Okay Erin, here's the deal. First I'll need you to sign an NDA, agreed?"

Erin chuckled, knowing she was about to get her exclusive. "Long as I know what can go on the record, I'm happy. But you've gotta leave me some meat for the story, Marty. This isn't my year for reporting on vaporware."

"I'm a vegetarian, Erin…but I'll give you plenty of meat. Listen, how about I prepare a briefing for you? It'll be rough, but you'll get enough detail so you know this is the real thing. Can you give me 72 hours?"

Erin paused. "No can do, Marty. This'll break in two days, tops. For all I know, you'll be hearing from Bernie Shaw later today."

Her answer confirmed his suspicion. Damn it, Marty thought, someone must be about to leak the story.

"Fine," Marty said with resignation in his voice, "can you be here tomorrow evening? We'll do dinner, you'll sign the NDA during drinks, and by dessert, you'll have your story."

"You romantic, you," Erin purred into the phone. Marty could imagine her dancing blue eyes and the sparkling teeth of her smile from 3,000 miles away. "I'll call you when I get into Logan."

Henry Chu was attending the Object Technology Conference in San Diego, more because of a business meeting than because he anticipated learning anything new. Henry had arranged to meet with a freelance developer on the West Coast. He hoped the developer would be able to help him nail down the viral deterrent problem on the OS. This guy was so quirky that he insisted Henry fly out to San Diego so they could discuss the terms of his freelance contract face to face. It was a most unusual request for a techie—most of these guys wouldn't even be receptive to a phone conversation, much less a personal meeting. Formerly a GWare employee, the developer now freelanced from the San Diego area, which was home to GWare corporate headquarters.

GWare, archrival of Incandescent, was one of the world's largest and fastest growing software companies. While San Diego had a considerable high tech community, it was GWare that caused the city to gain international attention, much like Microsoft had done for Seattle. In fact, GWare was the primary sponsor of the conference Henry was attending.

Henry was meeting the developer that evening for drinks, so he took the time to attend a few conference sessions. So far he had found the conference more stimulating than he had expected. Most everyone was talking about something that, only a few years ago, was unthinkable—making object-oriented technology a commodity by distributing it across enterprises. The implications were enormous, particularly to programmers. Distributing complex data types, such as voice, video, and high-level color graphics, required technical sophistication. Object-oriented programming was just emerging, but it could well become the accepted methodology. And with the growth of the Internet for commercial usage, there was no telling what the combination could mean for the future of computing.

Of course, the rise of the Internet also prompted heated debate about network security. Several of the conference sessions were to cover security in general and viruses in particular. Henry wanted to be sure to attend the latter.

Henry found himself sitting across from Jill Strathmore, a senior developer from GWare. He decided to make idle conversation with her. Maybe he'd learn something of interest.

"Jill, hi, my name's Henry Chu. What do you think of the conference sessions?"

Jill eyed his name tag quickly. Could this be THE Henry Chu from Incandescent? "I'm getting some value out of them. How about you?"

Henry nodded. "Yeah, good stuff. How long have you been at GWare?"

"Four years."

"Must be interesting, being a woman developer there."

She decided to answer his questions cautiously. "Working with all those chauvinistic geeks, you mean?"

Henry smiled. "No offense intended."

"None taken," Jill laughed.

"So what's this I hear about GWare, developing something hush hush?" Actually, Henry had heard nothing of the sort, he was just launching a trial balloon.

"Honestly, Henry," Jill said, shaking her head, "you don't really expect an answer to that question, do you?" She smiled sweetly.

Henry spread his hands out in mock innocence. "Can't blame a guy for trying."

"Actually," Jill continued with a glint in her eye, "I hear the same about Incandescent. I'd put money on the fact that you're not just here for this conference."

Now it was Henry's turn to smile. "Touché," he said, enjoying the parrying. He could see he wouldn't get very far with this little game, so he was about to drop the subject. But then Jill said something that renewed his interest.

"You know," Jill began, "GWare is actively recruiting. I'm sure TJ Gatwick himself would be delighted to discuss the possibilities with the renowned Henry Chu."

Henry blinked. "You know me?"

"Of course," Jill smiled, "your reputation is well-known around GWare."

"I'm flattered."

"You're somewhat of a local legend." She paused so the comment could sink in, then began anew. "I'd bet you'd find our dedicated development research center to be particularly impressive."

For the next half hour, Jill did an admirable sales job on Henry Chu. She talked about the environment at GWare, the people, the benefits, and she raved about the research center.

What Henry didn't know was that he was on a target recruitment list at GWare. Jill couldn't believe her luck running into him. There was a bounty on Henry Chu of up to ten percent of his first year's salary if he were to be hired by GWare. That would be a pretty tidy sum if Jill could be the one to make him bite.

Of all the things she said, what intrigued Henry the most was her description of the lavish dedicated research center. What Henry wouldn't give for something like that at Incandescent! He had tried to convince Marty to open a research center, but the cost of it was prohibitive. Marty made the point to Henry that they had MIT at their doorstep, and wasn't that the greatest research institution in the world?

In some respects, Marty was right, but Henry longed for his own research facility, one in which he could conduct software trials under real conditions. It wasn't just that, either. If Incandescent had its own research center, Henry thought the company would not only be in a better position to keep ahead of technology, but it would also be more likely to attract top candidates. A research center was a real draw for new talent, he thought.

As he listened to Jill go on about GWare, Henry had to admit she was quite convincing. She laid it on pretty thick, talking up the benefits of working with "world-class developers" and making sure to mention the liberal stock options.

"Listen Henry, here's my card. Think about what I've said, and if you have any more questions, e-mail me. Or call me if you'd like to talk more about the opportunities at GWare. No obligation, of course."

Henry was non-committal as he thanked Jill and said good-bye. He checked the conference program to see which session he'd want to attend next. But after the conversation he had just finished and the thoughts running through his head, Henry Chu wasn't at all certain he'd be able to concentrate on any of the sessions for the rest of the afternoon.

CHAPTER 2

"I don't want any more fucking excuses!" TJ Gatwick screamed, red-faced. "You're two weeks behind schedule already, and what you've got is a pile of crap…not code, but crap. I'm not fucking paying you for crap. You find a way to get back on schedule. Just get it done."

Another "TJ Tirade" was winding down. This time, the object of TJ Gatwick's furor and derision was a poor unfortunate junior programmer. The explosive development sessions were known as TJ Tirades because of the GWare founder's penchant for going ballistic on a regular basis. The development teams could almost set their watches by his outbursts, except they didn't have any watches, and they probably wouldn't work if they did.

Jill Strathmore found this aspect of her job particularly distasteful. But she had to admit she was always relieved when she knew she wasn't the target of a TJ Tirade. Actually, she'd been unusually lucky during this development cycle; the mercurial TJ had just gone off on her once, and even then it was more about her team's screw up than it was directed at her personally. Those were the worst ones—when TJ got personal. He had been known to reduce even some of the macho male programmers to tears.

On the other hand, it was the price you had to pay for the privilege of working for the incomparable Thomas James Gatwick. Even now, as TJ finished lacing into the cowering programmer, Jill sadly admitted that this raving lunatic was the most incredibly brilliant man she had ever known.

TJ had dropped out of MIT in 1973 to start GWare and now, twenty years later, it was the only software company ever to come close to rivaling Microsoft in both size and profits. The business press loved the rivalry. They had a field day comparing Bill Gates with TJ Gatwick. For one thing, their management styles were remarkably similar.

That is, if you could call it management. In TJ's case, it wasn't management at all, it was more like terrorizing the people who worked for him. The company's strategy, conceived by TJ himself, was to hire the very best talent available and pay them at least fifty percent more than they could make anywhere else. Then GWare waved stock options in the faces of its most valued prey. The money and stock, in combination with the promise of working with the best minds in the software business, and in the best facilities anywhere, were enough to convince almost anyone to join GWare. It was the software equivalent of the New York Yankees.

Once on board, these talented employees couldn't go anywhere else because GWare's golden handcuffs were just too tight. Putting up with TJ Tirades became part of everyday life. It was almost as if GWare employees were battered spouses living in an abusive relationship. They knew it was wrong but they were trapped and couldn't do anything to get out of it. Oh, there were a few employees who realized that this was no way to live…but they were mostly people who had worked for other companies and were experienced enough to know better. Since most employees were recruited right out of college, or from a company for which they had worked only a short time, they didn't realize it wasn't supposed to be like this. Besides, GWare's reputation was so superb that they figured being lambasted simply went along with the privilege of working there.

TJ's blistering attacks were admittedly cruel, but it seemed as if he was always fundamentally right. TJ had the unique ability to think faster than a parallel processor. He could identify the weakest link in a project and see several steps ahead of anyone else, before anyone even knew what the steps were. It was this unbridled brilliance, despite the tirades that came with it, that so attracted Jill Strathmore and every other outstanding developer to GWare...and kept them there.

The session was breaking up. The programmers and developers filed out of the room as if they'd just seen a gazelle get massacred by a hungry lion. The gazelle looked particularly pitiful as he shuffled out of the room, his tail between his legs.

TJ, his outburst over, looked calm now, even serene. As quickly as he lost control, he re-gained it. This was a man with the classic Type A personality. It seemed certain that he was headed for ulcers or heart disease or worse.

Jill used the moment of quiet to approach him. "May I have a minute with you, TJ?"

He gave her a brief nod and then exited quickly, expecting her to follow his long strides to his office. He whisked past his executive assistant, an older woman who was as much his surrogate mother as his relentless gatekeeper, with Jill following in his wake.

TJ motioned for Jill to sit in a guest chair as he perched on the end of his combination desk-work table, positioning himself so he could see his computer screen while still facing her. He swung his leg nervously over the side of the desk, looking at her with eyes that warned, "Don't waste my time."

"TJ, I ran into Henry Chu from Incandescent at the OOT Conference. It was quite a surprise to see him there."

TJ's eyes narrowed with interest, even as he scanned his computer screen. He was capable of multi-tasking, his mind typically in overdrive. Except when he was discussing technology, TJ was largely nonverbal, possessing few social skills. He waited silently for Jill to continue, his body language expressing supreme impatience.

"I don't know exactly what he was doing at the conference, but I used it as an opportunity to make a case for his coming to work for us. I've gotta say, I think Henry was interested if not intrigued by the possibilities."

"Good Jill, that's very good," TJ said, still eyeing his e-mail inbox. "Learn anything from him?"

Jill shook her head. "Nothing that would help us any. But I could tell from what he *didn't* want to say that he's fully engaged in an important project at Incandescent."

TJ chuckled. "You're shrewd, Jill." He stood up and began to pace in front of her. "Here's what I want you to do. I want you to start a dialogue with Henry Chu. Go after him and don't let up. Tell him we're very interested in making him an offer." TJ paused a moment, pushing his glasses up on the bridge of his long nose. "What the hell, tell him you spoke to me and that I said he'd be a leading candidate for Senior Evangelist."

Jill gasped inside, barely hiding her reaction. This was an unprecedented statement. TJ had never offered anyone coming from outside of GWare a Senior Evangelist position. Senior Evangelists were always home grown—TJ clones who had come up through the ranks at the company to reach the all-hallowed Senior Evangelist position that was now legendary. Every one of the five Senior Evangelists at GWare had already become a multi-millionaire.

Then it occurred to Jill what this was all about, and she had a momentary feeling of nausea. It wasn't just about Henry Chu working for GWare, it was about TJ gaining access to Incandescent's proprietary ideas.

If, in fact, Incandescent was working on a major operating system, as was rumored, then Henry Chu was surely the man at the center of it. He had access to the code and was likely heading up the project himself. This is what TJ was really after, Jill knew.

A cold sweat came over her. She wondered if what she was doing, and what TJ was leading towards, was even legal. But she felt that, if she were to protect her own neck, she had to comply with TJ's orders. Besides, there would be an incredible monetary incentive for her to do so, if Henry actually accepted, never mind the respect she'd gain as a result of having snared someone of Henry's caliber.

These were not small victories for Jill Strathmore. As the only female developer at GWare with any sort of status or seniority, Jill had silently endured the stares, the derision, sometimes the outright male chauvinism her position demanded. It was unusual enough for a female to succeed in software development, but all the more unusual at GWare. If money were the measure of success, Jill thought, I'll take it. And if I can prove my value in TJ's eyes by roping in Henry Chu, so be it.

TJ seemed to lose himself in reading his most urgent e-mails, which his assistant had carefully prioritized for him. Jill took his pre-occupation as a signal that their meeting was over, so she rose to leave.

"I'll do what I can, TJ."

He looked up at her, almost as if he had forgotten she was still there. Once again Jill was completely mesmerized by his eyes. One was blue and one was gray. They had a coldness and warmth to them at the same time. They seemed to be inhuman spheres that could penetrate into the mind and the soul. They looked deep inside her, as if everything she thought and everything she dreamed was exposed to him.

"Jill, I want Henry Chu. And I'm depending on you to get him." A crooked smile began to form on his lips. "You're smart. You're attractive. You figure out how to make it happen."

Jill smiled tentatively, somewhat taken aback at TJ's bluntness and his very obvious sexual innuendo. Could he really have meant...but what did it matter? For Jill Strathmore, her career at GWare was the top priority in her life right now. She knew she would do anything to succeed, anything to please TJ.

"I won't let you down," she said as she exited. TJ nodded absently. He was already answering an e-mail, his long fingers mercilessly attacking the keyboard.

"So tell me," Erin Keliher said, wiping a bit of tuna salad from her lower lip, "once you get the ODBMS operational, how do you figure to port it seamlessly from Windows to UNIX?"

TJ looked at her with something that approached admiration. "You're something else, Erin."

They were lunching at a little restaurant overlooking the water in La Jolla, as they did about once a month. Erin would make the quick flight from San Francisco to San Diego to see TJ on a periodic basis and it was always worth it. She maintained an unusually intimate relationship with TJ, but not at all in a romantic sense…it was strictly business. But if ever there were a platonic love affair that suited each other's distinct needs, then Erin and TJ shared it.

It was through these get-togethers that Erin learned the inner workings and deepest secrets of GWare—within reason. TJ wasn't about to expose the underbelly of his entire enterprise to Erin, but he did afford her a rare insider's perspective that no one else was privileged to obtain. In return and with her ascent, Erin shared news with TJ that pushed the limits of confidentiality but just stopped short of ethical suicide. What she was able to tell him gave him advance notice of important events and, in some cases, even contributed to increasing his vast fortune. It was, in Erin's view, a legitimate price to pay for access to one of the world's most powerful software entrepreneurs.

It was a remarkably symbiotic relationship that served both of them exceedingly well. When it first began, Erin had considered the possibility of seducing TJ if she couldn't get the information she wanted out of him any other way. Erin was an attractive woman—a petite 5'3", she was slim but well proportioned. Jogging had enhanced her calfs, thighs, and buttocks, which pleasingly rounded out the chinos she frequently wore. Her Irish blue eyes could sparkle with happiness or blaze with anger. Her slightly freckled face and pert nose were set off by high cheekbones. Other than her eyes, her most stunning feature was the thick reddish brown hair that she wore shoulder length.

With it all, Erin's one secret regret was her good looks. She thought they could actually be a stumbling block in the male-dominated software business. She was rarely taken seriously, until she opened her mouth, that is.

She would have used everything God gave her to gain TJ's interest, though she wasn't particularly interested in his physical qualities. Too tall, quite pudgy, too scruffy—nerdy, if the truth be told. Sometimes she wondered if he owned a comb, ever visited a dry cleaner, or knew how often to shower. But his power and his billions…now THAT had a certain attractiveness all its own.

As it turned out, Erin didn't even need to come on to him. TJ's attraction to her was, interestingly, not unlike her attraction to him. She was bright, articulate, successful. She could be as ruthless as he could when she was seeking out a story. And she could make or break a software product with one of her reviews. In short, she had her own kind of power and influence to wield. TJ liked it, because he was surrounded by men who generally cowered in front of him. Here was a woman who actually had the guts to stand her ground.

"I'm not letting up on you, TJ," she said with an impish smile. "Sooner or later, I'm going to find out if you're using smoke and mirrors to pull this off, whether you tell me or not."

She was one of the few humans on earth who could get away with conversing with TJ in this fashion. Not only did TJ accept it, he actually enjoyed the verbal jousting with her.

"You're actually quite attractive when you're on the hunt for a story," TJ said, taking a large bite out of a steakburger.

She let his idle flattery pass without so much as a smile, instead matching his stare with her own flashing eyes.

He put down his burger and wiped his mouth with the back of his hand, not bothering with a napkin. "Alright Erin, I'll level with you. We're gonna pull this off, for real. We're maybe three months behind where we need to be, but I'm kicking ass. And don't believe for a minute that we won't make up the time."

"So you are going to get there first, before Incandescent or anyone else," Erin stated rather than asked.

"Of course I'll get there first," he said, taking another chomp out of the burger. "GWare never loses, you know that."

This was where Erin couldn't cross the line. She wasn't about to tell TJ that he had the biggest challenge of his life ahead of him…and that maybe, just maybe, he'd finally get beaten at his own game this time.

What TJ had no way of knowing is that Erin had just returned from a trip to Incandescent. Her dinner with Marty Gladstone suggested to Erin that there would be a real horserace this time. What Erin had heard from Marty would indeed profoundly change the computing world, pure and simple…if, of course, Marty wasn't just talking through his hat. But Marty had promised to demo the system soon, and if it was anything like he described during their meeting, Erin knew the Incandescent operating system would be the system to beat. She didn't think that TJ had any idea just how far along Incandescent had progressed in their quest for software superiority.

Incredibly, here was Erin Keliher, perfectly positioned to break the story, not about one, but about two software operating systems. She had within her grasp a race of epic proportions…the classic struggle of a software David against Goliath. The potential was there for the upset of the century. Even so, she was in a precarious position. She knew she couldn't reveal to either TJ or Marty what the other was doing, at least not yet. This withholding of information made her uneasy, because she had gained the confidence of each of them and, in fact, she admired both men. Yet she had no choice but to keep quiet to maintain some sort of impartiality.

"So when can I see something that'll prove it to me?" she asked TJ.

He was signaling for the check, avoiding, as he always did, asking whether she wanted coffee.

"When, hmmm?" he said, as if to himself. "Oh soon enough, Erin, soon enough."

She hoped so, because the last thing she wanted was to break the news about Incandescent without the GWare story to accompany it. It would be so much more impressive to have two operating systems to talk about...to be able to break a story of such monumental proportions. Yes, Erin thought, this is the stuff Pulitzers are made of.

CHAPTER 3

Ever since attending the technology conference in San Diego, Henry Chu had kept in touch via e-mail with Jill Strathmore. It was dangerously audacious, but he couldn't resist. Jill's e-mails to Henry were increasingly enticing and tantalizing. She described the excitement surrounding GWare's latest development project. Of course, TJ was feeding her just what to tell Henry about it, and he had instructed her several times to make open overtures to Henry. Further, TJ told Jill to forward every one of Henry's e-mails to him, as well as to show TJ Jill's responses to Henry. This was the first time TJ had ever micro-managed Jill, but she was thrilled by all the attention she was garnering from him. He wanted her to keep him personally apprised of the developments with Henry Chu, and she was only too happy to oblige.

Jill knew this little game would pay off handsomely for her, both in monetary and political ways. And if Henry Chu defected to GWare…they'd make far better use of his skills and talents than Incandescent would, anyway.

Jill's most intriguing e-mail was, of course, when she said she was confident that TJ Gatwick would offer Henry a Senior Evangelist position at GWare. To Henry, this was indeed the ultimate prize of a lifetime. It was something he could not have dreamed of, something he never thought possible. It was this promise that, more than anything else, made Henry consider the most difficult decision of his career.

The sticking point for Henry was Marty Gladstone. Marty had become far more than a boss to Henry, he was his colleague and friend. In many respects, Marty treated Henry as if he were a business partner. Marty had demonstrated time and again his respect for Henry. Even when it came to Incandescent's most crucial project, Marty had encouraged Henry to take control, to put his own mark on it. No one at Incandescent, other than Marty himself, was granted this level of authority and responsibility.

Henry's relationship with Marty was rare and special. More than that, the trust Marty placed in Henry was even more special. This, Henry knew, would be incredibly difficult to abandon.

But even this paled in comparison to the greater dilemma Henry faced. He knew that if he left Incandescent for GWare, he would be expected to reveal the secrets of Incandescent's forthcoming operating system. He'd probably even be forced to turn over the crown jewel of the new OS, the newly developed viral deterrent. Henry's employment agreement with Incandescent expressly forbid this, of course, but Henry assumed that wouldn't stop TJ Gatwick from asking him to compromise himself. Henry assumed that GWare had been involved in such situations before, and with GWare's access to the best legal talent, the company could probably tie the matter up for years. By then, the damage would be done.

Even if GWare could protect him, however, Henry would have to deal with the moral consequences of breaking confidences. He would have to face Marty, who would no doubt view him as nothing less than a traitor. And Henry would have to live with his decision for the rest of his life.

Henry agonized over it, even as he read the latest e-mail from Jill. With his thoughts swirling in his mind, and no easy answer, Henry began his e-mail reply to Jill.

❧ ❧ ❧

What Henry didn't know, even as he tapped out a reply to Jill on his keyboard, was that he would be triggering a far worse dilemma than he ever imagined. For at that moment, a hacker who called himself Doomsday had gained access to Incandescent's mail server, and he was scouring for secrets by intercepting e-mail messages. This latest e-mail from **hchu@incandescent.com** to **jstrathmore@compuserve.com** was particularly intriguing. He couldn't believe his good fortune...Doomsday had learned of an impending treachery via his electronic eavesdropping. He shook his head in disbelief. How could a developer of Henry's stature and experience be so reckless as to send this type of message through his company's own server?

From an anonymous loft apartment on New York's Houston Street, Doomsday operated an invisible empire of sorts, coordinating a loosely affiliated group of hackers who wreaked havoc on the legitimate software world. The Internet sheltered him from authorities in a way that physical cover couldn't.

Doomsday was the moniker adopted by a troubled young man originally named Jeremy. At an early age, Jeremy was scorned by his peers because he simply wasn't like all the other boys. He spent the majority of his waking moments in front of his computer screen while they were outside playing stickball in the alleys of the Lower East Side in New York. His father, a construction worker who was drunk more often than not, had little use for his "weird-ass kid" who, day and night, stared at what looked to him to be a pint-sized television. But it kept Jeremy out of trouble, and the kid had paid for the computer with his own money, scraped together from doing neighborhood chores. Jeremy's weak-kneed mother could do nothing to change the perception her husband had of their son. She herself had to admit he was a bit strange.

All through grade school and high school, Jeremy rejected any connection with humanity in favor of his computer. He found others like him through bulletin boards and chat rooms…all of them malcontents who railed against their parents and the world.

As he matured, Jeremy escaped more and more into cyberspace, somehow developing a warped sense of perspective on the rest of the world. To him, there was something very wrong about capitalist society, particularly the software companies who preyed on computer users.

Jeremy attended a city college, but only because he thought it could help him better understand how to defeat his enemy, the civilized world. He was an uninspired student who formed no relationships with other students nor connected with any of his professors. He suffered through four years of hell as a social outcast just to get a B.S. in Computer Science.

Jeremy took a job as a programmer for a Silicon Alley firm so he could gain his independence and break free of parental authority. He honed his skills and discovered the truly awesome power of the Internet. He soon quit his full-time job because he hated the structure of the workplace, but his boss begged him to stay on as an independent contractor. This Jeremy did in order to support himself, and more importantly, to support his newly developing covert activities. Jeremy took an occasional freelance programming assignment to keep his skills up. He was able to handle the work over the Internet, from his dingy apartment. Luckily, one of those assignments was for Incandescent, so he got to know about the company and its product line.

He took the name Doomsday when it dawned on him that his true calling in life was destroying the commercial exploitation of software and the Internet. He believed software companies preyed on vulnerable computer users, who had no choice but to use their operating systems and applications. He saw Linux as the only true operating system of the people and felt software should be free to everyone.

He truly saw himself as something of an avenger, a cyber-Robin Hood. He saw himself as someone who had the moral responsibility to cleanse the world at any cost, even if self-sacrifice was necessary. In effect, he had all the makings of a cyber-terrorist. Doomsday was a legitimate programmer once, but he had "gone to the dark side," as he liked to describe his own awakening. To some extent, Doomsday modeled his activities after white supremacists, only he looked at himself as a software supremacist. He preached computer anarchy, and instead of burning crosses, he crashed hard drives.

He lived simply and alone, pursuing a monk-like existence, uncaring about his personal appearance. He was a hulking, portly figure with a full unkempt beard that framed a round face accentuated by granny glasses. Clothes were a necessary evil, food was needed only to avoid malnutrition. He cleansed himself infrequently and lived a single step above squalor. He often did not know night from day. His world was not without but within the confines of an illuminated screen that gave him the only sustenance he needed to survive. His obsession was his passion, his passion was his life. There was nothing physically significant about where he was, yet he felt as if cyberspace were the vastest universe he would ever know.

His skill at manipulating the Internet for his own twisted goals was impressive, and as a result, he had done some considerable damage to networks and computer systems over the past five years. He hurt governments and companies but in his view, not individuals. He penetrated security systems and launched viruses. Yet all of this was nothing compared to what he saw as his ultimate objective, the culmination of his efforts.

Doomsday had an ambitious if entirely mis-guided goal: to create the greatest, most unstoppable computer virus the world had ever known. His approach was chillingly simple. He had learned through his own network of hackers that both GWare and Incandescent were working on new operating systems. His plan was to infect both systems simultaneously, with a strain of computer virus that he was confident couldn't be stopped. Once the virus was launched, it would self-propagate and render users' computers useless. Doomsday was hoping that this would result in mass pandemonium and, with any luck at all, there would be class action suits filed against both companies. Then they would get what they so richly deserved.

Used to benefit the world, Doomsday's programming genius would have put software a quantum leap ahead. But instead, Doomsday's twisted perspective was focused on unleashing a series of chain reactions across networked systems that could wreak untold havoc on the emerging Information Economy.

> *The sheer beauty of it…this Asian bastard will be the perfect diversion! While all hell is breaking loose over Chu, with a legal battle sure to follow, I can plant my Doomsday virus deep within the coding structures of both Incandescent and GWare's systems…so deep the bastards will never find them until it's too late. Once and for all, I'll bring these profit-hungry dogs to their knees. They keep coming out with their damn systems and upgrades, more and more complex and expensive, with that over-written trash they call code. They don't give a shit about the developers they steal from, the programmers they abuse. Where's the purity, where's the elegance? All that matters to them is commercial success…more licenses sold, more users, more fucking profits. Interoperability—who cares? Easy applications—screw that! It's all in the name of shareholder value. The attitude of these corporate whores is unbelievable. They've got to be stopped, before it's too late. You and your corporate marauders will know that the Internet is the only true network, the network of the people. I won't let you bastards take that over too. Never.*

Erin was back in Cambridge, this time to view a demo of the Incandescent operating system. Marty had promised her a demo that, he claimed, would blow her away. While Marty certainly had something of the salesman in him, he wasn't known for hyperbole.

Erin maintained a healthy dose of skepticism. She had seen and heard enough in this business to know there was plenty of BS floating around. But even she had to admit she was excited as she stepped off the elevator at Incandescent headquarters.

The receptionist announced her arrival and it was just moments before Marty appeared. He grasped her hand warmly and led her to the company demo room. "Coffee? Water?"

Erin shook her head, waving him off. In the demo room was an Asian American, Chinese she thought. He looked disheveled—his shirt was wrinkled, his straight hair was uncombed, his face in need of a shave. He was busying himself at a computer keyboard.

"Erin, this is Henry Chu," Marty said, gesturing towards the man. Henry looked up ever so briefly, his eyes barely making contact with Erin's. He smiled slightly, nodded, and went back to work.

Marty allowed Henry to stay engaged while he began to brief Erin. He went into considerably more detail than he had at their dinner meeting. While he occasionally slipped into techno-babble, Marty was careful not to uncover too much...he didn't want to steal the demo's thunder. He told Erin about Incandescent's vision for hassle-free interoperability, multimedia integration and distribution—all within a networked environment that was as close to virus-free as possible. He explained how the company had examined the market and projected its growth. He related their quest to pioneering into areas that had just begun to be considered—a common operating system for compact discs, and linkage with interactive cable television, for example. He talked about the market niche that would most likely adopt the operating system first, and how Incandescent was prepared to serve those early adopters.

Erin mentally compared this operating system to what she already knew about GWare's new system. She was struck by the similarity in the way each organization thought about the technical aspects of interoperability.

As she listened to Marty and watched his enthusiastic delivery, she was impressed by his sense of software strategy. In marked contrast to TJ, who was a brilliant yet unpolished geek, Marty himself had business acumen. He was smooth, she thought, very smooth. She could see him subtly look over at Henry occasionally to see if he was ready yet. But despite his showmanship, there was a disarming sincerity about him that Erin found quite attractive.

"How are we doing, Henry?" Marty said, cuing his inscrutable developer. Henry just looked up, and while Erin didn't notice a signal of any kind, Marty said "Good." They must have worked together long enough to get vibes from each other or use subtle body language to communicate, Erin thought.

Marty directed Erin's attention to a large television monitor that was attached to the computer Henry was working on. There were three other computers next to Henry, each intended to represent different operating systems. Henry began the demo, explaining to Erin in a soft voice what he was doing.

"I have here completely different computers, completely different operating systems," Henry said. "The challenge is for them to work together, of course.

"Our operating system installs a 'technical overlay' onto each existing operating system. This unique characteristic gives the system the ability to instantly clone the qualities of the operating system beneath it, thus allowing total interoperability among platforms."

Henry used his computer to demonstrate how each other computer followed the commands he entered. "Our system is, in effect, a chameleon. It literally changes its form as needed, based on the operating system it detects, without any degradation of performance.

"In addition to detecting and preventing a virus from entering a computer system, the Incandescent operating system detects the host operating system and then molds itself to it. Through a higher level structure, our system forms a common umbrella, a technical overlay. It becomes a kind of hierarchical system taking over for every underlying system, embedding the qualities of each one, yet forming a universal communications link."

Henry wiped his brow with a handkerchief he pulled out of his back pocket. "Once in place on a single computer, our system uses the network to automatically overlap itself onto every other platform. It can do this across a LAN, a WAN, even the Internet. It takes fractions of a second, so even multiple networked systems are operational without delay. And the resident virus protection travels with it."

Henry smiled. "It is as if the individual computer hardware is irrelevant...the Incandescent operating system recognizes each separate device and seamlessly interconnects them."

As she watched the demo proceed, and listened to Henry's technical explanation, Erin had to admit that she was stunned. Incandescent had accomplished technological wizardry that no one, not even GWare, had ever created before. This was the dream of the truly open system—the ability to compute across all hardware and software boundaries. It was indeed a breakthrough of immense proportions.

To prove the system worked, Henry showed Erin how each computer responded individually to commands. Then Henry directed Erin's attention to the large monitor. He used charts to explain how cable television currently operated—basically a simple, direct link between the cable company and the end user. Henry explained that cable was moving to interactivity, which would give the viewer the ability to not only program individualized selections, but to interactively order products, play games or get information on demand. In fact, viewers could request individual movies on demand.

"The problem has always been building enough intelligence into the television interactivity so that it mirrors what is possible on high-end computer workstations," Henry said. "We have ported in prototype form to a multimedia application that drives the actual communication between cable company and viewer. This won't be available in the first release, but it is not far away from completion."

This was even more remarkable, Erin thought, as the potential for the new operating system was now reaching beyond the computer world, into the cable television world. Would cell phones or PDAs be far behind, she wondered.

"Thank you Henry," Marty said as Henry wrapped up the demo. "Well Erin, what do you think?"

Erin looked shell-shocked. "Marty," she said almost breathlessly, "I must admit, you've impressed the hell out of me. I mean, this is truly amazing. Unprecedented. I…I don't even know what to say."

Marty just winked at Henry and dead-panned, "I guess she likes it."

Erin started to regain her composure. "Marty, you know I need to ask you this. What you showed me just now, I don't see how it could be possible with today's technology. Everything I saw…it was real, wasn't it? You didn't…rig anything, did you?"

Marty looked at her with his most serious expression and shook his head. "No hoax, Erin. It's the real thing. You can try it yourself if you want. The fact is, this isn't anything like today's technology…we've come up with something better, that's all."

"When will you be ready to release?" Erin asked.

Marty looked at Henry and waited for him to answer the question. "Six weeks, eight at the outside," Henry said.

"Close enough for me to prime the pump," Erin said thoughtfully. "Marty, the rumors are already percolating. And you surely know that GWare has something up their sleeve as well."

Marty nodded.

"Well," Erin continued, "here's my proposal. Let me start talking about this in my column next week. No details, just an overview. It will give you the advance coverage you want at little risk." She paused for a moment, then smiled. "You can bet from my reaction today that my commentary will be positive."

"Erin, I can't have you saying too much about this," Marty said guardedly. "Now that you've seen it, you know there's too much here that could blow the lid off the market if anyone found out about it. The element of surprise will be to our advantage. I'm sure you can understand that."

"I signed your NDA, Marty," Erin replied, her eyes flashing, "and I won't break any confidences. I'll talk about it only in the broadest terms. You have my word on that."

Marty thought about it. He did trust Erin…but she was still a journalist. He knew that she was as close to GWare as she now was to Incandescent. But he also knew that she was the most influential technology writer in the country…and the demo she had just seen had obviously impressed her. He decided to take a calculated risk.

"Okay Erin, you win. Go public at your discretion," Marty said. His brown eyes held hers with a burning intensity. "But Erin, I'm trusting you. And I'm hoping that the first TJ Gatwick knows about this will be by reading it in your column, just like everyone else."

CHAPTER 4

Marty was running again, for the first time in a long time, very early on a cool September morning. His route paralleled Memorial Drive, with the Charles River on his right. Boston was just beginning to awaken across the river, its buildings showing faintly in the dawning light.

Normally Marty would be running to maintain his stamina, to relieve the general stress of owning and managing a software company. But this morning Marty was running to ease the pain.

Even as he ran, he couldn't remember the last time he felt this deflated, this low. Actually, what he felt mostly was the dull ache of betrayal.

It had happened only yesterday, although Marty had lost all track of time. Marty replayed the event in his mind as he ran…

It started like any other day, with he and Henry sitting at Marty's work table, sharing a cup of coffee early in the morning. Marty began to review their progress on the project, as they always did at that hour. He noticed, however, that Henry had a distant, almost vacant look on his face. Marty asked him if anything was wrong.

His question snapped Henry back to reality. Henry ran his hand nervously through his hair for a moment but didn't say anything. Then Henry leaned towards the table. He pulled a piece of paper from his shirt pocket and unfolded it slowly, his hands visibly shaking. He slid the paper across the table without saying anything.

Marty picked it up. It was a letter addressed to him. The first sentence jumped off the page: "It is with deep regret that I inform you today of my resignation, effective tomorrow."

Marty began to read the rest of the letter, but he couldn't process the words. They were a meaningless blur. Instead he looked up with a pained expression, as if he had been punched in the stomach. "Henry…" he began to say, but Henry quickly put his hand up, as if he could physically stop Marty's words and, more significantly, Marty's emotions. The word "Henry" lingered in the air for a moment as Marty just stared at this man who had been one of his best friends, one of his most trusted peers. Henry just shook his head, whispering "Not now." He stood up, hesitated for a moment, then turned his back on Marty and exited. Marty watched, dumbfounded, as Henry walked away, growing smaller and smaller.

As Marty ran, pushing against a breeze, he replayed these moments over and over again. The shock he felt at the time was immediate, but it was no less consuming now. He simply never saw this coming. Sure, Henry had been despondent at times, but no more so than usual. Marty had seen it hundreds of times in Henry…the stress of working on a big project, of balancing all the details, of handling the management headaches. Marty knew this was the biggest deal they had ever worked on, but Henry was getting it done, just like he always had. That was Henry's way: moody maybe, frantic at times, but he always succeeded, always came through in the end.

What was it this time that made Henry crack? Did he, Marty, push him too hard? Did he miss the signals, did he not care enough? Was he to blame for Henry's sudden and unexpected resignation?

Or was this something that was building up over time? Was it something Henry had contemplated for a while, hiding it from Marty until he had an opportune moment to spring it on him? Was it simply Henry's time to move on? And would it have happened no matter what Marty did to stop it?

Over and over, he considered it all, at times, blaming himself…at other times, reminding himself that you can lose people, that nothing is forever.

Nothing is forever, nothing is forever. The thoughts came and he couldn't control them. Thoughts of the biggest loss in his life.

It was also in September that it happened. It was September 1969, a month before Marty's thirteenth birthday. Marty, an only child, lived in a modest house in Brookline with his mom and dad. It was a Saturday, and he was about to go outside to play. The phone rang and, moments later he heard his mother screaming.

"My God, my God, he's dead, my God, he's dead!" He ran to her side, confused and frightened. A small woman, she collapsed in her son's arms, crying, screaming, shaking.

Marty knew at once she was talking about his father. He asked her over and over again what happened, but she was clearly in shock. He didn't know what to do so he called 911. An ambulance came and the EMTs tried to calm her. They took her to the hospital while Marty rode along. The emergency room doctor gave his mother a sedative and talked with Marty.

Marty remained quiet, not knowing exactly what was occurring. He felt as if he was outside of himself, watching what was happening from a safe distance. The doctor asked him a few questions. Marty told him his father was a shopkeeper in Brookline and that he didn't know for sure but he thought his father was dead. The doctor excused himself for a moment.

When he returned, the doctor confirmed what Marty had hoped could not possibly be true, but now he knew it was true. He told the boy that his father had apparently died of a heart attack at his shop. Ironically, his father had been rushed to this very same hospital, but nothing could be done. Marty's father had died before he reached the emergency room.

Marty just nodded and looked over at his mother, who was now sleeping, but fitfully, on the hospital bed, surrounded by a curtain. She looked small and helpless to him, as if she had lost some of herself. He felt much larger than her right then. He had to deal, at that moment, with his own pain and sorrow. He had loved his father dearly, in reality more than his mother. His father was so excited about Marty's upcoming Bar Mitzvah, and he was so proud of his little "Marteleh." He was looking forward to showing off his son at the celebration.

That was a shattered dream now. His father would never see him being Bar Mitzvah, would never experience the joy of Marty's transition to manhood. Marty realized then, as he looked at his mother, that indeed he had just made that transition, in an instant. A moment before he was a boy, ready to go out and play. A moment later, he was a man who had lost his father…and his childhood. Marty would never feel like a child again.

Why the hell had this moment come flooding back to him now, as he ran and ran? He knew why…because he was feeling that same sense of shock, of loss, of hopelessness. It couldn't compare to the death of his father, of course, but Henry's resignation was as much of a psychological blow to Marty now as his father's death was then. It occurred to Marty that, of late, he had so poured himself into his work that Henry had become not just his closest friend, but almost his only friend. There wasn't much time for anything else or anyone else. This project was so all-consuming, so important to the company, to Marty, to the world. And Henry, well Henry had been living it with him, feeling the joy and the pain with him. It was so close to completion, so damned near to being done…

Only now Henry was leaving, and somehow, Marty would have to see this thing through alone. He would have to call upon his inner resolve, the inner resolve that had gotten him through his father's death. He possessed that, sure, but he knew it would be tested now in a way that it hadn't been tested for a long time.

What would make it all the more challenging for Marty was the worst part: the revelation that Henry was going to work for Incandescent's mortal enemy, GWare. This was as stunning, if not more so, as the fact that Henry resigned. How could Henry betray him like this? They had shared the same feelings about GWare, at least that's what Marty thought. Henry had seemed to be as passionate about Incandescent's technical superiority to GWare as anyone. Yet here he was going to work for them.

Marty knew he had even more to worry about. Though he had always regarded Henry as having the highest ethics, Marty couldn't help but wonder if Henry would now reveal the inner workings of Incandescent's new operating system to GWare. Henry was bound by his employment agreement, of course, but Marty knew the contract would be tough to enforce, especially when he was up against the deep pockets of an organization like GWare. So he not only was losing a friend. Now Marty risked losing the competitive edge on his new operating system. If GWare got Henry to reveal the inner workings of Incandescent's new operating system, all could be lost, Marty thought.

Marty hoped against hope that it was too late to derail Incandescent's product launch. Marty was at the tail-end of the development process and the product release was imminent. If he could shorten the cycle even more, cut a few corners, and rush the product to market, maybe he could avoid any damage from Henry's defection, even if Henry did share some of the secrets with GWare.

Marty was physically and emotionally tired now. His breath came fast and hard, his legs felt leaden. But as he slowed to a walk, he vowed never to stop running when it came to his company and his operating system. He wouldn't let GWare defeat him, not this time. He would find a way to ensure success, in spite of Henry Chu. The future of Incandescent was on the line. Somehow, Marty would find a way to win.

Dueling Software Moguls:
How David and Goliath are Battling Over Releases of New Operating System
By Erin Keliher

Even as the Internet continues to become an attractive and viable means of networked computing, there remains a need for a computer operating system that leverages current computing technology and, to put it simply, makes disparate systems work together. While Microsoft Windows is the only game in town for PCs, Mr. Gates, head of Microsoft Corporation, would admit that an operating system that allows PCs to seamlessly integrate with workstations, minis, and mainframes in larger organizations is still uncharted territory.

This may not be true anymore. Today, there is not one, but two new operating systems about to enter the market. Either, or both, could dramatically change the way the world uses computers. And the companies behind these systems are betting their futures on the impending releases. In a race that has all the makings of a David and Goliath story, Incandescent, a well-respected but relatively small Cambridge software developer, and GWare, the San Diego giant second only to Microsoft, both plan to release new operating systems within weeks of each other.

While specific product details are sketchy, this reporter has learned enough about both systems to speculate that Microsoft does indeed have something to worry about. Both operating systems are impressive in their use of advanced technology to provide seamless interoperability, regardless of computing platform. In fact, both systems are remarkably close in the benefits they provide. In my estimation, however, the Incandescent system has an edge in terms of multimedia interoperability and growth potential.

But in the software business, the better product doesn't always come out on top. Microsoft has proven that you don't have to achieve anything close to perfection in a product release if you have dominant market share. Such Microsoft products as Word,

Excel, and even Windows itself have come under criticism for an over-abundance of bugs, sluggish performance, and interoperability problems. Despite this, Microsoft has been successful with these products due to its marketing muscle and, at times, its intimidation of competitors.

Only time will tell if the same will be true of the Incandescent and GWare product releases. Incandescent may have a better product, but GWare is the bigger company with the larger distribution channel and marketing budget. GWare has been breathing down Microsoft's neck for years, while Incandescent is smaller than either competitor in terms of market share or size. But Incandescent has consistently received high marks for product quality and has increased its share of market in certain application areas dramatically in the past three years.

GWare and Incandescent have actually been fierce rivals for almost fifteen years. GWare, founded in 1973 by 40-year old Thomas James ("TJ") Gatwick, has always managed to stay a step ahead of its smaller competitor. But the scrappy Martin Gladstone, a 37-year old self-made entrepreneur who started Incandescent in 1978, has been in relentless pursuit of GWare from the start. Mr. Gladstone's company has moved fast and could be on the verge of monumental success if its new operating system lives up to its pre-release hype.

Mr. Gladstone and Mr. Gatwick are as different as are their companies. While both attended MIT and in fact met each other there, Mr. Gladstone, a Boston area native, went on to graduate and work for another software company for a few years before starting his own firm. Mr. Gatwick, on the other hand, dropped out of MIT to start GWare in his hometown of San Diego.

That's not the only difference: Mr. Gladstone and Mr. Gatwick are a contrast in physical appearance, mannerisms and management style. Mr. Gladstone is perhaps 5 feet 8 inches tall, with bushy hair and an engaging smile. His associates report that Mr. Gladstone can be intense and focuses relentlessly on a goal, but he is universally well-liked. He is personable and humorous, and is known to be a caring employer who delegates well and gives his staff a lot of freedom.

Mr. Gatwick is 6 feet 3 inches tall, with straight hair that's prematurely gray and piercing eyes that hide behind wire-rim eyeglasses. He has a reputation for being driven and, at times, brash. A brilliant workaholic, Mr. Gatwick is known to be intolerant of employees who don't move at his breakneck pace. Nonetheless, Mr. Gatwick's firm has been wildly successful and is almost ten times larger than Incandescent.

With impending product releases that could make or break each company, this is one David and Goliath story that will possibly come to an end soon. In any event, it will be most interesting to see which of the two men's companies are successful in their quest to launch a new operating system…and whether the loser will have lost only a battle, or the entire software war.

CHAPTER 5

"Goddamn it Erin, how could you?"

TJ was standing in the middle of his office, the phone receiver clenched in his right hand. He was opening and closing his left hand into a fist in an attempt to physically channel his growing anger.

"TJ, really. What did I write that was so damaging?"

"Erin, I don't give a shit what you said about me. But damn it, you said Incandescent has a better product, for Christ's sake. How could you DO that?" TJ was practically screaming into the phone now, pacing around his office.

Erin sighed. Why not just level with him, she said to herself. "TJ, I wrote that because it's true."

She heard a sound on the other end of the phone that sounded like TJ had swallowed his tongue. He was silent for a moment.

"That's the way it is now, huh?" TJ said, his voice seething with contempt. "After all these years. OK then, Erin, you write what you want to write.You believe what you want to believe. But Erin…you've dug your own grave."

With that, Gatwick slammed down the phone. He was shaking with rage. He couldn't believe Erin could do this to him…write that kind of trash about him and his company. Hadn't he brought her into his confidence? Hadn't he had a relationship with her that paid off handsomely for both of them? And now to do this: the bitch was a TRAITOR, that's what she was!

Thinking about it made him furious. This was treachery, and he wouldn't have anything to do with her again. As far as he was concerned, their relationship was over.

He flew from his office, past his startled assistant. He walked briskly down the corridor of the massive building, not so much as nodding at the employees he passed. He exited the building by the front door so he could view the GWare campus. This gave him temporary solace. The campus lay outside San Diego on Torrey Pines Road, near the Scripps Oceanographic Institute. It was a testament to the sheer power of the American software business, but as much a monument to TJ Gatwick as anything else.

There before him was the physical representation of the company he had built, the massive construction project he had personally supervised. Five buildings sprawled outward, surrounding a central quadrangle, not unlike a university. Four of the five were two-stories, but the fifth was five stories. Construction was nearly completed on yet another building beyond the main campus. This would be the new home of the research center.

Looking from building to building, TJ felt a renewed spirit, a growing strength. He began to walk down the jogging path that wound around Building Two.

He had to focus, drive the anger from him so he could think clearly, consider all his options. Erin thought that Incandescent was potentially building a better operating system than GWare. Much as he hated her now, TJ cast aside his emotion for the moment and considered her viewpoint. She had to have seen something in Incandescent's product, something so special that she would risk his wrath. She had to know it would infuriate him if she even suggested Incandescent had built a better mousetrap.

So, for a moment, TJ assumed it was true. It wasn't the worst thing, after all. GWare had brought out a product or two that wasn't up to snuff...but they had always won the market share battle, except when they were up against Microsoft, of course.

TJ was confident that this time, he could win the marketing and distribution war against Incandescent. But it was much harder to control product reviews. He knew the inevitable head-to-head comparisons would be made, and benchmarks would be run. How would GWare's product REALLY measure up when it was being compared to Incandescent's, he wondered.

And then there was this other aspect of Erin's story that disturbed him...the part that he had to admit really got him riled up. It was the way she characterized the struggle: the David and Goliath analogy. He knew this perception could be especially damaging. In the software business, as in American business, the company with the biggest budgets usually came out on top. But the press and the public would have a field day with even the hint of a story about a true underdog rallying against its larger competitor. This could pit public opinion against GWare from the outset. It could hurt product demand and make distributors and retailers nervous. With a few bad reviews piled on top of the underdog story, TJ feared his product release could be a disaster.

He couldn't, he wouldn't let that happen. This new GWare operating system was going to be the biggest, most important damned release in his company's history. It was the product that could put him head-to-head against Microsoft. He could taste it. He wasn't about to let someone like Marty Gladstone take it away from him.

Gladstone and his ethics. Oh, he remembered Gladstone at MIT alright. The guy was filled with righteous indignation, an idealist who saw software as a cure for the world's ills. He had heard Gladstone pontificate in class, going after the "lack of morality" of American business. The guy should have joined the Peace Corps, not founded a software company. Yet Gladstone had somehow found a balance, he had somehow managed to reconcile his beliefs and start a software company of his own. More than that, TJ admitted begrudgingly, it was a successful one.

TJ's most recent victory over Gladstone was convincing Henry Chu to join GWare, of course. Even so, it wasn't working out as well as he had hoped.

Henry had started out by sharing some basic information about the Incandescent operating system, but now he was waffling on releasing any additional product details. He adamantly refused to share any of the code, saying he couldn't compromise his employment agreement with Incandescent any further. Gladstone's view of ethics must have rubbed off on him, TJ thought ruefully.

TJ was trying to pressure Henry but to no avail. GWare's law firm was feverishly reviewing Henry's employment contract and TJ told them they damn well better find a loophole. In the mean time, however, Henry was standing fast.

TJ couldn't depend on Henry to tell him anything useful, certainly not something that would hamper the Incandescent release, and even if Henry finally acquiesced, it would be too late.

TJ faced the growing realization that Incandescent would beat GWare to market. TJ knew that GWare was missing some important development milestones, and the delays were now mounting up. Would he be able to stem the tide? They were running out of time and he felt in his gut that they wouldn't make it.

He couldn't let that happen, he couldn't let anyone, certainly not Marty Gladstone, win the upper hand. GWare would make its product release date, even if TJ had to litter the halls with exhausted developers.

But TJ was not feeling confident that he could pull this off without assistance of some kind. What could he do to turn the tables on Incandescent? How could he find a way to assure his success?

Faced with almost certain defeat, TJ considered all of his options. It was then that TJ knew what he had to do.

The home of Senator John "Jack" Morrissey, silently overlooking the Pacific Ocean in La Jolla, was impressive in its stature as well as its location. The majestic views of water breaking upon rocks were visible from an expanse of lawn behind the mansion. Set back from the gated entrance, the house was fronted by the requisite circular driveway.

It was a home not acquired through political means but rather via the wealth of one of California's richest families. The Morrisseys were the West Coast version of the Kennedys...only they were of the conservative Republican variety. The Senator and Ron Reagan went back a long way and, before that, a much younger Jack Morrissey had been a Goldwater enthusiast, a little known fact that had been discretely eliminated from any biographical backgrounders on the Senator.

Jack Morrissey had been bred for either politics or real estate. He chose the former only after amassing enough wealth from the latter. Morrissey was a builder in more ways than one. He took over his father's commercial real estate firm and grew it into a business that couldn't help but be noticed by California's politicians. Morrissey got to know the state politicians well, and he became a good friend of the Governor. Wielding a fair amount of influence on the state legislature, Jack Morrissey realized that politics could lend him a kind of power that extended beyond wealth alone.

With the Governor's support, Jack mounted a campaign for the United States Senate. That was over twelve years ago. Jack Morrissey had recently been elected to his third term.

It wasn't an easy victory this time around. Morrissey had been on shaky ground in the most recent election. It had been alleged that he was having affairs, or worse, running around with whores, and it wreaked havoc on his public image. Despite his acknowledged edge as the incumbent, he had been vulnerable.

Even more so, the political climate was changing, and it wasn't such a good thing to be a conservative Republican anymore. In fact, it seemed as if Californians were fed up with his breed. The economy had been in a shambles and California was particularly hard hit.

The election was hard fought, and that liberal female mayor from San Francisco really had given Morrissey a run for his money. But it was money, and influence, that allowed Morrissey to squeak by one more time. And if it hadn't been for TJ Gatwick's money AND influence, Jack Morrissey might not have won the right to another six years in the Senate.

TJ pulled up to the black wrought iron gate of the Morrissey mansion in his silver Jaguar—one of the numerous automobiles in an impressive collection of rare and beautiful machines. They were essential playthings to TJ, objects that could fulfill his insatiable need for power and speed.

He pressed the buzzer and gave his name, and the gates silently swung open.

An attendant appeared as TJ reached the front of the house. The attendant opened the car door and nodded in recognition. TJ stepped out and moved up the brick path towards the front door, which was opened by a butler. Both the attendant and butler were naturally precise and measured, as if they had practiced their roles a hundred times before.

The butler led Gatwick into the spacious sitting room where the Senator sat in a leather chair. The room was an eclectic mix of California modern and antiques, perhaps as representative of Morrissey himself as a style of décor.

Jack Morrissey looked up at TJ, the inevitable martini glass in his hand. He was dressed in a three-piece business suit, as he always was, even though it was the cocktail hour. A large man, Jack's vest bulged with the evidence of too many good meals in too many fine restaurants. Yet his frame was broadly built to handle the extra weight, so he did not have the appearance of a fat man. His thinning silvery hair was combed straight back over a broad forehead depicting the creases of his years. But his face was surprisingly youthful, punctuated by blue eyes that held a twinkle still.

Looking at the man, TJ realized at once that the Senator had started his Happy Hour early. Morrissey's nose looked as if rosacea had already set in, and his eyes were twinkling just a bit too much. But then, TJ had gotten quite used to seeing Senator Morrissey in a state of light inebriation.

He was an alcoholic, TJ thought, who managed it well. The Senator had never been known to be a roaring drunk. He was the very picture of a social drinker.

The larger issue was that Senator Morrissey had become known as a two-timer who could barely keep his dick in his pants. Maybe that's why he drank so much, TJ thought. Everyone in the state seemed to know about Morrissey's transgressions, maybe everyone in the country. TJ figured the Senator's marriage to socialite June Morrissey could be nothing more than a sham to help keep public opinion from strangling him.

"Drink, TJ?" the Senator said as he motioned with his glass to the bar. TJ shook his head and, instead, walked over to the humidor, helping himself to a Cuban cigar and lighting it up with the silver lighter on the side table.

"You certainly like the finer things in life, Jack," TJ said, taking a puff of the cigar and rolling it between his fingers, a hint of sarcasm in his voice. "Thanks for seeing me on short notice."

The Senator just grunted and took a sip of his martini.

"I know your time is valuable, so let me get right to the point," TJ began. "You know GWare is about to release what is probably the most important product in our history." Jack nodded and TJ continued. "Well there's a little problem that I think you might be able to help me with."

"Go on."

"Ever hear of Incandescent, Jack?"

Jack smiled. "'Course I have. I've paid some attention at those goddamn technology council meetings." Jack was chairman of the Senate Technology Council, a sub-committee that was doing a landmark study of technology in America. Jack had become familiar with the country's leading computer and biotech companies.

"Incandescent," Jack said, looking up at the ceiling. "Lessee. Pretty hot software company in Cambridge, right? Started and run by a Jewish kid from MIT, Gladstone, right? Marty Gladstone, yeah. Industry leader, track record, makes solid products, tough competitor." He paused to take a sip and smiled crookedly. "Doesn't hold a candle to GWare, though."

TJ smiled. "True, Jack, but Incandescent is releasing a new multimedia operating system, just about the time we're releasing our new operating system. Fact is, they could beat us to market."

"Yeah, so what? You guys have faced stiff competition before."

TJ puffed on the cigar. "Not like this." He let the response linger in the air for a moment, like the wisps of cigar smoke.

Morrissey just shrugged. He wasn't following TJ's drift just yet.

TJ leaned forward. "I think I could use a little help on this one, Jack."

Jack looked at TJ absently. "What kind of help?"

"Well, I'm sure a company like Incandescent might raise a red flag with the Technology Council. You know, maybe there's been some questionable business practices or something. I mean, what if Gladstone had stolen the idea for the operating system, or what if they were getting secret funding from a foreign company, or something like that?"

"That's preposterous, I can't believe…"

"Jack, it could be anything, anything at all, you know," TJ said smoothly. "Your Council certainly has the right to ask questions, doesn't it? That's what the Senate is all about, investigations and so on. Why, I imagine if you did a little poking around you'd be sure to find something to look at a little more closely. You know, something that might distract Gladstone, tie up Incandescent for a while."

Jack pondered this in silence. He was high, but not high enough to be unaware of the implications of TJ's remarks.

"Y'know, Jack," TJ continued, "it's pretty easy to see that it would be bad for business here in California if GWare was upstaged by a Massachusetts company. In fact, I wouldn't be surprised if Gladstone was a bleeding heart liberal Democrat."

"You know what you're asking me to do," the Senator said quietly, almost whispering.

TJ looked at him blankly, almost innocently. "Oh Jack, I'm not asking you to do anything. We're just talking here." He paused to blow a circle of cigar smoke into the air. "You can figure it all out on your own, now can't you? Of course, I needn't remind you of the importance of our friendship, especially during the last election. As I recall, it meant quite a lot to both of us."

Jack shook his head. "The word blackmail comes to mind, TJ," he said with sadness in his voice.

TJ smiled, unruffled. "Don't be so dramatic, Jack. I'm hardly threatening you. I've told you of a situation, that's all. I think it might be helpful for you to give it your attention. I could see where it would be to your benefit to do something about it, but of course, it's entirely your decision."

Silence hung in the air for a long moment. TJ could hear the ticking of the clock on the mantle. The Senator took a long sip from his martini glass and slowly put it down on the table. He rose to his feet slowly.

"If there's nothing else, TJ, I don't want to seem rude, but I'm suddenly feeling quite tired. I think I'll nap for a while, if you don't mind," Senator Morrissey said, rising uncertainly to his feet. TJ also stood to leave.

"Good to see you, Jack. I know you'll give some serious thought to what I've said." TJ paused, then added, "I know you'll make the right decision. You always do, Senator."

CHAPTER 6

Another holiday season was approaching and the air was taking on its customary chill in Cambridge. Marty looked from his office window at the grayness of the day. Outside on the street the recently fallen snow was beginning to turn brown. He wished there were a new layer upon it to whiten up the scene again.

The day for his product launch was fast approaching. He had somehow overcome the loss of Henry Chu. His talented staff had picked up the pieces and kept the project on track, making a Herculean effort. Marty himself had worked virtually twenty-four hours a day to keep the project moving. Things were going along well, he had to admit, so well that he firmly believed they would launch the product on time, in mid-January.

What kind of year would 1994 be, he wondered, remembering that '93 had surely started with a jolt. Just two months into the new year, terrorists had bombed the World Trade Center, killing five people. At least they caught the bastards in March and locked them up.

That wasn't the only type of terrorism that was rampant in America. There had been an alarming increase in computer virus incidents as well. While some of the viruses were just inconveniences, others seriously hampered computer users. Computer viruses could result in major problems for corporations, infecting their networks, slowing productivity, and causing thousands of dollars in damage. Marty knew that software makers in particular were vulnerable, because it was their products that became the targets for the virus attacks. For example, Microsoft's Outlook e-mail system was a frequent target for frontal assaults by hackers. Marty hoped this year wouldn't bring even more virulent strains of viruses with it.

Marty's introspection was interrupted by the ringing of the phone. He could tell by the caller ID number that it was Erin Keliher on the line. Ever since Erin saw the product demo, she had kept in close touch with Marty. She had an insatiable appetite for information and made it clear that she expected to get even the smallest tidbit about the product from Marty himself. She was driving Marty's PR agency crazy, but since everything she was saying in her columns was positive, they reluctantly agreed to stay out of the way and allow her to have a direct line to Marty.

Actually, Marty enjoyed the attention for two reasons: One, because it was creating some truly valuable positive buzz about Incandescent's release. And two, Marty was growing increasingly fond of Erin herself. Though he had only seen her a few more times since the demo, they had spent many hours together, just talking. After they ran out of things to say about the software business, the conversations had inevitably turned personal, to their own lives.

It didn't take Marty long to figure out that they were cut from a similar cloth. Both Marty and Erin were classic workaholics, people who were so wrapped up in their professional lives that they had little time for anything else. That made having personal relationships difficult if not impossible, and they both commiserated over the fact that they were not only unattached but not even seeing anyone.

The fact is, Marty and Erin had a good laugh over it, sharing the absurdity of a lifestyle that was exhilarating but grueling. They both admitted to loving what they did, but each of them understood the sacrifices they made as a result. He was struck by the common feeling they had about their very public lives. As many people as she interacted with on a daily basis, Erin said, she felt a certain aloneness. Everyone was a business associate or a "story." Sure, she had her girlfriends, but they were slowly moving out of her life stage, getting married and having children. She, Erin, was about Marty's age and saw little hope of following the same path any time soon. Not that she wanted to, she told him. Her career was her life, and that's the way she preferred it, at least for now.

Marty could relate completely. He, too, had this feeling of aloneness, one that was fueled by long hours and an almost superhuman commitment to his business. Lately he had been asking himself if there was anything beyond this, if there was life after software. Every once in awhile, he even wondered why this operating system meant so much to him. How different it would be if he had someone to love in his life, he thought.

He wondered if that someone could be Erin. She seemed to be in the same place he was, and she certainly understood what he was going through. He found her to be bright, articulate, and a no-nonsense type of woman. He admired what she had accomplished in her life. And it wasn't lost on him that she was very attractive—that certainly was a bonus.

But how realistic was it for Marty to think that he could have any sort of relationship with this Irish Catholic who lived in San Francisco…he a Jew from Boston? Even if their different backgrounds could be overcome, how could he possibly carry out a long-distance relationship with someone like Erin? The thought was too crazy to even consider it.

"Hello Erin, good to hear from you."

"Well how is the boy wonder today?" she asked with a smile in her voice.

"No worse than any other day," he answered with a chuckle.

Erin's voice turned suddenly serious. "Marty, I have something you need to know about." She paused for a moment. "I've heard it on good authority that the Senate Technology Council is beginning an investigation of Incandescent."

Erin heard an audible gasp from Marty on the other end of the line. "Any idea why?" she asked.

"No, Erin, no idea at all," Marty said quickly. He was stunned at the news. Marty had been invited in the past by the Council's chairman, Senator Morrissey, to appear as a guest. He had testified on behalf of the Software Publishers Association. The SPA had launched an aggressive effort to crack down on pirated software, with the help of Federal authorities.

Marty's company had been victimized, just like numerous other software companies. His advisers had estimated revenue loss in the millions of dollars worldwide due to software that was illegally distributed.

Marty offered his expert opinion to the Technology Council, shared with them the estimates of Incandescent's losses, and made a strong plea for endorsing SPA's actions. But he also expressed considerable skepticism at the Federal government's ability to police such a pervasive problem. A few of the senators on the Council bristled indignantly at Marty's assertion but others, even Senator Morrissey himself, nodded in quiet agreement.

Was that enough to make some enemies, Marty wondered. Maybe he ruffled a few feathers, he thought, but he couldn't see why it would lead to an investigation. Senate investigations took time and money. The Technology Council was one of the few Senate sub-committees with a reputation for efficiency.

"Erin, I have no idea what they could possibly want with Incandescent."

"Any run-ins of any kind that you can think of?"

"I was just thinking about the time I appeared before the Council in support of the SPA initiative. I may have pissed one or two of them off."

Erin shrugged it off. "No, I don't think that's it. Sure, they have egos, but that doesn't sound serious enough to cause an investigation."

"I don't know of anything else." Marty paused. "Erin, of course I'll need to speak with counsel, but give me a little insight into how these guys operate."

"Well," Erin began, "the Technology Council has the same basic powers as the Senate itself. As a special committee, they can investigate as they see fit, with due cause, of course. They can subpoena people or documents or evidence, whatever they want, similar to a court of law.

"They don't have the power to prosecute, but they can make recommendations based on their findings. In short, Marty, they can make life pretty miserable for someone if they want to, that is, if their investigation has merit."

"What do you mean, 'has merit'?"

"There's been some sensitivity on the Senate floor lately as to the expense and the embarrassment associated with a questionable committee investigation," Erin said. "The Senate would rather stay out of the limelight when it comes to looking stupid."

Marty chuckled. "Lord knows they're pretty good at that. So what you're saying is the Technology Council better have a pretty solid reason to investigate anyone."

"Yes, or they could eat crow."

"Let's suppose they think they have a good reason. Then what?" Marty asked.

"Well, they could drag you and your employees before the Council, ask a lot of questions, waste a lot of your attorney's time, that kind of thing."

A warning signal suddenly went off in Marty's brain.

"Erin, hypothetically, if TJ Gatwick wanted to put a roadblock in the way of our product launch, wouldn't this be a great way to do it?"

Erin thought about it for a moment. "That's a pretty serious allegation, Marty."

"Yeah, but play along with me for a minute. Let's say TJ had some undue influence with the Committee. I figure the logical guy is Morrissey. After all, he's from California. Couldn't that kind of thing happen?"

Erin was following Marty's logic, and it was starting to make sense. "You have a point, and a good one. If memory serves me, TJ Gatwick was one of Morrissey's major backers in the last election...big bucks, come to think of it. Morrissey had his share of trouble, too. I wouldn't be surprised if TJ called in a few favors to help get Morrissey re-elected."

Marty was beginning to see this as a real possibility. "Erin, I think we may have nailed it. All we need to do is confirm the connection between Gatwick and Morrissey and I think we'll have a good reason for this investigation taking place."

"I can help you there, Marty. I'll get a look at *The Journal's* archive, and do a little poking around on my own. It shouldn't be too difficult to verify." Erin's investigative juices were flowing now. "But I have to tell you, even if we confirm the link, it may not mean much. It's just circumstantial evidence...we'll still need to prove that TJ engineered this whole thing, and that won't be easy."

"Maybe so, but it's all I've got. And whatever happens, Council investigation or not, I won't let TJ or Morrissey stop my product release, you can be damn sure of that."

After her phone conversation with Marty, Erin wanted to do more than just research the situation. She was so upset by the possibility that TJ would have done something like this that she decided to take matters into her own hands. She knew it could backfire but she just couldn't let this go if there was any chance she could do something about it. She hoped the power of the press would have some bearing on the man. She put in a call to TJ and when she got him on the phone she said she needed to meet with him right away, that it was urgent. TJ was noticeably cool at first, but he agreed.

Even as Erin's plane was touching down in San Diego, she was running through exactly what she would say to TJ for the hundredth time. The problem was, she never settled on the exact words, just the content.

But at least she had that part down, and she sensed that this meeting would be a showdown of sorts. TJ was, of course, furious with her anyway, and now, when she confronted him with this accusation, he'd probably go ballistic.

She had to do it, however, because she was indignant at the thought that TJ could stand in the way of the Incandescent product release. This product HAD to see the light of day, she thought. It was just too damned good not to, and no one, especially a competitor like TJ, should be able to suppress it.

There was another reason for her interest, though. She had to admit to herself that she liked Marty not just a little, but a lot. Here was a guy who was about as driven as anyone she had ever met, and yet, there was a softness, even a vulnerability to him. She was fascinated by the fact that he could be so strong, so forthright, that he could be such a dynamic personality—yet with such a private, personal side that was almost shy and innocent somehow. And with it all, he had a truly disarming sense of humor.

She had enjoyed their face-to-face meetings immensely, and their phone conversations had become longer and more personal. God, Erin thought, was she possibly falling in love with him?

It was time to deplane, and Erin put thoughts of Marty aside, preparing herself for the confrontation that was to come. She exited into the San Diego airport. It was far more manageable than San Francisco, and conveniently located in the center of the city. That would change, Erin realized, with the continuing growth of the San Diego area.

San Diego was expanding dramatically for many reasons, not the least of which was the prominence and success of GWare, one of the area's largest employers. The southern California weather was nearly perfect—idyllic, really. Erin couldn't think of a day she had visited the city that it wasn't sunny and pleasantly low in humidity…not like San Francisco, she thought with a grimace. Much as she loved the Bay area, it couldn't compare to San Diego's weather patterns. Frisco could get downright cold, and it rained often enough to remind her of Seattle at times.

She felt that San Diego offered its residents an unmatched combination of all the right lifestyle elements that made for gracious living. It was slower and less frenetic than Los Angeles, smaller and less cosmopolitan than San Francisco. Even the downtown buildings were not as tall because of the airport's proximity, and it gave the city a friendly skyline. It had the Pacific, great beaches, terrific attractions, lush countryside, wonderful shopping, history, the arts, beautiful surrounding towns, the Mexican influence…a paradise, Erin thought. And sure it was expensive as hell, but certainly no more so than Frisco.

As Erin exited the airport, she saw a limousine driver holding a sign with her name on it. TJ may be angry at her, but he still had some amount of class…he promised he would have a car waiting.

The limo was outside downtown in minutes, heading for the GWare campus, just twenty minutes away. It occurred to Erin that she hadn't been to the campus in quite some time, since she had always attended their monthly get-togethers at a restaurant in Lo Jolla.

Now she would be on TJ's turf…or entering his kingdom, really. The GWare campus was very much a world of its own in many ways. She wouldn't be surprised if it had its own time zone.

As always, she was impressed with the approach up the driveway to the main building. This was a company that, from the very first view, had the aura of success. The physical quality of it was stunning, with its buildings set on the rolling hills among the trees. It was all carefully planned to be in concert with nature, from the pond with the re-circulating fountain near the complex entrance, to the shaded parking areas and unobtrusive tennis courts behind the buildings.

The place had a casual informality, a youthful exuberance to it. Yet somewhere behind the scenes, another GWare existed, where workers lurked below the surface, being sucked dry of ideas, all but swallowed up by the all-consuming environment. She knew this truth because she knew people who had and who still did work there. She knew its reputation. And she knew the style of the notorious ruler of the kingdom, TJ Gatwick.

Erin entered the main building, a breathtaking structure with a giant atrium that spiraled upward, five stories from the first floor. Light crashed through the top of the building as if it were cascading from the heavens. Surrounding the atrium were the individual floors of the building, each of the major hallways traversing past the atrium opening. As she looked up, Erin saw people constantly moving, as if suspending in space, the light playing visual tricks on her eyes. The effect was startling, as if TJ's employees were angels walking on air.

A glass elevator whisked Erin to the fifth floor, where TJ himself greeted her. Now that was a major surprise.

"Welcome to my world," TJ said with a slightly condescending tone, leading her to a small conference room near the elevator.

"Help yourself," TJ said, pointing to a side table that had a variety of drinks and cookies on it.

Erin waved him off. "Good to see you, TJ."

"I'm sure," he replied off-handedly. "You said it was urgent."

Obviously, TJ was not going to engage in small talk or make this any easier for her.

"How's the product release coming?"

"Wouldn't you like to know. Come on now, Erin, don't waste my time with small talk."

Erin sighed. "Well, I *am* interested in it, TJ. My job is to report on software, you know. The word is you're close to hitting the street with it."

"Soon enough."

"But not as close as Incandescent," she said, challenging him.

He glared at her but didn't say anything.

Here goes nothing, she thought. "Funny thing is, Incandescent has run into a little problem. Seems as if they're being investigated by the Senate's Technology Council."

"Really?" TJ said, looking absently at the fingers of his left hand.

"Yes, and I thought maybe you could tell me something about that."

"What would I know about the investigation, Erin?"

She looked him straight in the eye. "Probably nothing. But then it's not the investigation itself I'm talking about. I'm wondering, TJ, if you had anything to do with *arranging* for the investigation."

"Are you accusing me of tampering with a Senate sub-committee, Erin?" TJ said with a laugh. "You reporters do have active imaginations." He emphasized the word "reporters" as if it were a dirty word.

Erin persisted. "So you're denying you had anything to do with it?"

TJ stood up to get a sparkling water from the side table. "Sure you won't join me?" he asked with mock charm. Erin shook her head.

"I would imagine that the Technology Council wouldn't be investigating Incandescent if it didn't have a reason to do so," TJ said, avoiding Erin's question. "You know, some software companies just cross the line a little too often."

Talk about calling the kettle black, she thought.

"You didn't answer my question, TJ."

"I'm not going to play your little investigative game, Erin. This isn't *60 Minutes*, and I won't accept your insinuation. Was there something else you wanted to discuss with me, because if not, I really think you wasted your time, and mine, coming here today."

It was obvious she had no further reason to stay, so Erin got up and straightened her slacks.

"I guess I did waste my time," she said. "But I'm not letting you off so easy, TJ. If I find out you had anything to do with this, anything at all, I'll break the story so fast you won't know what hit you."

TJ sniffed dismissively. "I'm not surprised. It's all about the story, isn't it? Well, you won't find one here, now or in the future. Wonderful to see you, Erin, as always. You know your own way out," TJ said as he turned and walked out of the conference room, leaving her standing there by herself.

"What a charmer," Erin said to the empty room, heading back to the elevator. She decided to ask the receptionist in the lobby to call her a cab…just so she wouldn't have to take TJ's damned limousine back to the airport.

CHAPTER 7

When Doomsday learned of the impending investigation of Incandescent by the Senate Technology Council, he was concerned that it could ruin his grand plan. He knew that the investigation could easily mean a delay in the release of the Incandescent operating system. If so, his carefully coordinated virus attack would fail.

He had already managed to embed the virus in GWare's code with the help of a confederate who worked at the company. This meant that, at worst case, half of what he wanted to accomplish would be put into motion. When GWare distributed their product to the world, they would also be distributing the Doomsday Virus. This deadly strain, for which Doomsday believed there was no cure, was designed to rapidly infect both networks and computer hard drives by self-propagating with astonishing speed. The result would be a meltdown of massive proportions. Doomsday was confident that his "product" was an inspired, ingeniously devised piece of software...one that would have easily won an award if it were legitimate. That would be rich, he thought, an award for the Doomsday Virus!

But it wouldn't be nearly as effective as launching the attack on GWare and Incandescent simultaneously. That would cause the most damage at once, dealing a devastating blow to the software industry and the networked world in general. He knew from industry news that Incandescent's operating system would be at least as hot a product as GWare's, maybe more so. With both of these systems launching at the same time, millions of copies of two operating systems would be distributed worldwide in a matter of weeks. He could imagine his virus lurking in all of them, waiting to be unleashed. It was too tantalizing an opportunity for Doomsday to miss.

If he could keep Incandescent's launch on track, he thought, he could still carry out his plan. It was ironic—here he was thinking about how to actually help a software company make its product launch date!

Doomsday realized that the only way to he could affect the current situation was to somehow block the investigation. If it could be delayed or postponed, then Incandescent wouldn't be deterred from launching its product. Of course, this was easier said than done. This was, after all, the United States Senate he was dealing with. Doomsday had an impressive network of hackers, but what could they do to thwart a Senate investigation?

He thought he might as well pose the problem to his inner circle…those few super-hackers in his covert network who he most relied upon. They were all instrumental in the plan, so why not let them brainstorm a solution. He quickly typed out an e-mail to them, explaining the situation. It didn't take long for members of the inner circle to share their ideas.

One of the hackers was located in the Washington, D.C. area and he said he had connections with an unsavory anti-American group that was always looking for excuses to draw attention to itself. He proposed to Doomsday that the network consider paying this group to do something quite outlandish to stop the investigation: kidnap the head of the Technology Council, Senator John Morrissey.

Doomsday found this idea intriguing. A successful kidnapping of Morrissey would certainly damage the investigation, as all attention would focus on the safe return of the Senator. What's more, the driving force of the Council would be gone, and Doomsday was certain that would mean the investigation would immediately lose its steam.

Doomsday also liked the idea that he could remain one step removed from the crime by having another group take responsibility. Shit, he thought, the group could even demand a ransom and keep it for their trouble!

Doomsday felt that this was a very good plan indeed. It would serve his purpose well, and it would wreak a little havoc in Washington to boot. It sounded like a win-win situation to him.

With growing excitement and optimism, he e-mailed his Washington operative in response and told him to move forward with the arrangements as soon as possible. The kidnapping needed to happen soon. At the same time, Doomsday would need to break into Incandescent's code. Since he had freelanced for the company, he knew one or two disgruntled programmers there who might possibly help him out. He contacted one of them at his home e-mail and was delighted to find that he was receptive to participating in subterfuge. This was turning out to be much better than he had hoped. Yes, Doomsday thought, this was turning into an excellent day indeed.

* * *

They had executed this routine countless times before, each time with success, but this was the first time they were doing it in Washington, and with such a famous American.

They parked several blocks away and proceeded on foot. Clouds hid the moon. They moved silently toward the gate. They knew about the security system. They had decided it would be simpler and safer to dig under the perimeter fence than to disarm it.

The earth was soft, but it was back-breaking work nonetheless. They sweated heavily. They alternated the task, stopping periodically to listen. But the night remained quiet as they dug the trench. One of them, the stronger of the two, could lie down in the trench and dig forward, sliding as he carved out the earth before him. He inched his way to the other side of the fence with agonizing slowness.

Finally, he was on the other side of the fence. He got up and stood quietly, looking around him in the blackness, listening to the silence. The other intruder followed, sliding on his back in the trench until he reached his companion. They stood still together, listening again. There was no sound.

They wiped their hands on their sweat-stained black shirts. They moved forward slowly, but with certainty. They knew where to enter the house, at a point were the alarm had already been disabled, the window left slightly ajar. Their accomplice had done his job well.

The Senator would be asleep in his second floor bedroom, apart from his wife. They knew it was his custom to have sex with her on a very rare occasion, but even when he did, it would not last long, and he would prefer to return to the privacy and comfort of his own bed in his own room.

Fortunately for the intruders, the Senator slept with an eye-shade. It made the flicker of their penlights indiscernible as they cased the room before approaching the bed. One of them brought out the cloth and gently but firmly put it across the Senator's nose and mouth. He jerked suddenly in momentary consciousness as sleep was interrupted by a strong chemical smell and a sensation that he could not breathe. Just as suddenly, however, he slipped into drugged unconsciousness. He would be incapacitated for more than enough time.

The stronger of the two lifted the Senator off the bed in a fireman's carry position. The other grabbed the Senator's robe and slippers on the way out. They were down the stairs moments after they had entered the Senator's room.

They next had to drag the Senator through the window to avoid the door alarm which they knew would still be active. The stronger one went outside and took the shoulders of the Senator. The other lifted the Senator's legs. They got him out but not without difficulty. Again, the stronger one hoisted the Senator over his shoulders and they made their way back to the trench.

They had dug the trench wide enough to accommodate the Senator's corpulent body. The stronger one crawled to the other side of the perimeter fence. They both pushed, pulled, and dragged the Senator until they got him through the trench. It was the most tiring, tedious part of the operation.

They stood over their prey on the other side, victorious. But there was still considerable danger. They still had to get the Senator to their car. The stronger one lifted him again. They moved quietly out of the area surrounding the Morrissey mansion, towards their vehicle.

Suddenly, they were startled by lights rounding the corner. They backed away quickly, the stronger one losing his balance momentarily, as he dropped to one knee. The Senator wobbled around as the man strained to steady himself. The lights were a momentary distraction—just a car in search of a destination at an hour when no one should be riding around.

They continued their surreptitious journey and finally reached the vehicle. They put the Senator in the back seat and threw a blanket over him. They hurried into the front and drove off in silence.

The elapsed time of the operation, including digging the trench, was a little more than an hour. It was a success. They would still have darkness shrouding their drive to their final destination.

The stronger one relaxed now in the passenger's set, his muscles aching. The other man drove north on Highway 78. They passed farms and open country, barely visible in the faint moonlight, vastly different from the congestion of San Diego. They saw an occasional car, but for the most part, they drove alone in silence for about 45 minutes.

"Heavy bastard," the stronger one said quietly. The other answered with a grunt.

They continued to Julian, sixty miles northeast of San Diego, 4,235 feet above sea level. The little town with its six-block Main Street was home to less than 1,000 people. It had sprung up during the gold rush of the late 1860s. Some eighteen mines were worked, producing millions of dollars of gold during the height of the rush. Now the sleepy town was better known for its apples.

They turned off the main street and headed into an uninhabited area. In fifteen minutes they had reached the remote cabin.

They had timed the event well. Dawn was just now breaking, showing its first light as the driver turned off the car engine. The stronger one uncovered the Senator and pulled him unceremoniously from the back of the car. He was still unconscious. The other opened the cabin door. Once more, the stronger one hoisted the Senator onto his shoulders, taking him inside and dropping him heavily onto a dusty bed in the corner of the cabin.

The other went out to the car, opened the trunk, lifted out a cooler, and brought it into the cabin. He opened it and pawed around, pulling out a beer. He motioned to the cooler for the stronger one to join him.

They stripped off their black shirts and wiped their faces. They sat at the wooden table, drinking the beer.

They did not speak, just looked over at the Senator, who conveniently still had his night shade on. The stronger one decided he had better tie up the Senator in case he awakened, so he went to get the rope from the car. He tied the Senators hands and feet, even as he slept.

They sat and waited as the sun signaled the beginning of a new day. The stronger one looked at his watch and finally spoke in Arabic.

"I'm going to make the call. He won't give you any trouble."

The other man just nodded, and the stronger one went outside and drove off.

In the hour that the stronger one was gone, the Senator barely moved. His captor wondered if they had used too much of the chemical, but as long as the fat man was breathing, his captor showed little concern.

The stronger one returned with some bags. He said in Arabic, "I have made the call. It is in Allah's hands."

Finally the Senator slowly regained consciousness. As he awakened, he had a familiar feeling of being hung over, but he could not remember drinking heavily the night before. He then became aware of the fact that his hands and feet were tied, and a cold fear swept over him. His night shade still in place, he could not see. The stronger one roughly undid the Senator's gag.

"What's going on? Where am I? Who's there?" Morrissey said weakly.

The stronger one answered with no discernible accent. "You are a prisoner, Senator. Do not try to yell for help. We are far away from anyone who could hear you." The stronger one pointed to the other man. They had previously agreed that they would switch off voices just to confuse Morrissey and make it difficult for him to focus on one of them.

So now the other man said, "Yell and we will gag you again. Or maybe we will slit your throat." He laughed.

Then the stronger one spoke. "On the other hand, cooperate with us and you will not get hurt."

Morrissey was afraid but indignant. His outrage unwisely rose to the surface. "What the hell is this all about?" the Senator asked angrily. "You're holding a United States Senator. I demand that you release me at once."

They both laughed at this. The stronger one said, "Oh yes, we know we are holding a Senator, Mr. Senator John Morrissey." He emphasized the last part of the name so it came out Morris—SEEE. He pointed to the other man, who added, "You will not be released just yet. And don't waste your time making demands. We will make the demands here."

Morrissey quickly understood these bastards were in control. He had to admit he was frightened, despite his heroic past. Morrissey had been something of a World War II hero. While it was nothing more than a brief altercation with a Nazi, it had led to his being awarded a Purple Heart. Morrissey's PR machine had made the most out of that.

Now he recalled the moment, that fleeting memory of so long ago. He remembered the mortal fear he felt, the whole unreal environment of that war, the smells and the sights of death and destruction. But somehow he had survived it all, even as many of his Navy buddies had not.

Morrissey conjured up the memory to give him hope. After all, he thought, he had been in battle, he had faced an adversary, he had overcome fear, he had survived. These thoughts were some consolation to him, as he lay there, frightened and helpless.

He forced himself to focus on the situation. Who were these adversaries, and what did they want? He quickly reckoned with the fact that it was a kidnapping and there would be a ransom to pay.

Last he remembered he was sleeping peacefully in his bed. How the hell did they get through his security systems? My God, he thought, was it an inside job?

But he couldn't think about that now. He had read accounts of kidnappings, and he remembered that it was important to put together details. A scene from the movie "Sneakers" flashed through his mind, when Robert Redford reconstructed the sounds he had heard during his abduction. In the movie, Morrissey thought grimly, Redford lives to tell about it.

He tried to concentrate on what had happened since he awakened. The sensation of a hangover—that had to be from a drug. The voices—there were two voices, he knew that. He thought about them. He wanted to hear them again, so he tried to engage his captors in conversation.

"Listen," he said with resignation in his voice, "I'll cooperate, whatever you want. I won't give you any trouble. But my arms hurt, can you at least untie me?"

"Shut up," is all he heard.

Morrissey needed to hear more of the voice, so he pushed it again. "Then please, a drink of water?"

He was stung by a kick to his shin, and he cried out in pain.

"Shut up, I said," the voice yelled at him. "You do not speak unless I speak to you."

Even in pain, Morrissey processed the voice. It had a formality to it, as if English was not the speaker's native language. He couldn't quite detect an accent, but there was a slight accent...European, Chinese? Maybe Arabic?

He knew he had heard two different voices before, so there were at least two of them. He figured they were alternating voices so he would not be able to analyze one of them.

Two voices, English as a second language, two men...it wasn't much, but it was something.

He was silent now, listening hard for any sounds around him, sniffing for any smells. He heard the occasional shuffle of feet creaking on a wooden floor, the pushing of a chair, but not much else. That meant something, didn't it? It was very quiet—no planes, no traffic. They had to be a fair distance away from San Diego, anyway.

He smelled the air—it seemed clean, but he could detect a faint smell of beer mingled with—what?—sweat maybe? He heard a clicking noise and then smelled smoke. Must be one of them lighting up a cigarette.

He sniffed the bed. It had a musty smell. He felt at the bed with his bare feet as subtly as he could. It felt like a wool blanket was covering the bed.

He tried to form a mental impression of where he might be. He imagined himself in a small cabin, away from civilization. That would fit. His kidnappers would obviously be using an isolated spot. If he could figure out how long he was unconscious, he'd know how far they'd traveled. But how could he possibly know that?

Morrissey mentally filed away the facts he had assembled. It wasn't much but maybe they would help. The bigger question now was why would these people risk kidnapping a U.S. Senator? It was pretty brazen just for the money.

There had to be another reason. Sure, Morrissey had enemies. But this was serious business, so the reason had to be something big. What was he involved in that could lead to someone doing this?

His wife…yes, she hated him, but she'd have to be nuts to get involved in something like this. The Democrats…ridiculous. The only thing he had been active in lately was the Technology Council investigation of Incandescent. Could that be it…could it be possible that Martin Gladstone had anything to do with this?

Morrissey couldn't see it—not Gladstone, he was an ethical businessman. It had been tough enough convincing the Council to proceed with the investigation—Gladstone was as clean as they come. Kidnapping just didn't fit his profile. On the other hand, if he were really desperate, if he thought it would deter the investigation, wouldn't he be capable of it?

But then Morrissey thought of another possibility, and even as it occurred to him, a cold chill ran down his spine. He could have been captured by terrorists of some kind…the kind that would be happy to do any sort of damage, even superficial and small, to the government. The kind that would be unconcerned about their own lives…that would do worse than kidnap, maybe even kill a Senator.

Unfortunately, this was the scenario that made the most sense to Senator Jack Morrissey. And as he lay there, helpless, alone and afraid, he said a silent prayer that he was wrong.

CHAPTER 8

Senator Morrissey Kidnapped

Taken from California home, ransom demanded

Marty was reading the words in the headline of the *Boston Globe*, but he couldn't believe it. Who in God's name would kidnap a Senator? What was the world coming to?

According to the article, the Senator had been kidnapped from his California mansion and was being held for a ransom of one million dollars. The kidnappers had made their demand via a telephone call to Federal authorities. Details were sketchy. The article went on to say, however, that the Senator was chairman of the Senate Technology Council, which was at the time of the kidnapping beginning an investigation of Incandescent. The Council, said the article, was postponing the investigation indefinitely.

Marty was, of course, thrilled and relieved to learn of the postponement. But he certainly did not wish any harm to come to the Senator.

When Marty arrived at his office, he had a voice mail from Erin. He returned her call immediately. She greeted him warmly but, as was Erin's style, she got right down to business.

"Read the paper today?" she asked, sounding a little breathless.

"Sure did," Marty responded. "Unbelievable about Morrissey. Heck of a way for me to get off the hook."

"I'll say," acknowledged Erin. "Look, I'm flying to Washington to interview the other members of the Technology Council. Maybe I can get a good quote or two…and as an aside, find out what they've got on Incandescent."

"Could you really do that, Erin?"

"What better excuse than the kidnapping to talk to them," she said. "If I catch them off guard, no telling what I could learn."

"That would be fantastic if you could pull it off," Marty answered. "At least I'd know what I'm up against."

"How about I do the interview and then catch the shuttle up to Boston? I'd love to see you."

"Y'know, that would be great. When do you think?"

"Shouldn't take more than a day or two to speak with the Senators. I'm thinking I could see you by dinnertime Thursday night."

"Thursday night…that's fine. It'll be a celebration of sorts…the impending release of Incandescent's operating system." Marty paused and thought a minute. "Tell you what. Let's have dinner together at a special place…I'll surprise you."

"It's a date," she said and hung up.

Marty had given Erin the address of his condominium on Beacon Street. While Marty wasn't extravagant with his money, he did believe his home should be a private and special haven, a place where he could truly escape from the rigors of running his business. He had found one of the most unusual condos in all of Boston, one that was literally his sanctuary, because it was created out of space in the spire of a church building. The church had been converted to a few exclusive units, with one—Marty's unit—taking advantage of the tallest point of the former church.

The security guard informed Marty of Erin's arrival and he came down to the entry-way to greet her. She looked exquisite to him—her blue eyes sparkled against a tanned face, surrounded by her auburn hair. She gave him a big smile and a hug. He responded with a slight peck on her cheek. There was the scent of perfume as his lips brushed her soft skin.

Marty led Erin to the door of his condo and heard her catch her breath when she entered.

"Unusual, isn't it?" he said as they walked inside.

"Unbelievable is more like it," Erin said wondrously.

"It's a church that was converted into condos. I got the unit with the steeple. Needless to say, I had never seen anything like it. It's all built on separate levels, four of them straight up, so I not only live here, I get plenty of exercise here."

She laughed. "Can you give me the 50-cent tour?"

"Love to." Marty led her from level to level, each small but impeccably furnished.

"How did you get the furniture in here?" she asked.

"With great difficulty," he answered. "Some of it, like the bed, had to be cut in half and re-assembled in the condo. Here, look at this."

He pointed out a Japanese sitting tub in the bathroom. "This the only thing that would fit. Pretty standard for Japanese homes, but not easy to find in Boston."

They walked up to the top floor. Atop the condominium was the highest point of the former church's spire. Oversized windows provided an unparalleled view of Boston and Cambridge.

"God," she whispered, turning 360 degrees as she looked out the windows in utter amazement.

"Yes, I like to think He's around here somewhere," Marty answered reverently.

She could do nothing but gawk at the city lights below her. He let her look around her and did not say anything to disturb the serenity.

It offered him an opportunity to admire her. He felt he could spend the evening just gazing at her.

"You can stay up here for awhile if you like," he said, breaking the silence.

"But I wouldn't want to make us late for dinner…" she answered, coming out of the spell she was in.

"Oh yes, dinner," Marty answered with eyes twinkling. "Well that won't be a problem. You see, we'll be having dinner here."

She graced him with a large smile that showed perfectly white teeth. "That's sweet. I had no idea you were a cook."

He shrugged it off. "We'll see if that's an accurate assessment when you sit down to dinner."

She laughed, following him down the narrow stairway, and then down another two stairways, until they reached the galley-style kitchen.

"Something to drink?" he asked as he made a show of putting on a chef's apron. "I have wine, soda, San Pellegrino…"

"White wine would be great."

Marty poured a glass for Erin and poured a glass of San Pellegrino for himself. He clinked glasses with her and said, "To journalistic integrity."

"I'll second that," she answered, sipping her wine. "Y'know," Erin said, "I don't think I've ever seen you drink wine."

"You're right," Marty answered. "Learned a long time ago that I don't have much of a tolerance for alcohol, so I stay away from it."

"And you're probably better off for it."

Marty smiled. "Yeah, but most people I know think I'm some kind of recovering alcoholic with a heart condition. I don't drink and I don't eat meat."

"More power to you," Erin said with a laugh. "Anyway, I like a guy who's health-conscious. Can I do anything to help?" she asked, as he busied himself with slicing tomatoes for a salad.

"No, I'm fine. You'll be proud of me, I left work early to get a start on this," Marty said as he stirred a pot of pasta sauce on the stove. "Cooking for a woman is something I take seriously."

"Not just any woman, I hope," Erin said with a twinkle in her eye.

He looked up with a smile and continued his work.

"How was Washington?" he said.

"Washington is Washington. But I did manage to get a little insight into the investigation."

Marty continued to work, but he listened intently.

"Jack Morrissey was definitely the instigator," Erin continued. "According to one of the Senators I spoke with, Morrissey was making quite a fuss about some highly questionable business practices pursued by Incandescent. When I pressed the Senator, though, he wouldn't give me anything specific."

Marty just shook his head. "That's because there's isn't anything specific, Erin. It's just not true at all."

She looked at him with those vivid blue eyes of hers. "I figured that," she said simply. "But then, Morrissey could've been full of it and the investigation would still proceed. He had that kind of respect, that kind of clout."

"He never would've found anything," Marty said firmly, putting a loaf of garlic bread into the oven. "There's nothing to find."

"Still," Erin answered, "he didn't need anything concrete, at least not at the outset. He could pretty much call the shots and get the Council to call you and plenty of others in for questioning, if nothing else. So he would have accomplished his goal of impeding your product release. Except now he's been kidnapped."

Marty nodded. "What I can't figure is, who would do something like that, and why? It's a hell of a risk, kidnapping a Senator."

Erin walked around the small kitchen. "Yeah. But there are enough crazies out there who might do anything to make headlines. And my reporter's nose tells me the kidnapping is too close to the investigation for it to be a coincidence."

"You think Morrissey was kidnapped…to keep the Council from investigating Incandescent?"

"That's what I think, but I don't know why," Erin said, taking a sip from her wine glass. "And I also think you'll be hearing from the FBI real soon."

"You serious?"

"Very," Erin replied. "These guys will look at everything…including the possibility that you arranged this kidnapping."

Marty laughed at the absurdity of the thought, but he quickly realized that's exactly what they could think.

"Oh man," he said, shaking his head in bewilderment, "I'm just tryin' to put out a software product, that's all."

Erin put her hand onto his arm. "Look, I know you've got nothing to worry about. Fact is, they can do all the questioning they want and we both know they won't find anything out of whack with you or Incandescent. Now you'll be able to get a great product launched…and get the recognition you deserve."

"Thanks for that, I really appreciate it," Marty said, putting his hand over hers.

She moved closer to him and, with a slow but sure motion, she brought her lips to his and kissed him gently.

Marty slid his hand to the small of her back, pressed her lightly to him, and kissed her tenderly in return. "Something's boiling over," he said, as he heard the bubbling pot on the stove.

"Oh, you mean the sauce," Erin said wickedly.

"Better check to see if my buns are burning," he dead-panned.

She laughed and squeezed his arm. "This dinner could get out of control in a hurry," she said. "I'd love to help."

"Okay, you may as well start lugging stuff up to the next level, where the dining room is. Part of the price you pay for eating dinner at a place as crazy as this one."

Erin dutifully brought the salad and salad dressing upstairs. Marty followed her with the garlic bread and a bowl of gorgonzola and walnut ravioli topped with marinara sauce.

He dished out the pasta, then served up the salad on two small plates.

"Need anything else?" he asked as he removed his apron.

"No, this is great. Please sit," she answered.

They enjoyed their dinner of pasta, salad and bread, talking about themselves. Erin told Marty about her family in the San Francisco area. Her mother was divorced and had not remarried. She lived alone in the city. Her father was living in Seattle. Erin had two brothers who both lived near San Francisco. Marty told Erin he was an only child and said his mother lived in Massachusetts but his father had died when he was thirteen.

Erin complimented the chef on the dinner. Marty offered Erin coffee or tea but she declined. He made himself a cup of herbal tea and invited her up to the top level. He put a Kenny G CD on. They kicked off their shoes, sat on the loveseat and gazed out at the magnificent view.

"I live in a lovely place where I can see Frisco at night," Erin said as she snuggled up against him. "Somehow, it doesn't compare to looking out over Boston from the top of a church."

He smiled. "It is definitely a religious experience," he said, stroking her auburn hair. "Sometimes I sit up here watching the snow fall and it's unbelievable," Marty said. "You can see each flake just floating past the windows. Other times, I just look across to Cambridge, that other country across the river."

"Have you ever thought about spending your life with someone, maybe getting married?" she asked.

"Now there's a serious question," he said. "Sure I've thought about it. But I fit the entrepreneurial stereotype, Erin. Married to the business, at least for now. And you?"

"Same deal. I fit the journalistic stereotype," she said with a sigh.

"Well we're both getting older and wiser," he said. "And I have to admit, at times I think it would be a lot more interesting to share my life with someone instead of a computer screen and a balance sheet. That is, if someone could put up with me."

"What do you think," she said, "it would take to make a long-distance relationship work?"

"A lot of frequent traveler miles," he said.

She hit him lightly in the stomach. "Really, I mean do you think it could work?"

"I guess anything could work if two people wanted it badly enough," Marty answered, "but I'm sure the logistics would be challenging. And you'd spend a ton of money on phone calls and plane fares."

"Yeah. I wasn't being suggestive or anything, I was just wondering how it might be, and how you might feel about it."

He pulled her from his shoulder, held her gently by the arms, and looked into her eyes.

"I'll tell you how I feel about it," he began. "I think it's absolutely ridiculous to even think a Jewish kid from Boston and an Irish journalist from San Francisco could have any kind of relationship that could be even remotely successful." He paused as she took his face in. "But I also think we'd be crazy not to try it," he said with a smile. Then he kissed her lightly on the lips.

"I don't know what to make of you, Marty Gladstone," she said smiling. She put her hand on the back of his neck and pulled him towards her. He kissed her forehead, then the tip of her nose. He stopped for a moment and said, "I've been wondering something."

She looked at him questioningly.

"…if you really have those freckles all over your body," he said innocently.

She looked at him as if he had been a bad boy, and then she put a finger to her lips, as if she was thinking about something. "There is one way to find out.," she said. Slowly but deliberately, she began to unbutton her blouse.

Marty chuckled. "Before you go any further, you may want to take another look at your surroundings." It was then that she realized there were no shades of any kind on the steeple windows. The city could look in on her, as easily as she could look out. "Thanks for stopping what could have been the most embarrassing moment of my life," she said, shaking her head and laughing.

"Let's move down one level to the bedroom. At least it has blinds."

He led her down the stairs with one hand, while he unbuttoned his own shirt with the other. He sat on the bed while she removed her blouse.

He lifted his arms towards her, slowly pulling down the bra from her shoulders. He looked at her firm breasts for a moment, then gently cupped one in his hand, leaned over, and kissed her nipple.

She shuddered momentarily, then reached out to bring his head towards her chest. He lay his head against her breasts, encircling her bare back with his arms. She moved his head from her with her hands and looked into his eyes. Then her fingers went to her slacks. She undid the belt, unbuttoned and unzipped her pants, and let them fall to the ground. Then she slowly dropped her panties.

She pulled off her socks and stood before him naked. He took in her lovely body, looking her up and down. Then he smiled and said, "Yup, they are all over you." He removed his own shirt, pants, underpants and socks and stood there as well.

"Now what?" she said with a gleam in her eye.

He went to the bed, laid down on his back, pulled a condom from the night-table and put it on, and motioned for her to join him. She lay on top of him and kissed him with her lips apart. He moved his hands gently yet firmly about her body, feeling all over as far as he could reach, starting from the back of her head, to her neck, to her shoulder blades, to the lovely mounds of her rear. He massaged her soft warm skin, kneaded her firm flesh.

She responded to his touch, kissing him gently at first, then opening her mouth and kissing him with growing urgency. They explored each other's bodies for the first time and then hugged tightly, their frames fitting well together.

She put him into her and they moved ever more rapidly, she at times sitting atop him, and at other times clinging to him tightly, their bodies growing moist and moving rhythmically together. Finally, with an exploding passion they became one, feeling as they did an intensity that was welcoming and special, an emotional release they had rarely felt before.

CHAPTER 9

Like a well-oiled machine, GWare had readied yet another product for release. The company was surely one of the best in the world at launching software. GWare had an established process in place that left no stone unturned. From advertising and PR through dealer and retailer distribution, GWare understood and applied their enormous leverage to infusing the market with excitement and enthusiasm, even if it was contrived. Some would say the company intimidated the channel and squelched competition by making sure that its own new products dominated the software business, no matter what.

Code-named "Release 1.0," the product was re-named GWare ONE for public consumption. It was an operating system that the whole company, especially TJ Gatwick believed was of historic significance. The advance publicity had certainly created anticipation in the marketplace. TJ Gatwick's PR organization had secured the obligatory appearances on a number of business radio and television talk shows. Massive amounts of printed and electronic literature were ready for release. In an unprecedented move, GWare had embargoed the software until its release. Normally, pre-release copies would have been distributed to influential industry analysts and journalists, but not this time. The operating system was a highly guarded secret, and GWare was taking no chances that a negative review would taint the introduction.

A major advertising campaign had been mounted, using the theme line "Now there's only ONE. GWare ONE." The line was appearing on everything from newspaper ads to TV commercials to billboards in a coordinated blitz on American business. There wasn't a major city in America that didn't have a GWare ONE advertising image somewhere.

With it all, however, GWare loyalists were somewhat concerned that the GWare ONE launch would be overshadowed by growing interest in UNITE, the competitive product from Incandescent. From a timing perspective, Incandescent's product launch was closely tracking to GWare ONE's. Incandescent knew it couldn't compete with GWare's media muscle, so the company's marketing organization, with the approval of Marty Gladstone, had made a strategic decision to delay its release until one month after the introduction of GWare ONE. It wouldn't give Incandescent time to make any product modifications, of course, but at least it would allow the hoopla over ONE to subside. Anything was better than entering the market in the midst of GWare's overwhelming hype. Hopefully, UNITE would gain its own window of opportunity to break through after the GWare ONE introduction had subsided, even with Incandescent's considerably smaller promotional budget. It wasn't a perfect strategy but it would have to do.

The encouraging aspect of the marketing battle was that UNITE had already created excitement equal to and in some circles even exceeding GWare ONE's buzz. Erin Keliher's unreserved enthusiasm for UNITE probably had much to do with it, given her influential position in the industry. In addition, word was getting around just how special a product UNITE was going to be. Others in the technology world had pumped up UNITE with write-ups and Marty was busily answering phone calls and doing one-on-one interviews. This was the kind of cachet UNITE needed to pull off an upset victory over GWare ONE. Marty hoped that Erin's David and Goliath analogy, which had resonated with others in the press, would turn out to be true. It was something Incandescent dearly needed for any hope of success in launching UNITE.

But none of the positive publicity surrounding UNITE deterred GWare from its launch plans. In a bold PR move, TJ Gatwick himself was booked to do an official product unveiling at GWare corporate headquarters. The event would be simulcast via closed-circuit television to invitation-only gatherings at hotel ballrooms and GWare technology centers worldwide. Erin, because of her stature, received a personal invitation to attend the event at GWare headquarters as part of the live audience. She may have broken ranks with TJ, but she was simply too important a person to snub.

She arrived at the GWare auditorium and presented her invitation at the door. A GWare greeter knew immediately who she was and showed her to a reserved seat in the first row. This was TJ's doing…Erin was certain he arranged for her to be right up front. No doubt he savored the opportunity to rub her nose in it. She was right. TJ intended to show her that GWare ONE was the superior product, and he couldn't wait to see her reaction to the product unveiling.

As the lights dimmed, a giant rear projection screen moved down from the ceiling of the auditorium, occupying the back of the stage. A multimedia presentation began…it was a piece of PR fluff, Erin thought, but ingenious in its simplicity of message. It was brilliantly edited, with a series of scenes from around the world, suggestive of people working together. These faded into scenes of individuals in homes and offices working on computers of all different types. The narrative made it sound as if only one company and one product could bridge the world's people and the world's systems…and of course that was GWare ONE.

As the brief presentation reached its climax, Erin couldn't help but admire GWare's marketing skill…it may have been a bunch of bullshit, she thought, but the company had set an emotional instead of rational tone for the introduction of GWare ONE. It reminded her of the simple, human emotion behind the Charlie Chaplin introduction of the IBM PC ten years earlier.

The presentation ended and then a voice said, "Ladies and gentleman, the president and CEO of GWare, TJ Gatwick."

Out came TJ to thunderous applause. Incredibly, TJ was dressed in a black tuxedo and a bright red bowtie. This signaled to the audience and the world how very different this event would be…Gatwick had rarely been seen even in a jacket and tie in previous public appearances. His standard uniform was a denim shirt with a GWare logo and chinos. Erin was amazed his publicity people could convince him of such a radical departure. But it certainly added to the theatre. TJ strode from stage left to a podium that had been set up to the right of the giant screen.

The screen continued to silently flash still images from the presentation on the giant screen behind him, then dissolved into a huge product logo for GWare ONE. The applause died down and at that point, the lights dimmed and a spotlight shone on TJ, clearly a signal for him to begin. Beautifully orchestrated as usual, Erin thought. They didn't miss a trick.

"Today," TJ began, reading from a video screen teleprompter to the right of the podium so he could look up at the video camera, "is a special event in the history of software. It is a day we have all been waiting for. A day when businesses will no longer have to abandon ONE computing environment for another. A day when all those who use a computer will be able to use ONE system to communicate and interact. A day when the benefit of a truly universal, single common language will bring the world together.

"This is the day I give you GWare ONE." TJ very obviously looked away from the teleprompter over towards Erin and smiled. The bastard knew exactly where I was sitting, Erin thought.

With that, the large screen transitioned into four quadrants. One fourth of the screen showed a close-up of a computer terminal from an over-the-shoulder perspective of a woman who was sitting in front of it. Two other portions of the screen showed similar arrangements, obviously in different locations. However, one of them appeared to be a television with a remote computer keyboard rather than a computer terminal. The fourth portion of the screen, in the upper right hand corner, was a close-up of TJ. On the left of the stage, a spotlight illuminated a woman sitting at a computer terminal, and it became clear that she was one of the people appearing in a quadrant.

TJ began to talk about the vision for GWare ONE and how it would pay off the lofty marketing promises he had made in his opening remarks. Then, he described what the audience would be witnessing as the product demo began. Each time an action was occurring in one of the three quadrants, he said, it would be transparently occurring at the other two locations, on completely different systems, one of which was a cable television connection. TJ made a point of indicating that one location was here on the stage at GWare headquarters in San Diego, but that the other two were in Europe and Australia, respectively. Everything that the audience would see was happening in real-time, live at these three locations. TJ heightened the drama by saying that independent auditors from the technology division of Price Waterhouse had been placed at all three locations to verify that this was not a simulated demonstration but the real thing.

As TJ described the actions, they did in fact occur almost instantly upon each computer terminal. Erin watched what was happening and felt as if electricity was coursing through her veins. That's because what she was seeing here in the GWare auditorium was something she had seen at least in part before. But it hadn't been at GWare…it was strikingly similar to portions of the demo conducted by Henry Chu at Incandescent.

Erin watched, horrified, as qualities and characteristics of Incandescent's product were revealed on the screen. She looked at TJ, astonished and disgusted. He was continuing his narration of the demo without looking at her; in fact, she could swear he was intentionally avoiding her stare.

By the end of the demo, Erin knew with certainty that Henry Chu had, very simply, sold out. There was no doubt in her mind that GWare ONE had incorporated large portions of the original code from UNITE. TJ had brazenly stolen not only Incandescent's thunder, but Incandescent's very product.

As the house lights came up, the audience jumped to its feet, cheering, in a standing ovation that shook the auditorium. TJ basked in the reaction, smiling and waving from the podium. Erin could not and would not stand; rather she remained in her seat, stunned and silent, glaring at TJ.

The audience began to exit the auditorium. GWare employees handed each audience member a brightly colored portfolio with the GWare ONE logo emblazoned across it. Inside was a copy of the GWare ONE software, along with numerous pieces of promotional propaganda. Erin lingered as the room cleared.

TJ, in a last act of defiance, walked down the steps of the stage and approached Erin. She looked at him with eyes that burned with resentment.

"I hope you're proud of yourself," she said, seething.

He simply laughed. "It's time you realized, Erin," he said casually, "that there will always be a winner in the software business. And that will always be GWare."

"You bastard," she spat. "You've turned this into a war, haven't you? A war where you'll destroy anyone and anything that gets in your way, you'll do anything to win…even if it means stealing someone else's intellectual property and calling it your own."

"That's quite an accusation," TJ answered, "and I don't intend to dignify it with a response. Now, I really must be going," he said, turning on his heels and walking away from her.

She watched the large figure in his tuxedo depart. "Damn you, TJ, you won't get away with this," she said after him. But he was already out of earshot.

* * *

Erin exited the auditorium and got back in her rental car. She was still angered by what she had witnessed moments ago. She called Marty on her cell phone. He was on another line but she said it was urgent and would hold for him. He finally picked up.

"Marty," she said breathlessly, "I just left the GWare presentation, and..."

Marty cut her off, his voice sounding tired and defeated. "Erin, I already know about it. One of my people attended the event at a hotel. I just got off the phone with him."

"I can't believe it...that bastard stole your code!"

"I can't believe Henry agreed to it," Marty said with sadness in his voice. "He had to know they couldn't get away with it, that we'd take action against GWare and against him personally." He paused. "But of course, the damage is done now."

"We have to fight them, Marty," Erin said fervently. "We can't let Gatwick win this one. We can't let GWare ONE masquerade as a great operating system when we both know it's UNITE that deserves the accolades. I mean, how can you introduce your product now? How can you go to market knowing what he did? We have to stop them, it's just too damned important..."

"Erin, calm down," Marty began. "I know, I know, I feel the same way. But let's be realistic about this. Gatwick's released GWare ONE and UNITE's release is a month away. I can't do anything to impact UNITE now unless I delay its release and trash everything that we've already committed to. Gatwick knows that. He's pre-empted us big time."

"But Marty, he can't get away with this. You can go after him, you can have your lawyers get an injunction against distributing GWare ONE.You can prove he stole your code."

"What I can prove," Marty said calmly, "is that Henry Chu went to work for GWare, and that GWare ONE ended up looking suspiciously like UNITE when all was said and done. But the onus is on me to go after Henry and GWare. If I want to make a case out of this, I'll have to pursue it aggressively. Sure, I can do that, and I will do that, but you have to understand that Incandescent doesn't have GWare's legal resources, Erin. Even if we sued, Gatwick would tie us up in court for years. That's the way the system works. By the time there's a verdict, people would have forgotten which product came first."

"I can't stand to hear you talk like this," Erin said tearfully. "Your company's too good, your product is too good. You don't deserve this. You can't give up on what you believe in. Marty, this is about right versus wrong, it's about integrity. You know that."

Marty sighed. "Yeah, I know that. In principle, I know you're absolutely right. Of course I still believe in myself, in my company, in UNITE. But it isn't easy for the good guys to win, Erin. I knew I was headed for trouble the minute Henry Chu walked out the door. I was hoping against hope that he'd honor the non-compete. But I knew the risk was there…that Gatwick could buy his loyalty."

"And steal what you've worked so hard to accomplish," Erin said, her voice cracking.

"Erin, we're both angry and upset," Marty said. "This probably isn't the best time to be talking about strategy. I'm feeling a little deflated right now. Maybe you're right, maybe we can fight this thing. But now I need to think about what I'm going to do next. Give me a day or two to mull it over. I need to talk to my people, my attorney. You'll be the first to know what I find out."

"Marty, you know I'll do whatever I can to help," Erin said, tears forming in her eyes. She added quietly, "I love you, Marty."

There was a momentary silence and then Marty responded, "I love you too. Good-bye, sweetheart."

Erin ended the call and dropped her head onto the backs of her hands, which were grasping the steering wheel so tightly that her fingers hurt. She cried silently for a few moments and then wiped her tears away. She was filled with a rush of mixed emotions. For TJ, it was an anger that grew into a raging need to fight his despicable act. For Henry Chu, it was a resentment that made her want to expose him to the world in her column. For Marty, it was an ache in her heart for his being hurt, combined with a burning desire to be with him right now, to comfort and hold him, to make tender love to him.

She took a minute to pull herself together and re-group before she began the drive back to the San Diego airport. She looked out through the windshield at the main building of the GWare campus. It was resplendent with a huge banner carrying the GWare ONE slogan. On flagpoles surrounding the building were GWare ONE banners. She looked from building to building, thinking this was an evil empire if ever there was one.

The sight of all of this brought to her a renewed sense of values, of determination that came from deep down inside of her. Erin had seen it all in the software business, the victories and the defeats, the bad and the good. She had been close to the most important companies in the world, had known the most powerful business leaders. Her product reviews had the power to make or break products. She had become a woman who was as influential as any person in the technology business could ever be.

As such, Erin knew she held a position of strength, a position of power, rare in the business world...one that now had implications beyond what she had ever imagined. At that moment, Erin resolved that she would use who she was and what she stood for in an all-out battle against TJ Gatwick and GWare. Whatever it took, whatever it meant, Erin Keliher would fight with every fiber of her being this injustice…and it would be all the more important because she would be standing beside Marty Gladstone.

CHAPTER 10

As TJ Gatwick had anticipated, the release of GWare ONE was met with a wildly enthusiastic reception from the press and the public. Copies of the software were rushed to worldwide distribution points as distributors, resellers, retailers, and end users clamored for it. The company could barely keep up with the demand, and the media covered the story as one of the great software success stories in recent memory.

But even as GWare ONE was taking the computer world by storm, lurking in its code, waiting to strike, was the insidious Doomsday Virus. The hacker Doomsday had been successful in embedding it in the source code, but he had gone one step further: the Doomsday Virus was programmed to activate only after a computer with GWare ONE installed was successfully logged into a network. That way it could wreak maximum havoc. The more computers on the network, the more damaging the virus…which was why it would be especially effective across the Internet.

The first sign of any trouble was a call that came into GWare's technical support hotline from a software engineer at a research center in Bethesda, Maryland. He had received one of the first copies of GWare ONE. The engineer had described something that looked innocent enough, but he knew from experience that it was in fact indicative of a deeper problem. He told the GWare Help Desk support technician to get his supervisor on the line immediately.

It was clear this was no hoax; the software engineer talked with the supervisor and walked him through what he had discovered in the software. In an unusual reversal of roles, the GWare supervisor was now the one being led by a customer through a series of steps. A chill ran down the supervisor's spine as he witnessed what was happening on his computer. He knew immediately this was no ordinary problem.

The discovery was escalated to the GWare Vice President in charge of Technical Support. He put in an urgent call to a senior engineer at SVAS, the Software Virus Alert Service, a consortium of software companies. The SVAS engineer said he'd check it out immediately and get back to the Vice President as soon as SVAS could complete a thorough analysis.

The SVAS engineer rushed a copy of GWare ONE down to the simulation lab, where SVAS could instantly test software in a controlled environment that simulated every type of networking. The simulation lab was staffed twenty-four hours a day, seven days a week, for emergencies such as this one.

"Looks like there's a potential worm in GWare ONE," the engineer said to the lab technician. "Called in by a software engineer. Need to check it out A—SAP."

The technician loaded a copy of GWare ONE and ran it through the most up-to-date virus scan available. Nothing out of the ordinary appeared.

"Whatever it is, detection's not picking it up. Must be a brand new strain," the engineer said. He was standing over the technician's shoulder, looking intently at the computer screen. "Lemme get on the other computer and let's run the Internet simulation."

The technician sent an e-mail message to the engineer over a LAN connection that simulated an Internet connection as closely as possible. The engineer attempted to open the e-mail by clicking on its subject line. The e-mail program suddenly froze, locking up the receiving computer's operating system. When the engineer re-booted the infected computer, it was clear that the hard drive itself had been damaged.

Meanwhile, the technician who had sent the message received an auto-response from the engineer's e-mail system. "I just got a message from your computer."

The engineer looked up, puzzled. "But I didn't send you one. Go ahead and try to open it."

When the technician did so, the same thing happened. The e-mail system froze, and the re-booted computer's hard drive was damaged. The virus had infected the recipient's computer, then re-sent itself to the sender's computer. It was set to assure that no computer would escape its deadly purpose.

The engineer shook his head and muttered, "Mother of God, we just wiped out the hard drives of two computers in a matter of seconds."

Unfortunately, the test had been a success. Now the engineer and technician knew what to expect from the virus. It had attributes they had never seen before. They went to another computer and loaded GWare ONE again. They began to examine the program's source code using proprietary software designed especially for SVAS. After about thirty minutes, they found what they were looking for.

"This is ingenious," the technician said, admiring the work of the creator of the virus. "It's a hybrid worm, different from any I've seen before. It looks like it's a combination of characteristics from a few previous ones, but it's far more virulent.

"See this? That's how it propagates." The technician continued. "It appears that the infected computer can transmit the virus across any network. When the recipient of an e-mail message from the infected computer even attempts to open it, the worm does its dirty work. It doesn't even need an attachment to infect.

"We'll try it with a few different e-mail clients, but it could be devastating even if it works only with Microsoft Outlook. Based on this code structure, I'm guessing the same thing will happen when you visit a Web page that's hosted by an infected server.

"But it gets better...I mean, worse," the technician said. "This virus is capable of blowing a security hole right through the e-mail system. That means anyone can get access to the contents of an infected machine...or an entire network."

The engineer just stared at the technician. "So you're saying this thing can spread like wildfire, through any network and onto any e-mail system. And it leaves the security of any computer or network completely at risk."

The technician nodded slowly. "Yeah, that's what I'm saying."

The engineer jumped to his feet. "Keep testing the damn thing, see if you can find any other attributes," the engineer said, running out of the lab. "I've gotta tell the boss."

It was only forty minutes later that the lab technician had discovered that the virus was indeed propagated not only by e-mail but by infected Web servers. In simulation, he saw that an infected server pushed a JavaScript "readme.exe" file to a computer that visited the infected Web site. The virus would then activate automatically upon transmission. By creating a new account without a password on an infected computer, the virus would make the computer susceptible to attack. As a result, any hacker could log on to the infected computer and gain unhindered access to the contents of the computer or network.

The insidious virus could also e-mail copies of itself to addresses in the infected computer's e-mail address book and Web cache folders. It could then scan the Internet for Web servers to infect. That meant the speed and severity of infection would be unprecedented.

The technician kept working on it, realizing that there did not appear to be an easy way to remove the virus from an infected computer or Web server. He wondered how it would be possible to cure the virus. There was no known antidote for this type of strain. No one had ever seen anything like it before. Short of shutting down every computer on a network, he didn't know what could be done to stop the virus from propagating. The consequences of this could be astronomical, he thought.

Within just hours of the discovery of the virus, SVAS was prepared to disseminate a Code Red Security Alert. This highest level of virus alert, rarely issued, would speed the alert across the news media and the Internet. SVAS would have to recommend that all copies of GWare ONE be embargoed by distributors, and that under no circumstances should the software be used on any computer. SVAS believed that using the software would risk launching a virus of massive proportions.

While SVAS had the authority to issue this strongest of warnings, the head of SVAS played it safe. Because of the reliance of SVAS on GWare for major funding, and because of the fact that this was GWare's most significant product launch ever, the head of SVAS insisted on getting approval from TJ Gatwick himself before issuing a Code Red. This delay turned out to be a fatal error.

Gatwick was unbelieving when he first got the urgent call from SVAS. He insisted on replicating the virus condition with the software himself to assure that it wasn't an isolated case. Despite pleas from the head of SVAS, Gatwick insisted on taking the time to do his own testing in his own research center. The head of SVAS reluctantly agreed. This second delay only added to the impending disaster that was to occur.

Another hour went by while SVAS anxiously waited for GWare's testing to be completed. Finally, Gatwick himself called the head of SVAS. He admitted with defeat that the virus was present in additional copies of the software, and that he had personally seen the virus launch itself on a number of computer systems. In despair, he agreed to the Code Red Security Alert.

But by now it was too late. Even as the Code Red Security Alert began to be distributed over the Internet with the most urgent priority, copies of the GWare ONE software had already been distributed, resellers had already begun to install them for important customers, and retailers had already begun to sell them. In fact, they couldn't sell copies of the new GWare ONE software fast enough. The product was already on its way into the hands of thousands of unsuspecting customers.

The impact of the initial delay by SVAS, coupled with the delay caused by testing at GWare, led to widespread distribution of GWare ONE and the virus that resided within it. The Doomsday Virus was capable of spreading much faster than any virus previously known. It was only a matter of days before the virus had infected millions of computers and Web servers. SVAS advised systems administrators to scan all incoming mail for the "readme.exe," but that didn't block individuals from opening their e-mail. Even clicking on the e-mails to select them for deletion activated the virus.

While SVAS feverishly worked on an antidote, the virus had spread so rapidly that the damage was already done. Ironically, the massive GWare ONE advertising and publicity campaign had worked exceedingly well, and the product had been widely distributed throughout the world. Within just three days, over seventy percent of computer systems running across the Internet had been infected with the Doomsday Virus.

TJ Gatwick had not slept for three days straight, working with SVAS and other anti-virus sources to no avail. He was unshaven and in need of a shower, but all he could think about now was the destruction happening around him.

One of his attorneys had just arrived and had been shown into TJ's office. TJ, despondent and exhausted, was at a loss for words. He simply motioned for the attorney to sit at the small table in the conference area of his office. TJ sat heavily in the chair opposite but was incapable of saying anything.

Clearing his throat, the attorney spoke first. "TJ, at this point, we are still trying to assess the real damage," he said quietly. "It appears the virus has done considerable damage to both corporate and individual users on a worldwide scale. In terms of liability, the exposure is severe. I believe we can expect a class action suit to be filed against GWare shortly."

TJ just looked at the young attorney with glassy eyes.

The attorney continued, "Unfortunately, class action is appropriate and will have a good chance of succeeding. A strong case can be made since the virus was in fact embedded in the program's source code. That means it originated with GWare ONE, rather than from any external source. That is a key point that will be used to lay major claims against GWare. Even if it was unintentional and you had no knowledge of its presence, we have a problem here. There is a reasonable expectation by purchasers that quality assurance procedures are stringent enough to prevent against the presence of anything that would have such a deleterious effect. In my judgment, the corporation is culpable, and I believe that is what any court would so find."

The attorney paused for a moment. He pulled out a handkerchief and wiped the perspiration from his upper lip. "Having the virus originate inside GWare ONE makes all the difference in the world, I'm afraid."

The silence was deafening. TJ leaned his chair back and simply bit one of his cuticles. The attorney was growing increasingly uncomfortable. He didn't know whether or not to continue since he was getting no signals from TJ nor any verbal response. He wondered if the king of software was ready to blow a gasket.

Finally, TJ said, "We have one of the best QA processes in the software business. How could the bastards have gotten it into the code?" He spoke this aloud without looking at the attorney, almost as if he was asking it of himself. The attorney assumed it was a question he wasn't expected to answer.

"This was going to be the best fucking product this company ever had," TJ continued, looking at an invisible spot on the wall. "The best." He stood up and paced around the office. Then, as if TJ realized for the first time that the attorney was present, he said off-handedly, "What are we going to do about this?"

"The firm is recommending you cooperate fully," the attorney said. "If and when the suit is brought, we will work diligently to keep it out of court. There's no point in spending additional money on a case we can't possibly hope to win.

"We'll have to be proactive about this, propose an out-of-court settlement that seems fair and just so no one goes after us for punitive damages." The attorney paused. "It will be a considerable sum."

TJ looked at him, his eyes asking the question he didn't want answered.

"I suspect it will easily be in the hundreds of millions of dollars," the attorney said quietly. "No other options, really."

TJ nodded and waved his hand dismissively. The attorney, relieved to be dismissed, stood and smiled weakly. He did not attempt to shake TJ Gatwick's hand, but rather turned and quickly left the office.

Once again TJ paced around his domain as if in a daze. He still could not believe his world had all come crashing down so suddenly, so brutally. Could it have been little more than a week ago that TJ stood before the crowd and announced the coming of the world's greatest operating system? It seemed like it was an eternity ago.

TJ began to process what had taken place: How did it happen? He asked himself. Who could have done this to me? He ran through the events in his mind over and over again. Erin, Erin Keliher…everything kept coming back to Erin. Was it possible she could have had anything to do with this? Could Erin hate him so much that she would sabotage his software program? Yes, he believed she could. He remembered how she had reacted so vehemently when she saw the demonstration of GWare ONE.

Or he thought, could it be Marty Gladstone? He could be capable of it, couldn't he? Then he thought, suppose Gladstone and Erin were in on this together. Erin had been so damned protective of Incandescent, so laudatory in her praise of UNITE. And Gladstone, he had been after TJ since their meeting at MIT, hadn't he? The two of them together, Erin Keliher and Marty Gladstone…wouldn't *that* be just perfect, TJ thought.

This conspiracy theory was beginning to make sense to TJ. If Erin and Marty had in fact teamed up together, he thought, wouldn't it be possible for them to hire some hacker to create the virus? Gladstone could have even used his own developers to create it. Then all they had to do was get someone at GWare, some traitor, to plant it. This was a ruthless business, TJ thought, he was proof of that. It was entirely possible, more than that, it was probable.

TJ Gatwick felt a surge of anger. He'd have to prove it was the two of them, but he would prove it all right. And when he did, TJ thought, they wouldn't get away with this…no fucking way.

CHAPTER 11

Part one of my grand plan is now complete. The reports of Internet disruption are beautiful, just beautiful. GWare doesn't know what hit them. And no one has figured out how to overcome my virus. I knew they couldn't! When part two of my plan kicks in, I'll have them screaming for mercy. That's when I'll tell the bastards who I am. Oh, they'll find out who's in charge alright. And they'll be sorry, they'll all be sorry…

In his demented reverie, Doomsday was dreaming of world domination. He had indeed brought the technology world to its knees with the most deadly virus ever launched, and he was far from finished.

Now Doomsday was setting his sights on part two of his plan: attacking Incandescent's UNITE operating system. There was a complication, however: Doomsday's contact within Incandescent had gotten cold feet. As a result, Doomsday was unable to infect the source code of UNITE from within. Instead, he needed to take a circuitous route.

His new plan was to go after UNITE through a back door. He had learned of a potential weakness in the product's security layer that would make it vulnerable in an externally networked environment. Doomsday believed he would be able to infect Web servers directly and they, in turn, would transmit the Doomsday Virus to networked computers using UNITE. It wouldn't be as effective as what he had accomplished with GWare ONE, but it would still crash enough systems to do some serious damage.

Of course, after the GWare ONE infection, Internet security was tighter than ever. That meant Doomsday had his work cut out for him, but his corps of like-minded hackers loved a challenge. They would help him pierce any security screen to wreak havoc on capitalism and harm the giants in the software industry.

Doomsday was corresponding via e-mail in encrypted code with several of his cronies, discussing how best to accomplish his newest act of cyber-terrorism when a high priority e-mail arrived from his Washington operative. When he decrypted the message, it read:

> Sorry to tell you this, but the kidnappers got carried away. They were more fanatical than I thought. Just learned that they slit Morrissey's throat. He's dead. Hope this doesn't screw up our plan.

"SHIT!" Doomsday yelled aloud as he read the e-mail. Everything was going well, despite the setback with Incandescent. That was something he could at least work out. But this...this was definitely NOT according to plan.

Even when Doomsday agreed to the kidnapping he had second thoughts about it. He didn't much care about Morrissey, but he didn't like to be in a situation where he wasn't in complete control. He had confidence in his hacker network...they had always demonstrated their loyalty. But even the Washington hacker had admitted the kidnappers were outside the norm.

What Doomsday had hoped for is the kidnappers would understand the objective, do the job, and get the extra bonus of a fat ransom if they could pull it off. The idea was for the kidnapping to interrupt the investigation of Incandescent, which it did. Doomsday thought that it would end there, that the kidnappers would turn over Morrissey once Incandescent had released UNITE. That's what the assignment was supposed to be.

Now the idiots had taken things into their own hands and killed the man instead. What most concerned Doomsday is that the kidnappers, who were now murderers, would be tracked down and caught. Christ, he thought, they had to be…this was a U.S. Senator that they'd killed! Every damned law enforcement official in the country would be looking for these guys.

And when they were caught, why wouldn't they simply turn right around and implicate the Washington hacker in the crime? Which means there could be a thread possibly leading to Doomsday himself, if his Washington ally turned on him.

Of course, it could work out another way. Doomsday figured that the kidnappers turned murderers had one reason to kill Morrissey…it was driven by their radical Islamic view of the world. Morrissey was the evil embodiment of a government and a way of life they hated. As such, in their eyes, their act was not one of murder, but one of heroism. They would be viewed as heroes by a twisted fringe group of Islamic extremists, the same type of maniacs who went after the World Trade Center and blew themselves up to kill people.

Doomsday grew increasingly heartened as he thought this through. After all, these bastards would WANT the credit for what they did. Even if they were caught, they'd want the world to think they acted alone because for them, it was a tribute to Allah. Maybe they'd actually keep their mouths shut about the hacker who hired them.

It made sense to Doomsday, and he felt better about it now. It was time for him to stop worrying about the ramifications of Senator Morrissey's murder and get back to his important work at hand…setting up the parameters for another attack on the Internet, this time with UNITE as his target.

The FBI had agreed to the ransom payment for Senator Morrissey and had left the money as instructed, but when the kidnappers didn't show up, they knew something was amiss. It took them three days to discover what Doomsday already knew. Agents stormed the cabin in

Julian, only to find the Senator's lifeless body, his hands and feet still bound, his sleep shade still covering his unseeing eyes. Senator Morrisey's throat had been slit.

Not surprisingly, Capitol Hill was outraged by the heinous crime, as was the President. He made a special statement to the press, which was carried during prime time, vowing to track down and capture the perpetrators, wherever they were. Intelligence had informed him that the likely criminals were Islamic extremists, but he and his advisors had decided to omit this fact from his statement. It was bad enough a senator had been murdered…why exacerbate the situation by giving the American public something else to get worked up about.

The FBI organized a massive manhunt that started in Julian and spread out nationally from there. They put a great deal of pressure on every informant they had, and went outside the U.S. to Interpol and the Israelis to see if they had any intelligence that might be useful. At the same time, the U.S. government was put on a high state of alert. Secret service protection had always been granted to the President and Vice President and their families, of course, but now, plain clothes auxiliary agents began to accompany key Senators and Representatives as they went from their home states to Washington.

The FBI was, in fact, able to confirm that the murderers were almost certainly associated with an Islamic terrorist organization, but they hadn't learned which one. The murderers themselves had disappeared, and the FBI suspected they had either somehow left the United States or changed their identities and faded into the country's woodwork.

A funeral was held for Senator John "Jack" Morrissey in the La Jolla he loved. As was appropriate for a man of his stature and style, it was attended by Hollywood's finest, along with luminaries from government and business.

TJ Gatwick himself was there. It was the first time since the debacle of his product introduction that TJ had been seen in public.

Whatever problems TJ was facing, he knew he owed it to Jack to be at his funeral. While theirs was a relationship sometimes built more on parasitic need than friendship, it had lasted nonetheless. Sometimes Morrissey had joked that he and TJ were both peas in a pod. They had their own definition of morality and ethics, he had said, and that's what made them special.

TJ couldn't help but think about Morrissey as he sat there, listening to the eloquent eulogies pouring forth about the Senator. The fact is, TJ had lost most of his respect for Morrissey in the past few years. The man had turned into an alcoholic whose marriage was in a shambles and whose position of power was mostly ceremonial. True, Jack Morrissey was still a respected Senator, at least by those who didn't know him well. But on the Senate floor, and in committee, Morrissey had slowly but surely been losing his credibility. If anything, he had become somewhat of an embarrassment to the younger Senators. But cronyism was Morrissey's shield, and the elder statesmen in the Senate, as well as the House, were only too happy to protect him in return for his support of their particular causes. After all, that was politics.

Yet here they all were, the senators, the representatives, the Hollywood stars, the leaders of American business, and TJ Gatwick…all paying tribute to the man. So be it.

After the service, Jack, even in death, would perpetrate one last act of theatre. He had requested in his will that he be cremated, and that his ashes be spread by his wife across the Pacific Ocean, in view of his beloved mansion. A navy ship from San Diego was pressed into service for this purpose. No doubt at least one newspaper photographer would try to get a close up of the ashes themselves as they were carried across the waters by the ocean breeze. Senator Morrissey would make one lasting grand impression on the world, even as he exited it.

Once again, Senator Morrissey made the headline of the *Boston Globe*, but this one was far more shocking to Marty Gladstone than the one about the kidnapping. He sat there in his kitchen, drinking herb tea and poring over the newspaper.

He had still not gotten over the kidnapping itself, and now Senator Morrissey was dead. It was irrational, but Marty had a sense of guilt about the Senator's death. Somehow, he thought, this whole thing is connected to me. How could it not be…no sooner was it announced that Morrissey's Technology Council was going to investigate Incandescent, than Morrissey was kidnapped and now, even worse, he had been murdered. What the hell is going on, Marty thought. How does Incandescent fit into all of this…and what does it mean for me?

He knew he wasn't really responsible for this tragedy, but somehow he felt involved. It was just too coincidental. Even the FBI had thought so…they had spoken with him shortly after the Senator's kidnapping. They too were trying to draw some connection between the kidnapping and the Council's abruptly cancelled investigation of Incandescent. They never implied that Marty himself had anything to do with it, yet the intention of their questions was clear. But Marty hadn't heard from them again since their interrogation. He fully expected they would be in touch with him once more, now that the Senator had been murdered.

Marty, sipping his tea, considered the chain of events. It seemed as if everything started to happen when Henry Chu defected to GWare. That was where Marty could draw the connection between UNITE and GWare ONE. It wasn't long after that, Marty thought, that he had been told the Senate Technology Council was going to investigate Incandescent. Of course, the result of that investigation would put a crimp in Marty's product launch plans. Whoever was behind that investigation had to know that.

It had to be TJ Gatwick, Marty thought, who somehow engineered the Senate Technology Council investigation. He knew about UNITE, through Henry Chu, so he knew what a threat UNITE would be to GWare ONE. By convincing Henry to sell out, Gatwick could build the best attributes of UNITE into ONE. Then all he had to do was get his release to market first.

Gatwick and Morrissey were connected, Marty knew that. Erin had mentioned it to him, and it had piqued his interest. He did a little poking around on the Internet and soon found that Gatwick had indeed been a major supporter of Morrissey in the most recent election. So it was true that Morrissey owed TJ, and owed him big. No question about it, he thought, Gatwick must have arranged for Morrissey to do the investigation in the hope that it would delay the UNITE product launch.

But then what about the kidnapping…that didn't fit. Obviously Gatwick had nothing to do with it, because that only would have interrupted the investigation that he had planned. Then who did, and why? If the kidnapping had something to do with me, Marty thought, whoever did it must have wanted to make sure UNITE was released without any delay. The kidnapping would interrupt the investigation of Incandescent, clearing the way for the product release. This was starting to fit together, Marty thought, but he still couldn't figure it out. There was a piece missing to the puzzle, and Marty wanted to solve it.

Maybe it was someone with a grudge against Gatwick…that wouldn't be hard to believe. Then something popped into Marty's mind. No sooner had GWare ONE come out than the industry's worst virus was unleashed. The virus had practically destroyed GWare…if it weren't for their cash reserve and huge worldwide installed base, they would have been ruined. It was a vicious attack on GWare itself, because the virus was embedded inside the operating system.

Okay, Marty thought, so the virus does its dirty work, again paving the way for UNITE to be released. And, of course, GWare ONE itself is destroyed by the virus, which means UNITE is free of any competition.

A chill ran down Marty's spine. If I didn't know better, he thought, I'd have to say I have a peculiar kind of guardian angel. Someone who wants to see Incandescent succeed at all costs.

Marty didn't want to accept the next thought that entered his mind, but he couldn't push it away. Who was the one person, he thought, who formed the link between GWare and Incandescent…the one person who knew TJ Gatwick and Marty Gladstone, and both companies, equally well?

Who was the one person who knew the details of Incandescent's product long before its release…and even knew of Henry Chu's treachery before anyone else did?

Who was the one person who was outraged by what Gatwick had done when he released GWare ONE?

Who was the one person who could had access to the Senate Technology Council members at any time?

Marty shuddered. He knew the answer…Erin Keliher.

Could it be…could it possibly be that Erin had anything to do with all of this? Marty truly believed she loved him, and that she would in fact do anything for him. He loved her too, with all his heart.

To think that she could be at the center of something like this was beyond belief. Yet he couldn't deny that Erin was the most likely candidate because of all the reasons that were becoming evident to him.

Jesus, Marty thought, was it even possible that Erin could mastermind such a plot? Could she be capable of anything so vengeful?

He decided then what he must do, and he could nothing less. He must confront Erin Keliher with his suspicion, even though it terrified him to think what it could mean. He'd look deep into those stunning eyes of hers to learn the truth…and he hoped to God what he'd see would tell him he was completely wrong about her.

CHAPTER 12

Marty was just coming out of a meeting with Incandescent's public relations firm, the last meeting before the planned launch of UNITE.

There was a significant difference of opinion between his Marketing VP and the principal of the PR firm. The Marketing VP thought they should move ahead now with the launch of UNITE, while the PR executive, an aggressive woman who minced no words, advised against it. She realized the business implications of a delay, but she felt that the market was still gun-shy because of the GWare ONE launch. The business world had barely finished mopping up from the damage the virus had afflicted on computer systems worldwide. She said the time just wasn't right to introduce another new operating system after the disastrous launch of the virus-laden ONE.

Incandescent's Marketing VP, on the other hand, was strongly in favor of the product release. He made the point that Incandescent's technical staff had scoured the source code, and an independent software testing lab had also confirmed the code was virus-free. The lab was even willing to put its stamp of approval on UNITE.

What could go wrong, the Marketing VP said. In fact, he felt the timing was ideal, precisely because of the problems with GWare ONE. The UNITE operating system would fill a gap left by ONE, at a time when GWare was reeling. There would never be a better marketing opportunity, the VP said, and he vigorously lobbied for Incandescent to make its move and enter the marketplace now.

Marty sighed to himself as he walked to his office. He had been through many successful launches with his Marketing VP and he trusted his judgment. But he also knew that the head of the PR firm had the wisdom of experience on her side. This would be a tough decision, one he would have to make by himself.

His first instinct was to call Erin for advice, but he couldn't. He was still bothered by his lingering doubt about her. He hadn't yet confronted her with his suspicion. It was something he wanted to do face-to-face.

Erin hadn't been East since that memorable evening they spent together. They chatted frequently by phone, but their schedules of late had been so hectic that they hadn't found a convenient time to see each other. After all, she was three thousand miles away. Unspoken between them was the realization that this was what a long-distance romance would be like. Neither of them expressed frustration about being away from each other, however, for fear of having it become an insurmountable obstacle.

Marty plopped into his desk chair heavily. He picked up a pen and nervously twirled it between his fingers. He reached for a lined pad, put it in his lap, and drew a line down the middle of the paper. He wrote "Yes" on one side and "No" on the other.

This was Marty's simplistic yet effective way of making the toughest decisions in his life. When such decisions loomed, he attempted to strip away the emotion and the subjectivity by writing down a bulleted list of pros and cons. He didn't use a computer to do it, because the very act of writing the list down on paper made him stop and think about the factors more carefully. He would analyze each side of his list and prioritize each bullet with his own private ranking system. This usually resulted in a decision he could feel comfortable making. He smiled ruefully at the thought that he had never gone through the exercise when determining whether or not to pursue a relationship with Erin.

After thirty minutes of writing and re-writing his bullets and shuffling and re-shuffling the priorities, Marty threw the pad on his desk in disgust. There were as many compelling factors that led to "Yes" as led to "No." In Marty's mind, launching the product was an inevitability…that wasn't the question. The question was whether to launch *now*, on the heels of the GWare ONE disaster, or wait for another time. He could truly see both sides of the argument for and against it. The problem was, he kept coming up with what amounted to a deadlock.

It would be just as easy, Marty thought, to throw a dart at a dartboard and make the decision that way. He wondered absently if he should leave it up to serendipity. After all, if he really couldn't make up his mind, maybe he should just flip a coin. But then, he thought, he would always wonder what would've happened if it had gone the other way.

No, Marty knew it couldn't be left to chance. He'd have to make the decision himself, and he'd have to live with it. If he was wrong, so be it. He had made big decisions before and, for the most part, he'd been right. So he would do what he had always done…he would rely on instinct. He admitted to himself that, in the final analysis, the rational was supplanted by the emotional in making the toughest decisions. That's what instinct was all about.

He closed his eyes, leaned back in his chair, and weighed the factors once more in his mind. Inside, he began to feel a sense of direction emerging. It was a feeling and nothing more, but it got stronger and stronger. With a growing sense of purpose, Marty opened his eyes, nodded to himself, and stood up. His decision was made. Marty would go with his gut instinct…and he'd have to live with it. He hoped to hell he was right.

Every Incandescent employee was geared up and excited about the impending product release. Incandescent's advertising and public relations agencies worked around the clock to help the company prepare for the launch of UNITE. This would be the biggest event in Incandescent's history. Media interest was extremely high, as much because of the recent GWare ONE disaster as anything. Not that the press wished Incandescent ill, but they were watching with baited breath for anything out of the ordinary to happen.

Erin Keliher played a lead role in creating positive pre-launch reaction to UNITE. She mentioned the product several times in her columns, heaping it with praise. Then, on the eve of the product release, she wrote her most glowing review ever. Other positive reviews followed, some of them wildly enthusiastic. Incandescent's Marketing VP had made certain that all members of the press, all analysts, all major resellers, and major customers received VIP advance copies of UNITE, and it paid off handsomely.

Marty, scorning TJ Gatwick's histrionics, did not himself engage in a theatrical product unveiling. Rather, he and his Marketing VP decided to let the product cause its own excitement in the marketplace. That's exactly what happened, despite the recent GWare ONE debacle. It was as if GWare ONE didn't even exist. After the outstanding reviews, resellers and retailers couldn't get copies of UNITE fast enough. Incandescent's U.S.-based software manufacturing facility had to be supplemented by hastily contracted offshore services to keep up with the demand.

Now, amidst the massive acceptance of UNITE, Marty believed he had made the right decision. He still had an uneasy feeling in his gut, though, and he wasn't quite sure why. He told himself he was just nervous because of the whole situation surrounding the launch of GWare ONE, because of the vulnerability of software to virus attacks. He knew UNITE had been tested and re-tested, and that gave him a sense of security. In fact, there had been no reports of anything unusual from the field as the product made its way through distribution channels, and Marty could take comfort in that.

Then why did he have this fear that something was yet to happen? He had no reason to worry…did he?

Marty pushed the feeling away, suppressing any negative thoughts. No, he said to himself, everything was going to be fine, he could be sure of it.

Doomsday was correct in his assumption that Incandescent would launch UNITE, despite rumors that the company was considering a product delay because of what had happened with GWare ONE. These American software companies just couldn't keep their greedy hands off of the people's profits, no matter what the risks, thought Doomsday. Now he would be able to complete his ultimate plan and sabotage UNITE. And this time, Doomsday planned to tell the world just who was behind this mass destruction. He wanted the Doomsday Virus to be universally known by name…and universally feared.

Doomsday and his cohorts worked feverishly to ready their Internet-based attack. Because UNITE's source code was a carefully guarded secret, they could not be sure that their plan would succeed, but they were optimistic. They had pieced together a good picture of the product from the detailed information provided in the prerelease materials. They had studied the product attributes as best they could and they thought they had found a potential security hole that could be the entry point for the virus. They planned to first target e-mail and Web servers they knew would be large UNITE installations. These would be their "test" cases. If the virus did its job at these initial sites, then they would know it couldn't be stopped until it was too late.

Still, they had to move quickly once the vulnerability was confirmed. After the havoc created by the virus-infected GWare ONE, Internet security had been tightened and systems administrators were on the highest alert. It would be a real challenge to break through the security screens and spread the infection.

The hackers' plan was to launch a coordinated invasion as soon as they knew UNITE was in place, confirm the fact that the virus had penetrated the operating system at select locations, and then follow-up with an all-out attack across the Internet. They would use steganographic messages to communicate instead of e-mail so they would be less likely to be detected. These covert messages were hidden in picture and music files that innocently appeared on normal Web pages. By hacking into the pages, Doomsday and his operatives were able to plant messages on any public Web site that were invisible to the average visitor but could be found by the hackers by using special software.

Doomsday wanted to create headlines with the initial incursion, so he decided to go after one of Incandescent's highest profile customers, the Massachusetts Institute of Technology. There was a long-standing relationship between the university and Incandescent, not only because Marty Gladstone had attended MIT, but because the company drew on the talent pool of MIT students for a large percentage of its employees. What's more, Incandescent had been generous to the university by funding numerous programs.

Doomsday thought it would be poetic justice to center his attack on the MIT Laboratory for Computer Science. LCS was an interdepartmental laboratory dedicated to the invention, development and understanding of information technologies. LCS members and alumni had been instrumental in the development of the ARPAnet, the Internet, the World Wide Web, and numerous other key information technologies. In fact, LCS was the breeding ground for dozens of leading technology companies, including Incandescent itself, which was now one of the sponsors of LCS. LCS was also the United States headquarters for the World Wide Web Consortium.

What better target to strike, Doomsday thought, than this bastion of technology? He savored the thought.

Doomsday decided to attack LCS through MITnet, the campus-wide system used by the university. He knew that MITnet was a computing environment with relatively unrestricted access. He would take advantage of the network's openness to try to penetrate the LCS' computing resources.

Finally the day came when UNITE was officially launched. Marty was incredibly proud of the effort his employees had put into the launch. He was also happy when Erin called to share his excitement. He had pushed his suspicion of her far back in his mind, rationalizing that at this point, it was of little concern to him. Right now he needed to concentrate all of his efforts on making the launch of UNITE a success.

As planned, UNITE would be showcased at a number of key strategic customers, including MIT's LCS. Marty had a special place in his heart for LCS, since it was very much associated with the launch of Incandescent. He decided that he would personally make a visit to the director of LCS and present him with copies of UNITE for installation.

Incandescent's PR firm arranged for select members of the press to be on hand for the occasion. Ironically, one of the individuals they invited was Erin Keliher. At first Marty resisted the idea. He desperately wanted to see Erin again, but at the same time he had mixed feelings because he knew he would have to confront her sooner or later. But he let the PR agency proceed with their plans and he fully expected to see her there.

With great fanfare, Marty was greeted by the LCS director, along with faculty, students and researchers. While these wizened technologists rarely got excited about a commercial software product, they had looked forward to the launch of UNITE with a great deal of anticipation. It was a thrill for them to be selected as one of the first installations in the country.

As Marty chatted with a group of the students, a few others loaded up the software. Marty felt a hand on his shoulder and turned to see who it was.

"Hello Marty," Erin said softly. He had almost forgotten how lovely she was. Her vivid blue eyes almost took his breath away.

"Hello Erin," he said warmly, taking her hand and holding it for a moment. He felt a spreading warmth. It started in his groin and made him tingle.

"I would've warned you I was coming," she said with a smile, "but I really didn't know if I could get here until the very last minute. I did a little arm-twisting. Told my editor that this was the ideal place to be for the launch of UNITE."

Marty drank in her face, realizing at once how much he had missed seeing her. "Well I'm glad you came for this historic moment," he said. "I hope you can stay a while."

"Flight out tomorrow," she answered.

He leaned close to her ear. "As the song says, 'We've Got Tonight.'"

She laughed and simply said, "Okay."

Erin stayed in the background as Marty held court. The program was successfully installed on a number of systems, there were accolades all around, and Marty spoke with other members of the press for a while. He then went over to Erin before departing. "What hotel are you staying at?" he asked.

She looked at him boldly. "Funny thing, I didn't have time to make a reservation."

"I know a nice place off Commonwealth," he said with mock innocence.

"Sounds perfect. How about if I play tourist for the afternoon, then call you later?"

Marty nodded. "That's great. Wish I could spend the day with you, but too much going on, as you can imagine. Call me around six and let's do dinner." He thought for a minute. "How about Mexican food?"

"Si, señor," she said.

Marty stayed at LCS a while longer and then hurried back to the office. He had a lot to do, and he wanted to get it done before he saw Erin that evening.

Later, Marty met Erin at Casa Romero, a restaurant located downstairs in an alleyway not far from his condo. It was small and dark, with an ambience that was quiet and romantic. The Mexican tiles set into the tops of the wooden tables glinted in the faint light. Erin was surprised when Marty ordered a half carafe of Sangria.

"You're not going to drink that, are you?" Erin asked when it arrived.

"I figured I'd splurge. Besides, it's more fruit juice than it is wine," Marty said. "Just a little to celebrate the launch." The real reason Marty ordered it, thought, is he thought a touch of alcohol would help him deal with his growing apprehension about the conversation he wanted to have with Erin.

Marty poured a little sangria in his own glass and some more into Erin's glass. He raised his glass and clinked it to hers. "Skol," he said.

"L'chaim," she answered.

He laughed aloud. "Where did you learn that?"

"Oh, I went out with a Jewish guy years ago. He taught me a few things about the religion, including that toast. Go ahead, ask me about Passover or Hanukah." Erin pronounced "Hanukah" with a straight 'H'.

He smiled. "Well I see he didn't teach you to pronounce Chanukah with a CHUH," Marty said.

Erin shook her head. "I'm Irish. I wouldn't even try a…chuh," she answered.

"There are a few things I don't know about you, aren't there?"

"Well," she said with some mystery in her voice, "I haven't told you *everything*."

God, he thought, what a portentous answer. She opened the door for him, so he figured why wait, he'd just walk right through it.

"Actually, I wanted to talk to you about exactly that," he began, swallowing a sip of the sangria. "I've been thinking about what a strange time it's been, how things have developed up to this point."

Erin had a puzzled look on her face. She wasn't sure where he was going with this conversation.

Marty continued, "What I mean is, there have been some things that have happened that have been pretty strange since..." He paused and looked her in the eyes. "Since you and I have been seeing one another."

Erin showed no sign of surprise or emotion, although Marty thought he noticed her right eye twitch ever so slightly. She sipped her sangria and said quietly, "Go on."

"I don't know quite how to say this," Marty continued, "but let me just go through it, get it all out, okay?"

Erin nodded warily.

Marty took a deep breath. "I've been replaying the events in my head over and over from the beginning. Let's go back to when you first saw our product demo. I know you got hooked on UNITE right then. I don't know what you knew about GWare ONE at the time, but I figure you were in a position to make a pretty good comparison between both operating systems, right?"

Erin nodded.

"So I think you had a tough choice to make...which bandwagon to get on. And I know you jumped on ours pretty early. Of course, I'm happy you did." He sipped the sangria, then swirled it around in the glass.

"But still, you had to keep your objectivity as a journalist. So maybe you saw that our product was better, but you figured you better wait and see if it was vaporware. How am I doing?"

"Pretty accurate so far," Erin answered.

"Then the whole deal with Henry Chu happens," Marty continued. "You've got to be thinking, would Henry Chu really sell out Incandescent to GWare? You go to the GWare ONE product intro and you find out it's true. That's when you call me."

"Yes, that's right," Erin said.

Marty took a breath. "Now this next part is just speculation, but bear with me. I'm looking at this saying, if I were Erin, after seeing what I just saw, I'd be so angry, so incensed at TJ Gatwick for what he did, not just to Incandescent and to me, but to the whole integrity of the software industry, that I'd never be able to forgive him. Maybe I'd even want to get back at him somehow."

Erin did nothing but quietly look at Marty as he weaved his story.

The waiter interrupted them and Marty brushed him away, saying they needed more time before they ordered.

Marty leaned over slightly, looking directly into Erin's eyes. "So then I get to wondering: How is it that GWare ONE, on the verge of the biggest software launch in history, has an undetectable virus inside? How is that a product like that, going through the kind of QA it has to go through, crashes and burns when it hits the market?

"And then, I think back to when Morrissey is about to investigate me. And I'm thinking, how did it happen that, just when UNITE was about to be delayed because of the Senate investigation, Morrissey is kidnapped? It's like I have a guardian angel or something, making all this stuff happen at the right time." Marty leaned back in his chair.

Erin picked up the half carafe of Sangria and poured herself some more. She let the sweet taste of the wine linger in her mouth for a moment.

She cleared her throat and spoke quietly. "So I gather from your story that you think I'm that angel."

He didn't say anything, but simply raised his eyebrows questioningly.

"Do you really think I'd be capable of planning a kidnapping, and of planting a virus, just to hurt TJ Gatwick and make sure UNITE would be the only operating system to successfully get to market?" She shook her head and smiled somewhat sadly. "Isn't that pretty absurd, Marty?"

He couldn't let up, he had to know if it was true. "I'm just putting it all together, one piece after another. But Erin, what I want more than anything else is for you to tell me that it isn't true."

"Marty, look," she began. "You're right that I was pretty damned indignant about everything TJ was doing. I figured he was behind the Morrissey deal, and I told you that. What you don't know is I went to see TJ after the Technology Council investigation was announced. I confronted him, accused him of arranging it. Of course he denied it and pretty much threw me out of his office.

"Then I saw that smug bastard at his product launch. He made sure I was seated right up front for his big show. When he demo'd GWare ONE, I realized immediately that the only way the software could have had that functionality was because Henry Chu built it with the code he stole from Incandescent. I was furious, of course I was, and I admit that. In fact, I'll even admit I could've killed the guy."

She looked at him, her eyes welling up. "And at the same time, Marty, I was falling in love with you. So," she said, "if I could have stopped the Senate investigation I would have. And if there was anything I could do to stop GWare ONE, I suppose I would have done that too. But not kidnapping, and not a virus. I just couldn't do anything like that, I couldn't."

She choked up, but then regained her composure and continued. "I'm a journalist, Marty, that's what I do. I may be an influential one, but I'm a reporter, that's all. My power is in the written word. I use it in the reviews and the commentaries I write. All I want is for people to read what I write, think about it, and make their own decisions. Sure, if I can get my opinion out there and people listen to me, then I can make a difference. And you're damned right that I felt strongly about GWare ONE and UNITE. But trying to change things by writing about them is as far as it goes. My job is to report on the news…not to make it." She sniffled and wiped her nose with her napkin.

All this time Marty was fixed on Erin's eyes. Not once did he glance away as she spoke. With an indescribable relief, he knew now that he had been entirely wrong about her. He felt an enormous sense of relief now. He reached over to take her hand in his.

"Erin," he began softly, "please forgive me for even imaging anything like this could be true. I just couldn't help but think that things were too coincidental for everything to fall into place this way. In a strange way, I half hoped you HAD done it because it would have shown how much you care for me. That's stupid, I know it is. Darling, what I really wanted was to believe it was impossible that you could do any such thing, but these crazy thoughts just kept filling my head. I didn't even know how the hell to talk to you about it."

Erin wiped away a tear. "I'm glad you did talk about it. I never want us to keep anything from each other. And I know the 3,000 miles between us didn't help the situation."

Marty wiped his mouth with his napkin, shaking his head. "I want you to understand that while I wondered about all this, while I thought it could possibly be you, what I really believed is that anything you would ever do would be for one simple reason: to right a wrong." He brought her hand up to his mouth and gently kissed one of her fingers. "I love you, Erin."

She returned the gesture by gently stroking his face. "Even if you do think I could've been a kidnapper?" she asked with a slight smile.

CHAPTER 13

Needless to say, the students working in MIT's Laboratory for Computer Science were not novices when it came to networking. It didn't take long for one of them to realize LCS was under attack from an outside source.

The student notified the LCS director immediately, who in turn notified the MIT Network Security Team. This team of members from MIT's Information Systems department and from independent departments, labs and centers at the Institute was established specifically to respond to threats to network and system security.

One of the team members rushed over to LCS. Another immediately instituted network virus scanning procedures while simultaneously issuing a security alert to all of MIT's networked users.

At LCS, the security team member removed all of the lab's computers from the network and launched virus scans on the machines. What he found was startling.

"This has the same characteristics as the virus that brought down the Internet not long ago, the one that traveled inside GWare ONE," he told the director. "Only this time, it's being propagated from an outside source.

"What's quite remarkable is that it appears to have targeted only select systems within your configuration, because I've only found three computers that are infected. I'm going to check each system for commonalities now."

The director and several students watched with growing fascination as the systems were being analyzed. This was the best live teaching experience they could imagine.

Finally, the security team member had his answer. "This is an educated guess," he said. "I'm going to verify it with the rest of the security team after further analysis. But I'm pretty sure that there's a strong connection between this virus and the operating system UNITE. In fact, it looks like the virus is seeking out a security hole in UNITE in an attempt to breach it."

The director had a stunned look on his face. "We just had UNITE installed. Marty Gladstone himself brought us the copies. We hadn't gotten around to installing it on all the systems."

"Lucky for you," the security team member responded. "But there's something that's even more amazing. It looks like UNITE had the ability to ward off the attack."

"How could it do that?" the director asked in disbelief.

"I can't be sure," the security team member said, "but if the virus was looking for a hole in UNITE's e-mail protocol, it appears UNITE didn't let it in. Looks like it put up some kind of shield when it recognized an attack. I've never seen a software program do anything like that before."

"Then you don't know Gladstone," the director muttered with respect.

"Listen," the team member said, "let me clean the virus off two of your systems that it attempted to compromise, get them up and running again. But I'd like you to quarantine the third infected system, under lock and key. I really want a few others on my team to look at how this virus works. I want to see if I'm right about UNITE...and maybe we might learn something that'll help us beat this one." He paused. "And if we do, that could be big."

The director didn't need convincing. "No problem. If I can get two of the three systems operational, that'll suffice."

The security team member nodded gratefully and went to work on the two systems. Within little more than an hour he had removed all of the infected files and run scans on both machines. The scans came up negative.

"All set," he said to the director. "I'll get back to you as soon as I can about checking on that third system. I know you don't want it tied up too long."

"Appreciate it," the director said. "And thanks for the quick response."

The security team member hurried off. He wanted to tell the others about what had happened...and he also wanted to make sure that MITnet was secure from further attack.

When the team member returned to his office, he was relieved to learn that the university's network had been secured. There were no other reports of viruses on other systems connected to MITnet, at least not yet. But there were thousands of systems, so it would take some time before every one of them was scanned and the security team could issue an All Clear. In the mean time, he was anxious to work with his colleagues to analyze the remaining infected system. This would be a rare opportunity to both understand how UNITE had repelled the attack...and potentially to get an inside look at one of the deadliest computer viruses in recent history.

Doomsday was anxious. It had been two weeks since he and his team of hackers had transmitted the Doomsday Virus to LCS at MIT. But he knew from scouring his Internet sources that MITnet was operational and had reported nothing unusual. Since the story hadn't appeared on C|Net or any other Internet news source, Doomsday could only assume that their attack had failed.

After checking again across the network, Doomsday got so incensed that he lashed out at the papers on his work table, scattering them about the dingy room. Red-faced, he jumped from his chair, gave a swift kick to one of the work table legs, and paced about furiously, pulling at his beard, wiping the sweat from his brow, and muttering obscenities to himself.

> *What the FUCK could've gone wrong?! This is the best damn virus anyone's ever created. I don't give a shit if it is MIT, how the hell could they stop it? Unless that son of a bitch Gladstone figured out a way to overcome it. I can't believe he could've come up with something to repel it, the bastard. But I'll find out, I'll find out. I'm not through with Incandescent yet…*

After his private tirade, Doomsday sat down and fired off an encrypted e-mail to his network of hackers. He told them he suspected that UNITE itself had some kind of virus repellent built into it, that it would be the only way the virus could've been stopped. He said he wanted all of his cohorts to work on finding out at any cost whether UNITE had anything special built into it, and what they could do about it. He said the success of their glorious mission hung in the balance, and he didn't want them to let him down.

Marty listened to the voice mail message again. Why would the head of the MIT network security team want to speak with him? But he did say it was urgent, and to please return the call on his cell phone as soon as possible.

"Bob Harris," a voice said, answering the phone on the second ring.

"Bob, Marty Gladstone. I got your message."

"Thanks so much for returning my call, Mr. Gladstone."

"Please, call me Marty."

"Okay. Marty, I wanted you to know of an incident at LCS that involved UNITE."

"Go on."

"A student working at LCS detected a virus attack coming in from an outside source. The director told us about it and one of our security team members got over there right away. He discovered it was the same virus that brought the Internet down…the GWare ONE virus."

"God, did it do any damage?"

"Well, luckily, it only infected three systems. But the three systems infected were the only ones with UNITE installed."

"And you think there's a connection?"

Bob cleared his throat. "We're sure of it, Marty. We quarantined one of the systems in its infected state and we've been studying it. We're virtually certain the virus was specifically targeting UNITE.

"Now I have to ask you this," Bob went on. "And I know you may not want to tell me, but I assure you I'll keep it confidential. It'll really help the investigation."

Marty was one step ahead of him. "You want to know about the anti-virus shield."

"Yeah, that's the most amazing thing I've ever seen."

Marty knew he would be taking a calculated risk by telling Bob about the closely guarded "secret weapon" of UNITE. But it was inevitable that at some point, word would get out about the shield. Virus attacks were just too common for it not to happen.

"Okay, Bob, but I'm telling you this to aid in your discovery process. I'd like you to keep this to yourself. If too many people know about this too soon, it'll lose its effectiveness, if nothing else because of the element of surprise when a virus attack occurs."

"I hear ya, Marty."

"We knew this operating system needed to resist viruses," Marty began, "especially after the GWare ONE disaster. We had already been working on a kind of virus shield, but we intensified our effort just before the product released. We didn't let on about this aspect of UNITE for two reasons: one, we really wanted it to be a hidden asset, so hackers wouldn't know about it…and two, we couldn't be entirely sure the damn thing would work with the most dangerous viruses, like the one that hit GWare."

"Makes sense to me," Bob said with admiration. "How does it work?"

"I can't give you the specifics, of course. Frankly, there's a lot on the technical side I don't fully understand myself. But here's the concept: The shield basically has a built-in detection feature that updates automatically during routine online maintenance. We've built free monthly online maintenance into the product cost of UNITE. We tell users to login at least once a month for a quality verification and to get updates. That's when we also update the virus detection."

"That's a cool feature in and of itself," Bob said, "but it's not a repellent."

"No, but UNITE takes it a step further. The detection feature is actually a sub-program integrated into the system architecture. The detection updates are more than that, they're actually components of the program that contain virus-deterrent elements. When the program detects a virus, it selects the appropriate set of elements that most closely match the virus attributes and sends them up through UNITE's networking protocol."

Bob was getting it now. "So that's why it looks like a shield…UNITE detects the invasion, then uses these elements via its networking protocol to ward off the attack. But that has to happen in a matter of nanoseconds."

"Yeah," Marty said, "that was the hard part…how to get the elements to the front line fast enough. That was a tough nut to crack for the engineers.

"That's why they approached it differently," Marty continued. "We developed a kind of security blanket that literally covers the core of UNITE as soon as any virus is detected. With the core protected, the detection program has the additional time necessary to pick the right elements and send 'em out." Marty paused. "Now you can see why we don't particularly want a lot of people to know how we do this."

"You convinced me," Bob said in awe. "If I didn't know better, I'd say it's all a lot of black magic. But I can tell you, from what I saw happen at LCS, it works."

Marty chuckled. "Believe me, that's a key data point. We kept hitting UNITE with every virus we could get our hands on in the beta lab. But it's never been battle-tested like this." Marty paused. "Listen, Bob, now that I've told you about UNITE's shield, it would really help if you could keep that system quarantined a little longer. I'd like two of my engineers to go over it with a fine tooth comb. This could really help us understand our own product and make it even better, maybe even detach the shield and see if we can make it work with other operating systems."

"That's the least I can do," Bob said. "I know you've shared a lot of information with me and you didn't have to. Just give me a call when they want to come over and I'll authorize the access. Thanks, Marty, for confiding in me."

Marty concluded his call and felt good about his decision to open up to Bob Harris. The man was clearly in a position to understand the sensitive nature of what was shared between them. More importantly, by engendering Bob's trust, Marty now had access to the quarantined computer. This would give his organization much-needed insight into virus attacks as they occurred in the real world.

This was a lucky break in many respects. But now, Marty knew, he could be facing a larger, more ominous challenge. Bob had suspected that this virus attack was targeting UNITE itself. He hadn't mentioned any other attacks across MITnet, so Marty was fairly certain the attack was localized. The circumstantial evidence was strong since UNITE was only installed at LCS.

It was weeks since he visited LCS and delivered the copies of UNITE to them, yet there was nothing on the news about a virus attack. Surely it would've leaked by now…the press was hungry for this kind of story. Marty figured that meant the attackers were selective. They must have targeted LCS, and LCS only, to be sure they could penetrate UNITE before spreading the virus. Who knows, maybe they suspected UNITE could repel it. Or maybe they just wanted to embarrass LCS and at the same time show that they could attack anywhere they wanted, when they wanted. What better place for a first attack than the legendary LCS, birthplace of the Internet.

Whatever the reason, Marty thought, these bastards were shrewd. Of course, what bothered him the most was they were obviously targeting UNITE. This was the GWare ONE virus, so Marty had to assume it was the same hacker or hackers behind this attack. It was one thing to have a known enemy like TJ Gatwick, Marty thought, but how the hell would he fight against this unseen enemy, someone who was completely invisible, someone who could attack without warning?

While it was some consolation that UNITE's virus shield had indeed done its job, and he was incredibly thankful for that, Marty was now entering a whole new stage in the lifecycle of UNITE. Now, his decision to launch the product flashed through his mind. Did he get this one right…or was it profoundly wrong to put this product into a marketplace riddled with viruses? Would UNITE now fall prey to the same fate as GWare ONE?

But there was no time to second-guess himself. Marty needed to take action on two fronts, and that's what he decided to do. First he would get two of his best engineers over to MIT to learn as much as they could about this particular virus attack. If these guys couldn't analyze that virus and find any vulnerabilities in it, no one could.

Next he would get in touch with the FBI. When the GWare ONE virus hit, he had been contacted by an FBI Computer Security Task

Force agent who said to call him anytime. That's exactly what Marty would do, and fast.

Even as he was thinking through his next steps, Erin suddenly popped into his mind. Marty wondered if he should discuss this with her. On a professional level, she was one of the best in the business, and her knowledge would be extremely valuable here. Since their dinner in Boston, Marty had felt better than ever about their relationship, although they were still finding it difficult to see each other very often.

He no longer had any suspicion of Erin, rather it was her role as a journalist that worried Marty at this moment. He had every confidence in her ability to be discreet, but this story was so huge, he knew she would struggle with the journalist's need to write about it. How could he tempt her like that? He loved her dearly and didn't want to put her in that kind of a compromising position.

No, Marty decided, he couldn't do that. This was one time he simply couldn't confide in Erin Keliher.

Marty looked up the FBI agent's phone number in his address book. He didn't have a moment to waste—he had to call him right away.

CHAPTER 14

The rare thunderstorm in San Diego matched TJ Gatwick's tempestuous mood. He had just come out of a planning meeting and he had about a million problems on his mind. Since the introduction of GWare ONE, the company had virtually been under siege. The class action suit against GWare was proceeding rapidly. While an out of court settlement was expected to come any moment now, it was anticipated to be somewhere in the neighborhood of ninety million dollars.

The company's stock price was being mercilessly battered, and TJ's personal wealth had already dropped twenty-five percent. GWare had announced a hiring freeze and was about to issue pink slips to several hundred employees in an effort to cut expenses. If it weren't for GWare's considerable revenue stream from its previously released products, the company would likely be teetering on bankruptcy. In effect, the introduction of GWare ONE, which was to be the company's crowning achievement, had brought GWare to its knees.

Yet all of this was dwarfed by TJ's decidedly irrational, vitriolic reaction to a single event: the apparent unqualified success of Incandescent's UNITE. With almost suicidal fascination, TJ had been closely watching the industry news of the way in which Incandescent's new operating system was sweeping the world. He would seek out all the information he could find about UNITE's continued market penetration, and then go into a rage as soon as he read about it. He was so uncontrollable of late that his closest advisors urged him to see a doctor and get a prescription to calm his nerves.

What his advisors didn't know is the real reason behind TJ's emotional outbursts. It wasn't the success of UNITE that tore at his guts, but rather his unrelenting conviction that UNITE's creator had brought about the destruction of GWare ONE. TJ was as sure of this as he had been of anything in his life: he believed without reservation that Marty Gladstone himself had engineered the downfall of GWare. And he was convinced he did it with his sweet little spy, Erin Keliher, helping him along the way.

TJ felt even more strongly about this now that UNITE had been launched without a hitch. He reasoned that if UNITE entered the marketplace unscathed by viruses, it could only have been Gladstone himself who sabotaged GWare ONE. How else could the little bastard get his product to market and win the software war?

TJ wondered when it happened that it became so important for Gladstone to defeat him. He remembered his brief experience at MIT when he and the founder of Incandescent had crossed paths. TJ recalled that first distasteful encounter with the pompous Gladstone. That must be it, he thought. That could be what set the tone for the conflict that would ensue so many years later…

"Now Mr. Gladstone," the Business Ethics professor intoned, "you have chosen to debate the topic, 'The Social Responsibility of Software Companies: People or Profits.' And Mr. Gatwick, you will present a counter-position. You each have three minutes to make your opening statements, then you'll be able to challenge each other's position by answering questions you ask of each other. Of course, you both will have the opportunity to rebut. I will then allow three minutes each for closing arguments.

"Do each of you understand the ground rules?"

Both Gladstone and Gatwick nodded.

"Very well. Mr. Gladstone, you may begin." The professor turned over an hour-glass egg timer to assure each debater would have the same allotted time.

Marty didn't really mind speaking in front of his class at MIT, but he was somewhat nervous because this was his first experience debating another student. He didn't know much about this Gatwick fellow, but he was certainly physically imposing. He towered over Marty. What's more, he looked to Marty like he was loaded for bear.

Marty began his opening statement. "Today, software companies have the ability to influence thousands if not millions of users worldwide. With the fundamental importance of computing, software itself becomes a means to create the functionality essential to the computer, but it also represents what the computer can truly do for people.

"Software applications are the building blocks of computing. Every application provides an opportunity for computing to help people improve efficiency, work faster and smarter, and solve problems. Where would we be without word processing, without spreadsheets, without presentation software? How would the world communicate? Isn't it computing applications that are behind telephones, ATMs and the Internet?

"While a software company makes huge investments in research and development to build these applications and bring them to market, the ROI can be nothing short of spectacular. We have only to look at the profit margins of leading software companies to know this is true. Granted, it takes considerable capital to launch each product and to market it, but the successful product then becomes a cash cow. The company can basically mass produce the product at a huge markup.

"My position today is not to debate the right of software companies to engage in free market capitalism, or to make reasonable profits from selling their products. Rather, I take the position that software companies have a social responsibility to produce products that advance human thinking, that help people aspire and achieve...products that can improve lives and improve conditions in the world.

"Further, I believe that software companies have a responsibility to allow free market competition...unlike Microsoft. Microsoft is a virtual monopoly in the software business who bullies its competition into submission. With Microsoft's financial might and industry influence, no other software company will be able to effectively compete in the PC operating system category, for example. Windows is the only real choice. It could be just as true of applications. Microsoft not only dominates some application categories, it basically locks out its competition in these categories. As a result, people have to accept products that may be lesser in quality...just because one company is more powerful than another company. This isn't good for business and it isn't good for the consumer whose choices become limited by unfair business practices.

"Finally, I believe that, while software companies have every right to profit from their products, and provide a reasonable return to their investors and shareholders, these companies should have a social conscience. I believe they should look critically at their profit margins and, when those profit margins are high enough, they should consider applying some of those profits to worthy causes...causes that help the society that supported their products in the first place."

Marty ended his impassioned statement and sat down.

"Mr. Gatwick, your statement please."

TJ Gatwick stood and looked about the room for a moment. He then glanced at Marty almost dismissively and began.

"This country is the greatest free market in the world. It has been founded on certain basic principles, like freedom of speech and expression. One of those freedoms in our modern society is the freedom to do business, to sell products people want to buy. Software companies, like any other American companies, enjoy that freedom, and they are controlled as in any capitalistic society by market conditions.

"If their software products are good, and they serve a purpose, there is a demand for them. If they aren't good, then competitors make better products that take market share. It's pretty simple when you think about it.

"Now I could say that software companies have a special social responsibility, because they produce products that help people improve their productivity and their lives."

TJ paused for a moment to look over at Marty with a derisive expression on his face. "But that is socialism, not capitalism. And that's not the society we live in.

"The reality is that software companies are no less or no more obligated to be socially responsible than automobile or pharmaceutical companies. These companies help people and improve their lives, too. Shouldn't they be held to the same high social standard as software companies?

"Furthermore, doesn't every company have an implied social responsibility when it operates in a free economy? Should we be singling out software companies and apply a different moral standard only to them?

"As for the current state of the software industry, let's be real. The reason Microsoft succeeds is because Microsoft has superior products that people want. It's all about survival of the fittest…and Microsoft just happens to be the fittest. I've heard self-appointed industry watchdogs complain for years about Microsoft's dominance. I say they wouldn't be dominant if other companies were any good at competing with them. There are stories in the software industry of smaller companies creating a product that becomes a big hit and sells millions of copies because it's a product people need, a product that isn't already on the market.

"Let me close by addressing the issue of software company profits. A software company does, in fact, make a major investment in bringing a product to market. If that product is a winner, then the company's investment pays off. There are times when the product isn't a winner, and the company's ROI just plain sucks."

Gatwick's bluntness elicited a giggle from several students. He continued, "The point is that software companies, like any company that wants to stay in business, need to make profits to survive. Those profits need to be re-invested in other products. And those profits are intended to return value to the company's shareholders, which is the first responsibility of any company in business.

"My view is that the profitability of the software company is good for the company, good for its shareholders and, ultimately, good for the people in the society served by the company. By being more profitable, and succeeding in the marketplace, the software company can produce more products that consumers want. That's the true way of achieving social responsibility in a society that depends on capitalism."

A few of the students licked their lips and sat forward in their seats after Gatwick concluded, their body language suggesting they couldn't wait for the questioning to begin. They realized this was turning into the classic debate between the power of the people and the power of profits.

Marty found TJ's position repugnant. He was fully prepared to defend his stance. He couldn't understand how Gatwick could be so insensitive to society's needs. Gatwick, on the other hand, saw Gladstone's position as thinly veiled communism. Gatwick was appalled at the holier than thou attitude of this diminutive idealist. Gatwick wondered if he was for real...and couldn't imagine how he'd gotten admitted to MIT. He couldn't wait until the first question was asked...

An intrusive tone from somewhere far away jarred TJ from his daydream. Absently, he looked around and blinked a few times. Then he realized it was his phone.

"Gatwick," he said abruptly as he punched the conference button. He rarely picked up the phone. He liked being in conference mode because it made the caller immediately feel uncomfortable, as if their words could be heard by anyone. TJ used it as a technique to dominate the conversation from the beginning.

It was one of his law firm's lead attorneys.

"I think we can close the class action case," he said. "I just need your approval to go with the amount."

"Which is?" TJ said.

"A hundred million," the attorney said. "Mr. Gatwick, I'm advising you to settle for that amount now."

There was silence on the other end of the phone. The attorney waited a moment and then said, "Mr. Gatwick?"

"Yeah, I heard you," TJ said.

"What's your decision?"

TJ exhaled audibly. "Fine," he said, fatigue tainting his voice. "Do it."

"Thank you, Mr. Gatwick. I'll draw up the papers and be over to see you, say in about three hours?"

"Yeah, whatever." With that, TJ hung up the phone.

One hundred million dollars because of a fucking virus, he thought. But it was a virus in MY company's product.

He could see that MIT debate again in his mind, hear those words spoken by Gladstone…

Christ, TJ thought, it's got to be Gladstone who did this to me. From that moment in Business Ethics class, from that encounter years ago, Gladstone must have hated him. He couldn't accept the fact that TJ told the truth about software companies, that TJ was a bold-faced capitalist. Gladstone's the one who planted this virus, TJ thought, to get back at me for debating him, for countering him. Social responsibility, my ass!

And his perfect accomplice was Erin, TJ thought. Erin, who from the very beginning misled him. She had been crafty, that bitch. She got into his good graces, got him to trust her and tell her about GWare. And then she turned on him, trashing GWare and supporting Incandescent. He wouldn't be surprised if she was fucking Marty Gladstone too. It was all becoming clear, too damn painfully clear. Now he was sure of it…these two were surely out to destroy him.

TJ's first responsibility, of course, was to save his company, to turn around a business that had been seriously if not mortally wounded. TJ felt that somehow, GWare would survive even the class action suit and the crushing bad publicity that resulted from the GWare ONE launch, if nothing else on past successes alone. Maybe his company would be smaller, but he'd make damn sure it would survive.

Even so, TJ Gatwick was anxious to take on another challenge…he wanted to devise a plan to bring the bastards, Marty and Erin, down. This would be what he would strive for, so that Gladstone could feel what he was feeling now, so Incandescent could reel from the same kind of disaster that occurred with GWare ONE. And he wanted Erin, too, to feel the pain, to get what she deserved, for betraying him.

If it was the last thing he'd ever do, TJ Gatwick would pay them back, they could be sure of that.

PART II

1999

CHAPTER 15

Decadence, sheer decadence, he thought, as he awoke and stretched lazily. Marty had always been an early morning person but lately, on Sundays at least, he took to staying in bed. The reason for this significant change of habit was lying right next to him.

Erin rolled over towards him and draped her arm around his bare chest. He lay there quietly, not wanting to disturb her. But he took the opportunity to turn his head and study the face of the sleeping beauty next to him.

How did I get so lucky, he thought.

They had been living together "part time," as Erin humorously described it, since Marty had opened Incandescent's Silicon Valley West Coast regional headquarters with much fanfare more than a year ago. The office was a fully staffed facility that was, in many ways, a smaller version of Incandescent's Cambridge headquarters. It had been an important strategic move for the company, of course, but it had the residual benefit of spawning a different living situation for Marty and Erin. Now Marty was able to share Erin's San Francisco condo with her when he was in town.

There was still a price to pay, however; the downside for Marty was what had become a true bicoastal lifestyle. He minimized the stress of constant travel by spending every other month in the company's Cambridge corporate headquarters, still maintaining his condo in Boston. During the months he worked at the Silicon Valley facility, he lived with Erin at her San Francisco condo. This one month here, one month there system was still better than traveling coast-to-coast on a weekly basis.

Marty's being in San Francisco was like a dream come true for both of them, especially those lazy Sundays. They had quickly adopted the tradition of staying in bed on Sunday and making long, languorous love. After so many years of a long-distance relationship, during which Marty and Erin had to steal an occasional weekend together, Sunday love-making had taken on an almost revered place in their lives.

They hungered for one another, making love each weekend as if it were their last days on earth. Erin was a delightfully sexy lover. She would often take the lead, and Marty loved it because she willingly took responsibility for their mutual enjoyment. He would jokingly call her his "CEO of Love."

Erin was particularly skilled with her mouth. She would flick her tongue over his nipples, then use her warm moist lips to suck them gently, and then pull at them with just the right pressure. It was excruciatingly delicious. Before Erin, Marty had never known a man's nipples could be so sensitive. And what she did with her mouth to the rest of him…well, Marty thought, she was a magician, a sorceress, a siren. There was no other way to describe it.

Marty certainly responded in kind. With the luxury of time, and the growing knowledge of her body and what drove her to ecstasy, he became a lover both passionate and patient. Afterwards, they would always hug, caress each other, and just talk for a while. They had an intimacy that he treasured, a closeness down to their very souls that they both believed was theirs alone.

But it hadn't been paradise early on in their long-distance relationship. The first few months of their living arrangement were challenging, to say the least. Marty and Erin discussed the fact that they were entering a new phase of their relationship. They talked about what it would mean to each of them. They thought they had anticipated the issues. They had, to a certain degree, but what they didn't and couldn't really understand was the emotional roller-coaster they would be riding together.

The temporary permanence of the arrangement became clear when Marty moved some "West Coast clothes" he had purchased into Erin's place. It wasn't a big deal to either of them; Erin had a guest room a few doors down from her bedroom with a closet that Marty could use. Conveniently, she had two sinks in the bathroom off the master bedroom, so they could wash up together in the morning.

That first month of his living there, they began their Sunday lovemaking, recognizing that there would be little time or energy for such intimacy during the week. All was working out gloriously...that is, until Marty reached the inevitable day that he had to return to Cambridge for his agreed-upon month on the East Coast.

As the time drew nearer, he half thought about extending his stay in San Francisco. After all, he was now CEO—he had hired a president, older and more experienced than him, who was extremely capable of running the company day-to-day. Marty knew, though, that he was still the spark-plug of the company's engine, and that engine was located in Cambridge, not Silicon Valley.

The challenges of product development and distribution were very different from the early days of UNITE. While UNITE had put Incandescent on the map as a global software company, the pressure to maintain the company's leadership position was enormous. With the rapid rise of Dot Coms, and the software industry's equally rapid transition to an Internet-based business model, it was all Marty could do to keep up with the pace of technology.

Marty believed in the Internet, but he also knew his company could not re-engineer itself overnight. He had taken the conservative position of maintaining the company's business model of producing hard-copy software, yet he aggressively pursued the strategic application of the Internet. By doing so, Marty felt he was hedging his bets. While his board sometimes grew impatient with Marty's methodical growth plan, they reluctantly deferred to his judgment. After all, the company had been wildly successful in the past five years, largely due to the acceptance of UNITE. Incandescent's stock price was high and revenue was growing. How could they complain about that?

Marty knew he could not shirk his responsibility. He was a driving force of the company, and that meant his presence in Cambridge was essential. It was one of the prices he paid as a founder and major shareholder. He had to look at the Silicon Valley operation as secondary, although important enough to warrant his attention. As it was, he wondered when the board would ask him why he needed to continue to spend every other month at the Silicon Valley office.

So after a month of living and loving together, Marty reluctantly returned to Cambridge. While he began to miss Erin the instant he stepped on the plane, he quickly got embroiled in the goings-on at Incandescent and subjugated his feelings for her, at least momentarily.

On the contrary, Erin found she was less able to cope with the loss initially. She thought she had prepared herself, but she ran head-on into emotional trauma. At every turn, she confronted something of Marty's in her home…his shaving gear in her bathroom, the mug he used for tea in her kitchen, the last bit of his dirty laundry she had washed the day after his departure.

It was so painful for her that she refused to change the sheets for a week after he left because she wanted his scent to linger. She would walk into the guest room frequently just so she could run her hands along his shirts and pants hanging in the closet. She found herself thinking of him at every time of day or night. Once she remembered waking up from an erotic dream that included him…only it was weirdly unsettling because in the dream he was making love to her but she couldn't physically touch him. That pretty much summed it up, she thought.

The loneliest time for her was, of course, Sunday morning. As she awakened that first Sunday, she naturally extended her arm towards his side of the bed. Half asleep, she felt a surge of shock as her arm met an empty space instead of the rise and fall of his chest. It jarred her to wakefulness as she suddenly remembered he was not there. She lay there momentarily, feeling sorry for herself. She impulsively picked up the phone and dialed his number. They had spoken just last night, but she felt a need to connect with him again.

She got his answering machine, though, and realized that he was already out and about. She didn't want to appear needy so she did not leave a message for him.

It was three hours earlier in San Francisco, and she knew without her by his side that he would have no reason to linger in bed. Maybe he was out running, or maybe he had even gone to the office.

It was easy for him, she thought with momentary resentment, he could distract himself at his place of business in Cambridge. But she had to live with his absence from her place in San Francisco, from her life. A tear welled up and she suppressed it. Get hold of yourself Erin, she thought, grow up girl! Be happy for what you have, and be happy he will return in a month. It's not like you won't ever see him again.

But it made her think. Before, it was a long-distance relationship. They had resigned themselves to a certain pattern of mandatory non-involvement in each other's lives. There was a growing love between them, yes, but it had no physical anchor. They did not live together, they spent time together. It was precious time, but temporary and fleeting time. In some respects, the longing was sweeter.

This was so very different, she thought. Now the longing was wrenching, because here she was, living together with the man she loved in a crazy, part-time, you're-here-but-you're-not-here kind of lifestyle. She assumed the first month would be the hardest, she just didn't realize how hard it would really be. Maybe it would ease up as time went on, she thought. It had to, she told herself.

While it took two installments of Marty's coming and going, Erin and Marty finally began to adjust to their new living situation. Once Erin resigned herself to the fact that he would need to leave but that he would indeed return every other month, she began to get over her underlying fear that he would not come back at all. Once Marty understood the fact that he was, in an odd way, an intruder in Erin's home, a part-time lover who abandoned her periodically, he made an effort to reinforce his presence when he wasn't physically there by calling her every day and sending her gifts and cards.

One time, he even surprised her by having a complete Sunday morning breakfast delivered to her door. He timed it so that he could call her and "have virtual breakfast together," as he said. They got back into bed, he in Boston, she in San Francisco, and talked as she had her breakfast. It was probably the most insane thing they had ever done, and she loved every minute of it.

After that, the next time he walked in the door, ready to begin another month together, she greeted him as if they had been apart for years. On that day they didn't wait until Sunday morning. Instead, he dropped his briefcase at the door and they kissed passionately for a long time. Then, standing in the entryway, they feverishly undressed each other, kicking their clothes off, embracing and kissing, making their way clumsily to her bedroom. They made love urgently, with an almost violent intensity that left him breathless and spent, and her shedding a tear of joy. Afterwards, they lay in bed together and he said with mockery in his voice, "So what did you say your name was?" She slapped his arm and burst out laughing.

From then on, they reached a new level of acceptance. They found it easier to cope with their living situation by acknowledging their frailties. They consciously put less pressure on themselves by not trying to make it so perfect. Sometimes on those precious Sunday mornings, they would lay very still in bed and talk quietly about their relationship, telling each other of the happiness they felt when they were together and the loneliness they felt when they were apart.

They consoled each other in this way and found solace in each other's arms, and their mutual understanding made it that much easier to survive those months when they were physically separated.

What they didn't discuss, but what surely lay just below the surface, was the unanswered question about the nature of their relationship. They both wondered what would happen when they reached a plateau, when being together every other month just wasn't good enough anymore. How long would this month-on, month-off lifestyle work for them? Wouldn't there inevitably be a time when they wanted more, maybe to get married, maybe to have children?

It was something Erin had begun to think about, had begun to consider, yet at this stage, she hadn't discussed it with Marty. Little did Erin realize that Marty, too, had given the same thing much thought. Surely that day of reckoning would come for both of them. And what Erin and Marty really wondered about on their own is when that moment came, would they both be ready to deal with it?

CHAPTER 16

From The Wall Street Journal, March 29, 1999:
You Got Mail, and You Don't Want It:
Virus Infects Computers Around the World
By Dean Takahashi
Staff Reporter of The Wall Street Journal

Computer experts grappled over the weekend with an insidious virus program that rocketed around the world by e-mail and could cause more chaos Monday.

The virus affects personal computers that have Microsoft Corp.'s Word software and its mail programs, Outlook or Outlook Express. Once activated by unwary users, the virus causes each PC to send 50 copies of a message containing a list of pornographic Web sites, generating a flood of traffic that brought many corporate e-mail systems to a halt on Friday.

Melissa, as the virus was dubbed by computer-security experts, causes no direct damage to infected PCs and, once it has been activated, can be deleted by using a software utility that is now widely available.

If anyone had told TJ Gatwick five years ago that the word "virus" would have brought a smile to his face, he would have thought they were demented. Yet reading *The Wall Street Journal* article, TJ could not help but smile.

There was good reason for his elation. Since that devastating introduction of GWare ONE back in '94, TJ Gatwick had completely reorganized GWare. The company had gotten out of the operating system business, and made a strategic move into Internet-related technologies. In fact, TJ led his developers to focus on anti-virus initiatives in particular, resulting in the creation in 1997 of GWare Guardian, an Internet-based virus monitoring and protection service.

It was a brilliant PR move, but certainly a double-edged sword not without its downside. It was risky on TJ's part and just as easily could have backfired if GWare Guardian had failed. TJ realized that the press couldn't help but dredge up the story about GWare ONE and the virus that nearly destroyed his company. But he also knew the positive spin was irresistible because of GWare's new role as a maker of an anti-virus product. It was the perfect positioning: a company teetering on bankruptcy stands up and fights against the very evil that brought it down. This was the stuff American dreams were made of.

It hadn't been easy for TJ to launch GWare Guardian in the first place. Still reeling from the GWare ONE legal settlement, and the subsequent downsizing of the company, the GWare board of directors had come close to forcing Gatwick's resignation. He used his considerable knowledge of the marketplace to convince the board that he could turn the company around by jumping on the Internet bandwagon. He made a compelling case for an anti-virus product structured as an Internet-based subscription service. If it worked, he said, the company would have a recurring revenue stream...an annuity that would stabilize the company and bring it back to an industry leadership position.

It was Gatwick's last stand. Reluctant at first, the board finally agreed to give Gatwick his chance to prove it could work. They had certainly seen first-hand the damage that could be done by a computer virus. Why not attempt to make a buck off of someone else's misfortunes, they reasoned.

With a renewed sense of optimism and a bold new mission, TJ threw himself into product development. He drove his staff mercilessly. They feverishly researched anything and everything about viruses and put several security experts on contract to accelerate the development process. The old TJ emerged from the ashes of GWare ONE. Once again, he became the brash but brilliant software guru. He knew this was his opportunity to show the board, and the world, that he could turn horseshit into gold.

Even from the beginning, the concept of GWare Guardian was deceptively simple. Users could subscribe on a monthly basis at three different levels of service. The most basic level was simply a virus alert service. The intermediate level included self-service protection, in which the user was responsible for downloading anti-virus software. The advanced level featured priority notification, automatic Internet-based updates, and personal attention from virus specialists. Each subsequent level cost more, but there were discounts for multiple subscriptions. The pricing strategy was as important as the service itself. Its flexibility meant that GWare Guardian had broad appeal to companies of all types and sizes. In effect, any company could use the service to some degree. And since GWare Guardian was Internet-based, product distribution was electronic. It could be easily delivered anywhere in the world, and "turned on" in an instant.

The concept was an instant winner. GWare Guardian took the industry by storm and became GWare's most successful product introduction ever. The company's stock and reputation rebounded, and TJ Gatwick went from chump to champ.

TJ couldn't help but gloat as he continued to read the article in *The Journal.* The Melissa virus would undoubtedly cause an industry-wide panic. There would be a rush to purchase anti-virus software, and GWare Guardian would very likely be the major beneficiary of the scare. The irony wasn't lost on TJ, and he basked in the glory of the corporate rebirth he engineered.

TJ thought back to that ugly time when a virus very nearly cost him everything he had. TJ continued to believe that Marty Gladstone was guilty until proven innocent. Just thinking of Gladstone made TJ's blood boil. The little bastard had, in fact, been wildly successful with UNITE. With the void left by the failure of GWare ONE, Incandescent became the only other major player in the operating system business, and now, UNITE was even giving Windows a run for its money. TJ was painfully aware that Incandescent was on the verge of overtaking GWare in total revenue, something that would have been unthinkable five years ago.

After all this time, TJ still couldn't accept the success of Incandescent without connecting it directly to the failure of GWare ONE. How convenient it was, TJ thought, that UNITE took off just when GWare ONE was going down in flames. He would never live that down.

Despite TJ's undying hatred of Gladstone, he was driven more by his company's current success and his personal gain than anything else. And that meant the ultimate irony for TJ—forming an unholy alliance with Incandescent. UNITE's position in the marketplace was such that GWare could not avoid the operating system's fundamental importance to computer users. Entering into an agreement with Incandescent was good for business, and in TJ's world, business came first. Under the agreement, Incandescent endorsed GWare Guardian and GWare certified UNITE. With the considerable impact this would have on revenue, TJ was perfectly willing to sleep with his mortal enemy.

The payoff was crucial for both companies. The anti-virus market was becoming a hotly contested segment of the software industry. There had been increasingly serious attacks in the years since the GWare ONE virus attack.

The problem had been exacerbated by the meteoric growth of the Internet, which now had 150 million users worldwide. The Internet was the ideal breeding ground for computer viruses. Its very nature, a loosely affiliated network of networks, created an environment that, at any given time, was highly vulnerable to attack. There were so many access points that an Internet-wide security solution would have been impossible to implement. As a result, every network connection and every computer that was networked required its own degree of individual security.

A company's e-mail system was particularly vulnerable to infection. As with Melissa, hackers often attacked Microsoft's Outlook because it was the dominant e-mail product in the marketplace. While Microsoft attempted to plug security holes as soon as they were discovered, by the time they did, the damage was already done. It was often too late.

The hacker who wanted to do serious damage recognized that e-mail was an excellent viral carrier. E-mail had already overtaken the telephone, direct mail and faxes as the most popular form of business communication. It enjoyed wide acceptance with consumers, fueled by the fact that every Internet Service Provider offered free e-mail as part of their package. With the ubiquity of e-mail, a virus could be spread to hundreds of thousands of users almost instantaneously.

The most common method was to infect an e-mail attachment. When the attachment was opened by an unsuspecting recipient, the virus was launched. Most viruses were worms—they literally wormed their way through the e-mail system, attacking not only the end user's computer, but the company's e-mail server. While some viruses were simply inconveniences, others had the capacity to bring down entire networks and do serious damage to computer drives, infecting each system's CPU and destroying the files residing on it.

The threat to computer security was so significant that the U.S. government established the National Infrastructure Protection Center (NIPC) in February 1998. Located in the FBI's Washington, D.C. headquarters, the NIPC's mission is to serve as the government's focal point for threat assessment, warning, investigation, and response for threats or attacks against the nation's critical infrastructures. These include telecommunications, energy, banking and finance, water systems, government operations, and emergency services.

According to the NIPC, "the same interconnectivity that allows us to transmit information around the globe at the click of a mouse or push of a button also creates unprecedented opportunities for criminals, terrorists, and hostile foreign nation-states who might seek to steal money or proprietary data, invade records, conduct industrial espionage, cause a vital infrastructure to cease operations, or engage in Information Warfare."

The NIPC uses three levels of infrastructure warnings which are developed and distributed consistent with the FBI's National Threat Warning System. According to the NIPC: "Alerts address major threat or incident information addressing imminent or in-progress attacks targeting specific national networks or critical infrastructures; Advisories address significant threat or incident information that suggests a change in readiness posture, protection options and/ or response; Assessments address broad, general incident or issue awareness information and analysis that is both significant and current but does not necessarily suggest immediate action."

In January 1999, President Clinton took another important step, announcing new initiatives to defend the nation's computer systems and critical infrastructure from cyber-terrorism. Among other initiatives, the President proposed a "Cyber Corps," enabling government agencies to recruit a cadre of experts to respond to attacks on computer networks. TJ Gatwick was selected as an advisor to the Cyber Corps. In addition, GWare had been consulted by the Defense Department in their installation of intrusion detection systems and creation of a network to warn key computers of an attack.

In many respects, the downfall of GWare ONE had begun a whole new era in computer security...and TJ Gatwick had been enough of a visionary to turn it to his advantage.

But there was a very personal aspect to TJ's battle as well. A few years after the GWare ONE attack, a certain audacious hacker identified himself as the perpetrator. He called himself Doomsday. At first, no one took him seriously, but soon a pattern of virus attacks emerged. Each attack was preceded by a warning from this hacker that he would strike. Of course he never announced where or when. The hacker directly challenged the NIPC and the FBI to try to stop him.

Doomsday was as ingenious at garnering publicity as he was at launching virus attacks. He selected a respected industry journalist and began to send the journalist messages. That journalist was none other than Erin Keliher.

Erin had no choice but to become Doomsday's conduit. It was her journalistic duty, even though she didn't relish playing this role. All of a sudden, Erin's position in the industry was vaulted to super-stardom, as everything Doomsday wanted to tell the world was communicated through her column in *The Journal.*

This was almost too much for TJ to bear. When GWare Guardian was first introduced, she had written a glowing review in her *Journal* column, and he begrudgingly appreciated it. But it didn't change his underlying distrust. While the passing years had cooled TJ's anger, his resentment of Erin had lingered. He had never been able to prove her collusion in the GWare ONE episode, but still he was convinced that she played a role in his personal misfortune.

Now TJ couldn't help but suspect that the reason Doomsday was speaking through Erin was because Erin was a sympathizer. TJ reasoned that it was the perfect cover…who would suspect Erin herself of anything, when she supposedly was chosen by a hacker as the distribution channel for his rantings and ravings? A respected journalist unwittingly brought into the situation…used as a hacker's voice. TJ was truly skeptical. He made it his personal vendetta to thwart Doomsday with GWare Guardian at all costs…and he wouldn't let Erin Keliher get in his way.

Of course, the media had a field day with the Doomsday-Erin Keliher "relationship." It was treated as if Erin were some kind of a medium holding a software séance, and Doomsday was the spirit speaking through her. Any pronouncement Doomsday made he sent to her via e-mail, knowing full well that she would dutifully mention it in her column.

Some people believed that Erin was doing nothing more than publicizing an evil-doer. In fact, she had a number of heated conversations with her editor about the ethicality of her actions. The editor had to ask if it was in the best interests of the newspaper or the public to print Doomsday's diatribes. Erin saw it differently...she could provide a unique picture of the hacker and maybe even draw him out so he could eventually be found. Besides, she said, all the national publicity could do wonders for increasing *The Journal's* circulation.

In the end, she won the argument for an even more important reason. The FBI entered the picture and backed her up. While the government agency had to tread very carefully when dealing with the press, a senior agent with the FBI made a compelling case to Erin's editor on the basis of national security. With Erin as the only link to Doomsday, the agent felt that keeping the lines of communication open was imperative. If Erin were to stop being Doomsday's mouthpiece, the agent believed the hacker would fade back into the deep recesses of the Internet and become invisible again. Then it would be that much more difficult to pursue and potentially capture him.

The FBI was banking on the fact that Doomsday would continue to crave the media attention and wanted the world to know that his "Doomsday Virus" was invincible. As long as Erin wrote about him, and the media attention continued, Doomsday was increasing his chances of being caught. Sooner or later, the FBI agent reasoned, Doomsday would make a mistake. The FBI agent didn't know how wrong he was.

CHAPTER 17

On an otherwise ordinary April day in Littleton Colorado, Eric Harris and Dylan Kiebold, two Columbine High School students, went on a rampage. They shot and killed twelve students, one teacher, and themselves, sending the nation into shock. A few days later, Marty Gladstone received an unexpected call in his Cambridge office. It was Henry Chu.

"Henry…it's been a long time."

"Yes," Henry said heavily, "too long. I thought we should talk."

"About what?" Marty said abruptly.

Henry caught the tone. "Marty," he began, "I know this will sound strange, but the Columbine shootings have changed a lot of things for me and I've been thinking." He paused. "Life's too short. I'm at a point where I need to reconcile some things." He paused again. "Our friendship is one of them."

Marty softened. "I see. Well I'm surprised after all these years…but I guess I'm glad to hear it."

Henry breathed what sounded like a sigh of relief. "Marty, I wouldn't blame you if you never forgave me for what I did. It was a time…a time when I thought I was making the right choice for myself. Nothing else mattered, Marty, nothing.

"Now I'm at another turning point, I dunno why. It's just something in me that says things need to be different, that's all. Listen,

Marty, I was wondering…if I were to come back East…would there possibly be a place for me at Incandescent?"

"Henry, I don't know what to say," Marty responded with astonishment. "You know how much I valued your talent…and your friendship. But this is pretty sudden. And after what you did, well, I'm…I'm not sure, not sure if I…"

"I understand," Henry interrupted. "But I'd just like to ask you to think about it. Marty, I've had it up to here with TJ Gatwick and GWare. Sure, I've been rewarded handsomely over the years, and I've been a major player in GWare Guardian. But I'm tired of the abuse. Like I said, life's too short." Henry added with a light laugh, "I can't remember a time that you ever belittled me."

"Yeah, TJ's got quite the temper, I hear."

"That's putting it mildly," Henry acknowledged.

"What's your timeline?" Marty asked, staying non-committal.

"My employment contract is up for renewal end of June. I basically have the next month to negotiate a new one…or to tell TJ I'm leaving. He won't be too happy about that," Henry said thoughtfully.

"And if I turn you down?" Marty asked.

"I've made up my mind…I'd leave GWare anyway. I've invested wisely, so money's not a problem. I'm living alone. I could always freelance. I don't want another job out here, I want a complete change. I want to come back to my roots, Marty. That's what's important to me now."

"I get the picture," Marty said. "Henry, you can appreciate that you caught me off guard. Let me give it some thought. Why don't you call me, say in a week, and we'll take it from there."

"I'll do that. Thanks, Marty," Henry said and hung up.

Marty put down the receiver and rubbed at his eyes. How strange life was, he thought, full of the oddest twists and turns. This was one twist he hadn't anticipated.

Marty's first impulse was to reject Henry's overture without consideration. Marty had always viewed Henry's act so many years ago as nothing less than traitorous. He had never gotten over the hurt and he had written him off as a friend immediately and forever. They had not been in touch since Henry walked out of his office that fateful day.

Could Marty now, after all these years, after all the hurt, possibly take Henry back? Could he truly let bygones be bygones and overcome the feelings he still had? It was unthinkable, he thought, out of the question.

Yet Marty himself was growing older and wiser. He had turned 40 not too long ago. He had always felt that he was older beyond his years, primarily because he grew up so fast when he was thirteen and his father died.

Marty didn't think he was going through any kind of mid-life crisis, but when Henry said he needed to "reconcile some things," Marty could relate to that. He had been doing a lot of thinking about a lot of things and wondering how they would play out in his life.

His relationship with Erin was foremost in his mind. In Erin, Marty had found a friend and a companion who had brought a depth of emotion to him that he had not known since his childhood. From the moment his father had left the world, Marty steeled himself against hurt and disappointment. He learned to shelter himself with a thin but impenetrable shell against intimacy. As a result, as he got older, Marty resisted any kind of serious relationship with a woman. He dated, sure, and even slept with a few women on occasion, but he never let anyone get too close.

Even his relationship with his mother had been distant and cold. When his father died, Marty was thrown into the role of the male of the household. He didn't realize what it meant, he only knew that his mother depended on him more than ever.

It seemed to Marty that she never really recovered from his father's death. She closed herself off from the world, turning their Brookline home into a kind of hall of memories. She did not work;

in fact, she did not do much of anything. It was as if she too had stopped living.

Marty dutifully stayed by her side, but he eventually came to resent her. He needed to spread his wings and start his life. He finally left home when he was admitted to MIT. His mother fully expected that he would continue to live with her through college and tried to lay a guilt trip on him. That's when Marty decided he had had enough.

As the years passed, Marty had called her weekly, but he did not maintain close physical contact. He had seen her only occasionally, making sure she was safe and secure in the house. He noticed, however, that she was not aging gracefully. He tried to get her to accept some sort of home aid, even on a part-time basis, but she stubbornly resisted.

He then began to worry about her ability to care for herself. On at least one occasion, she had fallen in the house. She said it was nothing, but he could see it was just the beginning of an inevitable deterioration.

As her sole heir, Marty had no choice but to make decisions on her behalf. Two years ago, he had to make the most difficult decision yet: he decided to put her in a nursing home. She was becoming increasingly senile, and clearly not able to negotiate the steps in the house or care for herself anymore. She still had her wits about her, though, and she did not make the transition easy. She vehemently fought against moving into the nursing home. She accused Marty of betraying her, of locking her away in a "place of death." It was a gut-wrenching experience for Marty but he prevailed in the end. He was confident that it was the best thing for her.

Erin helped him through that difficult time, even though they were physically apart as much as they were together.

Erin, in fact, had helped Marty make a life adjustment. He hadn't realized it until she supported him during his trying time with his mother. While Marty was generally a positive and confident person, he had a dark side that made him secretly fearful and oddly pessimistic. It caused him to look over his shoulder constantly. He always felt as if someone, or something, was chasing him, and his biggest need was to win the race.

It drove Marty to be a relentless businessman who rarely if ever let down his guard. He was relentless, not ruthless. He adhered to a high moral standard and consciously tried not to screw anyone.

Nevertheless, he was truly conflicted when it came to running a business. While his heart believed the glass was half full, his mind often told him the glass was half empty. He never felt entirely comfortable with his success, believing more in its fragility than its permanence. That's one of the reasons why he had finally turned over the day-to-day management of the company to someone else. He wanted someone else to make the decisions that tested his sense of morality.

Yet there were some decisions only Marty could make. And one of them was crafting an agreement with GWare.

The fact was that the business environment had changed so dramatically that today, arch-rivals could become partners. Co-opetition had become a way of life for software companies in the Internet era. Marty never could have imagined even a few years ago that Incandescent and GWare could have any kind of business relationship. The acrimony between Marty and TJ had never abated. So it was almost beyond belief that their respective companies would structure a deal to work together.

Marty agonized over the very notion of an agreement. He didn't know if he could go through with it given the circumstances of the past. Ironically, it was Erin who finally convinced him to do it. She was as passionate about her dislike for TJ Gatwick as anyone, but she made Marty (and herself) look at the other side of it. She asked him: Wouldn't he be hurting Incandescent more by rejecting the agreement with GWare? Wasn't it the right strategic business decision that would ultimately benefit the company…even if TJ Gatwick was involved? Ultimately, Marty realized it was one of those things that had to be reconciled, as Henry Chu had said. He signed the agreement.

Now, Marty thought, if he could look at the other side of it and sign an agreement with GWare, was he able to bury the hurt of the past and do the same with Henry Chu?

Marty had to admit it was the personal aspect of what had happened more than the business aspect that still bothered him. Henry Chu had not only walked out on Incandescent, he had walked out on Marty.

Marty believed his friendship with Henry was, in its own way, as special as his relationship with Erin. While Marty had many business associates, he had few friends. It was, in part, the demands of being a business-owner that made close friendships difficult to maintain.

Henry had crossed the line, becoming at once a valued associate and friend. Marty regarded him as more of a partner than an employee.

Marty and Henry had lived through so many trials and tribulations together. They had shared successes and failures, joy and sorrow. Through it all, they both maintained their sense of perspective. More importantly, Marty felt they shared and maintained common values.

He knew this was precisely what bothered him so much about Henry's treachery. When Henry made the decision to leave Incandescent, Marty saw it as Henry's repudiation of those values, a rejection of that friendship. That's why it hurt him so much.

What's more, it reaffirmed Marty's old ghost…the pain of loss. See, he had told himself when it happened, you let Henry Chu get too close, and now you got hurt. And now, Marty was faced with another monumental personal decision. Could he forgive and forget…this was something he would really have to ponder.

His thoughts were interrupted by the receptionist on the intercom. "Marty, I have an urgent call from Pleasant Manor Nursing Home." He told her to put it through immediately.

"Mr. Gladstone, this is Norah Samuels, the head nurse at Pleasant Manor. I'm afraid there's been an accident. Your mother has taken a fall and she's been rushed to the Beth Israel emergency room."

Marty thanked the nurse, hung up and darted out of the office, hurriedly telling the receptionist that he had an emergency and wasn't sure exactly when he'd be back. He caught a cab and arrived at Beth Israel within ten minutes of getting the call.

"I understand my mother is here, Ida Gladstone," he said to the emergency room nurse.

She checked her papers and nodded. "Your name and relationship please?"

"I'm Marty Gladstone, her son."

"Please take a seat for a moment, Mr. Gladstone."

Marty sat down. His heart was beating rapidly. He had been thinking about reconciliation just minutes earlier and here he was, quite suddenly and without warning, sitting in a hospital emergency room, awaiting news about his mother. Memories of his childhood flooded back…when he was in that emergency room so long ago. He had rarely been in a hospital since. He had avoided them whenever possible, simply because of his unpleasant memories. But then, how many times were pleasant memories associated with a hospital?

"Mr. Gladstone? I'm Doctor Harrison. Let's talk for a moment." Marty looked up at a pale-faced man with deep circles under his eyes who was gesturing for Marty to follow him. They went into a small room and the doctor closed the door.

"Do you know anything about your mother's condition?" the doctor asked.

Marty shook his head. "No, I just received a call from the nursing home and rushed over here."

"Apparently, she fell at the home," the doctor said quickly. "Seems she lost her balance during an attended walk. Unfortunately, that's not an unusual occurrence, but she hit her head pretty hard going down.

"She's unconscious now. We have her sedated so she isn't in any pain. I'm waiting for x-ray, but I can tell you what I think's going on." The doctor paused, gauging Marty's reaction. He was calmly listening.

"Chances are there's a significant subdural hematoma...bleeding around the brain. That's pretty serious."

"How serious?"

"Well, I'd rather wait until we get the x-rays. I'd also like to have a surgeon speak with you. Luckily, he was in the hospital, so he'll be here shortly. Why don't you wait here." The doctor got up and exited the small room before Marty could respond.

Marty didn't smoke, but he had a sudden wild urge for a cigarette.

Fifteen minutes went by. All Marty could do was hope for the best but prepare himself for the worst. It was his way of coping with anything major in his life.

Finally, another doctor entered the room. This one was considerably older than Dr. Harrison, but just as haggard-looking. He was dressed in hospital scrubs. He smiled warmly at Marty and put out his hand.

"Mr. Gladstone, I'm Alan Rosenthal. I'm a surgeon and I've been looking at your mom's x-rays."

The doctor had a relaxed and unhurried manner about him. He sat opposite Marty and began to speak in a soft voice.

"Your mom has suffered a severe blow to the head, Mr. Gladstone. Basically what happened is the fall she took resulted in some internal bleeding. The medical term is a bilateral cerebral hemispheric subdural hematoma. In simpler terms, it's bleeding that occurs between the skull and the brain."

Marty simply nodded and the doctor continued.

"Unfortunately this is quite serious. With someone your mother's age, it doesn't leave us with a lot of options. We could go in surgically to relieve the pressure and see if we could stop the bleeding. But the nature of the injury is such that, frankly, a successful recovery is questionable.

"I've seen many of these injuries in the elderly, Mr. Gladstone. I've also done a number of surgeries on them. Often, the surgery itself does as much damage as the injury when all is said and done. Even if the patient survives, the quality of life is such that it may not be the best thing to extend it.

"Of course, I can't make that choice. Only the patient's relatives can."

The doctor stopped and looked pointedly into Marty's eyes. "Please, ask me any questions you may have."

"If I understand you correctly, doctor," Marty began, "you're saying surgery is not a viable option."

The doctor nodded slightly.

"So," Marty continued, "what's the alternative?"

"I'm afraid that's the dilemma, Mr. Gladstone. There really isn't one." The doctor looked at Marty sadly. "Your mother has lived a long life. What we can do now is keep her stabilized and free of pain. She is unconscious and unaware in her current state."

"How long…" Marty asked, not needing to finish his question.

"In some cases, the patient survives only several hours. In other cases, it could be days. We would do everything possible to keep her comfortable." The doctor paused. "I don't expect, with your mother's injury, that this will last long at all.

"I'm sorry, Mr. Gladstone, I wish I had better news."

Marty took a deep breath. "Thank you, doctor. Based on what you've said, I don't think proceeding with surgery will be necessary. Please do whatever you can to keep her as comfortable as possible…until the end."

"I'll also need a decision regarding life support," the doctor said. "Your mother has a living will indicating she does not want her life to be maintained by artificial means."

"I'm aware of that, doctor. I will respect her wishes."

"Then just one last thing, Mr. Gladstone. Would you like to see her?"

Marty thought for a moment. Realizing this could be his final farewell, he nodded. The doctor led him to the bed where his mother lay. "Take as long as you wish," the doctor said, discreetly pulling the curtain around Marty as he left.

His mother was unconscious and had a breathing tube in her mouth. The quiet consistent "shush shush" of the machine, accompanied by the beep of the heart monitor, were the only sounds Marty heard. He could see some blood on the pillow below her head.

She looked frail but did not appear to be in any pain. He expected her to open her eyes at any moment but he knew it was an irrational thought.

He just looked at her for several moments. Then he reached out to touch the side of her head. Her leathery skin was warm. He stroked her gently and then pulled away his hand. He did not kiss her.

"Goodbye Mom," he said, choking back a tear. He felt a momentary swell of emotion but he regained his composure quickly. He swallowed hard, took a breath, and exited through the curtain. He did not look back.

Marty left the hospital, his head filled with mixed emotions. He felt a crushing guilt for having committed his mother to the nursing home, although he told himself it was still the right decision to have made. He felt a sadness for the fact that her life would be ending this way, the victim of an unfortunate accident. And oddly, he felt a sadness for himself, not because he was going to lose his other parent, but rather because he knew he did not feel much love for her. He drove the thoughts from his mind and returned to his office, but was unable to concentrate for the remainder of the day.

Twenty-four hours later Ida Gladstone was dead.

CHAPTER 18

As was Jewish tradition, the funeral was held a day after Ida Gladstone's death. Marty was extremely grateful that Erin flew in from San Francisco to Boston to be by his side. She arranged her schedule so that she could stay an additional day. She missed the funeral but was able to arrive so that they could spend a quiet evening together at Marty's condo. Marty used it as an opportunity to discuss Henry Chu with Erin.

"Everything comes full circle," Marty said philosophically. "What I remember now is when Henry Chu first told me he was resigning, I went out to run. During my run, I thought about losing my father. At the time I related the memory to losing Henry as an employee and a friend. Funny, sometimes you don't realize the impact someone has on your life until they're gone.

"It's the weirdest thing. Now, I get a call from Henry out of the blue, after years of silence, and as soon as I do, my mother dies. It's pretty eerie."

"Strange, sure," Erin said, "but it's just a weird coincidence."

"Yeah, I know. But it sure makes you think. And I don't know what to think about Henry." Marty grasped Erin's hand, rubbing his thumb gently across her knuckles. "Erin, what would you do?"

She smiled before answering. "What I would do might not be the answer you want to hear."

"But I value your opinion, so tell me anyway."

"You know, Marty," Erin began, "I surprised myself when I encouraged you to enter into a business agreement with GWare. I never thought I could have anything to do with TJ Gatwick again.

"Emotionally, I still detest the man. But the way I see it, a business relationship that benefits companies can over-rule personal feelings, especially if it's a win-win. It's tough for me to admit, but holding a grudge for years takes its toll…and you really have to wonder if it's worth it."

Erin leaned her head on Marty's shoulder and continued. "I know how you felt when Henry left you. It's how I felt when I sat there and watched TJ boasting about an operating system that he stole from you. I was angry and I was hurt. I felt as if all the trust was gone.

"I wouldn't blame you if you never forgave Henry, I wouldn't. But you asked me what I would do." She took a breath and went on. "What I would do is let Henry back into my life. I admit, I don't know if I could let him work with me again, but I'd try to recapture the friendship…if it were as special as you say it was."

Marty laughed lightly. "How did I know you would say that."

Erin put her arm around his waist and squeezed. "I guess you just know me too well."

Marty sighed. "There are never any easy answers, never any clear definitions of right and wrong."

"But it does make life varied and interesting, doesn't it?"

Marty kissed her forehead. "Yeah, it does do that."

"So what're you going to do?"

"You know me, no snap decisions," Marty answered, deflecting the question. "I still need some time to think about this."

"As well you should," Erin said.

Marty thought about it on and off for the next several days. He knew this wasn't one of those decisions for which he could write down the pros and cons on a piece of paper. So he just weighed the possibilities in his mind, knowing full well that ultimately, it would once again be a gut decision he would have to make. His mother entered his mind several times as he considered what to do. He would never see her again. Would the same be true with Henry?

When Henry Chu called him as he had promised, Marty had made at least one decision…he wanted to meet with Henry face-to-face. Marty told Henry he had to be at Incandescent's Silicon Valley office the following Tuesday. He asked if he could meet Henry in San Diego on Monday for dinner, and then he would catch a shuttle flight to San Francisco afterwards. Henry agreed.

Marty was glad he had the long flight to San Diego to think about what he would say when he sat opposite Henry. Marty had been to San Diego a few times and was taken with the city. If it hadn't been GWare's stronghold, Marty would have considered opening Incandescent's West Coast headquarters there…but it was too close for comfort. Besides, in San Francisco, he had an added benefit…Erin.

At the San Diego airport, Marty caught a cab and took a short ride to the Gaslamp Quarter in the city. This was one of his favorite areas of San Diego. It reminded him of Charles Street in Boston, with its old-fashioned lamps, buildings and trendy restaurants.

Marty and Henry had decided to meet at Croce's, which was on Fifth Avenue in the heart of the Quarter. Opened by Jim Croce's wife Ingrid in 1985, Croce's was the restaurant that helped pioneer the revitalization of the historic Gaslamp Quarter. Marty liked that the restaurant was a tribute to the late songwriter-singer. While Jim Croce was popular during the '60s, before Marty's college days, he had heard Croce's music on oldies stations. He thought the guy had something to say…the words were meaningful and they told a story, unlike some of the empty-headed music of the '80s and '90s.

Marty arrived before the appointed time and sat at the bar to wait for Henry. He looked around the place. Family photos, gold albums and guitars littered the walls. The black and white floor tiles gave it the look of an old-fashioned ice cream parlor. It wasn't crowded yet, but Marty figured it would fill up soon.

It was about fifteen minutes before Henry walked in. When he first did, Marty wasn't entirely sure it was him. The Henry Chu that Marty had remembered didn't look gaunt and pale, like this one did. Henry still had his trademark disheveled look, but his hair, previously jet black, now had several prominent streaks of gray. Even from a distance, Marty could see the lines etched into Henry's face, particularly his forehead, and the deep circles under his eyes. He had been to hell and back, Marty thought. Henry looked around and spotted Marty at the bar. Henry smiled crookedly and approached him.

"Hello Henry," Marty said uneasily, extending his hand.

"I'm so glad to see you," Henry said warmly, grasping Marty's hand with both of his. "Let's get a table."

They were seated. Henry ordered a light beer and Marty a sparkling water.

They chatted idly for a while about the software industry and about some of the people they both knew, both of them dancing around the real reason they were there. Marty asked Henry's opinion on the menu and Henry remembered he was a vegetarian, so he recommended a baby spinach salad and a pasta dish. That sounded good to Marty. Henry ordered a salad for himself and the swordfish.

Finally, Marty broke the ice. "It was a real surprise hearing from you again," Marty said. "It's still hard for me to believe you got in touch with me."

"Yes, I can imagine," Henry answered. "And it was big of you to want to see me."

"This wasn't the kind of thing I felt comfortable discussing over the phone," Marty answered. He paused and looked directly at Henry. "It takes eye contact."

Henry smiled and held Marty's eyes with his own. "Let me tell you my situation. Maybe it will help you understand why I'm so anxious to make amends."

Henry continued. "You remember Priscilla?" Marty nodded. Priscilla was Henry's girlfriend when Henry lived in Cambridge. It was a serious romance, and it was yet another reason Marty was so stunned when Henry announced he was leaving Incandescent.

"Well, she took it pretty hard when I left for San Diego. She followed me there about two weeks later. I thought she'd stay for a little while, then go back to her life and her job in Cambridge, but that's not the way it worked out. She moved in with me.

"I was happy at first, but it wasn't right. Of course, I was so wrapped up in myself I missed all the signs. Pris was miserable. No friends, no job. I was never there…and when I was, I complained about the pressure at GWare. Didn't take her long to get fed up. She left after about six months, had it up to here." Henry put his hand across his nose to make the point.

"I'm sorry," Marty said quietly.

"Yeah, well, there's more," Henry said. "I don't hear from her for another several months. Then I get this letter from her. She's telling me how much she misses me, but that she's not coming back. Wants to be near her family in Massachusetts." Henry paused to take a long swallow of his beer. "Tells me the reason is she's pregnant.

"She's sure it's mine and she's going to have the baby, she says. What do I want to do about it, she asks me."

Marty doesn't know what to say, so he doesn't say anything.

"I write her back, tell her I can't quit my job, not now. Say I'll support her, support the child, whatever she wants, but I'm not coming back. She answers me, says she's not happy about it, she thought we were in love, thought I'd want to be with her and our child. But she says it's my choice."

Marty shook his head, "I had no idea…"

"No one did," Henry says. "Not even my parents know about this."

"Anyway, that's the way it stays. I write her every Christmas, no more than that. She never answers me. Then this Columbine thing happens. It chills me to the bone. All I can imagine is my child, the child I've never seen, could be one of those kids someday. It could happen anywhere if it could happen in a place like Littleton, Colorado.

"I call Pris, but she hangs up on me a few times before I can finally leave her a message and make her understand why I want to talk with her. I pour out my heart to her one night on the phone. I'm crying, she's crying…before I know it, I'm agreeing to come back to Cambridge to see my kid, maybe to try and work things out. Then I figure, why not shoot the wad and call you while I'm at it. I mean, if I'm gonna do the reconciliation thing, why not go all the way."

Marty smiled. One of the things that always amused him about Henry was the way the man used very Americanized expressions despite his Chinese upbringing. His parents still lived in the Chinatown section of Boston and spoke little English. Henry was their first American-born son.

Marty whistled silently. "I gotta tell you, now I'm really glad I decided to see you face-to-face."

Henry nodded and smiled sadly. "It's been a wild ride since I left Incandescent, Marty. I never had any idea how wild it would be.

"The other part of it is…I never knew how good I had it with you or at Incandescent. That's the truth."

Henry's eyes were the windows to his soul; Marty knew he was telling the truth just by looking at him.

"GWare has been a living hell," Henry continued. "The price you pay to be a Gatwick disciple is just too high. I knew it as soon as I got there, I was just too scared and too confused to do anything about it.

"It got worse and worse, and then Gatwick forced me into breaking my confidentiality agreement with Incandescent. He played it real dirty, Marty. He blackmailed me. He found out about Priscilla and the child. Said if I didn't do what he wanted, he'd make sure I'd never see either of them again. The guy's a monster."

"You're joking," Marty said with true amazement. "He threatened you?"

Henry nodded. "The only smart thing I did was negotiate a renewable contract, and thank God it's up in June. There's no way I'd stay now. I'm getting out of here, one way or the other, going back to Cambridge. I'm gonna see if I can set things straight, put it back together with Pris. Even if it doesn't work out, at least I'll see Joey…that's my son's name.

"So you see, Marty, you'd close the circle for me, if we could start over." Henry lowered his eyes, his lips quivering. "I don't deserve it, but I'm asking you to just think about it."

Marty leaned back in his chair and considered the man for a moment. He looked broken, defeated…but somehow, Henry Chu seemed to have a spark of life left…at least enough to try again.

"That's one hell of a story," Marty said. He felt drained just listening to it. "I admit when I came here, I wasn't entirely sure what I'd do or what I'd say. On the plane ride, I kept going back and forth in my mind. On the one hand, Henry, your friendship meant so much to me, I desperately wanted you back in my life. On the other hand, I wanted you to be punished for what you did…and I thought, why would I ever take you back.

"Then I thought about something really odd that happened right after you called me. My mother was in a nursing home. She had an accident and she died a day later."

"I'm terribly sorry, Marty."

Marty waved him off. "Thanks. But maybe it happened that way for a reason. Because it struck me that you had talked about reconciliation right before she died. I never really reconciled with her. I never got the chance to." Marty paused and swallowed. "I'd like not to make that mistake again."

"Still," Marty continued, "it may take me a while to trust you. You need to understand that."

Henry nodded.

"Here's what I'd like to do," Marty continued. "I'd like to ease into this. It would make me feel more comfortable not to rush it.

"What I propose is a consulting contract, say, one year, with a 90-day cancellation by either party. We'll slowly work you back into the development process, but it'll be a while before you gain access to the most sensitive information, if you know what I mean." Marty paused. "I need to re-build that trust, Henry. We can work out the details, but that's the basic idea."

"I understand," Henry answered. "I know I'm asking for a second chance. What you're proposing is reasonable." Henry smiled sadly and added, "I couldn't ask for more. I only hope that I can win back your trust, Marty, and that somehow we can rekindle the friendship we had before. I didn't know how much it meant to me until I lost it."

Hardened as he may have been by the business world, Marty was touched by Henry's sentiment and his sincerity. While he still wanted Henry to prove he could trust him once again, this was an encouraging start.

"Do what you need to do," Marty said as he paid the check. "Take your time re-locating. You've got a lot of personal things to attend to. When you're ready, give me a call and we'll figure it all out."

Marty rose to leave and Henry followed. "I want to thank you, Marty," Henry said, grasping Marty's hand one last time. "If it means anything to you, now that I've seen both sides of this business, I'm certain of who the good guys are. And I'm glad I can still tell right from wrong."

CHAPTER 19

National Infrastructure Protection Center
Advisory 99-013
"Explorer Zip Worm"
June 10, 1999

> The National Infrastructure Protection Center (NIPC) has received reports that tens of thousands of computer systems in several major U.S. companies have had their files infected, damaged or destroyed by the Explore.Zip Worm. This program arrives as an e-mail message and utilizes MAPI commands and Microsoft Outlook on Windows systems to propagate itself. The virus e-mails itself out as an attachment with the filename zipped_files.exe. The virus selects addresses from the infected computer's e-mail in-box and therefore appears to come from a known e-mail correspondent. Most significantly, the virus searches through system drives and destroys a series of files by making them zero bytes long, resulting in irrecoverable data and/or systems.

Erin Keliher read the e-mail message from Doomsday again:

`Did you like the latest one?`

She was getting tired of this sick bastard's twisted sense of humor. He was obviously taking credit for the Explorer Zip Worm that had just been unleashed on beleaguered Internet users. It was now at a point where American businesses had come to expect a regular diet of viruses as the price they had to pay for the widespread use of the Internet and the massive adoption of e-mail communications.

It was hard to believe that any one individual could be responsible for the vast array of insidious virus attacks taking place with increasing frequency. But how else could Erin explain the fact that this Doomsday nutcase seemed to be one step ahead of every one of the attacks? Doomsday made sure to describe enough of the attributes of each virus, before it struck, so that Erin would know he was the genuine article.

While Erin secretly delighted in the knowledge that she had been the one journalist chosen to be Doomsday's voice to the world, she also had to admit it was beginning to make her feel dirty and violated. Why had he picked her, after all, and what did it mean? Yes, she realized she was influential and respected, but she wasn't the only journalist writing about the software business these days. She believed there was much more to it than that. She figured Doomsday was, in his own way, extremely knowledgeable of the goings-on of the software industry. She wondered what he knew about her. Had he followed her career? Was he aware of her public falling out with TJ Gatwick?

For all she knew, Doomsday knew a lot more than that. She shuddered to think that he knew she had a relationship with Marty Gladstone and was living with him. She assured herself that Doomsday couldn't do anything damaging with that information, even if he did know, but somehow it made her feel uneasy and vulnerable.

Erin was getting tired of being Doomsday's puppet. Lately, there were many times that she wanted to tell Doomsday to take a hike, to leave her the hell alone. Marty agreed with her. He didn't like this perverted relationship that had developed any better than she did, particularly because he felt it somehow put her in danger. Her editor didn't like it either. It was turning a respected newspaper into a sensational scandal sheet. But it was the FBI who wanted her to continue to communicate with Doomsday, and out of a sense of national duty she reluctantly agreed.

According to the FBI, Erin Keliher was the only thread the federal authorities could cling to in pursuing this super-hacker. The government had posted an unprecedented $5 million reward for any information leading to the arrest and conviction of Doomsday. He had become the Al Capone of software hackers.

For years, all they had come up with were dead-ends and bogus leads. The FBI suspected he had a secret network of hackers working with him, but they were hidden in the deep recesses of an Internet that had become unimaginably tangled and complex. With millions of users, hundreds of millions of Web pages, and billions of e-mails, all functioning in an informal, unregulated network of networks, these hackers could easily maintain their anonymity.

They were anything but anonymous when they struck, however, wreaking havoc across the Internet, sometimes causing untold millions of dollars of damage to corporate computer systems. Even worse, these hackers were breaking into sensitive government systems, potentially compromising national security. The FBI tried to keep a lid on this particular activity so the American public didn't know how vulnerable the government really was to a computer-borne invasion, but a few incidents that had leaked to the media were just beginning to garner attention.

Ironically, the same Senate Technology Council that years ago had started but aborted the investigation of Incandescent was now at the forefront of the anti-hacker investigations. And none other than TJ Gatwick was the Council's chief adviser. The Council did not, of course, interfere in any way with the FBI investigation, but rather worked cooperatively to provide legislative support to the effort.

One part of the joint investigation had revealed a startling possibility. It seemed that the 1994 murder of Senator Jack Morrissey, a crime that had never been solved, might have been connected to Doomsday himself. The pieces were still not all falling into place, but the circumstantial evidence was developing.

It had been discovered that the kidnappers were part of an Islamic extremist group, that much was known. But it also appeared that they were not working independently, that they had in fact been kidnappers for hire. They had been traced back to a starting point in Washington, D.C., possibly a hacker, but there the trail reached a dead-end. Nevertheless, the FBI was slowly making progress in the investigation, and they had an inkling that, if they could locate the Washington hacker, they could link him to Doomsday. The FBI knew that if this could be proven, Doomsday could be implicated in more than virus attacks alone; he would be at least an accessory to the murder of a U.S. Senator.

This would be a huge breakthrough in the battle against this demon. Doomsday had, in some circles, taken on the aura of a modern day Robin Hood. Erin had quoted some of his diatribes in her column. They were very much the anti-capitalist, power-to-the-people rantings and ravings that could make some believe that Doomsday's ultimate goal was to punish American software companies for their greed. His position resonated with those who felt American business was corrupt and out of control.

There were some in the government and even in American business who believed software companies and now Internet companies were indeed beneficiaries of unconscionable profits. The Internet boom was creating an over-zealous venture capital frenzy as anything with an "e-" attached to it became an instant money-maker. American business was about to spawn a new breed of under-forty billionaires in the frenzy of the Internet-driven economy.

While Doomsday was hardly gaining any kind of public support for his virus attacks, there was a fringe element that was sympathetic to his dramatic way of calling attention to corporate greed. If, indeed, the Internet was being commercialized to the point where its good would be undermined, there could be a real cause for concern. But surely, there were other ways to fight against the commercialization of the Internet rather than unleash deadly computer viruses on every unsuspecting user.

Now, if it became clear that Doomsday was an accomplice in one of the most shocking murders in recent history, the perception that he was some kind of folk hero could be irreparably tarnished. The FBI and the Senate Technology Council hoped this fact would not only expose Doomsday for what he truly was, a vile criminal, but also encourage someone close to him to turn him in. Still, the proof was not yet conclusive, so the jury was still out on this one.

Doomsday wasn't aware that the U.S. Government had suspected his involvement in the Morrissey murder. It was one of the few pieces of insider information he didn't know. Doomsday's ability to second guess his pursuers was uncanny. He knew they were no closer to cornering him than they had been when he brought GWare to its knees so many years ago.

The years hadn't been physically kind to Doomsday. The man's hermetic lifestyle had taken its toll on him. His eyesight had grown far worse. He had added to his already unhealthy bulk. His breathing was increasingly labored, exacerbated by his chain smoking habit. He hobbled around his small apartment, weak-kneed from lack of exercise, his back bent from constantly hunching over his computer terminal.

While he suffered the afflictions of an abused body, and the emotional scars of a recluse, his mind was as cunning as ever. He had, over the years, not only refined the Doomsday Virus, but produced variants and strains of it. Now he was launching them at will upon an unsuspecting public, making them increasingly wary of viruses as he announced his attacks through his unwilling accomplice, Erin Keliher.

Doomsday was pre-meditated in his madness. While the victims of his attacks thought them to be the random issuances of a sick, inconsistent mind, they were very wrong.

Rather, Doomsday was methodically testing and refining his virus variants. He would see how much damage each could do and analyze how quickly anti-virus software was introduced to combat it. He would then carefully record the results, very much as an exacting scientist conducting an experiment would do. By analyzing the impact of every variant, and the industry response to it, Doomsday was building up to a much grander scale. He believed he had the ability to develop a version of the Doomsday Virus that would once again be completely unstoppable, not unlike his original virus that destroyed GWare ONE. It was just a matter of time. Ah, that was sheer perfection, he thought.

He could feel now, more than at any time in the past, that he was very close to his goal. The Explorer Zip Worm had worked well and done quite a lot of damage in a brief period of time. But it was just one more in a series of carefully planned variants. It paled in comparison to his next planned attack.

The next virus Doomsday launched would be an e-mail-borne computer script that would not require a user to open an e-mail or e-mail attachment to infect its host. Doomsday targeted Internet Explorer 5.0 with Microsoft Outlook or Outlook Express. Doomsday had constructed it so that the virus could be activated in Outlook Express even if the user only used the Preview Panel.

The virus would take advantage of a security hole in Internet Explorer 5.0. Of course, Doomsday knew that as soon as the hole was discovered, Microsoft would issue a patch for it, but the damage would already be done. This would be another test on Doomsday's part. First he would determine if this strain would effectively penetrate e-mail. In particular he wanted to see how much damage it could do relative to his other strains. Then he would study the anti-virus measures, determining how long it took Microsoft to make the patch available. More importantly, he would see whether the patch would be no more than a temporary fix. It would be typical of

Microsoft if it were only that, and then he would know that the basic product weakness still existed.

Sometimes, Doomsday thought, reveling in his power, it was just too simple to put one over on these idiots. These software companies were in such a hurry to get their products to market, to make their obscene millions and billions of dollars of profits, that they didn't even care if their programs were flawed. So much the better for him, he thought. It just made his mission that much easier to accomplish.

Doomsday did recall with distaste that one time, the only time when his efforts were temporarily thwarted. That was an unexpected surprise, even if it was only a temporary setback. Thinking back to it, Doomsday had to admit Marty Gladstone was smarter than he had given him credit for. The bastard had built a pretty ingenious anti-virus system into UNITE. When Doomsday had tried to penetrate the MITnet through the Laboratory for Computer Science, UNITE actually repelled his virus. At first, Doomsday didn't believe it. He had never heard of any software system reacting this way.

Eventually, as word got around about UNITE's unique "shield," Doomsday learned more about the technology. He managed to get some of his associates to do some deep research into the shield properties and they were able to gain access to some of the early code, even though the most current code was a closely guarded secret. Doomsday studied it tirelessly. He sensed that the answer wasn't so much in the code itself as in the concept of the program. Once he understood the concept, he would get to the bottom of its functionality.

It was a challenge for Doomsday, but he took it on, meeting it with a fierce determination. All of his energy went into attempting to crack the code of UNITE's shield. The fact was that now, years later, Doomsday had not yet completely succeeded at understanding the full extent of the UNITE anti-virus system, but he was slowly making progress and he had yet to admit defeat. He knew he was getting closer and closer to figuring out the greatest puzzle yet of his unsavory career. It had become his obsession now, the reason for his lust for vengeance, his thirst for domination. Doomsday believed that when he found a way to do to UNITE what he had done to GWare ONE, the world would realize that he had the power to strike at will…and win. Of that he was sure.

CHAPTER 20

It was July 1999 and Marty, along with millions in America and around the world, watched in disbelief as the events surrounding John F. Kennedy Jr.'s plane crash unfolded. When the plane was finally located and Kennedy's death was confirmed, it ended yet another chapter in the annals of unthinkable Kennedy tragedies.

Few would ever know that the paths of Marty Gladstone and John Jr. had actually crossed. As a result, Kennedy's death had more than a casual impact on Marty. It was a brief and unremarkable meeting that brought JFK Jr. and Marty together, but Marty remembered it nonetheless. A Brown University professor had contacted Marty and asked him if he would come and speak to one of his classes about being an entrepreneur. It was not long after Marty had started Incandescent and he was more than willing to share his experiences with students who were only several years younger than him. It turned out that one of the students in the class he addressed was John.

John asked a few polite questions of Marty. He was obviously interested in how Marty started his business, but he didn't seem to be at all technology-oriented. His fellow students didn't appear to treat him differently from any ordinary student. At the end of the class, John came up to Marty and shook his hand. "I'd like to start a business someday, and I admire you for doing it," John said. Marty thanked him. That was the first and last time he would ever meet the man.

Marty remembered the moment, and that memory would remain with him years from now. It was Marty's brief brush with a living legend.

But now Marty had more pressing matters to attend to, not the least of which was setting up orientation meetings for Henry Chu. Henry was back at Incandescent as a contracted consultant. He had hurriedly left San Diego, moved into a Cambridge apartment, and was working on re-establishing his relationship with Priscilla. He had already seen his son Joey and was thrilled to be a father. From Henry's perspective, he was embarking on a whole new installment of his life.

Marty was hopeful that he could rebuild some sort of working relationship with Henry, if not rekindle his friendship of the past. He was cautiously optimistic that it would work out. Marty felt that Henry was being sincere, but he also knew there would be stresses on Henry that would have to be closely monitored. One of those stresses was Marty's old nemesis, TJ Gatwick.

As had been expected, Gatwick went ballistic when he learned of Henry's intention to return to Incandescent. While Gatwick couldn't prevent Henry from leaving GWare, that didn't stop him from unleashing a legal barrage in the form of strongly worded letters to both Henry and Marty. Basically, the letters reinforced the content of Henry's restrictive non-disclosure agreement with GWare, which was separate from his employment contract. Gatwick made it clear that he and his legal team would be scrutinizing the working relationship between Henry Chu and Incandescent to assure that nothing of a confidential nature Henry had learned at GWare would be used in any way, shape or form. He threatened Henry and Marty personally with the strongest legal action should he learn of any breach of the agreement.

Most of Gatwick's blustering was just posturing, but Marty knew he had to be extremely careful. Past experience told him that crossing Gatwick could lead to nothing short of war all over again. His unholy alliance with GWare was fragile enough without being further taxed by a legal dispute. Despite the fact that Gatwick's influence was nowhere near as great as it had been years ago, Marty knew any kind of confrontation would do nothing but cause damage to his business.

Marty was confident, however, that Henry's renewed value to Incandescent didn't rest on his knowledge of GWare's secrets. Marty would be able to leverage Henry's ingenuity in both improving future versions of UNITE and in developing new software products. He would watch Henry carefully, that he was sure of, but if Henry's contribution was anything like it had been before, then Incandescent would benefit greatly from Henry Chu's return.

One area in which Marty wanted Henry's involvement was the refinement of UNITE's anti-virus shield. Marty would have to tread carefully here, since Henry had been a key developer on the GWare Guardian project, but he knew Henry would be invaluable in this area.

The issue was that UNITE's anti-virus shield technology was no longer keeping pace with the virus-ridden Internet. In the early days, the shield was close to miraculous in its ability to ward off virtually any attack. But new more virulent viruses were being launched with increasing frequency. Marty's own testing lab had confirmed that it was only a matter of time before one of those viruses penetrated UNITE's shield. In fact, this was one of the primary reasons Marty had crafted an agreement with GWare in the first place—to use GWare Guardian as the leading edge line of defense against just such an attack.

UNITE itself had to continue to incorporate its own brand of virus protection, however. The anti-virus shield was a unique product property that set UNITE apart from all other software products and had yet to be duplicated by another operating system. Even Microsoft hadn't figured out how to incorporate such a shield into Windows. To maintain UNITE's continued growth, upgrading the product's internal anti-virus technology was essential.

Marty believed for UNITE to continue to maintain a leadership position, Incandescent would have to figure out a way to anticipate virus forms yet to be launched. Creating antidotes once viruses were known was already being done in the industry—that was the role of products like GWare Guardian. The real magic was in *predicting* the type of viruses that were likely to strike...before they even entered the marketplace.

While Marty's research team had studied every virus variant thus far, their ability to know with certainty what was on the horizon was limited. In this regard, it occurred to Marty that he had an inside track on one possible route to discovery. That route was Erin.

Doomsday used Erin as a conduit to pre-announce his attacks and to spread his propaganda—with the FBI's approval, of course. That's as far as it went, however. Erin was passive, a recipient of information and nothing more.

Marty wondered what would happen if the relationship Erin had with Doomsday shifted and intensified. What if Erin actually used Doomsday, instead of the other way around? Marty figured that Doomsday had probably gotten accustomed to the attention and coverage afforded him by Erin. He had to be basking in the glory, his ego feeding off the thrill of being a notorious celebrity.

What if Erin were to tell Doomsday she was shutting him off unless he gave her more than just propaganda? Suppose she told him she wanted the real scoop—some legitimate insight into his world and his viruses? Would he release more details to her, fearing that he would lose his mouthpiece? And could Marty then use that information to better anticipate all the variants of the Doomsday Virus and, as a result, know in advance how to defend against them?

Marty thought the idea of escalation would appeal to Erin. Marty knew she was tired of being Doomsday's lackey, and maybe this would at least shake things up a little and give her a way to get more out of Doomsday…and get a better story as a result. Marty wasn't sure how the FBI would react to it, but maybe they'd agree with the strategy as well. After all, they had been spending all this time pursuing Doomsday through Erin and didn't seem to be making much progress on the case.

As he thought about the idea, Marty liked it more and more. But he also realized that it was a calculated risk. Even if Erin and the FBI went along with it, Doomsday would have to be convinced. Marty was sure the hacker wouldn't like the feeling he was being coerced. More than that, Marty hoped it wouldn't set him off in some way. What if Doomsday reacted negatively to being pushed? What if it backfired and the hacker were to threaten Erin? The last thing Marty wanted was to put Erin in any sort of danger.

Nevertheless, the concept had merit, and Marty thought, what the hell, why not run it by Erin? It was still early, so Marty decided to call Erin at home. He thought he'd catch her before she left for work.

"Erin Keliher." Even on her home line, she answered the phone as if she were at work.

"Hi lover."

"What a nice surprise. What made you call?"

"Wanted to catch you before you headed out," Marty answered. "I just had a thought I wanted to run by you."

"Shoot."

"I've been thinking that these virus attacks are intensifying and the strains are more virulent than ever. Your buddy Doomsday must be working overtime these days."

Erin chuckled. "Yeah, he certainly has been prolific lately."

"Do you get the sense that the FBI is getting any closer to fingering him?"

"To be honest, Marty, they pretty much keep any information about their progress to themselves. They just tell me to keep the lines of communication open with Doomsday, but that's about all."

"That's the problem," Marty said. "They're not getting any closer to shutting this guy down, and the virus situation is worse than ever. So I thought, why not ratchet this thing up a few notches."

"Meaning?"

"What if you were to play a little hardball with our super-hacker, Erin? Y'know, tell him you're tired of being his spokesperson, that unless he starts opening up to you more, you'll shut him off."

Erin was quiet for a moment.

"Erin?"

"I'm thinking."

Marty waited until she spoke again.

"I see the point," she said. "It could work. But it could also backfire if Doomsday got pissed off about it."

"I know," Marty replied. "That's the part that bothers me. No way would I want to put you in any kind of jeopardy. But if it worked, maybe you'd get some more insight into this guy, some clues that would give us a better understanding of what he's got planned. That could be a win—win, Erin. You'd get a juicier story out of it, and maybe we'd get the facts we need to get to this guy. I must admit, I have a personal interest in this…I'm dying to figure out what's next on the virus horizon, so I can defend against it in UNITE."

"I assumed you weren't doing this just for the good of the country," Erin said coyly.

"Yeah, well, it's still for everyone's good, if we get the answers we're looking for," Marty said with mock indignity in his voice.

"Listen, lemme think it over. And I'll have to run it by my friends at the FBI."

"I expected you'd have to do that," Marty admitted. "But you never know, they may like the idea too. I figure if they aren't getting any further with the investigation the way it is now, they might like to shake things up a bit too."

"You could be right," Erin said. "I'll talk to them when I get into the office. I'm sure they'll have to send it up their bureaucratic ranks before they do anything about it, though. Call me later this afternoon and I'll let you know if I've heard anything."

"Fair enough. Have a great day. Love you."

"Love you too."

Marty was heartened by Erin's reaction. She would have told him right away if she thought it was a lame idea. Marty had no intention of using her as a pawn, and he really was concerned for her safety. Yet he had the feeling that the world had only seen the beginning of a long and ugly spate of viral attacks that would intensify in the next several months. The close of 1999 was just around the corner, and the hysteria surrounding Y2K was now beginning to reach its peak. There was already a growing concern in some circles that the nation's computing infrastructure was shaky, and that no one really knew what systems would stand or fall when the clocks struck midnight on December 31, 1999.

The media already made much of the fact that the Y2K "bug" had cost billions of dollars to fix, and that government agencies and insurance companies' legacy systems in particular were not yet in complete compliance. The computer industry would surely be holding its breath these next several months, waiting to see if the relatively simple computer programming error that would cause "99" to change to "00" would wreak havoc because computers couldn't identify the year as "1900" or "2000." The implications of a massive failure were so enormous it boggled the mind to think of the consequences.

The Y2K problem was certainly not lost on the world's hackers. It made computer systems especially susceptible to virus attacks. If nothing else, cyber-terrorists could use the Y2K scare as an excuse to launch cataclysmic attacks on the nation's or the world's computer infrastructures. Once again, the Internet could act as an electronic distribution channel for viruses that could do untold damage.

This was one of the most compelling reasons Marty had for wanting to get more information out of Doomsday. His sense of urgency was well founded. Marty assumed that virus attacks would be at an all-time high, and the slightest knowledge about these attacks could make all the difference in the world. Marty Gladstone didn't have any idea at the time how accurate his assessment would be.

CHAPTER 21

"They bought it," Erin said. "Of course, they said they were just thinking of proposing it to me, as if it were their idea."

"They can take the credit," Marty answered. "I don't care about that. The important thing is that they think it could work."

"Well I wouldn't go that far," Erin replied. "The FBI agent was somewhat skeptical but willing to give it a try, under one condition. He wants to call the shots."

"So how does he want to handle it?"

"This might surprise you," Erin continued. "He wants me to try to get Doomsday to agree to a face-to-face meeting."

"Whoa, Erin, I didn't say anything about confronting Doomsday in person. That's a little aggressive, don't you think?" Marty asked anxiously.

"At first I did," she admitted. "But the agent said I'd be wired as well as under surveillance. He said as long as it was in a public place where they could keep a close eye on me, he didn't see any danger in it."

Marty whistled. "I hope I'm not gonna be sorry I ever mentioned this crazy idea to you."

"Hey, no risk, no reward. Seriously, Marty, I don't see how I could be in danger if it happens out in the open. Besides, think what a story

I'd have if Doomsday actually agreed to it…a personal meeting with the world's most notorious hacker."

"That's a big if. Why would he expose himself that way?"

"It's spelled E-G-O. The guy's an egomaniac. Worse, he's a megalomaniac. If I tell him *The Journal's* decided to run a feature on him, but the condition is I have to meet him face-to-face, I bet he'll do it."

"You have your editor's approval to do the story?"

Erin laughed. "Are you kidding? He's salivating over the idea. This could be a journalistic coup if I can pull it off."

"Do I hear excitement in your voice?"

"Yeah, you do," Erin said with a laugh. "See what you started? I'm liking the idea already."

"Let's just remember that our main objective is to get Doomsday to give you some valuable information, not just to stroke his ego."

"Hey, who's the reporter here?"

Marty chuckled. "Okay, I'll shut up now. But Erin, if you go through with this thing, promise me you'll be careful as hell."

"Don't worry," Erin said reassuringly. "I've got the whole FBI looking after me."

Erin didn't waste any time. As soon as she hung up with Marty she wrote an e-mail to Doomsday. Her pitch was simple and blunt. She said that *The Journal* was pressuring her to end her coverage of Doomsday unless she could get a more in-depth story. She said she wanted to arrange a face-to-face meeting and in return she could guarantee a feature placement about Doomsday. She urged him to contact her at once.

Erin knew that her e-mail would go through some complex web of interconnected anonymous mail servers before it ever got to Doomsday. He had set up a routing protocol that protected his e-mail address from disclosure. The FBI had already run up against that brick wall.

It was several days before Doomsday responded, but he took the bait. Doomsday said he would agree to meet Erin but it would have to be in a public place, alone, and for only an hour. He also demanded that he be able to approve the article before publication.

Erin showed the communication to the FBI. Doomsday had made it easier by specifying a public place, so there was no negotiation necessary on that point. Erin didn't want to agree to his demand for prior approval, though—that undermined her journalistic integrity and she wouldn't stand for it. She e-mailed him back telling him she would respect anything he told her if he wanted it to be off the record, but that he could not approve the article for publication, and that was not negotiable.

Doomsday responded with a somewhat reluctant acceptance, letting his unhappiness be known about the condition that she set. He requested that Erin meet him at the outdoor plaza in Rockefeller Center in New York City. The FBI immediately speculated that New York could be his home turf and, if so, it would be the first lead they had to Doomsday's actual whereabouts. The hackers the FBI had captured and researched in the past were fairly limited in their geographic scope. They tended to act like hermits, not moving much beyond their immediate territory; instead, the Internet was their world. The FBI therefore hoped that this meant they had at least discovered Doomsday's home base, a breakthrough in and of itself.

Even if it were true, however, New York was such a large, impersonal place that the information in actuality had limited value. Doomsday could be operating from anywhere in the New York metropolitan area. They also knew this hacker was brilliant and shrewd; he could simply have arranged the meeting in New York and might not be located there at all.

Despite the fact that it was on the other side of the country, Erin's editor agreed to the trip. Erin decided she would make a detour to Boston on the way back to California so she could see Marty. The FBI agent Erin worked with in San Francisco put her in touch with an agent in the New York Field Office. She was to contact the agent upon arriving in New York so she could be wired and briefed before her meeting with Doomsday.

It was a crisp Fall day when Erin arrived at LaGuardia Airport. She took a cab to the Park Plaza Hotel where she was staying for the night. It was within walking distance of Rockefeller Center. Doomsday wanted to meet after dark, so she was able to rendezvous with the FBI agent at the hotel first.

When she checked in the desk clerk told her there was a message for her. It was from the agent asking her to call him as soon as she arrived. She went up to her room and placed the call immediately.

The agent was expecting her call. He asked her room number and said he and another agent would be over to see her within thirty minutes.

There was a knock on her door less than a half hour later. It was the FBI agent, accompanied by an attractive woman. They were dressed in business suits. The man held his identification up to Erin as he introduced himself.

"Ms. Keliher, I'm agent Sam Waterson. This is agent Liz Simon."

Erin ushered them inside. "Pleased to meet you."

For the next hour, Sam thoroughly briefed Erin on the way in which the FBI wanted Erin to handle the "encounter," as Sam called it. He showed her the wire and then allowed Liz and Erin to go into the bathroom so Liz could tape it to Erin's chest. It would be hidden by her bra and shirt.

Sam tested the wire when they returned and continued his briefing. Sam made sure that Erin understood what procedures to follow if anything unanticipated should occur. Sam didn't expect Doomsday to take any threatening action in the middle of Rockefeller Center but he wanted her to be prepared. He said he and Liz, as well as two other agents, would be close by and their first priority was to protect her from any harm.

Erin was impressed by Sam's professionalism and thoroughness. He was obviously experienced at such encounters and any apprehension she had about meeting Doomsday was quelled by the briefing.

It was about an hour before Erin's appointment with Doomsday. She asked Sam if it was okay if she walked leisurely down Fifth Avenue to Rockefeller Center. She wanted to window shop and calm her nerves a bit. Sam didn't see any problem with that and told her to go ahead, that he and Liz would be close behind but unobtrusive. He said the other agents were already taking their positions at Rockefeller Center.

Erin stopped at several store windows and admired the elegant jewelry and clothing that was Fifth Avenue's trademark. While she had always thought New York was too busy and bustling a city, the worldliness and sophistication of midtown Manhattan still never failed to impress her. She much preferred the charm of San Francisco, but she had to admit there was nothing like the store windows of New York.

Rockefeller Plaza was right off Fifth Avenue between 49th and 50th Streets, little more than ten blocks from the hotel. Erin enjoyed the leisurely stroll down Fifth Avenue. As she walked, she tried not to think about the risk associated with what she was about to do. She knew there was an element of danger, and that a man like Doomsday could be unpredictable. But she also knew that she was Doomsday's connection to the power of the press. She felt that he wouldn't do anything to jeopardize that, so why should he hurt her? Erin convinced herself that everything was going to be all right. When she arrived at Rockefeller Center, she was a few minutes early for her meeting.

She looked up at the buildings surrounding the plaza below, then walked down the steps. Doomsday had instructed her to meet him in front of the gold statue at the head of the sunken plaza. During the Fall and Winter months, the outdoor dining area was turned into one of the most famous ice skating rinks in the world. For a while,

Erin watched the skaters gliding effortlessly and silently on the ice from her vantage point near the statue. She looked around but was unaware of Sam, Liz, or anyone else who looked like an FBI agent. She felt strange but comforted knowing she was being intensely watched by hidden eyes.

Erin checked her watch. It was time. She was nervous, not really scared, but definitely nervous. There was an unpredictability to this whole thing that made her uneasy, though she felt confident that she would be safe and that the FBI would not let anything go wrong.

Fifteen minutes went by and still no Doomsday. Erin began to wonder if he would show. Then, as if from nowhere, a hulking figure appeared next to her. He was dressed in jeans, sneakers, and a t-shirt under a New York Yankees baseball jacket. His long hair ended in a pony tail and an unruly beard covered his face. Despite the darkness of night he wore biker-style sunglasses with reflective silver lenses. No one gave him a second glance because in New York, even the oddest appearances were nothing at all unusual.

"So we meet face-to-face," he said to her without a hello. He moved close to where she was standing, hands in his pockets, and talked to the night. He held his head straight, without looking down at her, as if she weren't even there. They could be two strangers watching the skaters.

"Do we talk here or go somewhere else?" she asked.

"Here is good," he answered.

"Thank you for coming," she said, looking at him sideways. He merely grunted. She pulled out a small reporter's notebook and a pen.

"No notes," he said quickly. She put the notebook away without disagreement.

For the next fifteen minutes, Erin asked Doomsday some basic questions about his background and his life. When he didn't want to answer a question, he just shook his oversized head slightly, as if he were shooing away a fly. Any question he did answer was vague and told Erin little. Doomsday was being obstinate, almost belligerent.

Finally she got to the heart of the interview…his life as a hacker and his penchant for computer viruses. Only then did Doomsday become more engaged and verbose. He talked about his viruses as if they were elegant software programs that were doing good and not evil. Erin quickly saw that Doomsday's entire world was the reverse image of normalcy. His upside-down reasoning seemed to make perfect sense to him.

"Let's assume, then, that your view of the software world is accurate," Erin said, "that all the software companies really want to do is to screw people and make huge profits. If that's true, then you're saying none of the advances in software have really done anyone any good."

"No," Doomsday answered. "That isn't it. It's their motivation I'm talking about. Whatever good has come out of software companies has been driven by greed, by the need to beat the shit out of their competitors. Any good that has come out of the products has been accidental. It's all about profits, profits above all else. You've been a reporter long enough to know this is true."

Erin decided to lend a sympathetic ear to see if she could cajole more out of Doomsday.

"Sadly, I have to admit you're right about the profits and the competition," Erin answered. "Sometimes it does seem like these companies' values are wrong."

For the first time, Doomsday turned towards her. "You're just saying that, you don't believe it."

"Well," Erin answered honestly, "I may not feel as strongly as you do about it, but I do understand your position. I saw it first-hand with the GWare ONE introduction. But you know, there's bad and good among people who run software companies, just like anywhere. We don't live in a perfect society."

Doomsday chortled and then broke into a fit of coughing. "Society," he said when his coughing subsided. "Society sucks."

Erin disregarded the statement and plowed ahead. "Tell me what you really hope to accomplish with your virus attacks, Doomsday. Aren't you hurting some of the people you say you want to help? Don't virus attacks just make things worse for everyone?"

Doomsday shook his head slowly. "It's the only way to let them know who is in control. They cannot be allowed to continue like this, driven by techno-capitalism without regard for computing purity. I have been chosen to stop them, and it is I who will do so.

"I can launch my viruses at will. My virus attacks are getting harder to stop, you know that. I'm just testing and refining now. But soon, very soon, the ultimate attack will come. It's coming, I can promise you that. It will be memorable and historic, you wait. Print that in your paper."

A chill ran down Erin's spine. This man was clearly demented, there was no doubt about it.

"And there's nothing anyone can do to make you re-consider this course of action?" Erin asked.

Doomsday simply laughed. "Time's up," he said. Without another word, he lumbered away. She watched the hulking man's back as he melded into the masses of humanity on the New York streets.

Erin realized that her meeting with Doomsday didn't accomplish nearly as much as she had hoped. He failed to reveal in words anything about his viruses that could be of great importance, other than his brazen threat at the end.

She certainly got a clearer picture of his personality traits and his physical appearance, though. This was the hacker stereotype come to life, Erin thought. Doomsday was physically a behemoth, yet clearly a brilliant man who could just as easily have been a positive rather than a negative force in the computing world. He was nothing short of a sociopath. She wasn't particularly surprised that he fit the mold, but she was somewhat saddened at the thought that whatever talents Doomsday had were wasted on his fanatical view of the world.

On the other hand there was a tiny part of Doomsday's righteous indignation that Erin understood and acknowledged had merit. She could never support Doomsday's way of dealing with the injustice in the business world, yet she could relate to his outrage. After years of covering the computer industry, Erin herself sometimes wondered how it got to be so jaded and profit-oriented. One of the reasons she had fallen in love with Marty was her belief that he was one of the few "good guys" left. His morality was rare in the software business. Somehow Marty had managed to balance growing a successful software company with maintaining a strong commitment to principles and values. He actually cared about what his company's products could do for the good of humanity. What a breath of fresh air he was!

More typical of the software business were the two Gs, Gatwick and Gates. Cut out of the same cloth, Erin thought. These two ruthless bastards were the symbols of everything Doomsday railed against. She could see why the actions of companies like GWare and Microsoft would drive someone like Doomsday insane.

But was he insane…or was he the modern-day Robin Hood that he claimed to be and that some thought he was? Surely infecting the world's computer systems with viruses wasn't the answer, she thought. There had to be a better way to get his point across. Yet his motives…were they all that wrong, she wondered.

Her thoughts were interrupted by Sam, who idled up to her and nodded a hello.

"You get all that?" Erin asked.

"Yeah, the wire worked fine. We also got some nice photos of our boy. At least we now have a physical description of him that we can circulate. The other agents are tailing him now."

"Thank goodness he was harmless enough," Erin said, relieved it was over. "But I didn't get nearly as much information out of him as I had hoped."

"Don't be discouraged," Sam said. "The fact that you got him out in the open was a major victory. Usually these guys won't risk any kind of physical contact. It's amazing that he even showed up at the appointed time. Who knows, maybe he'll grant you a follow-up meeting."

"Doubt it," Erin said.

Sam's cell phone rang. He answered it, listened for a moment, then said "Shit" quietly before disconnecting.

Erin's eyes questioned him.

"They lost him in the subway," Sam answered. "They think he was headed downtown, but they can't be sure. He changed trains a couple of times. Even a guy the size of Doomsday can disappear into the depths of the New York City subway system if he knows how. Probably figured he was being tailed."

"Yeah, well somebody like that belongs in the bowels of the earth," Erin said thoughtfully. "I only hope that when he surfaces again, all hell won't break loose."

CHAPTER 22

It didn't take long for all hell to break loose, but it wasn't because of Doomsday's next virus attack. Erin met her obligation by writing the featured story about Doomsday. She wanted to characterize Doomsday's position on the software industry as fanatical, but she also wanted her readers to consider the underlying message Doomsday was trying to convey. When he read the draft of the story, her editor balked at what seemed to be Erin's veiled support of Doomsday. He felt she might be going over the line, or at the very least, expressing a controversial opinion that could unleash a public outcry.

Erin showed the article to the FBI in its draft form and they endorsed it. They felt Doomsday might think he had done some good at his meeting with Erin. The FBI wanted to keep the lines of communication open and hoped a future Doomsday/Erin meeting was a possibility. Still, Erin's editor was gravely concerned about the tone of the article and urged Erin to consider a rewrite.

In the end, Erin did revise the article and soften her stance somewhat, but she still shared her personal view of what she thought Doomsday was trying to accomplish with his radical actions. She did not in any way show support for his position, but she cleverly incorporated some industry statistics about software company profits that would lead readers to the conclusion that they were, at the very least, unconscionable. Nonetheless, she was careful to express her disagreement with Doomsday's virus attacks as a solution to the issue.

The article had an immediate impact. The Software Publishers Association requested the right to author an article with an opposing viewpoint and challenged *The Journal* to publish it. Letters both reviling Erin's article and praising it flooded the newspaper's e-mail. The article itself became a story of controversy in computer trade journals and on industry Web sites.

As the controversy swirled around Erin, she wondered if she had made a big mistake. Writing a feature about the hacker was one thing, but editorializing was another. Over the years, Erin had become such an influential journalist that her reviews could make or break products, and her assessment of promising new technology could sometimes even affect a budding company's receipt of venture capital. She knew her words carried considerable weight in the industry.

Now she had stepped squarely into a pile of dog doo the likes of which she had never experienced. Of course she had expected a reaction to the article, but she hadn't anticipated the volume and emotional intensity of the responses. The power of the written word, especially when it appeared in as well respected and well read a publication as *The Wall Street Journal*, was awesome, she thought.

So, too, was the responsibility. And now Erin was questioning her own judgment in authoring the story and expressing what were obviously regarded as controversial views. The e-mails were running three-to-one against her article. Did she really think she could get away with being even the slightest bit sympathetic to someone who was an acknowledged cyber-terrorist, someone who had caused so much damage with his virus attacks?

Her editor wasn't sympathetic; he just informed Erin in an "I told you so" tone that it was the price a journalist paid for taking an unpopular position. It would blow over, he said, and it sure couldn't hurt the circulation numbers.

At least Marty was more understanding. During an emotional telephone conversation, Erin tearfully explained to him that she feared she would lose her credibility as a journalist. Marty saw it another way.

"Put it into perspective, Erin. This is an emotionally charged issue for the industry and for computer users in general. It took a lot of guts for you to tell it like it is, to write it the way you saw it."

"Maybe so," Erin said sniffling, "but you'd think I was supporting the overthrow of the U.S. government with the kind of reaction I'm getting."

"You've done worse than that," Marty said with a laugh, "you're attacking the almighty god of Profits...in America's business newspaper, no less. I don't know too many people who'd have the courage to do that.

"You know," Marty added seriously, "the older I get the more I realize just how warped our whole business model is. I mean, I think you've raised an issue that we, as an industry, don't want to deal with. I never thought about it as much as I do now, with what's going on with the Internet. Look at the venture capital that's being poured into even the craziest Internet ideas. Some of these companies don't even know what business they're in. They're raising millions of dollars just because they have an "e" in front of their names.

"It's nuts, Erin. Software companies like mine are scrambling and clawing to get a big piece of the newly wired world. Everybody's talking about e-business and e-commerce like it'll save humanity itself. Yet we know it's really about profits, ROI, shareholder value. That's what's fueling the Internet today, and that's why the venture capitalists can't throw money at it fast enough.

"Then you get someone like Doomsday," Marty continued, gaining steam, "an anti-capitalist looney tune who goes after us with a vengeance. He uses our own technology against us, distributes his own software programs across the greatest distribution channel we have to get back at us. He makes us stop what we're doing and take notice. We don't have a choice but to acknowledge his power, because he can bring us all down. We know it, and he knows we know it.

"Yeah, he's way off the scale, but Christ, the guy makes a damn good point, doesn't he? He gets noticed, that's for sure. Like most radicals he goes way too far, but if you look underneath the virus attacks and consider his motivation, it starts to make sense in a perverted way. Doomsday isn't right, of course, but he is a kind of a voice of reason in an unreasonably profit-driven world...someone who might see things for what they really are.

"That's what I think you see, Erin. You see it, you know it, and you're not afraid to talk about it. Who else would think to give Doomsday a fair shake, to even try to understand what he's out to prove? I don't think you made a mistake, Erin. I think we have you to thank for keeping us honest."

"Don't ever step off that soapbox, Marty," Erin said, wiping a tear away. "I love you for it."

"And I love you," Marty said, "even if you are the most controversial journalist in America right now."

Erin laughed as she hung up the phone. Marty always had a way of making her feel whole again.

Just then she noticed an e-mail in her inbox from Doomsday. She opened it and read it:

> I didn't think you had it in you. Maybe you are actually beginning to understand the injustice I fight against. When we met I promised you Armageddon soon. It is near, as near as year's end. It will come on the dawning of the new year 2000. But first there will be one more demonstration, one more test. Just a little taste of what is yet to come. Be watching.

As always, Erin immediately forwarded Doomsday's e-mail to her FBI contact, but this one she marked high priority. Erin found this communication particularly chilling. While Doomsday had always inserted some kind of warning into his e-mails, this was the first time he had mentioned Armageddon. And his statement, "It is near, as near as year's end," was particularly ominous. Was Doomsday planning the ultimate attack for the beginning of the new year, now just a few short months away?

But first, Erin thought, we'll have to survive "one more demonstration," as Doomsday had put it. Erin shuddered to think what his next attack would be.

National Infrastructure Protection Center
Advisory 99-028
"W32/EXPLOREZIP.WORM.PAK"
December 01, 1999

Various sources, including commercial anti-virus software providers, are reporting an outbreak of a new, high-risk variant of the W32/EXPLOREZIP.WORM (see NIPC Advisory 99-013). The new variant is called W32/EXPOREZIP.WORM.PAK or WORM.EXPLOREZIP(PACK), contains the same destructive payload found in the original EXPLOREZIP.WORM, and uses a commercial compression format called "NEOLITE" which may not be recognized by some anti-virus software.

Several Fortune 500 companies in the United States are reportedly infected with this new strain of the EXPLOREZIP.WORM; the potential for further infection is significant.

W32/EXPLOREZIP.WORM.PAK characteristics:

- The behavior of W32/EXPLOREZIP.WORM.PAK is identical to the original EXPLOREZIP.WORM. However, due to the different file compression technique, the file is 40% shorter than the original and does not need manual decompression to execute.

- W32/EXPLOREZIP.WORM.PAK propagates in the same manner as the original EXPLOREZIP.WORM. The e-mail containing the worm will have the content, "I received your e-mail and I shall send you a reply ASAP. Till then, take a look at the attached zipped docs." A file name "ZIPPED_FILES.EXE" will be attached to the e-mail. The worm uses mapi-capable e-mail programs on Microsoft Windows systems to propagate.
- When the attachment is executed, it generates a false error message, copies itself to the C:\WINDOWS\SYSTEMS directory with the filename EXPLORE.EXE, and modifies the mail addresses in a user's e-mail program. The worm will search for remote machines where the infected user has write permission and will install itself on those machines.
- The payload of W32/EXPLOREZIP.WORM.PAK is destructive. The worm searches all drive from C: through Z:, including network drives and zeroes the file size of all files with extensions*.C,*.H,*.CPP,*.ASM,*.DOC,*.PPT, or*.XLS. This procedure renders those files unusable and possibly unrecoverable. The payload re-executes every 30 minutes.

No sooner had news of the newest virus attack appeared on the Internet than Erin received a call from Senator Ted Chambers of Vermont, the recently appointed chair of the Senate Technology Council.

"What can I do for you, Senator Chambers?" Erin asked.

"Ms. Keliher, we've never met, but I am of course familiar with you and your…work," Chambers said with a voice that boomed, even across the phone line. "Let me be frank, Ms. Keliher. We're getting our teeth kicked in here in Washington over these virus attacks. And my Technology Council's taking the brunt of it. The latest attack, well, that pretty much put it over the top, if you know what I mean."

"I can imagine," Erin said, beginning to get the Senator's drift.

Chambers cleared his throat. “Now Ms. Keliher…”

“Please, call me Erin,” Erin interrupted. She couldn’t stand the formality, and she had the distinct feeling she’d be getting to know the Senator better real soon.

“Alright, Erin then. The Senate Technology Council is working feverishly with the FBI to break this case. I don’t need to tell you that this hacker Doomsday is at the center of it all. And that’s where you come in.”

“Go on, Senator.”

“Erin, I know you’ve cooperated with the FBI and we appreciate that. However, your latest article in *The Journal*, well, it raised a few eyebrows on the Hill, I can tell you that.”

Erin contained a laugh. It certainly wasn’t funny, but she could just imagine Chambers constraining himself from what he really wanted to say to her.

“In any event,” Chambers continued, “you know more about this Doomsday fellow than anyone, and we’ve got some real pressure on us to stop these virus attacks once and for all. I’m calling a special meeting of the Council and bringing together some experts for a kind of a summit on computer viruses. I urgently request your presence at it.” Chambers paused and then added, “This isn’t a subpoena or anything like that, Erin. It’s an invitation.”

“I do appreciate the difference,” Erin said ironically. “May I ask who else you have invited, Senator?”

“Why certainly,” Chambers replied. “From the government’s side, we’ll have the head of the NIPC there, as well as the lead FBI agent working on the Doomsday case. You know him, of course. And from the business side, I’ve asked TJ Gatwick from GWare and Marty Gladstone from Incandescent to attend. I couldn’t think of two more qualified individuals when it comes to anti-virus technology. They’ve agreed to be here. That’s everyone. I wanted a small group on this thing so we can move fast.”

Good God, Erin thought, TJ and Marty in the same room, and her thrown in for good measure! What a circus this will be.

"Well that's quite an interesting team, Senator. I'm flattered to be included and of course I'll participate. When is the summit being held?"

"Two days from now. I've blocked out the day. We'll start promptly at 9 AM here at the Capitol. Just ask at security where the Technology Council meeting is being held. Your name will be on the list. We'll be expecting you, Erin."

It wasn't difficult for Senator Chambers to observe the tension between Marty Gladstone and TJ Gatwick at his virus summit. He grumbled to himself, thinking that maybe he would've been better off if he had kept these two software moguls out of the picture.

Chambers sighed. He realized their input was valuable but he didn't have time for a pissing contest. The Senate's bad enough, he thought, but here Gatwick and Gladstone are bickering like little boys in a sandbox. Actually, Gladstone was just defending himself, it was Gatwick who was making it difficult to come to any kind of consensus.

"Gentlemen, gentlemen, please." The Senator broke in on the beginnings of another round between TJ and Marty. "We need to find common ground here and get on with it. It is of little consequence to this Council whether GWare or Incandescent has the superior anti-virus technology. What's essential now is a plan of action not just to repel but to prevent the inevitable attack.

"I must impress upon you again that the NIPC believes a major attack is imminent. Doomsday has made good on his previous warnings, so we are taking this one very seriously." Chambers waved in the direction of the NIPC director, looking for someone else to speak to distract TJ and Marty from their constant jibing.

The NIPC director took the cue and chimed in. "We have less than a month before January 1, 2000," he said. "The NIPC originally believed that large-scale infrastructure disruptions were not likely during the Y2K transition period. But considering the heightened awareness of and media focus on malicious activity, we're now on high alert.

"As the Senator said, when Doomsday makes a threat, we take it very seriously. The FBI is putting pressure on every channel to shake something, anything loose. They've learned a little something that might be of interest to all of us." The NIPC director nodded to the FBI agent who was the next to speak.

"We have a small bit of intelligence," the agent began. "Not much to go on, unsubstantiated at the moment, but it's all we've got. We expect there will be some increased activity via macro viruses. As you know, they're more of a nuisance than a threat, but there may be a possibility that new variants will be launched with trigger dates during the Y2K transition. They could certainly have destructive payloads.

"I think we're prepared to deal with most of those. I'm more concerned about PC CIH. We first saw it in mid-1998, I'm sure you recall that. It has a very destructive payload which will delete the first megabyte of data on all hard drives available to the infected machine and overwrite flash BIOS memory. The payload is triggered on different dates depending on the variant which infected the machine."

The FBI agent paused to wipe his brow with a handkerchief. "This is where our intelligence comes in. We've learned that a number of other viruses will become active in the next several weeks, like Padania and Prilissa, both macros. Again, I think we can cope with those. It appears that Doomsday and his cronies plan to unleash some of these macros, keeping us busy with them, in a kind of frontal assault.

"Releasing those viruses will be just a tactic to cover up the real attack, however," the agent continued. "We expect that the worst virus will be a strain of PC CIH. It could even be something else we don't know about at the moment."

"Doomsday warned of Armageddon at year's end," Erin said. "Has the FBI been able to confirm anything about that?"

The agent nodded. "We've heard from two different sources what the trigger date is likely to be." He looked around the table from face to face. All eyes were on him with anticipation.

"It looks like we're gonna see fireworks on New Year's Eve alright," the agent said, "but they won't just be up in the sky."

CHAPTER 23

The virus summit held by Senator Chambers led to a hastily formed coalition to fight against cyber-terrorism. After hearing what could be in store for computer users on New Year's Eve, TJ Gatwick and Marty Gladstone agreed to set aside their differences and work hand-in-hand with the NIPC and FBI. GWare and Incandescent would put their brightest and best developers on the project, functioning around the clock in an effort to find a way to protect against the anticipated attack. In a stroke of crowning irony, Henry Chu would be working in concert with a few of his former colleagues at GWare. One of them was Jill Strathmore, the senior developer who had interested Henry in GWare in the first place.

It was also decided at the summit that Erin should make a last-ditch attempt to convince Doomsday to re-consider. No one expected him to comply, but they had nothing to lose.

At the same time, the NIPC issued its most strongly worded Alert yet, warning the world about the imminent threat of an attack on December 31. The Alert was picked up by the media and it quickly became a major news story. The media, of course, hyped it as a Y2K story, almost trivializing the virus warning itself.

As the clock ticked inexorably towards the end of 1999, Marty Gladstone reviewed the progress of the coalition development team with Henry Chu.

"This isn't moving as fast as we had hoped, Doc," Marty said, shaking his head. "We're going to run out of time."

Henry wearily nodded in agreement. "Don't know what else we can do, we're all working 24/7. Our guys are cooperating with GWare, but only to a point. You know what the biggest challenge is, Marty. We can't make this stuff work together. We keep dancing around each other's proprietary code."

Henry was referring to the fact that GWare and Incandescent were being protective of their own unique virus-repelling programs. There was only so far two competing software companies would go in opening up their black boxes, even though they were supposed to be collaborating on a solution.

Marty thought about it for a moment. "That really is the heart of the problem, isn't it, Doc?" He stood up and began to pace around his office. "So if we have any hope of keeping Doomsday from obliterating our whole world just weeks from now, we've gotta lay all our cards out on the table. We've gotta open up our kimonos."

Henry looked at Marty, his eyes widening. "You'd do that? You'd share our code with GWare?"

Marty rubbed his chin thoughtfully. "Henry, I've been watching this Doomsday character for years. He's the most ingenious, insidious hacker we've ever seen. I really think this guy can do just about anything he wants to, at will. He's got virus strains up his sleeve we haven't even thought of yet.

"These aren't idle threats," Marty continued. "Every time Doomsday threatens to strike he tells us what he's planning and then he goes and does it, just the way he said he would. His viruses are getting more and more difficult to repel. No one in the industry can seem to muster up enough critical mass to beat him.

"I think we've reached the end game, Henry. This guy's ready to destroy everything we believe in, everything we depend upon. When he does, Incandescent and GWare won't matter anymore. Our shareholders won't matter. The profits won't matter. It'll be over, over for all of us. That's the reason we have to share the code. What other choice do we have?"

Henry nodded thoughtfully, considering the full impact of Marty's words. "You're right," he simply said. Then he got up, briefly put a hand on Marty's shoulder, turned, and slowly walked out of Marty's office.

Marty looked at his watch. It was approaching 11:30 AM. It would be 8:30 AM in San Diego. He thought he'd take a chance and see if TJ Gatwick was available. He called the cell phone number TJ had given him.

"Gatwick," TJ answered after one ring.

"TJ, it's Marty. We need to talk."

"I'm listening."

"I've been assessing our progress," Marty said. "I'm sure you realize as well as I do that we're running out of time."

"Yeah, I just reached that same conclusion last night."

"I don't think we're gonna make it, TJ."

"Looks that way. But I don't know what we can do about it."

"We can't let that happen. Doomsday'll take us all to the cleaners." Marty paused and swallowed. What the hell, he thought, I may as well just plow ahead. "TJ, I think we need to share our code for any hope of success."

Marty could hear TJ breathing into the phone but there was no response. He waited for what seemed to be an interminable minute.

"Share our code," TJ said, as if he'd been hit with a two by four. "You know what you're saying."

Marty sighed, "Yeah, I know what I'm saying. If you can think of a better idea, I'm all ears."

The phone line was silent again. Then TJ said with resignation, "This guy is gonna fucking destroy us, isn't he. Like he did to me the first time."

"Yeah," Marty said with feeling. He knew TJ was just now coming to the realization that it was Doomsday, not Marty, who was behind the GWare ONE disaster so many years ago. This was a hell of time for a revelation, Marty thought, but he gained some satisfaction from it.

"Shit," TJ said, "None of this will matter anyway if this bastard succeeds. Not GWare, not Incandescent." TJ paused to think about it. "You're right, Marty. It's the only way. We've gotta share our code or we'll never beat this maniac."

For the next fifteen minutes, Marty and TJ worked through verbally what would be an historic agreement in the software industry. When they were satisfied with the basic agreement in principle, TJ offered to have his law firm draft up a letter agreement and fax it to Marty's law firm for review and immediate signature.

The agreement called for broad cooperation between the two companies, such that their respective proprietary anti-viral code would be made available to the joint development team immediately. With all technological barriers broken down, Marty and TJ hoped that their combined efforts could result in a new more resilient virus shield, fabricated with each company's most confidential code playing a role in the final product.

The Incandescent and GWare developers began their work in earnest, weaving together the two companies' separate anti-viral components. Developers on both coasts, former bitter rivals, cooperated fully and openly in a team effort. With open code on both sides, they could work more rapidly, even though they still had to keep at it around the clock. At least they now had a common cause, a unified goal—to produce a single software product that could possibly repel The Doomsday Virus.

Finally, Christmas day arrived. Exhausted and spent, the team marked the occasion by giving to TJ and Marty the gift they wanted most—a jointly developed virus shield. It was far from perfect. It had bugs they didn't have time to fix, and they could only do alpha testing on the hastily formed product, but this was the best they could come up with given the enormous constraints they were working under.

GWare and Incandescent issued a public statement, endorsed by the NIPC, that the anti-virus shield was the best protection available to repel the forthcoming virus attack. The shield would work on top of virtually any computer or network operating system, although neither company could ensure complete compatibility. The companies cautioned that the shield was a deterrent but not an antidote. It was important to understand that it was basically an untested program with no guarantee of complete effectiveness, but it was believed it could repel any forthcoming virus attack.

The NIPC also announced that the federal government was taking the unprecedented step of funding the free distribution of the shield to anyone who wanted it. The shield would be downloadable at the GWare and Incandescent Web sites, as well as at additional download sites provided by the government and other cooperating software companies and Web sites. The objective was to make the shield as widely available worldwide in a compressed time period. In order to prevent hackers from gaining access to the product too far in advance, distribution of the shield was closely guarded and would not be made public until December 29.

A delighted Senator Chambers breathed a sigh of relief that Gatwick and Gladstone had finally worked out their differences and come together to fight as a team against the anticipated attack. He personally called them both to thank them and congratulate them on a superior effort. They told Senator Chambers they were indeed grateful they could get a shield to market, but each of them cautioned the Senator that the real test would be on December 31.

Marty had worked non-stop, alongside Henry, on the new jointly developed shield, providing encouragement and acting as an advisor. He had never been more tired, but he felt a certain satisfaction for the effort. The most remarkable part of the experience was, of course, the cooperative effort between the two companies.

Marty had never even conceived that it would be possible for Incandescent and GWare to work this closely together on anything. He believed the farthest the two companies could ever go was in reaching a simple business agreement over distribution rights to their respective anti-virus technologies.

Now, at Marty's urging, TJ Gatwick had agreed to the unthinkable—opening up the secret code that fueled GWare Guardian, the company's most successful product. And Marty's own company had responded in kind, revealing the secrets behind UNITE's anti-virus shield.

Marty realized it had been done out of desperation in a last-ditch effort to prevent what was sure to be a catastrophic virus attack. Still, he was heartened by the unprecedented cooperation between the two bitter rivals. If this could happen, he thought, there was still some sort of righteousness in the world.

In fact, Marty speculated, why couldn't this create a whole new way of doing business in the future? Now that GWare and Incandescent had, in effect, cast their fates to the wind together, wasn't it possible that their working relationship could last beyond the impending virus attack? Of course, the real issue wasn't the future, it was the present. Marty would know all too soon whether or not they had created a product that could repel the attack in the first place. That is what Marty had to concentrate on now…nothing was more important.

He wondered whether Erin had made any progress in approaching Doomsday. He called her to find out.

"No luck," she reported. "As we expected, Doomsday won't listen to reason. He's pretty much shut me off, I haven't heard from him since Christmas."

"I think we're gonna hear from him soon enough," Marty said quietly. "At least we've done everything we can. The cooperation between Incandescent and GWare has been unbelievable, Erin. Both development teams put their best efforts together. If anything can stop Doomsday, it'll be this new shield."

"That's encouraging, anyway," Erin said with some degree of doubt in her voice.

"Erin, I never thought Gatwick would be capable of this," Marty said with optimism. "It gave me a whole new perspective on this business. I mean, we both actually opened up our code to each other. I never thought it could happen."

"I hope it was the right decision…for everyone," Erin said, still distrustful of TJ Gatwick.

"It was the only decision," Marty said with conviction. "There's a greater evil than TJ Gatwick lurking out there, Erin. I think even he realized we had no choice. Maybe it'll change our relationship for the better, after this whole virus thing is over."

"Funny how adversity brings adversaries together, isn't it?" she asked thoughtfully.

"Now that was profound," Marty said.

She laughed and said, "I miss you."

"Miss you too," Marty said. "I would've loved to have spent Christmas with you, but you know I couldn't with all I had going on."

"Of course I know," she said quietly, and then added with a smile. "Saving the world is a just little more important right now. But I'm glad we're spending New Year's together." Erin was coming to Boston to join Marty for the city's renowned First Night celebration. Boston was the city that first pioneered the event.

"And what a New Year's Eve it promises to be," Marty said with nervous anticipation.

CHAPTER 24

The period between Christmas and New Year's Eve 1999 was the proverbial calm before the storm. There were no reports of any virus attacks and traffic on the Internet was generally lighter than usual.

Distribution of the anti-virus shield had reached a feverish pitch as the last day of the year came to a close. There were so many requests for downloads that numerous alternate sites had to be hastily set up to handle the Web page hits. The shield was now active on virtually every networked government agency, every Internet service provider's network, and very likely on a large majority of corporate networks in the United States. Distribution of the shield in non-U.S. locations had been slower to occur, but the servers in Canada, European countries, Japan, and Australia were seeing heavy download traffic.

The NIPC and FBI were on high alert. They had set up an emergency NOC in Washington—a Network Operations Center—manned twenty-four hours a day, to monitor the Internet and federal government agency computer systems.

Incandescent had set up a NOC in Cambridge and GWare had set one up in San Diego, in cooperation with the NIPC's NOC in Washington. All three NOCs were networked and in constant communication.

Erin's flight had landed on December 30, and Marty and Erin were spending New Year's Eve together in Boston. They attended some of the earlier events at the city's First Night celebration, but Marty was too pre-occupied to enjoy the evening. At about 11 PM, he and Erin decided to put aside any thoughts of a quiet, romantic remainder of the evening and head to the Incandescent NOC to watch and wait for the clock to strike twelve.

"How did I know I'd find you here?" Marty said as he spotted Henry Chu in the NOC.

Henry was looking intently at a computer monitor over the shoulder of a NOC operator. He acknowledged Marty with a smile and then waved a hello to Erin. Erin hadn't seen Henry since his return to Incandescent. She still had mixed emotions about the man, knowing that he was at the center of the bitter rivalry between Incandescent and GWare years ago, but she smiled and waved back.

"You really should be home with Priscilla," Marty said quietly to Henry, looking down at the monitor that held Henry's attention.

"Oh, I'll get there soon enough," Henry said distractedly. "But I knew this was where the action would be tonight, and I didn't want to miss anything."

One of the phones in the NOC rang and the supervisor picked it up. He listened for a few minutes, said a quick thank you, and hung up. He had a tense look on his face and, spotting Marty, quickly came over to him.

"That was the NIPC," the supervisor said. "They've had the first reports of an attack. NIPC says it's multi-pronged. They're detecting several different viruses, plus numerous DoS incidents. They suspect Trojans are involved as well."

DoS meant Denial-of-Service. It referred to when hackers overloaded Web sites or e-mail systems with bogus messages, causing the sites or systems to crash. Trojans were illicit programs that allowed unauthorized access to computer systems.

"Do they know if they're concentrated anywhere in particular?" Marty asked.

"It's too early to pinpoint...but the initial attacks seem to be targeting federal government agencies and utilities. The gov is being hit with the viruses and Trojans, a couple of the major telcos and ISPs are reporting DoS attacks."

Marty looked at Erin. "It's begun. Sounds like Doomsday's shooting the moon...he's going after the heart of the country's infrastructure first. Of course, that doesn't mean he'll stop there." Marty turned to the supervisor. "I'd like to go on chat so I can communicate with the other NOCs myself."

The supervisor nodded and led Marty over to a computer terminal. The NIPC had set up a secure chat so all the NOCs could communicate in real time.

Marty signed on. Almost immediately he saw a dialogue occurring between the FBI agent in charge of the Doomsday investigation, located at the Washington NOC, and TJ Gatwick, who was communicating from the San Diego NOC.

`TJ: What's been hit in the fedgov?`

`FBI: In the DC area, we have positive reports of viruses attacking Justice, HHS, EPA and the entire DOD. We've also identified Trojans at DOD.`

`TJ: Is the shield working?`

`FBI: Detection was absolutely effective across the board. Looks like prevention is holding with one of the viruses. But at least one other virus seems to be getting through. That's unconfirmed, I'm checking on it now.`

`Marty: Just joining you. TJ, any activity on the West Coast?`

`TJ: Just a few minutes ago we got an alert from Pac Bell. They've been DoS'd. Nothing else reported yet. How about up your way?`

`Marty: My NOC supervisor's checking, hold on. Yeah, looks like Bell Atlantic's just been DoS'd.`

FBI: So the pattern is becoming clear anyway. This looks coordinated and methodical. They're DoS-ing the utilities and launching viruses and Trojans against the government sites. If I had to guess, this is just the beginning of the fireworks.

TJ: I think you're right. We're now starting to get alerts from the major telcos West of the Mississippi. Coming in right now. All DoS'd. Occurred about the same time.

Marty: Getting East Coast reports coming in just now. We're showing telcos, Con Edison in New York, couple of other gas and electrics, all reporting DoS attacks.

FBI: I'm getting alerts from several other government agencies and departments now. Appears the shield has stopped one of the viruses cold. But another is definitely penetrating it at some sites.

TJ: Are you sure they had the shield properly installed?

FBI: No way to know that, I'll check and get back to you.

Marty: Can you get hold of one of these damn viruses and forward it to the dev team both East and West? We'll work on it and see if we can analyze it, maybe get an antidote working fast.

FBI: I'll see what I can do. Most of the departments and agencies are shut down for New Year's Eve, of course. Reports are coming from IT guys on duty. Some were beeper'd. They need to get to their Op Centers. Don't know if the virus getting through is via e-mail attachment or what.

TJ: We're getting alerts from all over. The map's lighting up like a damn Christmas tree.

Marty: Same here. They must've automated their attacks, they seem to be hitting all the telcos and utilities at once.

FBI: I'm getting reports of servers down at the FAA now.

Marty: We just got an unconfirmed alert that there's an ATM network down in the East. Looks like NYCE, but we're confirming.

TJ: Holy shit, the airport here is reporting air traffic control is down. Either of you guys hearing anything about this?

FBI: I'll ping the FAA with an emergency alert and see what's up. Gimme a minute.

Marty: Jesus, the ATC system went down at Logan. They're not getting any response from the New Hampshire backup. Logan is grounding all flights effective immediately. Thank God traffic's slow tonight.

FBI: Yeah, I'm getting confirmation now that air traffic control is down nationwide. Somehow they sabotaged the whole system.

Marty: Just got a confirmation that ATMs are out along the East Coast. Looks like they've gone after the banking network too.

TJ: The government, the airports, the utilities, the ATMs, what the hell is next?

FBI: What's next is the FBI and the CIA. They just crashed our main intelligence systems. Damn good thing we've got this NOC running on external servers. So far the ISPs are still reporting adequate uptime but Internet traffic is sluggish.

Marty: Volume should be light worldwide. TJ, what do you figure is slowing it down?

TJ: Lots of publicity for this…maybe people are jumping on to see what the hell is going on. Hopefully Doomsday hasn't screwed up the backbone yet.

Marty: So where do we stand?

FBI: I can't give you a full damage assessment yet. Reports are flooding us now. No details, everyone's too busy trying to fix their own mess. But I did get hold of one of the viruses that's getting through the shield. It's on its way to your dev teams.

Marty: OK, we'll jump on it.

TJ: Same here.

```
FBI: How fast do you think you can analyze it and
come up with an antidote?
Marty: No way to know until we see it.
```

Early into the first hours of 2000, Marty, TJ and the FBI agent stayed on chat, monitoring the situation and providing each other with updates. The development team members were called at home and got to their respective labs as soon as they could. Working collaboratively, they learned the virus that penetrated the shield was a multi-purposed variant, probably the most potent and destructive virus known to date. It launched simply when an e-mail was opened and irreparably damaged a computer's hard drive, at the same time infecting the e-mail server. It appeared to be from legitimate e-mail addresses and couldn't be identified by its subject line so it had a high degree of penetration. The e-mail also contained a disguised attachment that, if opened, could delete firewall and anti-virus files. The virus was a particularly destructive payload, as the NIPC would call it.

As dawn's first light began to break over the eastern United States, it was apparent to the FBI agent, TJ and Marty that January 1, 2000 would be like no other. The three exhausted men could do nothing else but watch the clean-up begin. Their worst Y2K fears had been realized, not because of systems that malfunctioned due to human error, but because of networks that had been completely devastated by cyber-terrorists.

The nation's computing infrastructure was in a shambles. Virtually every major branch and department of the federal government, almost every major utility in the United States, the nation's airports, and the entire monetary network had been paralyzed. The year 2000 had started not with a whimper but with a bang.

It would take untold days, even weeks, before the United States would recover from the worst virus attack in history. Doomsday had made good on his threat.

PART III

2001

CHAPTER 25

TJ Gatwick removed his glasses and tossed them on his desk. He rubbed his eyes wearily.

It was hard to believe that it was little more than a year since the devastating New Year's Eve 1999 virus attack had occurred. It was this one incident that had virtually shut down the nation's computing capability. It took close to six months to recover from the attack, and the resulting awareness of and concern about viruses had skyrocketed. Virus attacks by hackers had intensified since then. Just weeks ago, Microsoft.com, MSN.com, and MSNBC.com, all owned by Microsoft, were sporadically inaccessible for several days because of the actions of one or more hackers. The sites were flooded with large volumes of bogus requests in a Denial of Service-type attack.

All the news of hackers and virus attacks had been great for GWare's business. As a result, the demand for GWare Guardian was growing exponentially each month.

It should have been cause for jubilation for TJ Gatwick, but instead it was troubling him. He knew that GWare Guardian was winning battles but losing the war against computer viruses. Viruses were getting increasingly sophisticated and much harder to deter against. An incessant procession of viruses and virus variants was taxing GWare's anti-virus research capabilities and distribution channels to the limit. Every time a new virus strain appeared, the company had to react immediately, analyzing the virus and rushing out an antidote. Often, this meant hiring additional contract staff and authorizing massive amounts of overtime for existing workers to react quickly to the crisis.

Ironically, despite the spiraling number of subscribers to GWare Guardian, the service was actually taking a nose-dive in profitability. TJ knew what the reason was: the cost structure of the subscription service simply didn't work. The company couldn't raise its subscription rates high enough to match the real cost of anti-virus software development time. It wasn't like the old days when TJ could rake in the profits by selling a software product at fifty or even a hundred times its production cost. Even GWare's profitable technical service business had dropped precipitously, since the GWare Guardian subscription service didn't require nearly as much technical support as traditional software products. Most customers could self-solve their problems via the Web site. In 2001, self-service over the Internet was expected.

The financial situation was exacerbated by some bad investments GWare had made in Dot Coms. In an effort to latch onto to the shooting star of the Internet, TJ had aggressively pursued several Internet acquisitions in late 1999 and early 2000. Now in 2001, the picture had changed dramatically. Dot Coms were crashing and burning month after month with frightening frequency. One of GWare's key acquisitions had already imploded, and another was soon going to run out of money. What had looked like sure-fire winners during the Dot Com craze had turned out to be major cash guzzlers that were barely justifiable as businesses.

GWare Guardian had become a bottomless money pit, and the corporation's Internet investments had soured. It was a fatal combination that put GWare on the brink of financial disaster. The bottom line: GWare was bleeding red ink. It was hemorrhaging so badly that neither TJ nor the board knew how to stop it. Only a few executives within GWare knew how serious the situation really was. There had been the beginning signs of real trouble in the company's financials for the first quarter of 2001, and the stock took quite a beating. But that was just the tip of the iceberg. GWare was teetering on the precipice of bankruptcy...and it was coming fast.

TJ had been wrestling for days with an idea to save his company. He realized he had few options and little room to maneuver. It was dawning on him that there was little chance GWare could survive without help from an outside source. At least it could protect him against the huge personal loss he would suffer if he couldn't turn the company around. TJ put the tips of his fingers together and flexed them several times. He looked at his hands and thought for a moment how that simple action was like the expansion and contraction of his business. Only now it was contracting for good...dying a painful death. He took a breath, swallowed hard, and stared at the phone. Then he picked it up and pressed the speed dial number of Marty Gladstone.

Marty had agreed to meet TJ at GWare's San Diego headquarters. He had never been there, but the timing was good. He needed to be in his Silicon Valley office anyway, and San Diego was just a short flight away from San Francisco.

As he rode in the limo from the airport to the GWare campus on Torrey Pines Road, he wondered what could be so urgent that TJ had to see him immediately. The two companies had indeed put aside their rivalry since their fateful collaboration on New Year's Eve 1999. From that moment forward, GWare and Incandescent continued to share their anti-virus code structures to the extent that the original agreement hurriedly crafted by TJ and Marty had become permanent. Now both GWare Guardian and Incandescent's UNITE used the same anti-virus shield technology. This actually benefited both companies, since part of their agreement covered joint licensing and royalties. In effect, GWare and Incandescent were now financial as well as business partners.

Even so, TJ and Marty had kept a respectable distance from one another. Collaboration was one thing, personal friendship was another. Although it seemed like TJ had buried the hatchet, Marty never completely trusted the man. While there was little in the way of open conflict between them anymore, it was an uneasy relationship at best.

As the limo pulled up to the main building on the GWare campus, Marty couldn't help but be impressed. He had seen pictures of the facility, but he was overpowered by its physical presence. It put his Silicon Valley headquarters to shame.

Marty signed in at the main building and took the elevator to the fifth floor. An attractive young woman greeted him as he stepped off the elevator and led him to TJ's office.

TJ rose from his desk to greet Marty. He stuck out his hand to grab Marty's and shook it warmly, accompanying it with a big smile. Very out of character for TJ, Marty thought.

Marty looked at the man and was taken aback by his physical appearance. It looked like TJ had easily lost more than twenty pounds. His clothes hung on him; he clearly hadn't bothered to buy new ones since the weight loss. His eyes, bloodshot behind his glasses, were accented by dark rings underneath. His hair was noticeably grayer than Marty had remembered. It was obvious that TJ had been under a lot of strain.

"I appreciate your coming on short notice, Marty," TJ said.

"No problem. This is a magnificent campus. Pictures don't do it justice."

"Thanks," TJ said off-handedly. "Please, sit down." He motioned to a sitting area in front of one of his office windows. "Want coffee, water, or anything?"

"Water is fine." TJ went to a small refrigerator in the corner of his office and pulled out two Perriers. He grabbed a few glasses from a side table and brought them back with the bottles, handing one to Marty and sitting down in a chair facing Marty.

"How's business?" TJ said, taking a gulp of his water.

"Holding our own," Marty replied. "The Internet side is weak, but demand for UNITE continues to be as strong as ever, thankfully. And you?"

"That's what I want to talk to you about." TJ paused. He took a moment to remove his glasses, polish them with a handkerchief he pulled from a side pocket, and look through them intently. Marty watched the procedure. The man seemed very much on edge.

TJ replaced his glasses carefully, gulped some more water, and spoke quietly. "Marty, I'm not gonna sugar-coat this. GWare is in serious financial trouble. Worse than what you've probably heard. I'm looking for a white knight," TJ said, "someone who can bail us out fast."

Marty took a sip from his own glass and sat back in his chair. He had known GWare was having a tough time financially but TJ's voice was thick with desperation.

"How fast?" Marty asked, his mind already racing through the possibilities.

"A bankruptcy filing could be imminent. Two, maybe three months."

Marty was stunned. How could GWare have gone so sour in such a short period of time?

"I think there's a lot of compatibility between GWare and Incandescent," TJ continued. He was slowly rubbing his hands together as if he were washing them. "We already have a business arrangement that works. Bringing our two companies together could create one hell of an industry powerhouse. It'd probably be the only software company that could even come close to taking a serious run at Microsoft."

"I must admit, there's never been a better time for that," Marty said. "What are you thinking for a business structure?"

"On paper, you'd have to do the acquiring," TJ answered. "But operationally, I think it would be a true merger. Our product lines are different, except for the overlap in the anti-virus shield area, and we've already pretty much got that solved through our existing agreement. Staff overlap would probably be minimal. We'd have to consolidate operations, of course…things like finance and admin, HR, marketing…but I bet we don't have a lot of duplication in technical staff."

"What about management?" Marty asked, broaching the topic that he expected would be the most challenging to resolve.

"I've thought about that already," TJ said. "I'm prepared to accept a buy-out."

It wasn't the answer Marty had expected. "I'm surprised, TJ. You're saying you don't want to play a role in the new company?"

TJ looked at Marty with fatigue in his eyes. "We've been down a long road, you and I, haven't we? I supposed we could even co-exist if we had to." TJ paused to gulp some water. "But I've had enough, Marty. I've taken GWare as far as it can go. It's time to do something else. I'm ready to call it quits."

"We could try a CEO and President structure," Marty offered. "Run GWare as a separate subsidiary. You know the place better than anyone. It could work, TJ."

TJ shook his head. "I appreciate the thought," TJ said, "but it's time for me to go. I'm sure of it. Of course, I don't want to see what I built disappear. You could make it into something, I know that."

"You're an amazing guy, TJ," Marty said with sincere admiration. "Listen, this is the biggest deal I've ever had to consider. I've gotta run it by my board, of course. How long do I have to get back to you?"

"I'm not talking to anybody else, if that's what you mean," TJ answered. "We've already got an NDA in place that's sufficient for us to share some numbers. Let's have our CFOs and attorneys do some due diligence, see if it makes sense for you to pursue it. No obligation, of course."

"Yeah, that's a good place to start." Marty pulled out one of his business cards and a pen and wrote down the e-mail address and phone number of his CFO on the back of it. "Here's my CFO's contact information. I'll call him on the way back to the airport, tell him to expect someone from GWare to get in touch. Anything else we need to discuss?"

TJ rose slowly from his chair. "Probably about a million details," he said with a sad smile, "but all that can wait. I know you've got a lot to think about." He extended his hand. "I'll be in touch."

Marty returned the handshake as he stood, looking up at TJ. He saw a man whose spirit may have been broken, but it appeared as if a huge weight had already been lifted from TJ Gatwick's shoulders.

Marty returned to the lobby of the building, his head swimming. As he stepped into the limo, the impact of the meeting with TJ really hit him. His immediate instinct was to go ahead with it. A deal like this would undoubtedly catapult Incandescent into a strong second place in the software industry. The combination of Incandescent and GWare would be, as TJ said, a true industry powerhouse, one that could certainly rival Microsoft. It would have taken years for Incandescent to reach that plateau on its own, if it ever could.

Of course, it would not be without risk. GWare had to be in dire financial straits if TJ were willing to sell out. Buying a troubled company could bring down the whole new entity. Marty would have to make certain GWare's debt could be assumed without weakening the balance sheet. On the other hand, Marty figured he could get GWare at a bargain price, relative to its strategic value. But he'd let the financial guys figure all that out...what tantalized him was access to GWare's product line and distribution channels, not to mention the benefit of sheer size.

Marty called his CFO from the limo. He told him what was going on and to expect an e-mail or call from someone at GWare. He told him to keep this strictly confidential. Then Marty called Erin. He was fortunate enough to catch her in her office.

"Are you sitting down?" he asked when she answered the phone.

"What's up?" she said, her curiosity piqued.

"Erin, have I ever said to you, 'This is off the record'?

"No, I don't think you ever have."

"Well, this is off the record, and I'm serious," Marty said with a smile in his voice.

"OK, scout's honor. Now what have you got, honey?"

"What do you think of Incandescent acquiring GWare?"

"Jesus Christ," Erin murmured.

"He doesn't come with the deal," Marty dead-panned.

"My God," Erin said with a laugh, "are you serious?"

"About Jesus?"

"No, you jerk, you know what I mean."

"I just left TJ Gatwick's office. I'm totally serious." Marty paused and then asked without humor, "Erin, from a professional perspective, what do you think?"

"Well," Erin said thoughtfully, "you'd have to delve into their financials carefully. They're hurting pretty badly from what I hear. But as far as the fit, I can see it. In fact, there isn't much conflict between the two companies, and a lot of compatibilities."

"That's what TJ said. He said something else you won't believe."

"Which is?"

"He wants out."

Marty could hear Erin take a breath. "That's incredible."

"Yeah, I thought so too. I proposed to keep him on, let him continue to run GWare as a subsidiary."

"That was big of you."

"I really meant it. He knows the company better than anyone. But he turned it down flat. Says he's ready to hang it up."

"Do you trust him?"

"Probably never will completely trust him. But he's not playing any games. I think he's ready to sell, really wants to get out."

"So what's the next step?"

"We're gonna check out each other's financials, look everything over. He needs to move fast, Erin. They can't hold on much longer."

"Maybe you'll get GWare at a fire sale price, huh?"

Marty laughed. "That's for the lawyers to work out. Right now I'm just trying to picture what this new entity might look and feel like. Whether I want the headaches or not."

"You've already got the headaches now," Erin answered. "This'll just be an order of magnitude larger. You're just trading headaches for migraines, that's all."

Marty laughed. "You honestly think this could work?"

"I know it could," Erin answered with conviction. "It could work because you'd make it work."

"You're sweet," Marty said.

"It's true. You're one hell of a businessman, whether you know it or not," she said, then added in a husky voice, "one hell of a man, too."

"Don't start talking sexy to me. I'm in a limo and can't do anything about it."

"Limo, hmmm? Remind me we have to try that some time."

He laughed. "Listen, I'm almost at the airport. You gonna make it home for dinner tonight?"

"Wouldn't miss it," Erin answered with a purr.

They had finished dinner and were soaking in Erin's Jacuzzi together. Erin had lit a few candles and put on some soft music to set the mood.

"It's still hard to believe," Erin said, picking up where their dinner conversation left off, "that TJ will really sell out to you. After all that's happened, I would've expected him to want to retain at least partial control."

"I'm thinking he just can't deal with the difference between what GWare once was and what it is now. It's tough for a founder to see his company hit the rocks," Marty said, moving the bubbles around with his feet. He and Erin were facing each other in the tub. A stream of pulsing hot water was hitting his back and it felt good. "I'm also thinking, there but for the grace of God go I."

Erin rubbed one of her feet against his inner thigh, moving it slowly up to his groin. He caught it with his right hand and began to gently massage the ball of her foot.

"It is amazing how quickly things can change," Erin said. "Watching the Dot Coms crash around us is scary. The economy has cooled so much that we're even seeing a drop in circ at *The Journal*. Where's it all headed?"

Marty put his leg over Erin's thigh and touched one of her breasts lightly with his toes. "It's headed for a recession, that's where. If anything would make me think twice about acquiring GWare, that would be it. I have to wonder how the combined company would succeed in this environment."

"Yes, but in this business, size makes a difference," Erin said. She reached down into the water and wrapped her hand around Marty's member. "Mmm, size DOES matter," she said with a smile.

Erin sat up and moved Marty's leg off her chest. She raised her knees, and slid her buttocks along the bottom of the tub towards him. He spread his legs and wrapped them around her back. She stroked his hair and then pulled him to her and they embraced for several moments. She kissed him firmly, close-mouthed at first, then opened her mouth to admit his tongue.

"What's this all about?" he said, breaking away from her to take a breath. "Are you all turned on by the fact that I'm about to become the world's second most powerful software mogul?"

"That has absolutely nothing to do with it," Erin said, rising out of the tub and grabbing a towel. Marty got out of the tub as well. Then Erin put a hand down between his legs to gently squeeze his testicles. "I just like the feel of your balls."

"Oh you do, huh?" he said with a smile. Erin wrapped the towel around his shoulders and pulled him close to her. They stood there, still wet, kissing each other in the candlelight. In a few moments, Marty led her by the hand into the adjoining bedroom. "Well let's see how hard a software guy can get," he said.

"That," she said lying down on the bed and pulling him on top of her, "was a terrible line."

CHAPTER 26

In the next month, developments in the potential acquisition of GWare by Incandescent moved at breakneck speed. Both companies' attorneys and accountants worked to review legal documents and financial statements. The attorneys began the laborious task of structuring an acquisition agreement. The boards of GWare and Incandescent bought into the concept and neither had any objections, although Incandescent's board wanted to be assured that GWare's debt load wasn't onerous and that the viability of the company going forward was sound. Of course, the Incandescent board found the potential price attractive. It would essentially give Incandescent a bargain in GWare, substantially below market value. What they really needed to be concerned about was whether or not someone else came in to start a bidding war.

After flying back to Cambridge to meet with his board a few times, Marty returned to Incandescent's Silicon Valley office and stayed there so he could be close at hand for face-to-face meetings with TJ. The two of them met at least weekly to hammer out organizational issues and determine how best to merge the two companies' operations for maximum efficiency. TJ also spent quite a bit of time orienting Marty to GWare's product line and reviewing the company's senior staff.

Marty recognized how much TJ Gatwick was an integral part of GWare. He became concerned about losing the value of TJ's presence. It was incredibly ironic, Marty thought, that the man he once detested was now so important to him.

Marty appealed to TJ to reconsider his decision to leave the merged organization. He told TJ he would be more than willing to accept a dual management role; in fact, the more he thought about it, the more it made sense to run GWare as a separate subsidiary anyway. But TJ resisted Marty's arguments and, in the end, Marty realized getting TJ to stay was futile. For whatever the reasons, TJ wanted out, and his decision was final.

Marty noticed every time he met with TJ that Gatwick looked increasingly pallid and gaunt. What had happened to the man who years ago had leaned towards pudginess, his ruddy complexion always noticeable? Marty wondered if there was anything about TJ's health that had something to do with his desire to be bought out.

Nevertheless, Marty had to respect the fact that TJ did not want to be involved in the new organization, and his plan to run GWare without TJ began to take shape.

Marty began to think about what he wanted out of all of this. The acquisition was coming at a good time for many reasons. Marty had become somewhat tired of leading Incandescent, although he never admitted that to anyone but Erin. He certainly had never let any lack of enthusiasm show to his employees, but he had slowly and methodically distanced himself from the day-to-day operations over time, turning over the primary responsibility for running the company to the president he had brought in several years ago. The president was competent, loyal, and operationally skilled. He didn't have much of a personality, but that's where Marty complemented him well.

On the technology side, Marty had also backed away from the in-depth involvement he had had previously, although he stayed close to product development. Henry Chu had proven himself beyond a shadow of doubt in Marty's eyes after a stint as a consultant to Incandescent. As a result, Marty offered Henry a full-time position once again. Henry was so anxious to regain Marty's trust that he became more dedicated and valuable than ever.

Now, with the GWare acquisition, Marty saw a new opportunity emerging for himself. He played it out in his mind. With Incandescent's president continuing to run the company, Marty could appoint Henry Chief Technology Officer of Incandescent. In so doing, he would essentially replace himself. That left him with a new challenge, one which now excited and invigorated him as he considered it: running GWare.

Marty had become familiar with GWare's anti-virus technology over the years since the New Year's Eve '99 disaster. He was intrigued by both the technology and the way it was being delivered via the Internet. Moreover, Marty had grown increasingly interested in the fight against cyber-terrorism.

As head of GWare, Marty would be in a position to directly contribute to the war against criminals like Doomsday, who had yet to be stopped. Doomsday had stayed active since the '99 attack, but his subsequent attacks had been far less damaging. Everyone was waiting for another big strike, and Marty wondered if and when that might come. He felt he would be in a good position at the helm of GWare to help thwart it.

Marty felt running GWare would breathe new life into him. He wasn't focused on the money or even the power he'd gain from the GWare acquisition, it was the sheer exhilaration of this new challenge that meant more to Marty than anything. Of course, Marty wasn't naïve; he knew that he couldn't just slide into managing GWare without any complications. He would be under significant pressure to turn the company around quickly, and there would be the complexity of merging GWare and Incandescent operations together. But that was part of the excitement. Marty enjoyed the thrill of building something, and now he had the opportunity to build something new and different from anything he had done previously.

An added bonus to taking over GWare for Marty was, of course, the fact that he could now re-locate to California. That would be a dream come true for him: he would finally be able to spend more time with Erin. It would be so much easier on their relationship for him to be 500 miles away from San Francisco instead of 3,000.

He thought it would be best to maintain GWare's headquarters in San Diego. It was a fabulous facility, and relocation would probably mean losing valuable employees. Since he planned to run GWare as a subsidiary, it didn't need to be physically merged into Incandescent's other West Coast location. It would be easy enough to communicate over their private network to get things done and it was a short plane ride from San Diego to San Francisco when visits were necessary.

With GWare in San Diego, Marty could get a place on the ocean in La Jolla. He already had enough money to buy whatever he wanted and still maintain his residence in Boston. With a La Jolla residence, he and Erin could spend some of their weekends in San Diego and some in San Francisco. And with Incandescent's Silicon Valley location, Marty still had reason to go to San Francisco during the week as well. This would be a win-win for him.

Maybe this new living situation would even precipitate a more serious discussion about marriage. Marty had brought up the idea of getting married to Erin several times over the past few years. He was absolutely convinced he wanted to spend the rest of his life with Erin. He loved her deeply.

Yet each time he had broached the subject, Erin said she was happy with their relationship just the way it was. When he pressed her, she admitted to the reason for her hesitation. Erin had almost married once before, just prior to meeting Marty. She thought she was very much in love with the guy, a successful attorney, but it turned out he was two-timing her. She was devastated by the experience.

She told Marty that, although she loved him dearly, she was afraid of being hurt again. She felt that their long-distance relationship was the best it could be, but because they still lived apart for half the year due to Marty's responsibilities in Cambridge, she simply couldn't accept the idea of a commitment like marriage. She needed to be with Marty all the time for a marriage to have any hope of succeeding, she said. She told Marty she completely believed that he was faithful to her. That wasn't the issue, she said; it was more a matter of her need to feel that their togetherness was complete.

Erin had said the physical distance became an emotional distance for her. While she could handle it under their current "part-time" living situation, she was not sure how it would affect them if they were married. She was afraid it could strain a marriage to its breaking point.

A move to the West Coast could be the very thing they needed to solve the problem, Marty thought. At the very least, Marty would be seeing her every weekend, and possibly during the week when he visited the Silicon Valley office. Sure, he'd have to go back to Cambridge headquarters periodically, but that would be an occasional business trip instead of a regular part of his life.

Maybe he could convince Erin to move to La Jolla with him, Marty thought. As a journalist with a national beat, she really didn't need to stay in San Francisco. She could easily write her columns from La Jolla and check in for meetings at the San Francisco office as required. Marty knew Erin loved Frisco and had family there, but wouldn't the beauty and tranquility of La Jolla be a compelling draw to her…especially if they could be together all the time?

Marty was flush with anticipation. Here he was, on the verge of breathing new life into his own career by taking on this brand new, exciting challenge. And at the same time he would have the opportunity to live closer to Erin and see her frequently, maybe to even have her live with him in La Jolla. How lucky I am, he thought, for things to work out this way.

Reports of the impending deal between Incandescent and GWare began to appear in the media after Erin herself broke the story. "Consider it a gift," Marty had said with a shit-eating grin when he told Erin she could be the first to write about it.

Marty had also told her about his plan to run GWare and move to La Jolla. She was thrilled with the news, throwing her arms around his neck and smothering him with kisses. Marty asked her if she'd like to help him pick out a place to live and she enthusiastically agreed. He told her they would of course have to wait until the deal was finalized before they contacted a real estate agent.

On the other side of the country, however, the announcement of the Incandescent/GWare merger was met with a much different reaction from one individual in particular...

> *Isn't this perfect...the profits aren't big enough for these two alone, so they figure they'll join together and become more powerful and more profitable at our fucking expense. Don't they see the Internet boom is melting and all those bastards who tried to make a fortune with their Dot Coms by appropriating the people's network are now getting their payback? Those venture capitalist assholes are losing their shirts and they'll burn in hell. Incandescent and GWare together, huh...well I'll show them what I think of the idea, that's for damn sure.*

Doomsday felt the bile rising in his throat. He recalled with great satisfaction the light-headed feeling of ultimate superiority he had after his massive attack on New Year's Eve 1999. It had wreaked such havoc that it took almost a year for the country's computing infrastructure to recover completely. Doomsday had succeeded beyond even his wildest dreams. As a testament to his victory, he had covered one entire wall in his dank apartment with the front pages from newspapers reporting on the devastation.

But the attack had brought with it a new barrage of activity from law enforcement agencies. It had led to an intense manhunt by the FBI for Doomsday and his cohorts. The government had raised the stakes and was now offering a $10 million reward for information leading to his arrest.

As a result, Doomsday had submerged even further underground. He had stopped all communication with Erin and the outside world. He was now resorting to much more covert means of communicating with the members of his own network. Through an intricate combination of encryption, re-directs, and hidden messages on Web pages, Doomsday was able to maintain contact with his primary operatives. But launching and disseminating viruses had become much more difficult since the computer industry and the federal government had gone on high alert. In fact, GWare and Incandescent had become increasingly effective in guarding against virus attacks. Their business agreement had worked to Doomsday's disadvantage, of course, and now, with their plans to merge, there was no telling the impact it might have on virus detection and prevention.

Doomsday thought about the merger with increasing hostility. There was an underlying reason he was outraged by their intentions. The combination could in fact be a direct threat to his own illicit activities. Doomsday was now involved in far more than computer viruses alone. His meager income as a freelance programmer hadn't been nearly enough to support his development efforts and his network's ongoing operation, so Doomsday had become a skilled cyber-launderer.

Doomsday had put his considerable programming talents to work in another way, opening dozens of accounts at Internet banks and transferring money anonymously. In addition, he was finding novel ways to steal money electronically and then add it to numerous debit card accounts. Then he would insert the cards into his PC-based card reader so funds could be transferred to dummy Web-based businesses he had set up. Doomsday had mastered the art of money laundering in the Internet Age, creating a complex hidden web of activity that was paying him big dividends.

All of his illegal activity was completely under the radar screen of government authorities. What Doomsday was doing was quite invisible to traditional means of detection. There were no receipts, no records of transactions that could be traced, no physical banks that were involved. Doomsday conducted everything electronically and anonymously, and he was stockpiling a tidy sum of money as a result. He would then move the necessary funds around to keep his network in business.

In some respects, Doomsday's occasional virus attacks were nothing more than a cover-up for his growing interest at accumulating money illegally via the Internet for himself. It was the ultimate irony: Robin Hood was using the very Internet he wanted to protect from the profit-takers to take profits of his own.

But Doomsday still regarded the software companies as his mortal enemy, and now he had more proof of their willful desecration of the people's Internet. He felt newly invigorated by his anger. Once more, the industry he detested was consolidating. It was a brand new opportunity, he thought, to go after Incandescent and GWare as one. He had fatally wounded TJ Gatwick a long time ago, and now Gatwick was leaving the business he built. It was time for Doomsday to focus solely on a new target: Marty Gladstone.

Gladstone would now be almost as powerful as Bill Gates. He would be in control of a company second only to Microsoft in size and profits. That would certainly be worthy of Doomsday's full attention. Besides, he wanted to show Gladstone and the world that he was still quite capable of executing virus attacks at will. He was anxious to prove he could overcome even the most advanced anti-virus technologies that he knew Gladstone would be developing.

Doomsday looked forward to the battle with anticipation. And Doomsday delighted in the fact that he'd also be hurting that bitch, Erin, whom he knew was Marty's girlfriend. She could have made a difference, but she had sold out a long time ago, Doomsday thought. She was no better than the scum who ran the software industry.

Doomsday decided on a strategy: he would watch and wait patiently as Gladstone began to stitch together the two companies. He knew that Gladstone would be pre-occupied with making the new organization work, and that would be the time the company would be most vulnerable and unsuspecting. That was when Doomsday and his cohorts would strike quickly and violently, much as a venomous snake would do. Doomsday would find a way to bring Gladstone down. Doomsday thought to himself, *My days of glory are far from over.*

CHAPTER 27

The boards and shareholders of both companies approved the acquisition of GWare by Incandescent without further ado. There was a rumor that Microsoft would try to top Incandescent's bid for GWare, but it was unfounded. Microsoft had its own problems—the corporation was busy enough defending itself against the federal government's anti-trust law suit.

The Incandescent/GWare deal didn't meet with any resistance from the government since the two companies' product lines were in very different areas. While eighty percent of Incandescent's income came from UNITE, GWare was primarily an anti-virus software company, relying on its flagship product, GWare Guardian, for the bulk of its revenue.

Once the final papers were signed, Marty shook hands with TJ Gatwick and watched the man leave behind what he had worked so hard to build. But even as he departed, Marty noticed that there was a certain peacefulness in TJ's demeanor. Marty decided the first thing he'd do is address the staff of GWare.

GWare's internal corporate communications group hastily arranged to broadcast Marty's talk via the company's private satellite TV network. The address was simulcast via the Internet to all Incandescent locations worldwide. Marty gave the address on the very same stage that, so many years ago, was the platform for the nefarious introduction of GWare ONE.

The auditorium was filled to capacity with GWare employees, anxious to get a look at the man who had bought out TJ Gatwick.

Marty decided not to use the podium. He wanted to seem approachable and informal. He used a hand held microphone instead, walking to the edge of the stage and looking out at the crowded hall. The faces looked back with nervous anticipation.

"Good afternoon, everyone. I'm Marty Gladstone, and I guess I'm the new boss around here."

There was scattered laughter throughout the auditorium.

"I want to welcome you to the new GWare. It's a GWare that will be stronger and better than ever. And it's a GWare that will, with your help, continue to grow, to thrive, and to be successful. You are all important and I hope you will want to remain here and share in the company's future.

"I have the utmost respect for this company and for all of you, its employees. Incandescent has of course had a business relationship with GWare, even before this most recent development, and I've personally come to know what a wonderful company this is. We may have acquired GWare, but I promise you we do not want to change the way you work or what you have achieved. That's why we will continue to operate GWare as a separate subsidiary.

"GWare will maintain its distinct identity and its own product line. And just to put any rumors aside, GWare's headquarters will remain right here, in San Diego."

Applause broke out.

"And it will be an honor for me to run GWare. I'm truly looking forward to the challenge. I only hope I can do as good a job at growing and leading this company as its founder, TJ Gatwick, has done.

"As a long-time Boston resident, I can honestly tell you that one of the best things about this acquisition is that I'll be moving to San

Diego. Although I can't say that the traffic here is much better than what's going on in Boston with the Big Dig."

Marty's remark was met with laughter.

"There will be a lot more detail coming in the next several days and weeks. For now, it's business as usual. I hope to be able to meet many of you personally, and I want to encourage all of you to communicate with me and tell me your thoughts on how I can make this a better company for all of our employees, our customers, and our shareholders. Thank you."

Marty got a round of sincere applause as he stepped off the stage. His main objective was to let employees know the kind of person he was, and to make sure the transition of power was a smooth one. He was confident he had accomplished that goal.

An attractive woman approached Marty and put out her hand. "Marty, I wanted to tell you I appreciated what you said," the woman began. "I'm Jill Strathmore."

Jesus, Marty thought, hiding his surprise, he knew that name. She was the woman Henry had mentioned to him long ago…the one who told Henry all about GWare in the first place.

"Pleasure to meet you," Marty said pleasantly, returning her handshake. "How long have you been with GWare, Jill?"

Jill laughed, "Seems like forever. Going on ten years. I've absolutely loved the work and the people," she said. Then she gave Marty a knowing look and added, "But truthfully, I can't say I'm going to miss TJ's tirades."

Now it was Marty's turn to laugh. "Yeah, I guess they were his trademark. Well I can tell you that's one thing that'll be different around here. I'm not the tirade type."

"I'm happy to hear that. The change will be refreshing. And I'm happy to have you here. I look forward to working with you."

"Come see me anytime, Jill. I'm sure your perspective on GWare after ten years will be valuable."

Jill smiled and turned to leave.

How quickly allegiances change in business, Marty thought. Enemies can become friends in the blink of an eye. It would be remarkable for Henry Chu to know that the first employee to welcome Marty to GWare was Jill Strathmore.

Marty went up to the fifth floor into TJ's office, which would now be his. He walked around it for a while, looking at the furniture and gazing out the window at the pristine GWare campus. It was a very strange feeling, knowing he would be living here, working here, running this company.

He went over to the phone and dialed Erin's number.

"Erin Keliher."

"So how does a quiet evening with the new head of GWare sound?" he asked.

"Let me think about that for a second or two."

"I think I'm gonna like this place. I just addressed the employees and I think they all took it in stride."

"That's the first big step."

"Yeah, now I'm ready to take the next big one. How'd you like to look at houses in La Jolla this weekend?"

"Love to," Erin said excitedly. "What have you got in mind?"

"Oh, I dunno, something very Californian, I guess. As long as it's overlooking the ocean, I won't be particular."

"Well," Erin said, "you might be a lot more particular when you see the asking prices around there. It's about as bad as Frisco."

"You forget, I'm from Boston, home of the million dollar condos."

Erin laughed. "I don't think I've ever heard you so happy, Marty. I'm happy for you…and happy we're going to be together."

"That, Marty said with excitement, "is the best part."

By the time the weekend came, Marty and Erin had already done some searching on the Internet for potential properties in La Jolla. Marty was unconcerned about price. It's true that his wealth had increased more than ten-fold from the GWare deal, but he wasn't flaunting it; rather, his focus was entirely on what he and Erin thought would make them happiest.

There were some basics that they both agreed upon. They wanted a place that overlooked the ocean, of course, that was secluded yet fairly close to the shops and restaurants in town so they could walk there. They knew they wanted an open floor plan with large expanses of glass and plenty of room for outdoor living. They each needed their own offices, and Marty liked the idea of a separate den or library with lots of room for books.

They flew to San Diego and were picked up at the airport by a real estate agent they had arranged to meet. They agreed to spend both Saturday and Sunday looking at properties with the agent. Marty was heartened that Erin wanted to be so involved in finding an appropriate place for them to live.

By Sunday afternoon, they had fallen in love with and made an offer on a $9 million modern home with lots of interesting angles and glass that sat on oceanfront bluffs overlooking the coastal preserve. It was within walking distance of the village yet at the end of a one-lane road. A footpath led to the edge of the bluffs and the views from all sides of the house were breathtaking.

The house was nothing short of paradise, and Marty and Erin talked about it excitedly on the flight back to San Francisco. Marty had virtually been living in San Francisco while the negotiations between Incandescent and GWare were taking place, making the short flight to San Diego on a frequent basis. Now that he would be working at GWare, he would have to fly there daily. He hoped their offer would be accepted and they could close on the La Jolla property quickly.

It was early evening when they returned to Erin's condo. They relaxed for a while before dinner, Marty reading the Sunday paper, and Erin puttering around. Just as they began to prepare dinner together, the phone rang.

Erin answered it and handed the phone to Marty. "It's the real estate agent."

Marty took it, listened for a moment, said "That's great," and hung up.

He went over and hugged Erin, whispering, "We got it" in her ear. They kissed and then embraced, and continued their dinner preparations as they talked.

"I can't believe it," Erin said. "I can't believe it's going to be ours."

"Yes, ours," Marty said. "Erin, I'd like to ask you to consider something. I'd love it if you would consider moving to La Jolla and living with me." He paused and took her hand. "Actually, what I'd really like for you to consider is marrying me."

Erin smiled and tears began to form in her eyes. "Are you officially proposing?"

Marty smiled and kissed the back of her hand. "I guess I am. Although I must admit, I don't have a ring handy. I've been just a little busy."

Erin returned his smile. "That's okay," she said. "Marty, I want to be with you more than anything in the world. And yes, I would consider leaving San Francisco to be with you in La Jolla…and to be your wife."

She took out a tissue to wipe away a tear.

"But there's something I have to take care of before I can," she said nervously, sniffling and blowing her nose. She tried to compose herself before she went on.

"I…I have to tell you something. It's hard, but I want you to know."

Marty didn't know what was coming. She took a deep breath, wiped another tear from her face.

"On Friday," Erin said, "I went for a routine mammogram. They…they found something."

Marty squeezed her hand tightly.

"It's some sort of a mass. It isn't necessarily cancerous. But I need to see a surgeon about it."

"Oh God," Marty said, shaken. "When's the appointment?"

"I was lucky enough to get one this Wednesday. It's just a consultation, of course. The radiologist at the mammography center told me what to expect. After they did the first mammogram, they took another one. That's when I got nervous...they never did that before.

"The radiologist spoke to me. He said he saw a small, contained mass that looked suspicious. He felt fairly confident that it was nothing to be too concerned about. He said about eighty percent of the time these things aren't malignant. But he also said they just couldn't be sure until I had it checked."

Marty felt a lump form in his throat. "Erin, I'd...I'd like to go with you to the doctor if you don't mind."

Erin nodded. "I'd like that."

"It'll be okay," Marty said, his voice trembling, "I'll be here for you, no matter what."

Erin stroked his face gently and kissed him softly on the lips.

"I know. I love you, Marty." She leaned her head on his shoulder. "But I'm scared," she whispered.

He stroked her hair and held her to him.

"Maybe...maybe I should wait on the house..." he said.

"No," Erin replied. "You go ahead with it. It'll give us something to look forward to, and maybe keep your mind off of this. You know, you have a lot to do now. You've got to get GWare back on track, keep Incandescent going strong. I don't want you to worry about this, Marty."

"Listen," he said, "nothing is more important to me than your well-being. I want to help you through this, and I will."

She smiled with sadness. "My Marty," she said, "always trying to control fate."

On Monday morning, Marty went to the Silicon Valley office of Incandescent. He decided to spend the next few days there, so he could be near Erin, and then accompany her to the doctor on Wednesday. He felt as if he were in a daze on Monday and Tuesday. He found it difficult to concentrate on anything. Each night that he came home to Erin, they held each other for long periods of time. Once, during the night on Tuesday, he was awakened by Erin's soft crying. He turned and held her to him, stroking her hair, kissing her forehead.

On Wednesday, Erin went with Marty to a surgeon referred to her by her general physician. They sat together in the small waiting room at the surgeon's office. There were several other patients there, all women. Marty wondered how many of them had the same condition. He had read all he could about breast cancer on the Internet and he was guardedly optimistic, knowing that the statistics were in their favor. But he also had read about the treatments for breast cancer if a malignancy was found. The radical mastectomy and chemotherapy were among the most frightening options. And the statistic about death from breast cancer was staggering. He forced these thoughts from his mind, taking Erin's hand in his.

Erin's name was called. Marty looked at her questioningly, asking with his eyes if he should come in with her. She hesitated, but then shook her head slightly, kissed him, and said, "I'll be alright. I want to go in alone." He let her go and he remained in the waiting room.

Erin was nervous. She had enjoyed excellent health and had rarely been to see a doctor other than her general physician and gynecologist. She was greeted by the surgeon's nurse, a woman probably in her late fifties whose take-charge manner made Erin feel immediately comfortable. She had quite the personality, chatting away while she took Erin's medical history.

Erin went into the examining room and sat for ten minutes before the doctor came in, introducing herself with a warm smile. Erin had asked her physician, a woman, for a referral to another woman surgeon. She couldn't imagine that a man could relate to what she was going through.

The doctor talked to Erin about the mass that was detected during the mammography. She said it could very well be benign, and she repeated the statistic that she had heard from the radiologist—that eighty percent of the time the mass was, in fact, non-cancerous. The only way they could be sure, however, was to do a biopsy. She explained to Erin that the mass was located on the side of her left breast, and given its location and type, the doctor wanted to do a procedure known as a stereotactic biopsy.

This procedure, said the doctor, was simple and virtually painless and it could be done in day surgery. It was minimally invasive, involving the use of a needle that was guided by stereo images—pictures of the breast taken from different angles—to determine the exact location of the abnormal tissue. Erin would lie on her stomach on a special table with her breast extended through an opening. The table would be raised and the biopsy would be done from below it. She would be given a local anesthetic and the surgeon would use a needle, aided by pictures to confirm the precise needle placement. Multiple tissue samples would be taken through the needle. The doctor said the entire procedure would last less than thirty minutes.

The doctor's clinical, casual description eased Erin's mind. Apparently the doctor had done the procedure hundreds of times and more often than not it revealed a benign condition.

"What happens after the biopsy?" Erin asked.

"We'll examine the extracted tissue," the doctor answered, "and I'll discuss it with you. It could be benign or it could be cancerous. It could also be pre-cancerous, which basically means it isn't dangerous yet but could be if it was left unchecked. We'll discuss the options at that time...there's really no need to do so until we know exactly what type of mass this is. I'll have the nurse arrange an appointment for the biopsy."

Erin thanked the doctor. The nurse came in a few moments after the doctor left and led Erin to a small office. She was the picture of efficiency. She made the appointment for the biopsy and the follow-up visit, gave Erin a few additional tips about the biopsy, joked a bit with Erin about getting "a needle in the boob," and sent Erin on her way.

Erin knew she still had reason to be concerned, but both the doctor and the nurse had at least calmed her fears. She told Marty everything the doctor said and he seemed somewhat relieved as well. Nevertheless, they both knew that the worst part of this was waiting for the biopsy, which was scheduled for next week, and then waiting to find out the results of the biopsy the following week. It was as if they had no control over what was to be. They both understood that, based on what the biopsy revealed, their lives could change in an instant.

CHAPTER 28

Marty threw himself into his work that next week in an effort to drive any negative thoughts from his mind. The most difficult time for him was the middle of the night. He could barely sleep. He would often awaken to make sure Erin was still lying next to him. He would sometimes dream that she was gone and wake up with a start, reaching out and being relieved to find her by his side.

While Marty was exhausted during the day because of his sleepless nights, he had much to accomplish. The purchase of the house in La Jolla was moving along well. The real estate agent turned out to be competent and attentive. She was handling the house inspection and following up on financing for Marty. It relieved Marty of a lot of the time-consuming details and he was thankful for it.

Marty was quickly acclimating himself to GWare. He spent the majority of his time talking with senior staff, reviewing the company's organization, and studying the product strategy. One thing he quickly learned was just how much TJ Gatwick was a part of the fabric and personality of the company. Marty got the distinct impression there was an overwhelming sense of relief on the part of most of the employees that Gatwick was gone. Some of the senior staff had shared with Marty the nature of Gatwick's outbursts and his almost abusive management style. But it was this very tension between

Gatwick and his employees that had created a unique environment, a group of people that was driven to succeed at all costs.

Marty realized that one of his biggest challenges would be to maintain that drive, despite the fact that his own management style was not confrontational. How would he keep these people motivated, he wondered, with positive instead of negative reinforcement? How would they respond to management that was based more on tenderness than toughness? Marty knew these wouldn't be easy questions to answer.

Also on his mind was the urgent need to overhaul GWare Guardian. As a subscription service, the product had achieved phenomenal success in terms of raw numbers. But it was the high renewal rate that was keeping the service alive. Renewal was almost automatic because of the great and continuing concern over viruses. As a result, the renewal cost of the subscriber base was minimal to GWare. It was the acquisition cost of new subscribers, coupled with the expense of ongoing research and development, that was killing GWare.

Marty had to find a way to reverse the pattern. The company could not keep investing so heavily in new customer acquisition, because it was costing them over two dollars for every new subscription dollar. When you added in the cost per subscriber of continuously adding new anti-virus programs, it ended up costing more than four dollars for a new subscriber's dollar. The fact that a large majority of subscribers renewed their contracts for the second and subsequent years at a far lower cost was the only saving grace.

Marty knew it wasn't just a matter of raising prices. He thought GWare Guardian needed to be re-structured into more tiers, so the company could charge large users more money for the service. He also saw the need for premium services that could offset some of the company's anti-virus research costs. Of course, anything he implemented had to be done in such a way as to not alienate the existing subscribers.

As he was pondering this, his assistant buzzed him and told him Jill Strathmore was asking if she could have a few moments. She didn't have an appointment but said it was important. Marty told his assistant to let Jill come in.

After Jill had introduced herself to him, Marty became curious. He looked up her personnel file and learned that she was an employee who had steadily gone up the ranks at GWare. There were numerous commendations in her file, one from TJ himself. Apparently, Jill had become one of the company's most valued developers. It was a particularly fine accomplishment for a woman, since the field was dominated by men.

Jill came into Marty's office. He looked up and couldn't help but admire her appearance. She was wearing a tight melon-colored top that accentuated her breasts. In fact, the nipples were decidedly prominent, protruding through her bra and the thin fabric atop it. Her top was set off by a pale green skirt cut well above her knees. Her shapely legs were bare and she was wearing sandals. A matching scarf the color of the skirt was loosely tied around her neck, completing the outfit. Very Californian, Marty thought.

Marty hadn't so much as thought about another woman since he fell in love with Erin. But he wasn't blind to the allure of an attractive female, and Jill was certainly in that category.

He rose to greet Jill and led her over to the small conference area in his office. Jill sat opposite him. As she crossed her legs, her skirt hiked up to reveal an expanse of tanned thigh. Marty involuntarily looked at the spot where her legs crossed, then quickly up at her eyes. Jill noticed the slight transgression and gave Marty a knowing smile. She remained motionless, doing nothing to pull down her skirt.

"What can I do for you?" Marty said, making a concerted effort to keep his eyes on Jill's face.

Jill leaned forward in her chair slightly so that her chest would be all the more obvious. "I'm hoping it's what I can do for you," she answered.

Marty just looked at her quizzically.

"TJ had asked me to work on a model for streamlining our anti-virus development process," Jill said. "I think we've made a breakthrough."

"The timing couldn't be better, Jill," Marty replied. "One of the biggest challenges we have is how to cut down the cycle. It costs us a lot of money each time we introduce a new virus patch."

"That's exactly the problem TJ wanted me to look into," Jill said. "We've been following a pretty standard process, but it's been decentralized, for the most part. I've finally been able to customize a rapid development software tool and run it in our dev environment. I've tested it with a couple of the programmers to see if they could learn to use it and work more closely together. It's been a struggle, but I think they're beginning to see the value of interactive collaboration. But they're a tough bunch, and they're only just now coming around."

Marty chuckled. "Yeah, I know what you mean. We've got our share of independent code jockeys in Cambridge too."

"Anyway," Jill said, "I've made enough progress with these guys that I think we're ready to implement the process on a wider scale. I just need some support from senior management on this."

"And that's why you're here," Marty said.

Jill nodded. "To be honest, Marty, my manager isn't being very supportive. He doesn't think getting the programmers to collaborate more closely with a centralized tool will work. Thinks we can't teach old dogs new tricks." She paused, then added with a little laugh, "He's kind of an old dog himself."

Marty smiled. "You're not afraid to speak your mind, I'll say that for you."

"After ten years of working at GWare with mostly guys, being blunt is something I've learned. It's about the only way to rise above the testosterone level around here."

Marty laughed. "You report to Ray Davis, right?"

Jill nodded.

"Well let me do this. I won't say anything to Ray about the discussion we've had today. But I'll nose around a little, pay a visit to the development lab, see things for myself. When I'm there, I'll take a look at your new process first-hand. And if it's as good as you say, I can promise you it will be adopted."

"Oh it's good," Jill said, reaching over to lightly touch Marty's hand. The gesture wasn't lost on him. "Otherwise I wouldn't have asked to see you."

Marty stood up and Jill stood as well. "Thanks for coming to me, Jill. I'll follow up on this."

She gave him a radiant smile. "Thanks, Marty. I appreciate you giving this your personal attention." She looked at him with what could only be described as bedroom eyes. "I hope I can always come see you when I have something important to discuss."

"Of course," Marty answered, trying not to read too much into her comment.

Jill smiled again, batted her eyes once or twice, and turned to leave his office. She did have a lovely figure, Marty had to admit, scanning her rear end and her legs as she departed.

Marty had a sudden pang of guilt as Erin popped into his mind. For Christ's sake, he thought, it doesn't mean anything if I admire another woman's body. At least it means I'm a normal male. He had to wonder, though, if Jill was a naturally provocative woman, who used her obvious charms just to make an impression in an all-male environment, or if she was making a concerted effort to win his personal attention and favor with her female allure. It certainly wouldn't be unusual, given his new position of authority, for her to come on to him. But did she think she would need to play that card if he hadn't been receptive to her development breakthrough? Maybe this was the kind of world TJ had created, Marty thought. Or maybe it's what Jill did out of necessity to survive at what may have well been a male chauvinist company.

Whatever it was, Marty was thankful Jill had approached him. If the methodology she had described was a way to reduce the time and increase the efficiency of the development process, he would be all for it. In fact, it could very well be the key to profitability that the company so badly needed. Jill could be of real value to the organization, Marty thought. But he made a mental note to be on guard for any potential future advances from Jill Strathmore.

Marty accompanied Erin to her appointment with the surgeon. The stereotactic biopsy had been performed and it was time to get the results.

Again, they both sat in the small waiting room, but this time they were far more apprehensive than on the first visit. While still optimistic and hopeful, the suspense of the moment was all but unbearable. Marty looked up to see a woman and a man come out of the office area. She had clearly been crying, and she was holding a tissue up to her nose. There was a look of abject fear in the woman's eyes. The man went over to the receptionist to make another appointment. Marty assumed the news they had received was not good.

Erin's name was called and this time, when Marty asked if he could accompany her, she agreed. Erin and Marty were led to an examination room by the nurse. The nurse was her jocular self, but she seemed a bit more pre-occupied today. She said the doctor would be right with them.

In several minutes, the doctor entered. She said hello to Erin and introduced herself to Marty.

"Well, Erin, the results of the biopsy are in and we're fairly certain that the mass is not malignant, so that's the good news."

Both Erin and Marty breathed a sigh of audible relief.

"But the mass is not benign either…it's what is known as a pre-cancerous condition. The medical term is apocrine metaplasia. Basically, that means the mammary cells are somewhat abnormal, and there is the possibility they could become cancerous. The biopsy we did is able to analyze portions of the mass, but it doesn't analyze the entire mass. Because of the nature of the biopsy, we can't be one hundred percent certain that the mass isn't cancerous.

"On the positive side, the area is quite contained. It is a small mass and there doesn't appear to be any spreading at this stage. However, I am still recommending surgery to remove it. I consider this minor surgery—you won't even need to spend the night. But you will be under general anesthesia, so plan on having someone drive you to and from the hospital."

The doctor continued, "Only when I remove it can we be certain it hasn't spread. But I can tell you that I think we caught this in time. I've seen this type of mass many times before and it's more than likely we can take care of it with the surgical procedure."

"Is there a possibility you'll find more of it when you go in?" Erin asked.

"Anything's possible. I can't tell you not to worry at all about this, Erin, but based on my experience, I'm anticipating that everything will come out fine. I'll have the nurse schedule you for the surgery."

The doctor said goodbye and left. Erin looked at Marty and smiled. He squeezed his hand. "It'll be okay," he said hopefully. Erin nodded.

The nurse returned and brought Erin into her small office. She made the appointment for the surgery and gave Erin some literature to read about the surgery and pre-op preparation. "Don't worry," she said, "the worst part of it is the anesthesia. The doctor does hundreds of these surgeries, and more often than not, everything turns out fine."

Everyone reassuring Erin made her more rather than less apprehensive. It was still surgery, she thought, and still too damned close to breast cancer for her to dismiss it as simply a "procedure."

Marty was somewhat apprehensive as well, but he strove to put on an optimistic face to Erin. He saw it as his duty to be positive and supportive, despite any fears he might personally have.

For the next ten days, Erin and Marty went through the motions of daily life and work. Sometimes in the evening they'd discuss the surgery that was approaching, but more often than not, they would avoid the subject. They spent most evenings together, talking, reading, and holding hands. An interesting dynamic had changed in their relationship. They seemed to have formed a stronger, more intimate emotional bond, the kind of bond that occurs when two people live through a defining moment in their lives. Maybe part of it was that Erin knew Marty was now going to be a permanent California resident. Part of it could be the fact that Erin was facing her own mortality…and Marty was pondering just how precious life really was.

The day came for Erin to undergo surgery, and Marty wanted to be by her side. He drove her to the hospital and waited nervously while she underwent the procedure. In a few hours, the doctor came out.

"Everything's fine and she's doing well," the doctor said in a business-like manner. "I excised the mass and some surrounding tissue to make sure there was no possibility it had spread. She'll be sore for a while, but I anticipate a complete recovery. The scar will be noticeable, but nothing major.

"She'll be regaining consciousness shortly. You'll be able to see her soon."

Marty nodded, smiled, and choked back a tear that was welling up inside him. He was so relieved that Erin was all right that he couldn't even say anything to the doctor. It was only now that he began to realize how concerned he really was about the operation. Erin meant so much to him. He knew they had dodged one of life's bullets and he vowed to be thankful for every day they could spend together from now on.

He waited another forty-five minutes until a nurse came and said he could see Erin. The nurse said Erin was still a bit disoriented from the anesthesia, but she was slowly recovering. She told Marty that they wanted to keep Erin for observation for most of the day. As long as the doctor cleared her for release, Marty would be able to pick Erin up in the late afternoon.

Marty went into the recovery room. Erin looked pale and weak but she recognized him and smiled. He come over to the bed, took her hand and leaned down to kiss her forehead.

"Hey lady, nice to see ya."

Erin nodded sleepily.

"You don't have to talk," Marty said, stroking her cheek. "The doctor says everything is fine.

"I just wanted to see you and tell you how much I love you. But I'm going to let you get some rest. I'll call you later, ok?"

Erin nodded and closed her eyes. Marty kissed her forehead again and left.

He had something to buy before returning to work: an engagement ring. Marty decided he would ask Erin to marry him this weekend...and he wouldn't take no for an answer.

CHAPTER 29

Henry Chu marveled at how life had changed for the better. When he had begged Marty for an opportunity to return to Incandescent, he had never suspected the developments that were yet to come.

Henry was Chief Technology Officer of Incandescent…but it was a brand new Incandescent that he had never dreamed would be possible. Now he was not only in charge of the company's own development projects, he had the development operation of the subsidiary division, GWare, reporting into him as well. Henry was thrilled with the responsibility, and he basked in the delicious irony of the situation. It was not all that long ago that he was miserably unhappy at GWare, his life seemingly in a shambles.

Henry knew that it was a giant leap of faith for Marty Gladstone to take him back. But he also knew that Marty was a special kind of person. He had believed in Henry, even after Henry had deserted him, and Marty had given him a second chance. For this Henry would be eternally grateful. He promised himself he would work hard to keep Marty's trust from now on.

Thankfully, Henry's personal life had also been turned around by this remarkable chain of events. Henry had reconciled with Priscilla. They were living together with their son, Joey, now in elementary school, in Cambridge.

What continued to drive Henry Chu in his life, though, was his love of technology. Henry was a builder of a different sort from Marty. He was a true builder of software, an architect of programs that were as special and unique as any in existence.

Henry's latest venture was perhaps his most ambitious yet. He was working on an advance in anti-virus technology that he hoped would revolutionize the industry.

Now that Incandescent and GWare could completely pool their resources and development talent, Henry could see the evolution of the UNITE anti-virus shield into a stand-alone product.

It was an entirely new approach to anti-virus technology. Henry had come up with a novel way to create a kind of artificial intelligence software wrapper—Henry called it a "deflector"—that adhered to an incoming suspicious message or attachment and stopped it from propagating. The deflector could instantly analyze the nature of the virus and isolate it. As a result, it neutralized it from being harmful.

But the deflector was a brand new concept. The development team was just now running it through extensive testing and working out some significant flaws. One of those flaws was that the deflector couldn't yet discriminate between a bad message or attachment and good ones—so it could potentially stop any incoming communication in its tracks, not just a virus or a worm. In its current form, it was a powerful barrier, but one that would virtually shut down all networking activity. That wouldn't be acceptable to mission-critical operations. Henry's deflector needed a lot more refinement before it could be implemented.

Nonetheless, Henry realized that the deflector had enormous potential…the kind of potential that had far-reaching implications in the fight against computer viruses. It was the kind of potential that could fundamentally end the threat of virus attacks forever.

Henry had, of course, shared the news of his breakthrough with Marty. With excitement, Marty had enthusiastically encouraged

Henry. He said he would give him any resources he needed to push ahead with the development process. He also asked that Henry and his team keep any information about the deflector in strict confidence. Marty couldn't afford for any word to leak out about it, both for competitive reasons, and for the fact that he didn't want any hacker, especially Doomsday, to get wind of the new product.

Doomsday had been strangely silent this past year, Marty thought. He wondered if the man had dropped out of existence, as did many hackers. But Marty thought that would be too much to hope for. Marty had the inexplicable feeling that their paths would cross again.

Was it possible that Doomsday, even now, was silently working on and planning another attack? The thought had crossed Marty's mind that the "new" Incandescent, with its GWare subsidiary, would be an even larger target for the likes of Doomsday. And wouldn't he find the company irresistible…a reason for the hacker to emerge from hiding and attempt to disrupt the software industry once again?

Marty recognized there was that distinct possibility, and he desperately wanted to be ready for it. That's why he was so encouraged by Henry's latest project. True, the deflector had a ways to go before it was ready for beta testing. Marty knew that Henry and the team were having difficulty with the last crucial step—"teaching" the product to discern viruses. But if anyone could do it, Marty reasoned, Henry could.

At the same time, Marty had slowly started to turn GWare around. It was as if he were changing the course of a massive ship. Interestingly, it was Jill Strathmore who was one of the big reasons for the turnaround. When she had come to Marty to tell him about her development process breakthrough, Marty had to admit he was somewhat skeptical. But then he did as he had promised Jill. He visited the development lab to check it out for himself.

Marty had to be carefully diplomatic with Ray Davis, Jill's boss. Ray was a GWare "lifer," he had started his career at GWare straight out of college and had never worked anywhere else. He was one of those employees TJ Gatwick had trapped at a tender young age.

But it paid off for both GWare and Ray...the company had gained a naturally talented developer who, over the years, had risen to the occasion and been involved in numerous successful products. Finally, Ray had become a vice president in charge of the entire development effort. The position was more in recognition of what he had achieved, rather than for his management ability. And that was the problem.

The fact was, Ray wasn't much of a manager at all. His real love was developing, not mentoring others or solving personnel problems. As a result, the development group was a loosely run band of renegade developers, not a tightly-knit organization of workers committed to a common goal.

Marty had been aware of this fact through confidential discussions with other senior managers, and it was a problem he was trying to figure out how to address. He hadn't seen it first-hand, but now, by visiting the lab and doing some observing of his own, he had the opportunity to do so.

Jill's assessment of Ray being "an old dog" turned out to be true. After some personal investigation, Marty could see that it was quite possible that Ray was an obstacle in the implementation of Jill's new development process. It was obviously hard for Ray to admit that someone else, especially a woman, could have devised a way to work together that would streamline and improve the development process.

While Marty had to tread lightly because of Ray's longevity with the company and the importance of his position, he knew he had to assure that the development process Jill had brought to his attention was fully implemented. After working on Ray for several months, Marty finally got the man to see the light. That was one of Marty's leadership skills—finding a way to make others accept sometimes harsh realities.

Fortunately, Marty won this time. It wasn't always that way.

The result was that the new development process was indeed fully implemented. Jill had been more than right about it...once the developers were strongly encouraged by Ray Davis and Marty himself to try to make it work, they came around quickly. The process cut the development time in half, and that meant anti-virus patches could be brought to market much faster and at much lower cost than previously. In addition, Marty had started to gradually re-structure the way GWare Guardian was packaged and priced. These two factors alone were having a positive impact on GWare.

Another contributing factor was more difficult for Marty. He had to make the painful decision to authorize some layoffs at both Incandescent and GWare in overlapping functional areas. While the layoffs were anticipated and kept to a minimum, Marty hated to do it. But he realized it was a necessity to help GWare recover.

Marty had confidence that all of these steps would, in fact, lead the GWare subsidiary to profitability within a year.

Marty did have another challenge, however, that he wasn't quite sure how to deal with: the continuing advances of Jill Strathmore.

He had let her know that he was grateful for her coming to him about the development process, and he also wanted to encourage her to continue to be an innovator. Marty believed Jill's intelligence and dedication were valuable to GWare and he wanted to keep her motivated.

Yet Marty was increasingly uncomfortable with what he regarded as an unusual amount of interest in him by Jill. She knew she had won an important victory with the adoption of the development process, and she took this to mean that she could have access to Marty when she needed it. She requested meetings with him often, under the guise of progress reports on the development process. The meetings were, in fact, legitimate business discussions, but Jill was unfailingly dressed in a provocative outfit, and her physical signals to Marty were unabashedly sexual. Sometimes she would make suggestive comments which, although subtle, clearly let him know her intentions. He hadn't the slightest doubt that she was trying to seduce him. Of course, his love for Erin would have caused him to resist any advances from Jill, no matter how obvious they might have been.

Marty did find the attention flattering, he'd be a fool not to, but he had to find a way to extricate himself from what could become a dangerous situation. Marty took his responsibility as an employer very seriously. He viewed his relationship with employees as strictly professional. It was a sacred rule of his not to mix business with pleasure. He rarely had any kind of personal relationship with an Incandescent or GWare employee; in fact, Henry was the only one with whom he had developed a friendship.

He knew there could be trouble brewing if he so much as gave even the slightest encouragement to Jill Strathmore. His meetings with her had to be kept strictly on a business level.

It got even more complicated, however, If Marty confronted Jill about her advances and told her to back off. Then he would be accusing her of taking a personal interest in him, of coming on to him. That could backfire as well. The fact was, either way, Marty could easily find himself to be the target of a claim of sexual harassment. He didn't believe Jill was capable of this; in fact, he felt that her career would be too important to her for her to make any such accusation. But she also had to know that, if she were to do so, she could quite possibly make it look like an employer wielded power over her in return for sexual favors.

Marty had heard of this happening before, and although it seemed unthinkable and almost ludicrous, he realized it could become a real predicament for him. He was in a quandary about it.

Marty hoped it wouldn't come to some sort of showdown with Jill. For now, he decided to keep things on an even keel, hoping that he could maintain a strictly business relationship with Jill. Maybe it would be a good idea, he thought, to start holding meetings with her in the presence of Ray Davis. Then at least he'd have another employee available as a witness.

Marty shook off his mental meanderings about Jill Strathmore. He had to attend to more important issues right now. He wanted to call Henry Chu to discuss his progress on the deflector. He hoped it would soon be ready…before Doomsday or anyone else launched the next virus attack.

CHAPTER 30

Erin awoke suddenly. A wave of relief came over her as she realized that she was just having a nightmare. She remembered bits and pieces of it. She was running, running, running, being chased by some absurd man-woman combination comprised of Doomsday and the surgeon who had operated on her breast. She was running towards Marty but she could never reach him: the closer she got the further away he moved. She shook her head in an attempt to push the frightening image from her mind.

She looked at the clock. It was 4 AM. There was Marty, her husband of two months, sleeping peacefully beside her. She wanted to snuggle with him, to wake him so he would hold her just now, but she didn't have the heart to disturb his sleep.

Things had happened so quickly since the surgery. Marty had asked her to marry him and she didn't hesitate this time. The fleeting nature of life, and her brush with breast cancer, told her she'd be crazy not to. She had loved him from the beginning, so that wasn't the issue. It was all about loss for her. She didn't ever want to lose him and she had put off marriage until she was sure she could be living with him each and every day.

Now, she thought, she had almost lost herself. She recognized that she could just as easily have had breast cancer as just a pre-cancerous mass that had been removed. She shuddered at the thought that a cancer could grow inside of her. How different it would have been had the pendulum swung the other way. It could still, someday. Life was too precious, too short, for her not to enjoy it with the man she loved.

So she had said yes, happily and self-assuredly, and she had agreed to move to La Jolla. Still, she retained her San Francisco condo, and Marty retained his Boston condo, so now they had three residences. They could easily afford it on Marty's income alone. It gave them entirely different venues to enjoy…although it was quite a responsibility to own three properties, one of which was on the other side of the country.

The La Jolla house was, in every respect, a dream come true for her. She had her own office, overlooking the ocean. At first, it took some getting used to. How can I write a column, she thought, gazing out at the sea? But as she became acclimated to her new environment, she loved it more and more. Erin was surrounded by the majesty of nature in all its raw, unspoiled glory. She could work for a while, then stop and take a walk and look out at the cliffs, listen to the birds, smell the foamy water. It was incredibly idyllic. And she loved the fact that this was not hers alone, but the place she and Marty had chosen together.

She was particularly thankful that Marty had a unique ability to balance his work life with being so connected to her. Despite his awesome responsibilities, he'd call her every day to see how she was doing. On occasion, he'd even ask if he could join her for lunch. He would break away from the office, pick something up at a restaurant in town, and bring it home so they could eat together on the deck. She suspected that part of his attention was because of her recent surgery, but she didn't care. She loved the priority she played in his busy life, and the way he treated her. How could I have waited so long to have married him, she thought.

There was nothing they couldn't share, nothing they couldn't talk about. He had been her most intimate friend for a long time, but their bond had strengthened in marriage. There was one thing, however, that she hadn't shared even with him.

It was the fact that, out of the depths of the past, Doomsday had re-surfaced and contacted her again.

Quite without warning, he had sent her an e-mail, and then another, attempting to once again strike up a correspondence with her. She did not answer the first one, but her journalist's curiosity got the better of her and she answered the second communication. His tone was as vitriolic as ever. While he never said it in his e-mails, it was clear to her that he was craving the publicity he had once enjoyed by being associated with Erin. Doomsday had fallen out of the media spotlight as the Dot Com crash and the softening economy had taken over as lead stories. Doomsday's virus attacks had been few and far between. What's more, GWare Guardian in particular had been so effective in deterring them that they had been of far less concern in recent days.

But Doomsday wasn't finished, he told Erin. He was preparing to launch another round of attacks, and he wanted her to know it because he was confident of his ability to succeed. He threatened a repeat performance of the New Year's Eve 1999 debacle...only he said he was preparing a few new surprises. Erin's rational side told her he was bluffing, that he couldn't possibly pull it off, not now, when the government had put so many safeguards in place. How could anything that drastic ever happen again?

Still, Erin's old fear was creeping back. The fact that Doomsday was daring enough to re-contact her suggested she had better take it seriously. This guy wasn't the kind to make idle threats, he had proven that too many times before. In fact, the pattern was the same: Doomsday had said he would launch a preliminary attack first, just to make a statement, and then follow it with the finale.

Jesus, Erin thought, just when you think it's safe to go back into the water...

But this was no laughing matter. Erin had a sense of dread just thinking about the possibility of a renewed Doomsday-style attack. She contacted the FBI immediately. She tried to call the agent she had worked with previously, but he had been transferred. She was routed to another agent. He knew who she was and he was well aware of Doomsday. He got all the details from her and then urged her to not tell anyone about the contact with Doomsday. This time, he said, the FBI didn't want Doomsday to get any publicity at all. It would only fuel Doomsday's ego. That's why he requested that Erin keep it to herself. He said it was a matter of national security.

This presented a double dilemma for Erin. Again she was in a position to break a major story, but this time, she had to keep the information embargoed from her editor. Because of what the FBI agent had said, she hadn't told Marty either. It was a terrible burden keeping the secret from him and she felt a pang of guilt thinking about it. She knew she could trust Marty, but the agent had said to tell no one. She thought about it and reluctantly decided to keep it to herself.

No wonder I'm having nightmares, she thought as she lay there, unable to get back to sleep.

National Infrastructure Protection Center
Alert 01-016
"Code Red Worm"
July 29, 2001
A Very Real and Present Threat to the Internet: July 31 Deadline For Action

Summary: The Code Red Worm and mutations of the worm pose a continued and serious threat to Internet users.

Immediate action is required to combat this threat. Users who have deployed software that is vulnerable to the worm (Microsoft

IIS Versions 4.0 and 5.0) must install, if they have not done so already, a vital security patch.

How Big is The Problem? On July 19, the Code Red worm infected more than 250,000 systems in just 9 hours. The worm scans the Internet, identifies vulnerable systems, and infects these systems by installing itself. Each newly installed worm joins all the others causing the rate of scanning to grow rapidly. This uncontrolled growth in scanning directly decreases the speed of the Internet and can cause sporadic but widespread outages among all types of systems. Code Red is likely to start spreading again on July 31, 2001 8:00 pm EDT and has mutated so that it may be even more dangerous. This spread has the potential to disrupt business and personal use of the Internet for applications such as electronic commerce, e-mail and entertainment.

The Code Red Worm was the first real test of Jill Strathmore's new development process at GWare. No sooner had the Code Red Worm been introduced than GWare Guardian had a virus patch available to its subscribers. The speed with which GWare was able to create and distribute the patch was nothing short of remarkable. The new process worked, not only proving the value of the GWare Guardian service, but saving untold thousands of computer users the agony of being sabotaged by the Code Red Worm.

The achievement did not go unnoticed by Marty Gladstone. He acknowledged Jill's breakthrough in a congratulatory e-mail to the entire company, also announcing her promotion to Director of Software Development. While Jill would still report to Ray Davis, the Vice President of Product Development, the promotion was significant recognition of her achievement. Jill was also confident she would continue to have a direct line to Marty when she needed it.

Thwarting the Code Red Worm was one more in a series of recent successes for GWare Guardian. Still, Marty wrestled with his senior managers over continuing to improve the profitability of the service. They were close to deciding on a sweeping restructure of both the service offerings and the pricing strategy, but they were hesitant to implement it in the midst of what was clearly becoming an economic recession. The current plan called for laying the groundwork in the Fall for the roll-out of a revamped GWare Guardian service in early 2002. Marty wondered if he would be in a position by then to wrap Henry Chu's deflector technology into the re-introduction of the service.

Not long after the news of GWare Guardian's success against Code Red, Marty received a call from Senator Ted Chambers.

"Hello Senator, it's been a long time."

"Yes, too long, Marty, too long," answered Chambers, sounding very much like he was delivering a speech on the Senate floor.

"What can I do for you, Senator?"

"Marty," the Senator began, "as you probably know, I'm still running the Senate Technology Council. Of course, the '99 disaster made us take a whole new look at everything. As you know, soon afterwards, the government took steps to shore up the national computing infrastructure. You and your predecessor have done a lot in the way of anti-virus technology, and we're very thankful for that."

"We can't underestimate the threat of virus attacks, Senator," Marty replied.

"That's right. Now I've just learned of the speed with which GWare was able to get to market with a patch for that Code Red Worm and, damn it, that impressed me. I know you've recently taken over at the helm there, and frankly I don't know if that has anything to do with it. But it seemed to me this was a good time to renew our acquaintance." The senator paused. "And frankly, Marty, I need your help."

"How can I help, Senator?"

"Well, off the record, Marty, the FBI believes this Code Red thing is just a warning shot across the bow, so to speak. They've gotten some inside information that suggests another major attack is imminent. You may remember that the same pattern developed before the

New Year's Eve disaster. First it was a warning, then all hell broke loose." He paused for a moment to emphasis the gravity of the situation. "Marty, it seems the FBI thinks we're in for an attack on that same grand scale."

"Good God," Marty answered. "Do they have any idea when it could occur?"

Ted Chambers sighed. "Christ, it could be September, it could be New Year's Eve again, who the hell knows. The point is, they're telling us that something's coming, and it's something big.

"Now I don't know if your technical gurus over there can help…but Marty, we've got to find a way to prevent against anything like the New Year's Eve debacle from ever happening again. With the economy in trouble, it could have a disastrous effect, even more so than in '99."

"I don't have to tell you, Senator, that half the battle is early detection," Marty said. "The more the FBI can find out about how the attack will occur and when it will take place, the more prepared we can be. More importantly, if we could just get a tip on the type of virus strain we might have to deal with, we could be in a position to repel the attack more rapidly. I've got a pretty advanced R&D lab here, and we've already developed our own virus variants.

"I'll tell you, Senator," Marty continued, "it's pretty frightening to see the kinds of viruses that can be created now. I've seen some things in the lab environment that scare the hell out of me. Code Red is a good example, and that doesn't even represent the worst of it. It's essential that we know the virus type, because once we do, we've got a process that we can use to bring antidotes to market faster than anyone else."

"That's what I wanted to hear, Marty. Now as for early detection, we've got the whole goddamned intelligence community working on this. The FBI is putting a lot of pressure on informants and maybe they'll shake something loose. They're following up on every lead and looking under every rock. In the mean time, I'd like to stay in close touch with you. Of course, you'll have to keep our conversations in strict confidence. We don't want anyone to know about this, Marty. It could create a major panic if they do."

"You'll have my complete cooperation, Senator, you can count on that," Marty said. "I may be in the anti-virus business, but the last thing I want to see is a repeat performance of the New Year's Eve disaster."

"I appreciate it Marty. You'll hear from me soon."

"Oh, Senator, one more thing."

"Yes?"

"Just asking…does the FBI think our old friend Doomsday is behind this?"

The Senator snorted. "Yeah, the FBI is certain of it. No question about it, they think that son of a bitch is still the kingpin, head of the whole dirty operation. He's been responsible for launching most every virus attack, far as they can tell. They figure if they can bring him down, they can pretty much stop the majority of them dead in they're tracks." Then Chambers added with resolve, "Marty, I can promise you that the FBI is working around the clock trying to get Doomsday. And this time, they'd better catch his ass before it's too late."

CHAPTER 31

It began as a gradually rising structure the color of the water it stretched across. At first a highway to heaven, it changed direction in a remarkable arc vaulting across the bay, as if the architect decided to abruptly return the steel structure to earth. Then it descending gracefully to its final destination. Its 20,000 tons of steel and 94,000 cubic yards of concrete had no suspension cables of any kind; rather the Coronado Bay Bridge was an unencumbered span that stretched 11,179 feet from bustling San Diego to the quiet, posh island of Coronado. Over 2,800 feet of it was curved steel, which gave it a shape unlike any other bridge in the world. Its grade and 90-degree angle were designed specifically to allow an empty aircraft carrier from the naval base on Coronado to pass beneath it.

It was this monument to the ingenuity and skill of mankind that tonight would witness the end of one of mankind's own.

He drove slowly but with a sense of resolve and purpose, up the grade from the San Diego side until he reached the mid-point of the bridge. It was 3 AM on a weekday evening and the bridge was empty except for an occasional delivery truck. He stopped his car near the side railing, only 34 inches high, an inadequate barrier to the bay below.

He looked out over the darkened sea, first back towards the lights of San Diego, the city he loved, and then over towards the few flickering twinkles of Coronado. He thought briefly about all those he knew and those he would never know. The consistent cough came again and wracked his relentlessly thinning frame. He would no longer have to endure it, nor would he have to feel the daily pain that afflicted him. He had never felt as free and peaceful as he did this night, standing atop the world. He had made his decision, and it felt good.

He took the air of the sea into his lungs for several moments, gulping it hungrily, breathing deeply, even as he risked another fit of coughing. He went back and killed the engine of his car and left the driver's door ajar. He leaned into it and checked once more to be sure that the letter he had written was in the glove compartment.

With a moment not of hesitation but of sad finality, he stepped upon the concrete barrier and closed his eyes. God forgive me, he thought, and he launched himself into the darkness, without a sound.

His body began the free fall as his mind cried out in terror. There was nothing he could do now to reverse his trajectory. He had become a human missile, hurtling some 200 feet to the water below. It seemed an eternity to him but in no time at all, his body crashed into the surface of the sea with such force that his bones were instantly pulverized. There was little time to feel pain. Death came mercifully and quickly.

From above, there was a growing recognition of what had occurred. A delivery truck driver was unsure, but he thought he had seen someone teetering on the edge of the bridge and then the apparition was gone. He had screeched to a halt and raced over to the side, keeping a safe distance back, himself squeamish about heights. He looked into the abandoned car, a silver Jaguar XKE. He was about to call the police on his cell phone, but he didn't need to. Flashing lights appeared and a trooper got out of his car. After a brief exchange of words, the trooper nodded and the truck driver went on his way. The trooper called in his report. In moments a police boat would make its way to the place below where the empty car sat on the bridge. The boat would find nothing but the swells of the sea.

Marty's assistant buzzed him and told him there was a San Diego policeman who needed to see him on official business. He told her to show him in.

"Mr. Gladstone, Lieutenant John Romano, San Diego Police." The man showed Marty his identification.

"Pleased to meet you," Marty said, extending a hand. Romano shook it with a strong grip. Marty led him over to the conference area in his office.

"Thanks for seeing me. This won't take long." Romano pulled out a pad and pen. "Mr. Gladstone," Romano said with a voice that was toneless, "TJ Gatwick is dead. He apparently committed suicide early this morning."

Marty was visibly stunned. His eyes widened in disbelief and he sat back in his chair as if the air was knocked out of him.

"How...how did he..." Marty began. Romano interrupted him.

"It appears Mr. Gatwick jumped off the Coronado Bay Bridge," Romano stated simply. He was a man of concise description, a man without the luxury of time or emotion. "His car was found on the bridge, abandoned. A witness thinks he saw a man step off the side, but he can't be sure. Mr. Gatwick left a note in the glove compartment of the car. The note strongly suggests that he took his own life."

"I can't believe it," Marty said quietly, still in shock.

"How well did you know Mr. Gatwick?" Romano asked.

"We were business associates," Marty answered. "My company recently purchased his company, as I'm sure you know. We had been business acquaintances quite a long time, actually. I met TJ at MIT when we were both students there. He went on to start GWare, and I eventually started Incandescent. Our paths crossed years ago when we produced rival software operating systems. I guess you could say we were adversaries, at least in business."

Romano took notes as Marty spoke. While his expression didn't change, he was intrigued by Marty's use of the word 'adversaries.'

"Time went on," Marty continued. "GWare fell on hard times, primarily because a virus destroyed the credibility of their primary product, an operating system called GWare ONE. TJ re-organized the company and it became known for anti-virus software instead. It was his crowning achievement, to create software that could fight viruses. I guess it was his revenge of sorts.

"But TJ had made some bad investments in Dot Coms, and his company's primary anti-virus product, a service called GWare Guardian, was losing money. That's when TJ contacted me about buying his company."

Romano nodded, looking up from his pad. "What was your reaction?"

"I was surprised," Marty admitted. "Very surprised. We had buried the hatchet over the years, I'd say. But still, it must have taken a lot for him to contact me. We met and talked about it. He urged me to buy the company, said he thought I was the one who could save it. He was a changed man from what I had remembered years earlier. TJ always had a hell of a temper, a real fiery side to him. But when I met with him he was quiet, subdued."

Marty reflected for a moment and then went on. "That's not all that was different, though. His physical appearance had changed as well. TJ had always seemed to be on the pudgy side. He could get away with it, because he was tall. And he had a ruddy face. But when we met, I was struck by how thin and pale he looked. He didn't look well, actually."

"You're very observant," Romano said without emotion. "How did he handle the negotiations with you?"

"There wasn't much disagreement about anything," Marty responded. "TJ was most concerned about what would happen to

GWare, not about himself. He wanted to make sure I didn't change the nature of the company. I offered him the opportunity to stay on, to keep running the company as a separate subsidiary, at least for a while. He declined. So we agreed to a buyout. He didn't seem all that interested in the actual terms of the deal. Just said he was ready to get out, to do something else. It was kind of odd."

"In what way?" Romano asked.

"Well, here was a guy who had founded the company, who obviously had a lot of himself tied up in it. I've done the same thing, I know what it means. If I were selling my company, I'd have some real emotional attachments to it, probably I'd make it difficult for the buyer, if you know what I mean. He just kind of let it happen, almost as if he didn't care anymore."

"Did you have any contact with him since the deal?"

"No. After the papers were signed, that was the last I saw or heard from TJ Gatwick."

"Other than his obvious loss of weight, and his seeming to be more subdued, did you notice anything else different about Mr. Gatwick?" Romano asked.

"I dunno, this is more of a perception really, but it seemed to me like TJ had just lost his spark. Of course, he had reason to, here he was, selling his baby, the company he founded, under tough circumstances. That had to be a defeat for him, I'm sure. He said he was ready to go on to other things, and I believed him, but he seemed like he had lost his vitality, that's all."

"One last question, Mr. Gladstone. Anyone you know of who could have wanted Mr. Gatwick dead?"

"I thought you said this was suicide," Marty asked, puzzled.

"Yeah, that's what we think alright," Romano said. "But we gotta follow up on everything just to make sure."

"I know from talking to GWare employees that TJ wasn't everyone's favorite around here. Apparently he was pretty well known for his outbursts, and he was capable of chewing up employees in front of others. It wasn't a pleasant experience for an employee on the receiving end, but it seemed like everyone took it in stride. It just went with the territory...kind of expected as part of working at GWare. Maybe they didn't like it, but I can't see any of them being hurt so badly by his tirades that they'd want him dead." Marty thought about it a minute longer, then said, "No, lieutenant, I can't imagine who might want to have murdered TJ Gatwick," Marty said.

Romano rose from his chair. "Thank you, Mr. Gladstone. I appreciate your taking the time to speak with me." He handed Marty his card. "If there's anything else that comes to mind, please give me a call."

Marty nodded. "Lieutenant, you may not be able to answer this, but I'd like to know: Do you have any idea why TJ might have killed himself?"

Romano hesitated for a moment, as if he didn't want to reveal any part of the investigation. Then he said, "Yeah, we think we have a reason." He paused and then added without emotion, "According to his note, TJ Gatwick was dying from AIDS."

When Marty got home that evening, he learned that Erin had received a visit from John Romano as well. She was as shocked as Marty was to learn of TJ's death, even more so when she learned from Marty that TJ had AIDS.

"Who would've thought?" she said as they had dinner together out on the deck. "It's amazing what you don't know about people."

"I thought he didn't look well," Marty said, "I knew there was something wrong, but I had no idea, no idea at all. Erin, you were a lot closer to him years ago. I have to ask you, did you suspect that...that he was gay?"

"That's the first thing I thought of when you mentioned AIDS," Erin answered, taking a sip of white wine. "Y'know, I often did wonder why TJ never came on to me. I mean, there was a time we were seeing each other, professionally that is, every month like clockwork. He'd tell me all sorts of things about his business. Every once in a while he'd compliment me on my appearance or something, but he never really made a pass at me."

"Maybe you just weren't his type," Marty said with a smile.

"It's not as if I would've resisted his advances," she said impishly.

"Oh really? You mean you had the hots for TJ Gatwick?" Marty asked with an eyebrow raised.

"Hardly," Erin said, laughing. "But after all, he was a very powerful man, and power can be, well, attractive."

"So *that* explains it," Marty said, mocking her, "you married me for the awesome power I wield."

"Don't be so impressed with yourself," Erin answered, laughing dismissively. "Seriously, now that I think about it, sure TJ could've been gay. It's a distinct possibility, but I had no proof of it."

"Yeah, anything's possible. Or he could've gotten bad blood during a transfusion, too. Whatever it was, if he did have AIDS, and he was dying from it, it goes a long way to explaining the suicide."

"Still," Erin said thoughtfully, "For a guy like TJ to be capable of taking his own life...it just doesn't add up."

"I know what you mean. In the old days, Gatwick was as full of piss and vinegar as anyone I ever knew. And after the buyout, he had more money than God. Could have pretty much done whatever he wanted to, or done nothing for the rest of his life."

"Do you think there could've been something else?" Erin said, adopting a new train of thought. "I mean, suppose he did have AIDS, but suppose it was at least under control, you know, enough so he could live with it. Couldn't there be some other reason he did it?"

"What are you getting at, Erin?"

"Just wondering, that's all. Must be my journalist's antennae going up. What if there were something else, not just AIDS, but an even more terrible secret that TJ had, that he just couldn't live with?"

"What might that be?" Marty asked.

"I'm not sure, but TJ was involved in all sorts of crazy stuff, always scheming and figuring out one deal or another. Maybe he got himself into real trouble with one of those Dot Coms, you know, maybe he did something illegal that he didn't want anyone to find out about. Or maybe it was drugs. I dunno, it could be anything."

"That's pretty wild speculation, don't you think?" Marty asked.

"Call it woman's intuition," Erin said, tapping her wine glass with her fingernail. "I'm not sure why, but I have the feeling there's more to TJ's death than we, or the police, know about."

CHAPTER 32

Marty hadn't been to Incandescent's Cambridge headquarters since the acquisition of GWare. He decided he'd better pay a visit, if for no other reason than to maintain a symbolic presence. He suggested to Erin that she accompany him and that they escape to Nantucket, a small island off the Massachusetts coastline, for a few days when he was through with business. She had never been there and happily agreed, despite his warning that mid-August would be the height of the tourist season.

Marty and Erin took a cab from Logan Airport in Boston to his condo. He told the cab to wait while he got Erin settled.

"I still remember that first night we made love here," she said wistfully, climbing to the top room in the former church. She looked out upon the city as he came up behind her and gave her a hug.

"That's what did it for me," he said. "It was a completely religious experience."

Erin laughed and shook her head. "Just like you to trivialize a most enchanting evening."

"Oh no, dear heart, it was far from trivial for me," Marty answered, kissing her cheek. Then he looked at his watch.

"Listen, enough of this clowning around. Why don't you relax here for a while. If you feel like it, take a walk a bit later, do some window shopping. I'll head over to the office. I'll try to get through early so we can have some time together, I promise." He kissed her good-bye and headed downstairs. He got back into the cab and drove over to the Incandescent building in Cambridge.

He still found a lot of charm and warmth in these two cities, Boston and Cambridge, separated as they were by the Charles River. They each had their own distinct personality. Boston was small and provincial in many ways, yet it could be sophisticated and worldly. Cambridge was bohemian and hip, yet it was a cultural mecca. In some respects he missed living here. But how could he be any happier than living with Erin in his idyllic home overlooking the ocean in La Jolla?

When he arrived at the Incandescent building, Henry Chu was waiting for him in the lobby. "Welcome back," Henry said with a huge smile. "I've been lonely too long."

"The Rascals," Marty said, returning Henry's smile and putting a hand on his shoulder. They often played the game of "song titles"—one of them spoke a song title, and the other had to answer with the name of the artist. "How are you, Doc?"

"Fine, fine. And more importantly, how's married life treating you?"

"Couldn't be better," Marty answered with conviction. "Best thing I ever did was marry that girl."

"I know what you mean. Gotta admit, I'm a happier and more stable guy since getting back with Priscilla," Henry said.

"Good to hear, Henry. I'm glad for you. How's Joey?"

"Growing like a weed. Nearly killed me the other day with his bicycle."

Marty laughed and walked with Henry down the corridor. Everyone who passed by greeted him with a happy smile and lots of "Good to see you's."

They had set up an office that Marty could use for his now infrequent visits. It was much smaller than his original office, at Marty's request. No reason to waste the real estate on someone who was there only a few times a year.

There were already several voice mails waiting for him. One of them was from Jill Strathmore. She said it was important he call her as soon as he arrived in Cambridge.

"Know anything about a call from Jill?" he asked Henry. Since the acquisition of GWare, the ultimate in ironies had occurred and Henry had actually collaborated with Jill on building new anti-viral technology into UNITE.

Henry shook his head.

"Lemme put her on conference and see what this is about," Marty said. He dialed Jill's direct number and she picked up on the second ring.

"Jill, I just got in and got your voice mail. I've got you on speaker. Henry's here."

"Thanks for calling back right away. Hi Henry."

"Hello Jill," Henry answered.

"Marty, we got word today that there's a 'Code Red Two' hitting the Internet," Jill said. "We're developing a patch as we speak. Henry, you'll be getting it as soon as it's live, of course."

Jill and Henry had worked out a procedure by which any GWare Guardian patch was immediately transmitted to Incandescent so it could be integrated into the next electronic alert for UNITE. It was a smart way to keep UNITE updated...but it also helped to maintain the product's competitive edge in the marketplace.

"What's different about Code Red Two?" Marty asked.

"It's particularly nasty," Jill said, "smarter than the original."

"In what way?"

"It's installing a back door onto the target computer. Once it's there, anyone with a Web browser can remotely access the server and execute commands. Obviously that makes it vulnerable to any sort of hacker attack. This thing installs itself and gains full access to the system. Then it launches a hundred additional worms on pre-programmed dates to invade other computers.

"The FBI told us the Defense Department had to shut down its Web sites for a while," Jill continued. "Code Red Two has already infected maybe 150,000 server computers. This one is pretty sophisticated, Marty."

"How're you doing on working up a patch?"

"We won't be able to get out there as fast as we did with the original Code Red. But we'll have something live probably late tomorrow."

Henry interrupted. "That's not bad, Jill. You know, I heard about one interesting aspect to Code Red Two. *The Wall Street Journal* broke the story that the new variant of Code Red is almost identical to another worm that attacked the Department of Energy in April. That one didn't make headlines because it didn't work. While that attack was unsuccessful, they think it could be the same person who was involved in both."

"So," Marty said, "if they think Code Red Two was created by the same hacker who created the April worm, can they trace either back to the hacker?"

"They're not saying," Henry said. "Problem is, they haven't been able to find Code Red or Code Red Two's Patient Zero yet." Patient Zero was hacker talk for the worm's first victim. If the FBI could identify where Code Red or its variant originated, it could give them another important clue to the creator.

"Well, we could do with a breakthrough, that's for sure," Marty said to Henry. Then he addressed the speaker phone. "Jill, the sooner you get that patch out for Code Red Two, the better."

Marty and Henry ended the call with Jill and they talked more about Code Red Two.

"Marty," Henry said, "There's something about this I don't get. You know Doomsday's work. The guy is a genius, I mean, he's an artist at creating viruses and worms. If the FBI can connect Code Red

Two to the April virus, that means the hacker had to leave something behind, you know, greets or something like that."

Greets were a kind of electronic greeting that hackers put into their programs to privately contact other hackers. They were like a hacker's own unique signature.

"I know he's been out of circulation for a while," Henry continued, "but it's just not like Doomsday to leave anything in his code that could identify him. He's too careful for that, too much of a professional."

"Are you saying what I think you're saying, Henry?" Marty asked.

"Yes," Henry said slowly, "I think it's quite possible Code Red Two and maybe Code Red itself are someone else's products. I think we may have another hacker out there who could be just as dangerous as Doomsday."

"It's certainly possible," Marty said. "You're right, it's hard to believe Doomsday would leave any clues behind. Of course, he is unpredictable. In fact, I wouldn't put it past him to identify himself just to challenge us. But why open himself up to that kind of risk?

"If you're right, Henry," Marty continued, "we could have yet another character in addition to Doomsday to worry about. And what's even more disturbing is if Doomsday's modus operandi of old holds true, and he had anything to do with either of these attacks, we know they're just a warning. Which means he has much bigger plans."

"Not a repeat of the New Year's Eve disaster…" Henry said quietly.

"Yeah," Marty said, "I'm afraid so. Off the record, and I really mean keep this to yourself, I have it on good authority that another major attack is imminent. I'm telling you because we've gotta pull out all the stops, Henry. We've got to get that deflector of yours ready for prime time a lot sooner than we thought."

"Easy to say," Henry said, shaking his head, "hard to do. I'm still not happy with the thing. It's got too many flaws to go public just yet. Besides, Marty, we need a handle on typing the viruses, you know that. If we have no idea what strains to expect, how are we going to prevent against them?"

"I know, I know," Marty said perplexed. "Ted Chambers himself called me. He said that the FBI is working diligently on trying to get something that would give us a clue as to the type of viruses Doomsday could be using. But they just don't have anything yet. As for the deflector, Henry, we can't afford to wait much longer. I know you're doing the best you can, but we're gonna run out of time. Even if it isn't perfect, find a way to get it ready to launch, and soon. Heaven help us if we have to go through anything approaching New Year's Eve 1999 again."

Marty spent two more days in meetings and catching up with the staff in Cambridge. The news Marty received from Jill and the subsequent conversation with Henry weighed heavily on his mind. He had every reason to believe that the warning signs were there, and that Doomsday was all but announcing by his actions that a massive attack could come at any time.

But Marty tried his hardest to bury his thoughts, at least temporarily, so he and Erin could enjoy a few precious days of rest and relaxation on the island of Nantucket. Thirty miles out to sea from the mainland, Nantucket was reachable only by ferry or airplane. It was more remote and less developed than its bigger sister, Martha's Vineyard. But over the past several years, Nantucket had exploded in terms of tourist interest, probably because everyone with money wanted to "get away from it all." Nantucket had seen its summer traffic swell and, with it, some of the charm of the isolated island was lost. Nonetheless, Marty knew there were parts of it that Erin would fall in love with.

Marty and Erin took an early morning forty-minute flight from Logan Airport to Nantucket. They didn't want to be burdened with a car. Besides, cars were frowned upon on the tiny island especially during high season.

Marty arranged for a room at the Jared Coffin House, a quintessential island inn. Located near the center of Nantucket town, the inn had grown into a collection of six buildings with sixty guest rooms. It was fully occupied, as the town was bustling with activity this time of year.

Despite the summer crowds, this brief sojourn would be a welcome respite from their busy lives, Marty thought. Erin found the cobblestone streets and gaslight lamps charming. It reminded her of a tiny version of the gaslamp district of San Diego.

It was a warm, sunny day but there was a refreshing breeze off the water and the humidity was entirely bearable. Marty suggested they take a leisurely bike ride and Erin said she was up for it. He said he knew a special place, but it was six miles away. She gave him a questioning look. He smiled and said, "It's just about all flat road. Trust me."

After checking in to their room, they changed into t-shirts, shorts and sneakers and headed off. They rented two bikes at a shop in the town center and began their journey with Marty in the lead. He took them down Orange Street, out from the center of town, to Milestone Road. There, a bike path would take them to Siasconset, pronounced "Sconset" by the locals.

As Marty had promised, the path was virtually flat. Erin gazed out over at the sea. With the island only 3-1/2 miles wide, she could see water all around her. She noticed it smelled distinctly different from La Jolla; more salty, perhaps.

They rode side by side at a leisurely pace, watching the mile markers go by, simply enjoying the experience. It didn't seem at all like six miles. Finally, up ahead they came upon a view of the cranberry bog, and Marty pointed to the picturesque Sankaty Lighthouse in the distance. The village of Siasconset lay in front of them.

As they rode into the sleepy town, they were greeted by a collection of cottages with weathered gray shingles, many graced by wild roses adorning their sides and fences. Erin now understood the wisdom of the lengthy ride Marty had planned. Siasconset was so quiet, so far removed from the mainstream of the island that there was barely a tourist in sight.

Marty led her to a cottage surrounded by gardens full of climbing roses. A small sign read Chanticleer Inn. She marveled at the beauty of the place, with its multi-paned glass windows fighting for attention amidst the rose-covered walls.

They got off their bikes for a well-deserved rest. "Here before you," Marty said, "is one of the best restaurants in the country, maybe the world. I called in a favor and was able to get us a reservation for tomorrow night." He bowed, as if he were a medieval knight, then added, "Of course, we'll take a cab."

"My, you do have pull, don't you," Erin answered smiling. "It looks lovely. I can't wait."

"Well I thought you might want to check out the locale first, which is why I took you on this little excursion."

"I loved the ride," Erin said. "You were right, I didn't even feel the distance."

"Wait 'til later when your legs stiffen up," he said lightly. "But isn't it nice to know there are still places like this on the earth to escape to," Marty said, "especially when we have things to escape from."

"Oooo, that sounded serious."

Marty sighed. "Erin, I've got to admit I'm worried. Much as I love being here with you, it's hard for me not to be pre-occupied. I've got something on my mind I've been hesitant to tell you about."

Erin didn't say anything but rather looked at him expectantly.

Marty took a breath and continued, "There's a chance, a very good chance, that there'll be a major virus attack coming soon. It could be huge…on the scale of the New Year's Eve disaster. I just told

Henry about it. He's working on something new that I'm hoping will be ready in time to repel the attack."

Erin looked at him without surprise. "I know about the attack, Marty," she said, lowering her eyes. "I've heard from Doomsday again."

"What! When?" Marty asked with surprise.

"A while ago," she answered guiltily. "Marty, I wanted to tell you, I was dying to tell you. As soon as I heard from him, I contacted the FBI immediately. They asked me not to tell anyone as a matter of national security. They wanted to keep it quiet because they didn't want Doomsday to get any publicity this time. And they didn't want it to get out because it could create a panic. So I agonized over it, and decided I'd better keep it from you and from my editor. I'm sorry, Marty, I shouldn't have."

Marty thought about it for a moment, then reached out to caress her cheek with the back of his hand. "You did the right thing, Erin. That's what the FBI asked you to do. You had no choice.

"Besides, I did the same with you. I got a call from Ted Chambers. He told me what was happening, requested my help. And he asked me to keep it in strict confidence."

She smiled. "Well aren't we a pair," she said. "We weren't even tortured and we spilled the beans."

Marty took her hands. "I was stupid to keep a secret from you. It was tearing me up inside. Never again, I promise."

"Me too," she said simply. "But what are we going to do, Marty? What can we do to stop this maniac?"

Marty shook his head slowly. "I've got the best team of developers I've ever seen, Erin. Between GWare and Incandescent, they can do anything I ask of them. Henry's close to coming up with a breakthrough, but he's still working out the kinks in it. I just don't know if he'll have it ready in time. The worst part of it is, we know what's coming, I'm just not sure we can stop it. It's like '99 all over again.

"But Erin, somehow, at least for the next two days, we can't think about it, we musn't," Marty said decisively. "This is our time. Let's enjoy it."

She nodded and laid her head on his shoulder.

They sat on the grass and, after a while, they mounted their bikes for the ride back to the inn.

That evening, they had dinner at a quiet little restaurant in town and returned to their room early.

"Now I'm beginning to feel that bike ride," Erin said as she sat on the side of the lovely canopied queen-size bed.

"How about I give you a nice massage?" Marty said.

"I'd like that," Erin said. She lazily took off her clothes and lay face down on the bed.

Marty became aroused, as he always did at the sight of her naked, but he suppressed the feeling. The bed was high off the ground, so he was able to stand beside her and reach her body comfortably with his hands. He began to gently but firmly massage her neck and shoulders.

"That's wonderful," she said dreamily.

He continued to work his fingers and hands into her shoulders and then moved down to her upper and lower back. Occasionally she would emit little moans of pleasure. After a while, he massaged her legs and then her calves. He slowly picked up each of her legs, bent them at the knee, and massaged her heels and the balls of her feet.

"If you ever get out of the software business," she said, almost in a daze, "I know the perfect job for you."

He chuckled, enjoying her pleasure. "Your personal masseuse?"

"Mmm-hmm."

"All relaxed now?"

"Mmm-hmm."

"Then how about we try something else?" he said, kissing one of the rounded cheeks of her rear.

She slowly turned over and looked at him through half-closed eyes. "What did you have in mind?" she asked with a smile.

He pulled his shirt over his head, undid his shorts, and stepped out of his sandals. His erection was just about at her eye level, and she looked over at it.

"Hmm, happy to see me, huh?" she asked, reaching out to pull his penis to her mouth. She kissed it and put it in her mouth momentarily. "Love my lollipop," she said, stroking him.

He laughed and got onto the bed. He lay beside her and kissed her tenderly at first. Then their kisses grew more passionate. They embraced and kissed for a while longer.

She stopped abruptly and looked deeply into his eyes. "I was thinking," she said with a smile. "Let's make this trip really special." She paused for a moment, running a finger along his chest. "Let's make a baby."

Marty couldn't believe his ears. They had talked about having a child a few times before. Erin had told Marty she'd know when she was ready.

"Right now?" he said, smiling like a country boy who had just bought the latest Garth Brooks album.

"Yeah. And if it's a girl, we'll name her Nan," she said.

"Hmmm," Marty answered, furrowing his brow. "And if it's a boy…let's see…Tucker?"

She made a face and he laughed. Then he looked at her seriously. "You sure about this, Erin?"

She nodded. "I've never been more sure of anything in my life," she said.

And they made love as passionately and as tenderly as they ever had before.

CHAPTER 33

No sooner had Marty gotten back to his office in San Diego than he had an urgent message for Ted Chambers to call him.

"Senator, it's Marty Gladstone."

"Marty, thanks for getting back to me. Things are heating up here in Washington. I'm sure you've heard about Code Red Two. Thankfully it wasn't nearly as severe as Code Red, but it still caused widespread problems."

"Yes. We were able to get a patch out pretty rapidly and we contained the damage, at least for our own subscribers."

"Well, Marty, that's great. But now listen to this. The FBI thinks they've finally got a break in their investigation. They've been using a new Internet spying technology. They can actually plant a Trojan horse keystroke logger on a suspected hacker's PC. It hides itself on the computer and captures all keystrokes, even passwords. They don't need to have physical access to the computer."

"Kind of like a virus sent by the good guys, huh?"

"Exactly, Marty," Chambers answered. "It seems to be working. They're narrowing down their search and they're closing in on a suspect. They could make an arrest at any time."

"That's terrific news, Senator. But then, why the urgent message from you?"

"The problem is," Chambers said, "the FBI has confirmed they have *two* hackers to worry about. Of course, there's Doomsday, but now there's a Doomsday look-alike. Doesn't appear they're working together, either."

"Is the FBI sure?"

"The new technology they're using confirmed it. It's the other hacker they're closing in on. Seems he's the one responsible for Code Red Two."

The Senator cleared his throat. "Now I've got to tell you something that may disturb you, Marty. They think the hacker is somehow associated with GWare."

"Jesus," Marty muttered. "Can that be confirmed?"

"Not yet, but they're pretty confident that's where the road is leading them. You could have a traitor in your midst, Marty."

Marty couldn't say anything—he was too stunned to reply.

"Now listen Marty, I know how you must feel, and once they find him, I know you'll have your hands full. But I must tell you, we can't afford to be distracted by this second hacker. The FBI will get him, you can be sure of that. But Marty, they're coming up empty on Doomsday, and they know with certainty that he's still the real threat. The latest intelligence says his big strike is coming soon. We've got to do something to repel it. We've got to be ready, no matter what."

"I understand, Senator. But with a hacker somewhere inside GWare, I also have to be certain whatever we might be planning isn't compromised. After all, it's still possible this guy is in collusion with Doomsday. If they're working together, it could be disastrous."

Chambers sighed. "I know, Marty, I know. What a mess! But the FBI should get the bastard any day now. In the mean time, I need you to focus on the possibility that Doomsday and Doomsday alone is setting up another monumental attack. He could strike at any moment."

"Senator, you know I'm still looking for even the slightest indication of what kind of virus we'll be dealing with," Marty said, somewhat exasperated. "Can't the FBI find out anything about it from their sources?"

Senator Chambers let out what sounded like air escaping from a tire. "All they can tell me is they're working on it."

"What about the primary targets, any word on those?" Marty asked hopefully.

"Well that's a bit more promising. They think they know where the first strikes will be. But if it's true, we'll have hell to pay." The Senator paused, then he added hoarsely, "This time, Doomsday's targeting every one of the 104 licensed, operating nuclear power plants in the country."

Marty whispered a profanity to himself, then said goodbye to Ted Chambers and hung up. His mind was racing. He didn't know whether to be more concerned about Doomsday's imminent threat or about "the traitor in his midst," as Senator Chambers called the second hacker. Chambers was exactly right, Marty thought—if it truly turned out there was a traitor at GWare, this was a traitor of the worst kind. How could *anyone* working for GWare, a company with such an outstanding reputation for anti-virus technology, possibly be a virus-launching hacker himself? It was beyond Marty's comprehension.

What could be a reasonable explanation for such treachery, he wondered. How could this person justify his actions, on the one hand working to fight viruses and on the other hand subverting that very goal. And who could it possibly be? Marty was perplexed and disturbed by the revelation.

Still, he had to focus his attention on the impending attack that Chambers told him about. He wondered exactly how Doomsday could go after nuclear plants with a virus in the first place. Each plant was independent of the other, and their internal operations surely wouldn't be vulnerable to outside viruses. Whatever computer programs they used to operate the plants themselves would certainly be protected from attack.

So what were the possibilities, Marty thought. Doomsday could have confederates in some of the plants, but that wouldn't be likely. Or he could plant a virus that would automatically use each plant's e-mail address book to send out infected messages to all the others, since it was highly likely that they had each other's e-mail addresses on file. That might work for a while, Marty thought, but it would soon be discovered before it could do any serious damage.

There was a more likely scenario that Marty played out in his mind. What if Doomsday could get into the NRC's system, and maybe sabotage it with a Trojan horse instead of a virus? Marty remembered that he had penetrated the NRC before, during the New Year's Eve disaster. The Trojan would give Doomsday unauthorized access to the NRC's network. Then it was conceivable that Doomsday could simultaneously send infected messages that looked official to the plants themselves. He'd have to come up with something ingenious to do any damage in this way, but Marty wouldn't put anything past Doomsday.

Marty thought about an even more likely scenario. Doomsday could be using the whole nuclear plant scheme as a decoy. He was cunning enough to leak the story to the FBI through a phony source—to make them think he was going to attack the nuclear plants, while he had a completely different target in mind. Marty felt there was a pretty good chance that was the real threat.

Whatever Doomsday had planned, Marty now felt a renewed sense of urgency to get Henry's deflector to function properly, and fast. Marty knew his one hope was Henry Chu. No one he had ever met could even approach Henry's technical wizardry.

The problem was the deflector still couldn't yet discriminate between a bad message or attachment and good ones, so as it stood now, it would virtually shut down all networking activity. That wouldn't be acceptable to mission-critical operations such as the

NRC. Henry's deflector needed more refinement before it could be implemented effectively.

Nonetheless, Marty thought, it was all they had at the moment. They'd just have to find a way to make it work. Marty picked up the phone and put in a call to Henry. One way or the other, he thought, we'd better be ready to launch the damn thing.

Erin had been receiving increasingly belligerent e-mail messages from Doomsday. This latest one was filled with invective and profanity. She cringed as she read it. He was enraged that she hadn't written anything about him in her columns. She hadn't even answered any of his e-mails.

She was following the instructions of the FBI, and they had told her to do nothing, absolutely nothing. They said to just let Doomsday rant and rave in his e-mails. With Erin's permission, the FBI had set up split access so they could monitor her incoming e-mail continuously. That meant they were reading the e-mail Erin had just received from Doomsday and analyzing it at this very moment.

One of the things about this latest e-mail that disturbed her most was Doomsday's ugly reference to Marty. Doomsday said he intended to make Incandescent and its subsidiary GWare a prime target. "What will you think of your kike husband when I have him crawling on his knees?" he had written in his e-mail. Erin was disgusted at Doomsday's vulgar bigotry. She didn't know whether to be terrified or angry. She choked back a tear thinking about the destruction this monster had caused before, and what he might be capable of doing again.

Doomsday's e-mail correspondence had put Erin in a difficult position. She was glad she had told Marty about Doomsday's contacting her again, but she had also recently told her editor. Now she was getting a lot of pressure from him to go public with the story. He said it was her journalistic duty, but she had resisted, steadfastly following the instructions of the FBI. Her editor made a strong case for freedom of the press, but Erin weighed both sides and stood her ground. She understood and agreed with the FBI's strategy of keeping Doomsday out of the limelight.

She kept asking her FBI contact when they thought something might break, and she told him honestly that she may have to go public with the story soon, before it somehow leaked out to someone else. The FBI agent urged her to continue to cooperate by keeping it confidential. They felt an enraged Doomsday would make a mistake, and that's when they'd be able to nab him.

To placate Erin, the agent had said they were about to collar a second hacker, not Doomsday, and Erin would be the first to know when they did.

Just then, the phone rang. Erin picked it up and it was her contact, the FBI agent.

"I was just thinking about you," Erin said. "Can you guys wiretap brainwaves now?"

The FBI agent chuckled. "Not yet, but we're working on it. I just read Doomsday's latest diatribe and I figured you must be pretty upset by it. I thought I'd better call you."

"Thanks, that was thoughtful of you," Erin answered.

"Listen, he's getting really nasty now, I know that. But he's desperate, and that's why you've got to hang on a little longer. He's gonna make a mistake soon."

"I'm trying," Erin said with resolve, "I'm really trying."

"I do have something for you," the agent said. "I promised you'd be the first to know about the other hacker. We've made an arrest."

Erin perked up. "When?"

"Only minutes ago. I got authorization to let you have the story first...consider it a little gift for all your cooperation with the FBI."

"Can you keep it under wraps until I get it into tomorrow's print edition?" Erin asked.

"Not likely."

"Okay," she said thinking fast, "then I'll talk to the editor about running an exclusive on WSJ.com. What are the details?"

"This is a juicy one, Erin," the FBI agent said. "The hacker was pretty high up in GWare, as we suspected. The hacker left an identifier in the Code Red Two virus that connected it to the April virus, the one that never made it to wide distribution. We were able to trace it back to a covert e-mail address, and that led us to GWare. We've just taken a suspect into custody and confiscated her computer and disks."

"Did you say *her*?" Erin said with surprise.

"Yeah, her," the FBI agent answered. "Hell of a thing. It's a woman named Jill Strathmore who's the hacker."

Erin spoke with the agent another few minutes. He authorized her to break the story and told her who to contact in the San Diego office for additional details. He said not to expect much more in the way of information until they had interrogated Jill.

Erin thought, Jill Strathmore! Marty had told Erin that it was Jill who had turned GWare's development process upside down and come up with a way to dramatically speed up the release of virus software patches. It was Jill, Marty said, who had been responsible for the company's latest successes. In fact, she had just been promoted. This just didn't make sense, Erin thought, it didn't make sense at all. She picked up the phone and dialed Marty's cell phone number.

"This is Marty."

"Honey, it's Erin. Can you talk?"

"Yeah, but I've just been in with an FBI agent. He went to make a phone call but he's coming back any time now."

"I'll be quick. Obviously you already know what I'm calling about," Erin said guardedly.

Marty sighed. "Yeah, I sure do."

"The FBI authorized me to break the story. Figured it was the least they could do for me being such a good girl."

"Well it's gonna break one way or the other," Marty answered, "so it might as well be you who goes public with it. This is a really tough one to believe."

"I know, I know. I feel terrible about it. Listen Marty, this is going to sound weird, but I'm talking to you as a journalist now, not as your wife, okay?"

"Well that *is* why you kept your maiden name...so I could identify the two Erin's I live with."

"Happy you haven't lost your sense of humor, even now," she said with a small laugh.

"It's about the only thing that keeps me sane, and even that's questionable," he responded.

"Okay now Mr. Gladstone," she said, sounding official, "can you comment on the arrest of Jill Strathmore by the FBI today?"

"I'm afraid I can't comment on that, Ms. Keliher, other than to confirm her arrest," he answered.

"Okay," Erin said, "we got that out of the way. Now off the record, what the hell is going on?"

"Off the record," Marty said, "it looks pretty conclusive that she's the creator of Code Red Two."

"Why in God's name would she have done that?" Erin asked.

"Well, we have to wait for the official word from the FBI on that." Marty paused. "But I have a theory."

"Which is?"

"These developers, they live in a different world, Erin," Marty began. "They're working so hard, all the time. Sometimes they don't sleep, they just work for days on end. What for? For the glory of personal gratification. They just want their programs to be the best, it's as simple as that.

"When some of what they do gets recognition," Marty went on, "when their work becomes famous, I think they go a little crazy. They never wanted that kind of glory, that kind of attention. But there it is, the spotlight's shining brightly on them. They tend to be shy introverts, and all of a sudden they're celebrities.

"Y'know Erin, we've really been in the limelight with our anti-virus technology lately. GWare developers are like the computer world's great American heroes right now. I've gotta believe it's going to their heads. These guys aren't used to it."

"I get all that," Erin said, "but it still doesn't explain why Jill actually *created* a virus."

"Oh, I think it does," Marty responded. "She's one of the very few women in this crazy business who's made it big, Erin. And she's clawed her way to the top. She finally got the recognition she deserved. And it was all because she was a virus expert, something the world needed and respected.

"Well if I were Jill, I'd be terrified that my moment of glory would end, that I'd go right back to where I was before, fighting for recognition amongst the males. So what do I do? I find a way to *sustain* that glory that I hunger for. I *create* the enemy...a virus...so I've got something that I need to keep fighting against, something that keeps getting me noticed, that keeps me being needed. So I continue to be a hero.

"*That's* why I think Jill Strathmore did it, Erin. She got a taste of the glory and simply didn't want it to end."

"God," Erin said, "it makes sense the way you explain it. But that's pretty warped, Marty."

"Yeah, like I said, these developers live in a different world. It's funny, but there's a very fine line between developer and hacker. A hacker is as much a genius at his craft as a legitimate developer. Unfortunately, it's the hacker who's completely misguided in his motives."

"So what now?" Erin asked. "If Jill is guilty as charged, that could be a big loss for GWare."

"True, but we'll survive. We've got a lot of talent here, I just have to tap into it. Besides, Henry's working some magic back in Cambridge right now. I think he's getting close to another Henry-style breakthrough."

"You mentioned that to me before," Erin said, always playing the journalists. "Are we on the record yet?"

"No," Marty said firmly, and then followed it up with a laugh. "This is NOT for publication, Erin. But Henry is damn close to getting this thing up and running. I swear, as soon as we've got something, you'll be the first to know. I just hope it's not too late."

CHAPTER 34

It was Monday, September 3—Labor Day in the United States. The summer was officially coming to a close and, in most states, children would be returning to school tomorrow.

Marty and Erin both had the day off and they were spending a rare three-day weekend together at their La Jolla home. Marty was a morning person and although it was only 6 AM, he was already up. He had too much to think about to sleep. He kissed Erin gently on the cheek and padded into the kitchen to make himself a mug of tea. He took it outside and sat on the deck in his t-shirt and boxers, his standard sleepwear, putting his legs up on the railing.

There was a slight chill in the air but nothing like what it would be in Boston this time of year, he thought. While he would miss the turning leaves and the brilliant Fall colors of New England, he was certain he wouldn't miss the snow. He was beginning to truly enjoy the consistent temperate climate of San Diego. He looked out over the water. It was just becoming visible in the dawning light. He watched a bird quickly dive towards the water's surface and come up again.

Suddenly his cell phone rang. Thankfully it was in the living room so he hoped it wouldn't disturb Erin. He jumped up and hurried inside to grab it. Who the hell would be calling him at this hour?

"Marty, Ted Chambers. Hope I didn't wake you."

"Actually, I'm up already, Senator."

"It's damn early there, isn't it?"

"Yes, it is. I'm just an early morning person."

"Good for you. Marty, I hate to bother you on a national holiday, but I'm afraid it's started. Our boy Doomsday has launched his first strike."

"The nuclear plants?" Marty asked.

"No, that must've been a decoy," Chambers answered. "It's the Federal Reserve. He's planted a virus in their main network that launched itself this morning. The FBI's anti-virus people have contained it so far, but I'm sure this is just the beginning."

Marty was hurrying to the bedroom to throw on some clothes. "I'm getting dressed now, Senator. I'm going to call Henry Chu in Cambridge and get him over to Incandescent's NOC. I'll also get some emergency staff over to our NOC at GWare.

Give me a number where I can reach you and I'll call you as soon as we're situated."

Chambers gave Marty his cell phone number and Marty disconnected. Christ, Marty thought, here we go again. Obviously, Doomsday felt national holidays were a prime opportunity to strike. Marty thought back to New Year's Eve 1999, when he and Henry Chu and TJ Gatwick and the FBI watched in horror as they couldn't do a damn thing to prevent the massive destruction to the country's computing infrastructure caused by Doomsday in a matter of hours. He hoped to hell it would be different this time.

Marty awakened Erin—he knew she wouldn't forgive him if he hadn't told her what was going on. She said she wanted to check in with her editor to see if they knew anything about the developing story while Marty rushed over to GWare. They agreed to meet at GWare as soon as she was dressed.

As Marty was driving to GWare headquarters he called Henry Chu. His wife answered the phone and said Henry was in the shower.

Marty said it was urgent and to please tell him to come to the phone right way.

"I'm dripping wet, so I guess this must be important," Henry said into the phone.

Marty was just approaching the entrance to the GWare campus as he spoke. "Sorry, Henry. Blame it on Doomsday. Better get over to the NOC pronto. Log onto chat when you get there."

Marty didn't have to say anything more. He and Henry had discussed just such an eventuality many times in the past month. Henry was ready and he knew what to do. Then Marty called Ray Davis. He woke him up, apologized, and told him what was happening. Ray said he'd get right over to GWare and contact a few more key employees on his way.

GWare's Network Operations Center was open around the clock because of the company's need to be ready to supply anti-virus patches any time of the day or night, so there was already a skeleton staff there when Marty rushed in. He placed his hand on the security scanner and a green light came on. The door unlocked and he hurriedly entered the NOC.

Marty went up to one of the operators and explained the situation. The man nodded and started emergency procedures. Marty requested that he set up an online chat immediately. He wanted to communicate in real time with Henry Chu, Senator Chambers, and the FBI. He called Chambers, told him he was initiating the chat, and gave the Senator the URL and password to access it. Chambers said he'd get the information to the FBI agent. Then Marty signed onto the chat.

Marty: **Marty@GWare** signing on. Who else is here?

Chambers: This is Chambers.

Henry: Henry here.

FBI: Jerry Henderson, FBI Washington here.

Chambers: Jerry, please brief them on what's happening now.

FBI: This morning a virus was launched during routine maintenance of the e-mail system at the headquarters of the Federal Reserve. With the national holiday, only on-call staff was available. The virus was set to send infected e-mails to every district. It didn't appear that it had gone outside the Fed's headquarters to any of the twelve district banks but we're still confirming that.

Marty: Any read on the virus type yet?

FBI: Still working on it. Looks like the worm is a mass-mailing type. It sends itself to all addresses in the address book. It also sets itself as a server process so it doesn't show up in the task manager. And it deletes any anti-virus definitions it finds on the target computers.

Henry: That's pretty clever. It must have a fair amount of intelligence built in.

FBI: Affirmative. It also searches out and terminates firewall product processes.

Marty: We've got a sophisticated virus on our hands then.

Chambers: Jerry, any other attack incidents reported yet?

FBI: Just getting word from New York that a similar virus was found at NYSE and NASDAQ. Also the NYCE and CIRRUS ATM networks are starting to get DOS reports coming in.

Marty: So he's targeting all the financial networks.

FBI: Looks like it. No way to tell what's next on his hit list, but we'll have our hands full with these alone.

Chambers: But why on Labor Day? He knows there'll be minimal damage during a national holiday.

FBI: But there's also minimal Federal staff available, Senator. He's got to be figuring we won't be able to contain it fast enough. He'll just keep filling the glass until it overflows.

Marty: Same strategy as with the New Year's Eve event. It's a Doomsday trademark. Senator, Henry's been working on a universal virus antidote, a type of virus deflector. It's proven effective with every virus we've tested against it. But we're still working out some flaws in it. I'm pretty sure it can shut down these attacks, but there's a risk. It could paralyze communications for a while because it blocks all messaging, good and bad. Henry, is that still the case?

Henry: Actually, I've improved the deflector somewhat. I can minimize the disruption by setting a recognition factor for certain types of communications. It's still screening out some valid transmissions, but deflection of valid e-mail should be minimal. Bottom line is the deflector will likely deter the virus, but it might prevent some legitimate e-mail from reaching its destination.

Marty: We can deploy this immediately, Senator. Henry can ftp it to any server, as long as you understand it isn't the perfect solution.

Chambers: Jerry, are you willing to take the risk? It sounds like a small one to me.

FBI: We have no choice, Senator. I'd settle for even minimal disruption at this stage. Otherwise, the country's whole financial infrastructure could be taken down. Doomsday timed this right. Fedgov doesn't have enough personnel to cover all the intrusions. Even if we did, the virus is deleting anti-virus protection as it goes. That means we're toast. Let's go for it.

Marty: OK then it's a go. Jerry, just give us the addresses of the servers to send the deflector to. I don't want to make it available on the public Internet so we need to ftp it across a secure network. I'll need access to it.

Jerry: No problem, we can accept it across the FBI's private network and then get it distributed from there.

Marty: Henry, can you put together a fast read-me and send it along with the deflector?

Henry: Already working on it. I'll have it ready in half an hour.

Marty: Great. Just make sure you add a warning about the valid transmissions the deflector could potentially interrupt.

Henry: Will do.

Chambers: Will this really work Marty?

Marty: Like Jerry said, we don't have any other options. It better work.

Henry: It WILL work.

Marty: That's good enough for me.

Marty, Henry, Jerry and Senator Chambers continued to stay online and report on the situation. Henry ftp'd the deflector to the FBI's site, and Jerry got it distributed to all of the financial institutions and networks immediately, along with an urgent alert. There wasn't anything more they could do except wait and see if they had acted quickly enough to prevent another New Year's Eve-type disaster from occurring.

Erin arrived at GWare just as Marty was signing off from the online chat. She waved to him through the glass window of the NOC. He went outside to meet her and briefed her on what was going on.

"Do you think the deflector will work?" Erin asked.

"If Henry says it'll work," Marty said confidently, "then it'll work. He's the best we've got, the best I've ever met. If anyone can stop Doomsday, it's Henry."

Marty put his arm around Erin and began to walk her towards her car.

Erin opened the door to her car. "Sit down for a minute," she said to Marty. "I've got something to tell you."

Marty slid into the passenger's seat beside Erin, leaving the door open and turning towards her.

"What is it?" he asked.

"When I was speaking to my editor, he told me about a story that had just come over the news wire," Erin said. "Apparently the San Diego Harbor Police Dive Team located a body a few days ago. They kept it quiet until it was ID'd. They confirmed that it's the body of TJ Gatwick."

"Well that closes the Gatwick case, anyway," Marty responded.

"Not entirely," Erin said. "It seems that they found a gun stuck in the pocket of Gatwick's pants."

"You mean he shot himself?"

"No, there wasn't any evidence of gunshot wounds. They believe it was the impact of the jump that killed him.

"But the gun they found was unusual, some kind of dueling pistol," Erin said. "They figure it must've come from Gatwick's personal collection. When they searched his mansion after his apparent suicide, they found out he was quite the collector. He collected a lot of stuff, some of it weird, like dueling pistols."

"He had to spend his money on something."

"Well he wasn't spending it just on collecting."

"What do you mean?" Marty asked with growing interest.

"It looks like Gatwick had quite a private life. His interest other than software was hard core. They found quite a stash of porno videos and magazines at his place, mostly homosexually oriented materials."

"What's all that got to do with the gun?"

"Remember how I said I thought it was more than just AIDS that caused TJ to take his own life?"

Marty nodded.

"Well," Erin said, "I could be right. The news wire said police are investigating a possible connection between the gun they found and the recent murder of a homosexual prostitute. Someone who went by the name of Jimmy Ritual. Seems TJ was one of Ritual's regulars. One night, Ritual was found dead from a gunshot wound. Only it wasn't an ordinary bullet."

"The dueling gun?" Marty asked in disbelief.

"Exactly," Erin said.

Marty shook his head sadly. "Gatwick committing murder? I find that hard to believe."

"Not really," Erin answered. "You heard about TJ's tirades. He was obviously capable of uncontrollable rage. You have to wonder if he just completely lost control."

"I guess so, but enough to murder someone?"

"Gatwick was a strange guy," Erin said. "He was always somewhat of a geek, but he had succeeded in the software business beyond even his wildest dreams. He achieved a lot, was a real self-made man. Kind of macho in an odd sort of way.

"My guess is Gatwick despised himself for being a homosexual," Erin continued. "Maybe when he discovered he had AIDS, he flew into a rage over it, went after the likely source. Maybe his anger finally got the best of him and he killed Jimmy Ritual, couldn't help himself."

"Still, murderer or not, TJ Gatwick built one hell of a company," Marty answered, "and it's one that I'm proud to be part of."

"You mean owner of," Erin said, smiling.

"Let's go home," he said.

CHAPTER 35

One week later, Marty was talking on the phone with Ted Chambers.

"The final report from the FBI on the Labor Day attack showed a high virus infection rate," Chambers said. "Even though we took action early on, Doomsday still had managed to already penetrate the network of the Federal Reserve and all its branches. His virus also got into the New York Stock Exchange, NASDAQ, and the ATM networks. He obviously intended to crash our entire financial system, and he knew where the vulnerable points were. With the economy heading in the wrong direction, the timing of the attack could've had a chilling effect on the country."

"We confirmed that the virus was a nasty new strain this time," Marty said. "It was not only self-propagating, it was fully capable of neutralizing most commercial anti-virus software."

"Frankly, Marty," Chambers said in his baritone voice, "I think we would've had a major disaster on our hands if Henry Chu's deflector hadn't worked. Doomsday did some damage, but we caught it before it became a lot more serious."

"Funny thing is, Henry's such a perfectionist, he was kind of embarrassed to release the product so early," Marty answered. "He didn't like the fact that it still had some bugs in it."

"Bugs or not," Chambers said with relief, "the damn thing worked like a charm. So what if it caused a little inconvenience here and there. A few legitimate e-mails being quarantined is nothing in the greater scheme of things. It was a small price to pay."

"I agree," Marty said. "Now that we know Henry's new virus deflector works under battle-tested conditions, we're gonna clean it up, work out those bugs, and put it on the market." Marty paused. "But I've got a novel twist to this you might like to know about."

"What's that?" the Senator asked.

Marty took a breath. "Anti-virus technology is just too important for us to profit from," he said. "We can't risk a maniac like Doomsday doing anything of this magnitude again.

"That's why I've decided to set up a non-profit foundation—The UNITE Foundation. Under the auspices of the foundation, we'll make Henry's deflector available to anyone who wants it, anywhere in the world, free. We'll fund the foundation with donations from our corporate profits and from other corporations and individuals who care about the future of computing. It'll guarantee that the deflector can be freely distributed forever…and we'll use any additional funds to continue to refine the product."

"Why that's…that's amazing, Marty," Chambers said with genuine surprise. "I can't believe you'd do such a thing. I mean, you could make a fortune from the deflector."

"This isn't about profits," Marty said quietly. "Look at a guy like TJ Gatwick. He had all the money in the world and what did it matter." Marty paused. "We've got to show the world we're gonna take a stand against virus attacks. Besides, money isn't the only way to demonstrate value." Then he added with a laugh, "Although my shareholders might not entirely agree."

Chambers chuckled. "You're a special kind of man, Marty Gladstone. God bless you."

"Goodbye, Senator."

When Marty hung up he realized he didn't even ask Senator Chambers about the follow-up investigation into Doomsday's whereabouts by the FBI. But somehow, he already knew the answer.

He had to believe that Doomsday would escape their net once again, staying one step ahead of the authorities as he had done all along.

Except now, Marty thought, Doomsday would be well aware that he had been soundly defeated. Once he realized that the deflector had worked to neutralize his latest virus attack, he'd know he didn't succeed.

And when Doomsday learned that the deflector was going to be made available free to anyone in the world who wanted it, Marty believed Doomsday's threat of any future virus attack would be lessened, maybe even eliminated. Henry Chu's deflector was years ahead of anything else on the market, and it had the potential to virtually eradicate a computer virus threat. Marty firmly believed the deflector would keep Doomsday and any other hacker at bay…at least until they developed a virus strain that was so sophisticated it could reach beyond the deflector's capabilities. That's why part of Marty's mission would be to continuously improve the deflector's potency.

The concept of a non-profit foundation wasn't a sudden brainstorm of Marty Gladstone. For some time, he had been thinking about a way to pay back the world for his success. He now thought about what that success had meant to him. Marty had lost his father early in his life, and his mother later in life. He couldn't remember a time when he didn't feel solely responsible for his own survival. Even growing up, there was a drive and desire in Marty that moved him to succeed against all odds.

Succeed he did, in ways he couldn't even imagine as a child. And now Marty had turned Incandescent into one of the great software companies in the world, greater still with the acquisition of GWare. This despite the fact that his best friend Henry had turned on him and sold him out, despite the fact that TJ Gatwick tried to crush him. But that was ancient history. Marty had succeeded, and all the while, he had played the game with class.

Marty had a sense of morality that was unusual and rare. His decision to distribute the deflector at no charge would be unprecedented in the software business. It was heretical to do anything that didn't lead to a profit, and he was certain his judgment would be questioned by both his board and the shareholders...but he hadn't the slightest doubt that he was doing the right thing.

As Marty had told Senator Chambers, this wasn't about profits anymore. Now he had other goals. He would continue to lead Incandescent and GWare, of course, focusing on the profits necessary to make them a success, but to Marty, this was about something that transcended business alone.

This was about doing the right thing, about overcoming true evil. It was about defending against viruses launched by hackers who were dedicated to the destruction of the software industry.

Marty decided right then that he wanted to make a major announcement about the foundation and the deflector as soon as possible. The momentum of the victory over the latest virus attack made this the best time to do it.

He knew he would be giving up huge profits, but the corporation would at least benefit from the publicity. The announcement would surely make Doomsday cringe, maybe even drive him back into his rat's nest for good.

Marty wanted Henry to be there for the announcement. After all, it was Henry who was responsible for the technology. He called Henry immediately and excitedly told him about his plan.

"You know what the deflector could be worth. You sure about this?" Henry asked skeptically.

"Absolutely," Marty said. "Henry, these hackers are terrorizing us and it'll only get worse. In the long term, if we don't stop them now, it won't matter what kind of company we have, or what kind of products we make. Remember when we opened our code and shared it with GWare? Look what happened...we ended up benefiting from that in ways we never even thought about. Now the two companies are one.

"We'll always be living in the shadow of the next attack," Marty went on. "This is the time to act. We've got to put an end to this, and your deflector is the way to do it. Besides, the publicity alone will do us more good than any profits we could ever make."

Henry sighed. "I suppose you're right. But it'll be tough to watch those royalties go up in smoke."

Marty laughed. "Yeah, but Henry, think of the psychological benefits you'll get out of this. Listen, I want you to be here for the announcement. How soon can you get to San Diego?"

Henry looked at his watch. He never knew exactly what day it was without checking first. It read Monday, September 10.

"I'll try to book a flight tomorrow morning," Henry said. "I'll e-mail you with my flight arrival time."

"Great. You're gonna feel good about this, Henry, I promise."

"You haven't steered me wrong yet," Henry said with no doubt in his voice. "See you soon."

Marty hung up. He was so elated he had to call Erin and tell her about his decision.

"So what do you think?" he asked when he finished explaining to her his vision for the foundation and the distribution of the deflector.

"I think," she said with emotion, "that you're the most wonderful man I've ever met."

"Aw shucks," he said.

"And soon," Erin said, "Nan is going to know all about the wonderful things her father is doing for the world."

Marty felt like he had just walked into a wall.

"Nan?" he said, a lump forming in his throat. "You mean…"

"That's what I mean," Erin interrupted. Marty heard her crying, but she was shedding tears of joy. "You're going to be a daddy."

Epilogue

On September 11, 2001, Henry Chu boarded United Airlines Flight 175 at Logan Airport in Boston, bound for Los Angeles. It was the earliest flight he could get, and he planned to catch a flight from LA to San Diego.

The 767 took off on time, at 7:58 AM. It would never reach its destination. Instead, its flight number would be indelibly burned into the memories of the entire country, even the world. Henry would become world-renowned, but not for his virus deflecting software. He would be one of the passengers who met an untimely death, crashing into the south tower of New York's World Trade Center at 9:03 AM.

Marty Gladstone, watching the World Trade Center disaster unfolding on a television at his office, would have a terrible feeling when he saw the second airliner slam into the building. He felt that Henry Chu was on that flight. When the news reports confirmed that it was United Flight 175, Marty was devastated. Rather than postpone his announcement, however, he went ahead with it. He renamed his foundation The Henry Chu Foundation to honor his friend who had perished, killed by a different kind of terrorist from the kind Henry had fought during his last years. Henry's son, Joey Chu, would grow up to follow in his father's footsteps, becoming a programmer with a special interest in fighting computer viruses.

The deflector would be distributed by The Henry Chu Foundation, free of charge, as Marty had promised. He fought a tough battle with his board but he won in the end. The deflector would become the most widely used software in the world, and no one would pay a cent for it. The resulting publicity would create an aura around Incandescent and it would become one of the most revered companies in American business. Its profits would multiply handsomely as a result, and Incandescent would become firmly entrenched as the number two global software company, second only to Microsoft.

The deflector would be as effective as Henry Chu had intended it to be—so effective, in fact, that the Doomsday Virus would never reappear. However, Doomsday would still remain at large, continuing to occupy a prime position on the FBI's Most Wanted list.

It was confirmed by the San Diego police that TJ Gatwick had indeed used his dueling pistol to murder Jimmy Ritual the night before Gatwick took his own life by jumping off the Coronado Bay Bridge. Gatwick's suicide and the story released about the murder he committed would be what everyone remembered about this otherwise remarkable and brilliant software entrepreneur. He would be all but forgotten as the founder of GWare.

The murderers of Senator Jack Morrissey of California would never be found. One rumor would connect them to Doomsday; another rumor would have them being part of Al Qaeda, the organization responsible for the September 11 hijackings.

Jill Strathmore would be tried and convicted in Federal court for creating the Code Red Two virus. She would be sentenced to ten years in Federal prison and be paroled in three years. She would never return to the software business.

Senator Ted Chambers would be re-elected to several more terms by an enthusiastic populace in Vermont. He would remain chair of the Senate Technology Council. After a successful 25-year career in the Senate, Chambers would retire and return to private life. He would become a board member of the software firm, Incandescent.

Marty Gladstone would become Chairman Emeritus of Incandescent, and relinquish his daily responsibilities to run The Henry Chu Foundation. He would never be happier than as the head of a non-profit foundation.

Marty and Erin would give birth to a healthy 7 pound 4 ounce girl. They would name her Nancy. Nancy would have her mother's blazing blue eyes and her father's quick intellect. She would grow up to have her mother's passion for life and her father's moral convictions.

Author's Note

While *The Doomsday Virus* is a work of fiction, it is based on virus attacks that have occurred and continue to occur with increasing frequency. There is a real National Infrastructure Protection Center (**www.nipc.gov**), and all of the NIPC alerts used in this book are real. Doomsday is a fictional character, but he is based on hackers whose activities are known to the FBI. Some of these hackers have been captured, while many others are still at large. As of this writing, there is no known software product that can do what the "deflector" described in this book could do, but anti-virus software becomes more sophisticated every day.

Is the threat of a virus attack of the magnitude described in this book real? In a landmark article in *Scientific American*[1], four IBM researchers found that, even by 1997, more than 10,000 viruses had already appeared, and hackers were developing viruses at a rate of six a day. The article indicated that macro viruses are a major threat today because they can spread very rapidly through the increasing usage of electronic mail, file transfer and document exchange over the Internet.

1. "Fighting Computer Viruses," Jeffrey O. Kephart, Gregory B. Sorkin, David M. Chess and Steve R. White, *Scientific American*, November 1997

The NIPC, in a report[2] on extremist groups, stated that "increasing technical competency in these groups is resulting in an emerging capability for network-based attacks, including those targeting our nation's infrastructures. Extremist groups have proven themselves capable of carrying out acts of violence, and the leaderless resistance strategy makes it even more difficult for authorities to foresee actions by such groups."

So the question is not if a large-scale virus attack will occur, but when. And when it does, will we be ready? One thing we can be sure of: September 11, 2001 has proven that terrorism knows no boundaries.

2. *Highlights*, Issue 10-01, November 10, 2001, National Infrastructure Protection Center

For more information and to purchase additional copies of this book,

please visit this Web site:

www.thedoomsdayvirus.com

0-595-26883-8